Ab

Georgie Lee loves c̶ ̶... and storytelling thro̶ ̶... writing professionall̶ ̶... ̶ ̶ ...̶ ̶ moving to Hollywood to work in the entertainment industry. When not writing, Georgie enjoys reading non-fiction history and watching any movie with a costume and an accent. Please visit georgie-lee.com for more information about Georgie and her books.

Amanda McCabe wrote her first romance at sixteen – an historical epic starring her friends as the characters, written secretly during algebra class! She's never since used algebra, but her books have been nominated for many awards, including the *RITA*® Award, Booksellers Best, National Readers Choice Award and the Holt Medallion. In her spare time she loves taking dance classes and collecting travel souvenirs. Amanda lives in New Mexico. Email her at: amanda@ammandamccabe.com

A Regency
Christmas
Wedding

GEORGIE LEE

AMANDA McCABE

MILLS & BOON

First Published in Great Britain 2022
By Mills & Boon, an imprint of HarperCollins*Publishers*
1 London Bridge Street, London, SE1 9GF

www.harpercollins.co.uk

HarperCollins*Publishers*
1st Floor, Watermarque Building,
Ringsend Road, Dublin 4, Ireland

A REGENCY CHRISTMAS WEDDING © 2022 Harlequin
Enterprises ULC.

His Mistletoe Marchioness © 2018 Georgie Reinstein
The Wallflower's Mistletoe Wedding © 2017 Amanda McCabe

ISBN: 978-0-263-31782-4

MIX
Paper | Supporting
responsible forestry
FSC™ C007454

This book is produced from independently certified FSC™ paper to ensure responsible forest management.

For more information visit: www.harpercollins.co.uk/green

Printed and bound in Spain
by CPI, Barcelona

HIS MISTLETOE MARCHIONESS

GEORGIE LEE

To my wonderful readers,
may you have a happy and
hope-filled Christmas season.

Chapter One

Kent, England—December 20th, 1806

'I still can't believe you talked me into coming back to Stonedown Manor for Christmas,' Lady Clara Kingston complained to Lady Anne Exton, her sister-in-law, for the second time during their journey. The first had been when they'd set out two hours ago from their estate, Winsome Manor. Conversation with Anne had eased Clara's initial misgivings and for a while the carriage ride through the snow-covered countryside had been soothing. But as the rolling hills of Surrey had changed to the flatter lands on the edges of the Weald in Kent and the familiar landscape surrounding Stonedown Manor, Clara's apprehension had returned. With Stonedown looming on a nearby rise, the creamy stone front of it fading into the stark and leafless trees and frost-covered hills behind it, Clara's unease increased.

'You're too young to cloister yourself at Winsome,' Anne said. 'And what better way to return to society than surrounded by people you know who will be glad to see you? It's been ages since you've attended one of Lord and Lady Tillman's annual Christmas house parties.'

'For good reason.' It'd been six years since the last time Clara had travelled this road. Back then she'd been heading home with the disappointment and embarrassment that had marred the remaining days of that Christmas visit accompanying her. It had been one of the worst Christmases that she'd ever endured and one of the best and most memorable.

'That was a long time ago, Clara, and far behind you. Think of the better times,' Anne encouraged.

'I'm trying.' Clara traced the outline of her wedding ring beneath her glove. She'd been unable to take it off despite the two years that had come and gone since Alfred's passing. With him beside her, she could have returned to Stonedown without the regrets and doubts weighing her down, laughing at the less-than-pleasant memories of her last visit instead of allowing them to torture her as much as his loss. The surety of his love and protection was no longer there to help her and never would be again. Whatever waited for her at Stonedown, she must face it alone, as she had the humiliation that had marked that Christmas morning six years ago before Alfred's caring had driven it away.

Clara nearly rapped on the roof of the coach to

tell the driver to turn around and take her back to Winsome, but instead she clasped her hands tight together in her lap, her wedding ring pushing into the crook of her fingers. She couldn't run away from this like a scared spinster or that was exactly what she would become. She was tired of being the widowed aunt, of living through Anne's and Adam's lives while hers remained mired by a loss of love and purpose. This more than all of Anne's urgings had brought her to Stonedown. After two years secluded in the country, even she could see how the isolation and loneliness weren't good for her.

Anne leaned across the carriage and clasped Clara's hands, giving them a reassuring squeeze. 'Don't worry, Clara. Everything will be all right. You'll enjoy yourself and who knows what might happen. You met Alfred here. There might be someone equally special waiting for you this time.'

The light of hope in Anne's pale green eyes surprised Clara as much as the sensation rising in her heart. Hoping for such a thing felt like a betrayal of Alfred's memory, but she needed to believe that there was something more waiting for her than the endless lonely days at Winsome Manor, many of which she spent lamenting what hadn't been. Alfred wouldn't want her to stop living, but the chance of lightning striking twice at Stonedown was remote, as was the possibility that she and others would not recall that her biggest embarrassment had also happened here. 'Assuming people can see me as I am and not always think of me the way I was and what happened before.'

'Few people will be so bored during their time here as to dwell on that unfortunate incident. There's no reason for anyone to remember or to bring it up.'

'I pray you're right.' Clara didn't wish for people to view her as the simple girl who'd allowed herself to be duped by a fortune hunter, but as the poised Marchioness of Kingston that she'd become in the years since. It was the other reason she'd decided to come here, to prove to herself and everyone how much she'd changed. As for love finding her twice at Stonedown, she wasn't that hopeful. 'I doubt there will be anyone waiting at the house party for me. Most of the guests our age are married and the rest are old enough to be our parents. But you're right, this is a good chance for me to venture out again and remember what it's like.'

'Don't be too safe,' Anne suggested with a mischievous smile as she sat back against the squabs. 'An innocent risk every now and then is good for a woman.'

The plotting look in Anne's eyes made Clara wonder if Anne knew something about Lady Tillman's guest list that she didn't. There wasn't time to ask as the carriage made the turn on to the main drive leading to the massive front staircase.

A number of other carriages stood before the entrance, disgorging their passengers who strode up the numerous steps to the house. Spying the carriages and all the familiar faces, the excitement and anticipation that used to seize Clara when she and Adam were children and their parents would bring them here for the week before Christmas swept her again. Yes, she would enjoy herself in a way she hadn't done in years and perhaps for a little while forget the lingering sadness that had been draping her for far too long.

A footman opened the carriage door and a gust of cool air with a hint of snow rushed in. Clara stepped out and peered up at the tall façade and the wide columns stretching up to support the triangle-shaped entrance giving Stonedown Manor the appearance of a Greek temple. It had seemed so much taller when she'd been a child holding on tight to her mother's hand while they'd climbed these same steps. Coming to Stonedown had been as much a family tradition as Christmas pudding or carols. After their parents' passing eight years ago, Clara and Adam had continued to come to Stonedown, to keep the tradition and their memory alive until that awful Christmas six years ago.

With a sigh, she started her ascent, but Anne took her by the arm, giggling like a new maid. 'Do you remember how old Lady Pariston used to pinch the footmen on the cheeks?'

Clara tossed back her head and laughed, having quite forgotten. 'I do. Didn't she catch one on the bottom once?'

'She said her shoulder hurt too much for her to reach the higher cheek. She will be here.'

'Then no footman is safe.'

They almost doubled over in laughter when they reached the top, the old memory and the chance to see the charming Dowager again giving new life to the prospect of being here. It didn't have to be all pain and regret, and Anne was right, Clara must think about the happy memories instead of dwelling on the unfortunate ones.

She and Anne stepped into the main entrance hall and craned their necks to take in the tall-ceilinged room with wide-eyed wonder. Despite the marble floors, the stone and iron of the curving front stairs and the high plastered ceilings and stark white moulding, there was a cosiness to Stonedown, an air of family and comfortable living one often didn't find in estates this grand. This was the seat of the Earls of Tillman, but also their true home and, where it once rang with the noise of their five children, it now echoed with the sound of their grandchildren and the children of the guests and all the people gathered to celebrate Christmas. Fresh boughs of holly adorned every table and garlands of evergreens draped the long banister of the wide staircase leading up to the first floor. The crisp and spicy scent of cinnamon and nutmeg mingled with the earthy aroma of pine while the tinkling notes of someone playing Christmas carols on the piano in the music room drifted through the air. Clara took it all in, allowing the many happy memories of Christmases with her family here to fill her and make her doubts about coming fade. This delight was exactly what her tired soul needed.

'There's Lady Tillman. She will be so happy to see you.' Anne guided her to where their stately hostess stood beneath a magnificent painting of the Italian countryside.

Lady Tillman, with her grey hair done up and decorated with a sprig of holly, and her thick figure regal in a dark green velvet frock with long sleeves and fur cuffs, reminded Clara of her mother and the way she used to appear whenever she'd greeted house party guest at Winsome Manor. The Countess smiled while she watched a group of children race past her. One of the little boys bumped into a half-pillar and made the vase on top of it rattle, causing the footman near it to leap at the ceramic to make sure it didn't fall. Lady Tillman uttered not one word of reprimand, the near loss of a vase a worthy price to pay to have this much joy echoing off the overhead frescos.

Clara watched the children dart between the guests, the ribbons of the little girls' dresses fluttering while the shoes of their brothers and cousins and friends slapped against the stone. Clara smiled at the sight, but it slowly faded as the familiar sadness she'd endured too many times in the past six years dropped over her like a blanket. At one time she'd dreamed of returning here for Christmas with a son or daughter who could play with her niece and nephew and enjoy the festive season the same way she had as a child but it hadn't been. As with his first wife, she and Alfred had had no children. With Alfred gone, her dreams of having a family of her own were in danger of never coming true and it left a hole in her heart that made her want to weep.

'Lady Kingston, Lady Exton, how magnificent to see you both.' Lady Tillman strode up to Anne and Clara. Clara struggled to push aside her melancholy and greet their hostess. This wasn't the time to cry and lament. She'd done enough of that at Winsome and there would be plenty of opportunities when she was alone in her room at night, but no matter how much she smiled, she couldn't shake off the sadness completely. Alfred wasn't even here to comfort her. 'Lady Kingston, you don't know how thrilled I was when Lady Exton told me you were coming. You've been away from my parties for far too long.'

She wagged a reprimanding finger at Clara before clasping Clara's hands, her gracious and heart-felt greeting soothing Clara's sadness. 'You're right, Lady Tillman, and it's a mistake I intend to rectify.'

'You already have.' Lady Tillman patted her hand, then let go. 'You both must go on through to the dining room and have your tea before the children eat all the tarts. The little cherubs, how I adore having them here.'

'Are my children somewhere in this crush?' Anne

glanced about to see if she could spy the tow-haired heads of James and Lillie.

'Oh, yes, they went running through here some time ago and your husband is in the billiards room with Lord Tillman and many of the other men.'

There hadn't been enough room in the carriage for them all so Adam and the children had gone on ahead while Anne had ridden with Clara. Clara felt sure she'd done it to offer her support and she was thankful for the company, especially as they waded through the guests on their way to the dining room. Clara gave and accepted greetings from many old acquaintances, all the while enduring their consolations. It made her feel loved and wanted, but even these kind words reminded her of the loss of Alfred and how grief had made her stay away. It was a bittersweet arrival.

'Lady Kingston, is that you?' Lady Pariston stopped them. Wisps of her grey hair stuck out from beneath her white lace mobcap and she stooped a bit where she gripped a walking stick in her frail hands. Clara had never remembered her as robust or young, but she seemed even older today, but no less cheerful than she'd been before. Nothing ever appeared to dampen the Dowager Countess's delight in everything. Lady Pariston leaned forward on her stick with a little too much amusement and no small amount of mirth. 'What trouble do you intend to get up to this time, Lady Kingston? Plan to get jilted by another marquess while you're here? I don't think there are any in attendance, and if there happens to be more than one then you must share. It was awful of you to keep both of them to yourself last time, even if you did land the better of the two.'

Clara stiffened, struggling to maintain her smile. 'I'll be sure to share this time if there's more than one marquess.'

'Good. I know you won't believe it to look at me, but I used to have to fend off marquesses, and even a duke, with a stick.' While Lady Pariston waxed on about her past, Clara glanced around to see if any footmen stood in danger of her fingers, but none was so close. 'If I hadn't loved Charles so much I never would have consented to becoming a mere countess, but he more than made up for the step down by the size of his manor.'

She nudged Clara with her elbow and Clara laughed.

'A sizeable manor does make a great deal of difference, doesn't it?' Clara could enjoy Lady Pariston's jokes because they were not cruelly meant. She spoke plainly and frankly and expected everyone around her to do the same.

'I'll say. Now go on through to your tea and pick out the man you want to catch this time.'

Lady Pariston strolled off, her gait, despite the walking stick, as spry as her laugh.

Clara crossed her arms and trilled her fingers on them as she turned to Anne. 'So much for no one remembering that unfortunate incident from the last time I was here.'

'Well, if anyone was going to bring up what happened, you know it would be Lady Pariston.'

'I doubt she'll be the only one.' Clara nodded to where Lady Fulton in her lace-cuffed dress that did little to contain her large chest and slender Lord Westbook with his sharp nose and slicked-back dark hair stood whispering together, each of them throwing Clara sidelong glances and then casually strolling away when it was clear that they'd been seen. Clara was certain they were not discussing the size of her diamond earrings. 'What was it that Lady Fulton called me? A plain country mouse?'

'And you are no longer that any more. Chin up, my dear Marchioness. There are tarts to eat.'

They strolled to the dining room, their progress slowed by more greetings, and Clara tried to shake her irritation at Lady Fulton and Lord Westbook. Their catty remarks had made a bad situation much worse six years ago and, unlike Lady Pariston's silly and innocent reminder of Clara's past, she knew anything they said was designed to inflict the most damage. The two of them were notorious gossips and Clara's story must have greatly amused them, and who knew how many other country families six years ago.

As if to add insult to injury, it was then that she and Anne passed the small hallway leading to the ballroom. A sprig of mistletoe hung from the chandelier in the centre of the hallway, just as it did every year. Clara paused, noticing the white berries adorn-

ing the branch, and the memory of that Christmas
Eve six years rushed back to her...

'We should probably return to the ballroom,'
Hugh had suggested, rocking back on his heels before planting himself firmly in front of her.

'Yes, we wouldn't want people to notice our absence and talk.'

She didn't care if they did. She yearned to stay
there in the hallway beneath the mistletoe alone with
him. He must desire it, too, for neither of them made
a move to return to the dancing and she enjoyed this
rush of boldness, the first one she'd ever experienced
in a man's presence.

He stepped forward and clasped her hands in his.

She straightened, struggling to stand still against
the excitement coursing through her at the press of
his fingers against hers.

His pulse flickered beneath her grasp and a shiver
of excitement made her tremble. She wished to feel
not just his fingertips against her skin but the en-
tirety of him and everything promised by the longing in his eyes.

He wanted her as much as she wanted him, not
in the sordid way spoken of in gossip, but in a deep
and binding union of their lives...

Until the next morning, Clara thought wryly, the
memory of crushing the berry he'd plucked for her
from the mistletoe beneath her boot heel in the drive
the next morning equally potent. Hugh might not
have asked for her hand in so many words, but it had

been there in every look he'd cast her that night and across the table and sitting rooms of the days before. The ones everyone in the house had seen, too. How people like Lady Fulton had sneered at her when Hugh had left to marry another. Despite his kiss and everything they'd shared that week, she'd been nothing more to him than a way to pass the time until someone more lucrative had come along and she'd been too much of a simple country girl to see it.

Clara swept off to follow Anne into the dining room. *I'm not that naïve girl any more.*

And she would make sure that people like Lady Fulton recognised it.

'Oh, Clara, Lady Tillman has set out her mincemeat tarts.' Anne eyed Lady Worth's small china plate as she passed them. 'I must have one before they're all gone for it isn't the start of the Christmas season until I've eaten one.'

'Don't you wish to greet your husband?' Clara was somewhat curious to venture into the billiards room and see what men were in attendance, almost ashamed to admit she did hold out some hope for this party. After all, it was the season of miracles and she could do with one.

'Adam can wait. The tarts will not.' Anne took a tart from the magnificent selection of treats arranged on the long table and enjoyed a large bite, sighing at the sweet taste and the aromatic holiday spices.

'You're right.' Clara took a bite of her selection,

savouring the cinnamon-laced confection. 'It isn't Christmas until I've had one of these.'

Anne dabbed the sides of her mouth with a small napkin, then set it on the tray of a passing footman. 'No, it isn't. Oh, there's Adam. I must tell him that I brought his cufflinks and will have my maid send them to his valet. I'll be right back.'

She rushed off to take care of this domestic matter, leaving Clara to enjoy more tarts. While she finished her last treat, her stays already growing tight from the bounty of delights, she noticed the open door to Lord Tillman's library across the hall from the dining room. Through the white-corniced frame, she could see the warm fire burning in the grate, its light glistening off the many gold-tooled titles of the books lining the walls. If there was one other Christmas tradition she could not do without, it was perusing Lord Tillman's illuminated manuscript outlining the Nativity, the one he set out every year for his guests to enjoy. The last time she'd admired the Nativity had been six years ago when Hugh had glanced at her from across the wide pages, his fingers brushing hers when he'd turned the aged parchment. It had been the place where Hugh had first become more to her than her elder brother's longtime friend and sometime houseguest at Winsome Manor and everything between them had changed.

No, I will not think about that, but of better times.

She left the bright dining room and crossed the hall to the library. It was just as she remembered it, with the shelves filled with antique manuscripts and more recent novels. The heaviness of the wood bookshelves and mouldings and the dark leather of the furniture made the room much darker than any of the others in the house, but with a large fire burning in the grate and the medieval illuminated manuscript perched on the tall bookstand by the window, it was one of the cosiest places in Stonedown. Lord Tillman was generous with his collection, making everything in it available to his guests. She'd spent many hours in this room with her father during the Christmases when he'd been alive, with him helping her to puzzle through the Latin text of the manuscript or to select a novel to read while she was here. She would take the book up to her room and every night before falling asleep she'd devour a few pages, relaxing after the excitement of the festive days. The next day at breakfast, she and her father would discuss the story, for he always urged her to choose ones he'd already read and he would make her guess how it might end. She used to beg him to tell her, but he never would spoil the story no matter how well he knew it or whether or not it was one of his favourites.

Taking a deep breath of the smoke-tinged air flavoured with the faint must of old paper, she closed her eyes and almost forgot for a moment that her father and mother were gone, and that she'd spent too many of the last eight years missing people the most at this time of year.

She opened her eyes and crossed the room to the

illuminated manuscript. The sunlight coming in from outside, despite being muted by passing clouds, still sparkled in the glittering gold of the chorus of singing angels' halos and in the fine calligraphy of the first letter of the page. The book was in Latin and she peered at it, trying to make out what words she could remember from her lessons with Adam and their father so long ago. Unlike her brother, she'd never mastered the old language, but a few words and phrases were familiar and she worked them out in a whisper, her effort making the noise and chatter in the hallway and rooms outside fade away until one voice rang out above them, stopping her cold in her reading.

'Lady Kingston, it's a pleasure to see you again.'

Clara's finger froze over the red calligraphy, her pulse pounding in her ears. She took a deep breath and turned slowly around to find Hugh Almstead, Fifth Marquess of Delamare, standing at the bookshelf in the corner holding an open book. He didn't flinch at the sight of her, but his confidence was betrayed by the subtle shifting of his weight on his feet. In her eagerness to view the manuscript and to remember everything she used to love about being in this room with her father, she'd walked right past him, unaware this entire time that he'd been watching her from the shadows.

He closed the book and stood up a touch straighter. He'd gained some height and his chest had grown wider along with his shoulders since the last time

she'd seen him. His dark blue coat highlighted the
darker strands in his sandy brown hair and made
the copper flecks in his light brown eyes stand out.
He appeared more like a man than the boy who'd
courted her six years ago before abandoning her for
a richer woman.

She worked hard to swallow down the old anger
while she straightened the line of brass buttons on the
front of the spencer covering the top of her London-
made mauve dress. The entire time she prayed that
the shock and agitation of seeing him again didn't
show on her face. No one had thought to tell her that
he would be here. With so many other memories and
feelings already leaving her raw, she didn't need his
presence conjuring up more for her to struggle with.
'Lord Delamare, what a surprise to see you.'

If he was shocked by her presence, he hid it well,
his piercing brown eyes taking her in with an earnestness she couldn't read. 'I find myself in need of
some Christmas joy. I always remembered finding it
here at Stonedown, especially in the people.'

He traced the leather corner of the book with a
weariness she knew well. She'd lost interest in so
many things after Alfred's death and now faced the
challenge of rediscovering life instead of wallow-
ing in sorrow. Then, when she was on the verge of
reclaiming the simple pleasures of a house party at
Christmas, here was Lord Delamare to remind her
of more unpleasant times and the awkward young

woman she'd once been who'd fallen for his deceptive charms.

She ceased her fiddling with the buttons and dropped her hands to her sides, striking as confident and regal a pose as she could muster. 'One would think London would hold more joy for a lord of your reputation than the woodlands of Kent.'

She tried to sound light, but the remark came off as sharp as the pop of sap on the logs in the fire. Given the tales she'd heard of him and his preference for London actresses in the last three years since his wife's death, he'd appeared more bent on emulating his grandfather's vices than his level-headed father's virtues.

'Not any more.' He slapped the book against his palm, chafing at the remark before regaining his former composure. 'My condolences on the passing of Lord Kingston. I met him a number of times in the House of Lords. He was one of the few men there who kept his word. He gained an admirable reputation because of it.'

'Yes, he was a very trustworthy and loyal man.' She fixed him with a pointed look. 'If only all lords possessed such integrity.'

He shoved the book back into its place on the shelf. 'Sometimes, life has a way of beating the integrity out of a person.'

'It didn't beat it out of Alfred.'

'Then he was a fortunate man, for many reasons.'

She wondered if he included her in those reasons,

but she doubted it. He'd made his decision and not looked back—neither should she. She reined in her irritation, determined to be cordial and polite. It would be a long week if she didn't master that skill and her tongue in Hugh's presence. 'I'm very sorry about Lady Delamare, to be stolen away so young is a tragedy.'

He laced his fingers in front of him, running his thumb over the empty place where his wedding ring must have once been, the loss in his expression striking a chord deep inside Clara. 'Thank you.'

A log in the fireplace collapsed, sending up a sea of sparks. The scent of burning oak permeated the heavy air between them.

'My brother is here,' she offered, trying to lighten the mood with the kind of small talk she preferred to engage in with Lord Worth or any of the other guests. Except she'd never imagined she'd be chatting with Hugh of all people.

'I know.' Hugh faced her with the same stern countenance he'd worn when she'd first turned to see him. 'He wrote to me and told me that he and you would be here.'

This made her stiffen with surprise more than his having interrupted her private moment.

'Did he now?' She needed to end this conversation and have a very much needed other one with Adam and Anne as to why she hadn't merited the same warning.

'It was his letter that gave me a reason to come.'

The tender yearning in his eyes struck her as hard as a well-packed snowball, but it didn't stun her enough to make her take leave of her senses.

He hadn't really loved her years ago. That he held a candle for anything more than perhaps her inheritance, which was now even more substantial than it had been before, was preposterous. Perhaps, having run through all the actresses in London, he was here for other, more lucrative amusements. The anger his grief had pushed aside slipped slowly back to her and she narrowed her eyes at him. 'In search of another heiress to help fill the family coffers? Or did you think a widow would serve you better?'

That wiped the tenderness off his face. She'd insulted him and she was glad, for the mistakes of six years ago along with Lord Westbook's and Lady Fulton's snide whispers were not experiences she wished to repeat. 'My motives for being here are not as base as you believe.'

'I'm sure they're not as noble as you've convinced others to believe either.' She marched up to him, fingers closed into fists at her sides. The humiliation of standing before him in this very room years ago while he'd told her he'd decided to marry another instead of asking for her hand was made sharper by the rich scent of his bergamot shaving soap and his stance. He didn't so much as step back or flinch, but stood there, taking her disdain with irksome stoicism. She didn't expect him to crumble in shame, but at least he could have the temerity to blush or look away in guilt. 'Whatever your true reasons for coming here, be perfectly clear, they will not include me. Good day, Lord Delamare.'

Clara stepped around him and out of the room, pausing in the hallway to drag in a deep breath and settle the nervous tremors coursing through her. It wasn't like her to lob insults at people, but she hadn't been able to help herself. Nor was it like her to reveal to anyone so bluntly the depths of the injury they'd inflicted, but Hugh must see that she was no weak widow all too ready to run into his arms and surrender her fortune and her person to his control. The sooner he recognised the futility of coming here, the sooner he might leave and she could enjoy her week in peace. Until then, there was the matter of Lady Tillman's guests list to discuss with Anne.

Clara marched into the dining room and up to Anne. She laid a stern hand on Anne's arm, stopping her from taking another bite of her holiday delicacy. 'Lord Delamare is here.'

Anne peered at Clara from across the pastry before slowly lowering it to her plate. 'Is he now?'

Her surprise wasn't convincing.

'You knew he'd be here, didn't you?' Clara pulled her out of the dining room and down the hall to a secluded alcove adorned with a large vase filled with fragrant hothouse flowers.

Ann hesitated, giving Clara her answer before she even managed to stammer out a few weak lies. 'Well, no, not exactly. Adam told me Lady Tillman had said she'd invited him, but she gave him no indication that he'd accepted.'

Clara glanced down the hall to make sure no one, including Hugh or anyone else, was listening. 'You're lying. I can always tell because your cheeks go red.'

With Anne's fair complexion and blonde hair it was difficult for her to hide even the slightest of blushes.

'Yes, we knew,' Anne mumbled, suddenly very interested in the button on her spencer. 'Lady Tillman wrote to us about it a week ago, wanting to make sure there would be nothing awkward between the two of you. I assured her there wouldn't be.'

'Without consulting me first?'

'I was afraid if I told you, you wouldn't come and I wanted you to. I see the way you are at Winsome, and how lonely and sad you appear sometimes, especially while watching the children or when you think no one is looking, and it breaks my heart. I want you to be as happy as Adam and I are and to have children of your own and all the things you lost when Alfred died. You won't find them sitting in your room at home, but here with people.'

Clara swallowed hard. Only Anne could stop Clara from being angry at her when she should be steaming. She thought she'd been better about hiding her grief, but she hadn't if Anne and Adam had gone to such lengths to make sure she came to this house party. Anne was right. Clara had travelled to Stonedown to take her first steps towards finding a new life. She'd already seen a number of new faces among the usual guests. Perhaps one of them would be someone like Alfred with caring eyes and a trustworthy heart, the kind of man who'd readily comfort a grieving and rejected young woman one Christmas morning instead of laughing at her. That man was not Hugh.

'I realise Lord Delamare being here might be a little awkward,' Anne continued, 'but what happened between the two of you was a long time ago and since then he was happily married and so were you. There's no reason why you can't be polite and cordial to one another and no reason why his being here should spoil your week.'

Except Clara had already been less than cordial to him because he'd reminded her of the worst embarrassment she'd ever endured. This wasn't at all how she'd imagined this house party beginning. 'Even if we can be cordial to one another, more people than Lady Pariston are bound to remember what happened and bring it up, especially Lord Westbook and Lady Fulton and you know how cutting they can be. I told you what they said about me the last time we were here once the entire household heard of what happened.'

'And a great deal has changed since then.' Anne laid her hands on Clara's shoulders. 'There's no reason why they and everyone won't see anything but the confident woman before me.'

Clara wasn't so generous in her perception of what

people would see when they looked at her. She hoped it was a mature marchioness, but she feared, especially with Lord Delamare present to remind them, that they'd see nothing but the awkward young girl she'd once been. No, she was no longer an easily tricked country heiress, but a woman of experience and sophistication who would not have the wool pulled over her eyes by a scheming man and she would prove it to everyone, including Hugh. 'Yes, you're right. Just because he's here doesn't mean I have to speak with him or give him more than a curtsy and any required manners. In fact, if I can avoid speaking to him entirely, I will.'

'Except that because of precedence, you'll be sitting next to him at every dinner,' Anne reminded, dropping her voice so as not to be heard by the gentlemen and ladies passing them as they went from the dining room to the billiards room.

Clara let out a frustrated sigh. If the footman hadn't already dragged her travelling trunk up the stairs to her room, and if Mary, her lady's maid, wasn't already busy arranging dresses in the wardrobe, Clara would order her clothes packed up and the trunk put back on the carriage so she could return home. Except there was nothing for her at home except more nights alone, more days spent in reading and solitude or watching James and Lillie play and regretting that she had no child to play with them. She could leave and allow the melancholy to claim her or stay and remain on this path to being out in the world and open to the possibility of love and a better life. That, and proving that she'd changed, was why she was here and she wouldn't allow Hugh to steal this from her the way he'd tried to steal her faith in herself six years ago. She intended to enjoy the season and she would. What Hugh did was immaterial to any of that.

Hugh examined the pages of the illuminated manuscript, trying to concentrate on the beautifully drawn and painted figures, but all he could see was Clara. The moment she'd entered the room, the only thing he'd been able to think about was the Christmas Eve ball when he'd held her in his arms. Her petite body had been languid against his when she'd curved into him with sighs as tender as her fingertips against his neck. Beneath the silk of her gown he'd been able to feel the press of her hips against his and when he'd caressed the line of her back, the sweep of his fingertips over the bare skin above the line of her bodice had made her shiver.

He'd sat across the table from her at Adam's family home over the years, paying her no more heed than he would the younger sibling of any of his friends. It wasn't until she'd entered Lady Tillman's sitting room at the beginning of that fateful Christmas house party, her dark blonde hair done up in ringlets and secured with red ribbons, the plain cut of her dress unable to hide her curving hips or the fullness of her breasts, that he'd viewed her as a woman. Even when dressed in the simplest of fashions, she'd taken his breath way and he'd struggled not to stare at the womanly changes that had come over her while she'd spoken about the falling wheat prices and how they plagued the major landowners. Her girlish interests had changed as much as her figure. In those few moments she'd transformed from the gangling young sister of his closest friend into a lady he couldn't take his eyes off, one worthy to become mistress of Everburgh Manor.

There hadn't been any trace of that smitten woman in the one who'd turned to face him today, her full lips opening with surprise before she'd pressed them tight together in disgust. Marriage and loss had changed her as much as it had changed him. The simple young woman he'd fallen for had matured, her plain country styles exchanged for the elegance of London fashion, her once-adoring looks now cutting, but he deserved her anger. It was the grief he'd seen when she'd pored over the vellum that she didn't deserve.

He turned the manuscript pages until he reached the one of the women crying at the foot of the cross. The mournful looks on their faces reminded him of how Clara had appeared when he'd watched her from across the room, hesitant to interrupt the private moment or to intrude on a sadness he was all too familiar with. While he'd watched her, the anguish and torment he'd suffered after he'd received the Christmas Eve letter six years ago informing him that Lord Matthews had finally agreed to Hugh's requests for his daughter's dowry, and that Hugh and Lady Hermione Matthews's engagement could proceed, had rushed back to him. Along with it had come the regret that had tortured him in the carriage that Christmas morning when he'd ridden away from Stonedown and Clara. The memory of her distraught face when she'd faced him in this very room had torn at him along with the same accusation she'd thrown at him moments ago.

'Fortune hunter. Bollocks.' He slapped the book stand, making it rock before it righted itself. He hadn't married Hermione simply for money, but out of duty to his family. The cold winters at Everburgh when his parents used to struggle to heat even a few rooms while his grandfather had squandered the family fortune on his actress second wife still haunted him, as did the strained and worried faces of his parents. After his grandfather's hard living had finally killed him, the massive debts had fallen to his father to pay and their quality of life, which had never been high, had declined even further. Although his parents had done everything they could to shield Hugh from the reality of their situation, there was nothing their stories of knights and dragons could do to stave off the cold or place more food on the table. Then, when they'd been on the verge of leaving those days behind them for good, Hugh's father's heart had given out, worn down by years of struggles. At his funeral, Hugh had vowed that he would do everything he could to make sure that his mother would one day experience the comfort and ease that a marchioness deserved. His marriage to Hermione had given him the chance to do that and he'd never regretted his decision. He still didn't. It was his youthful indiscretion at not being more cautious with Clara's feelings that he lamented, especially today, but there was nothing he could do to change the past, not his one with her or the last three years. He could only move forward and he would.

Hugh left the library in search of Adam and society, needing both more than solitude and regret. Solitude and the constant torment of remorse had already led him to make too many mistakes in London after Hermione's death, ones he'd have to work twice as hard to overcome if Clara's reaction to him offered any indication of how people currently regarded him. She and they had heard the stories about his behaviour in London. Most of the tales weren't even true, or they were exaggerated far beyond recognition, but it didn't matter. Until recently, he hadn't worked to check them and enough of them were true to give credence to the rest. At one time he'd been admired as much for himself as his old title and had been known to everyone as an honourable and respectable marquess who hadn't inherited his grandfather's taste for ruin. It'd taken a lifetime to build that reputation and three years to throw it all away and make everyone believe he was no better than his grandfather, but he was and he would prove it again.

Striding down the hall, he found Adam in the billiards room with a number of other gentlemen. They bent over the table to examine the shots, change the score on the marker or watch the game, each of them carrying glasses of brandy and sipping them between bits of conversation and breaks in the play. A gaggle of children ran through the room, swarming around the table before running out the opposite door, their noisy chatter barely breaking the conversation of the lords who were willing to tolerate their antics in this season of forgiveness. Hugh hoped everyone was willing to forgive more adult mishaps, especially his.

'Delamare, good to see you.' Adam clapped him on the back, then moved to hand him a glass of brandy from a nearby footman's tray before remembering and setting it back on the salver for someone else to enjoy. 'Sorry, I forgot you'd given it up.'

'There are times when I think that might have been a mistake.' He glanced at the brandy, tempted to throw back a good portion of it and savour the burning in his throat. It was a pain he deserved, but he wasn't a man to go back on his promises, at least not any more.

Adam tilted his head to one side in scrutiny. 'I assume you've seen Clara, then?'

'I have. She wasn't pleased to see me.'

'I'm not surprised.' He didn't look at Hugh, but swirled his brandy in his snifter before taking a generous drink. 'She didn't know you would be here.'

'You didn't tell her?' He wanted to take the snifter and break it over his friend's head. 'The entire reason I wrote to you was so you could warn her in the hopes it might ease any tension between us.' The tension that had dominated every word that had passed between them in the library.

'If I'd told her you'd be here, she wouldn't have come. You know how it is, no one likes to be reminded of past mistakes and such.'

No, they didn't. Not Hugh, not Clara, no one.

'Anyway, it doesn't matter now,' Adam continued. 'You're both here and now you've got your awkward first meeting out of the way, I'm sure the two of you will get on splendidly.'

'I wish I shared your optimism.'

'Well, the season of miracles and all that.' He rapped Hugh on the arm and took up his cue stick and bent over the table to take his shot, the conversation about Clara and Hugh being here together over. Hugh allowed it to drop. Adam was one of the few friends from his past who saw the better in Hugh even when he couldn't see it in himself. Hugh owed it to him to be respectful, especially of Clara. Adam, having inherited young, knew well the responsibilities of a titled man, but for all of his patience and understanding of Hugh's mistakes, and the family duty that had forced him to marry another, Adam would draw the line at intentional injury to those he loved.

'Marvellous shot, Exton,' Lord Tillman muttered through his bushy moustache, one hand on his round belly, the other clutching his brandy. He was tall with spindly legs and long thin arms, his full head of hair a striking contrast to his less-than-robust form. An earl from a long line, he didn't lord his title over anyone, taking it all in stride. He and his wife were two of the most congenial hosts that Hugh had ever known and the most forgiving. Neither of them had baulked at inviting him after he'd placed a gentle request with Lady Tillman when they'd met at the theatre at the end of last Season. He was thankful for their support and this chance to take his first steps towards redeeming himself with good society. If Clara's reaction to him was any gauge, he had a great deal of work to do.

Hugh tried not to sigh in weariness while he watched the game. He intended to some day hold a house party like this at Everburgh, but with no Lady Delamare to help him welcome his guests and no children to run with the guests' children, he would have to live once again off someone else's generosity. It was yet another dream that was on the verge of never coming true, especially if the court ruled against him in the last case concerning Everburgh.

He glanced at the brandy, wanting to knock the drinks to the floor, but he maintained his self-control. He'd done all that duty had required of him when he'd become the Fifth Marquess, paying off the last of the debts with Hermione's money, using Lord Matthew's connections to woo influential lords and hire expensive barristers to settle remaining court cases in his favour or on better terms, but still it hadn't been enough. The estate was in danger once again from a Scottish lord who claimed that Hugh's grandfather had signed over Everburgh to him in exchange for a life annuity and the payment of some debts. The Scotsman had a few letters indicating some sort of deal between him and Hugh's grandfather, and receipts of payment to his grandfather, but he had yet to produce the signed contract. If he did produce it, it would become a matter for a judge to decide. If the court ruled against Hugh, then everything that Hugh, his parents and Hermione had done to save the estate would mean nothing.

Hugh stood up straight and greeted Sir Nathaniel with a hearty welcome, determined to remain polite and solicitous. He would face this unexpected challenge with the fortitude his parents had always shown during their trials, the one he'd demonstrated, too, until Hermione's death had sent him into a dark spiral, but those days were over. He'd made a number of mistakes since Hermione's death, but they and the damage they'd done would soon be behind him. He would enjoy the respect and esteem of these men again, and, if given the opportunity, Clara's, as well. He was the Marquess of Delamare and he would bring dignity to the title and himself once again.

Chapter Two

'My dear, are you sure that's the dress you wish to wear tonight?' Anne asked, entering Clara's room to collect her for dinner. In a short while, everyone would line up according to precedence on the main staircase before going into the dining room. Clara prayed someone had arrived to outrank her, a dowager duchess or a dowager marchioness with an older title than hers who would bump her back a place or two in the line away from Hugh. As much as part of her wanted to be at the head of the line where everyone might see her, she didn't wish to be there beside Hugh.

Given that this wasn't likely to happen, she'd dressed as she would for any other dinner at Lord and Lady Tillman's, careful to pay no special heed to her attire. She didn't wish Hugh to think she'd changed her manner of dress simply because they happened to be beneath the same roof. If Anne's half-frown were any indication, Clara had succeeded a little too well in her desire to under-dress. 'What's wrong with my dress?'

'Nothing, except it's a tad dark.'

'It's winter.' Clara opened her arms and looked down at the black velvet dress devoid of any decoration, trying to sound sensible and failing.

'But the season is so cheerful and you don't want to come across as dour. Perhaps your green dress would be better. You want people to speak with you, not offer consolations.'

Clara dropped her arms in defeat, her desire to be seen as a refined and chic lady fading in the face of her current wardrobe. This dress might be fine and of excellent material but it bore the hallmarks of her grief, as did most of the dresses she'd brought with her. The bright gowns she'd worn before Alfred's death were still packed away in trunks at Winsome Manor. She wished she hadn't left them behind.

'You're right. I appear as if I'm going to a memorial, not preparing for a festive week. I'll wear the green dress.' She waved for Mary to undo the buttons on the back so Clara could change. 'I don't want to scare whomever I'm paired with for the week's events or give them the impression that they'll be stuck with a stick in the mud.'

'No, you don't.' Anne laid a finger on her cheek, her frown drawing up to one side in a smile that made Clara suspicious. 'Especially since you're sure to be seated beside Lord Delamare.'

'You needn't remind me.' He was the reason she'd

already devoted too much time to preparing for dinner. Her inability to find an appropriate dress reminded her of the many times she'd stood before this mirror six years ago, feeling heavy and uncomfortable in all her country finery and inherited jewels, the reflection staring back at her one of a young lady who used to turn down dances for fear that she would step on toes and embarrass herself. Every evening before dinner, she would try on all her dresses, lamenting to Mary about her inability to look like a refined London lady. She'd once thought this was the key to securing Hugh's heart. Instead, the way into his affection had been through more pounds and political influence than her family had possessed.

'I think you should consider yourself very lucky,' Anne said, drawing Clara back to the conversation.

'Lucky? I am far from lucky.' If she were lucky, then Hugh wouldn't be here and she wouldn't feel the need to prove herself to the likes of him or Lady Fulton. She had changed a great deal since the last time she'd been here—now the trick was proving it to everyone else, including herself at times.

'Of course you are. If you forgive him, then there are no barriers to anything happening between the two of you this Christmas.'

Clara gaped at her sister-in-law, unable to believe the words that had just come out of her mouth while Clara was standing in her shift and chemise of all things. Clara stepped into her green dress, yanked it up and stuck her arms in the sleeves. 'Life in the country has become quite dull if you're suggesting something between me and Lord Delamare, a man who is nothing more than a fortune hunter who'd go through my money faster than he does actresses in London.'

'He isn't as bad as you and so many others think,' Anne responded with surprising seriousness, having seen and heard a great deal more of Hugh than Clara had when she'd followed Adam to London every Season. But while she'd been discreet with her tales of him, others had not and a very different picture of him had emerged for Clara.

When Hugh had been a student at the Reverend's school with Adam he hadn't been so bad, but it wasn't the case any more as she sadly knew from experience. During Hugh's many visits to Winsome when she was a girl, he'd seemed so friendly, straightforward and predictable, enjoying riding and hunting like any young gentleman, but the candlelight had never caught in his eyes or his smile been as wide or charming as it had during that Christmas week. Some time between their meeting in the sitting room on the first day and the snowball fight in the garden, Hugh had stopped being simply her elder brother's friend and had become very much more.

It wasn't until the morning that he'd told her he would marry another that he'd suddenly become someone Clara didn't recognise. After that disastrous Christmas, Adam and others had tried to convince her that Hugh wasn't the rake Clara believed him to be. Hugh's behaviour in London had proven them all wrong, making her brother's continued faith in his old friend perplexing. Adam had always had their father's gift of seeing the best in even the worst people. It was a trait she didn't often share and Clara wondered what Hugh hid from Adam and Anne to keep them so enamoured of him. 'What about the duel he fought? Only a true wastrel resorts to that kind of theatrics to resolve a dispute.'

'You know how men are when it comes to their honour. Even the best of them can lose their heads at times.'

'He isn't the best of them, as proven by the tale of him and Miss Palmer at the theatre, the one that was in all the London papers that Lady Bellworth was kind enough to send us as if I'd wanted to hear news of Hugh, good or bad.'

'According to Adam, the story is quite overblown. I think once you speak with him at dinner you'll see that he isn't the rake those rumours make him out to be.'

'I doubt it.' Clara peered at Anne while Mary did up the back buttons, amazed, after her earlier show of concern downstairs, that she would be this cavalier about Clara and Hugh. 'Even if he is, I don't care. I learned the hard way about him once before. It's all I need to know about his character.'

She viewed herself in the mirror, silently admitting that the green dress did suit her better. Good.

It would make her diamond and emerald necklace stand out and help banish the old self-consciousness nipping at her. While Hugh's rejection had wounded her burgeoning confidence years ago, Alfred had made her certain of it, but he was gone and it was up to her to maintain her belief in herself.

She glanced at the door to her room and at the shiny knob reflecting the firelight. Just on the other side of it was where she and Alfred had truly met for the first time, on that Christmas morning after she'd come upstairs from meeting Hugh for the last time.

She'd struggled to remain composed until she'd been able to reach this side of the door and cry, but Alfred had been there to help soothe her broken heart...

'Lady Exton, are you well?'

Genuine concern and not just the nicety of manners had driven Lord Kingston's question. It had been there in his blue eyes with their faint lines at the corners.

He was older than her—thirty-five, perhaps—with dark hair touched with grey at the temples and the regal air of his class. He stood straight and tall, his strong features making him more debonair than a man like Lord Westbook, but there was a kindness about him that called to Clara.

'Since the passing of my parents I sometimes find the holidays difficult to endure.'

If she'd known him better she might have wailed

on his shoulder, as she wished she could still do with her mother who would have rushed to comfort her. But her mother was no longer there to offer her love or wisdom or even the strength to face the other guests.

All day today she'd have to sit beside everyone in church and across the table at dinner and pretend to be cheerful while her heart continued to break. Everyone had seen her and Hugh walking and playing cards and spending almost every moment they could in one another's company. His having left and her looking more like it was All Hallows' Eve than Christmas morning would make it obvious to everyone what had happened.

Hugh hadn't just trifled with her and jilted her, he'd done it in the most public way imaginable, making the pain even more deep.

'I understand. It was a great many years before I could enjoy Christmas after my wife passed. I assure you, Lady Exton, it does get easier with time.'

'Does it?' she whispered.

Her mother would have seen Hugh for the fortune hunter he really was and she would have warned Clara off him as she had the other fortune hunters in London. The lack of her mother's love and guidance further tarnished an already clouded morning.

He reached into the pocket of his coat and took out a white handkerchief and handed it to her. 'It does.'

She took his handkerchief and dabbed at her eyes,

embarrassed for almost losing her poise. 'I'm sorry to cast a shadow over the merry day.'

'Don't be. A pretty young lady like you is allowed to be sad from time to time. If you weren't, one would think you didn't have a heart. May I escort you down to breakfast?'

He'd held out his arm to her, the tenderness in his eyes difficult to abandon for the cold emptiness of her room. There'd been enough of those sorts of mornings in the last two years, between her father's death and then her mother's passing. That Christmas had been supposed to be better—and it had been until that morning.

It could be again. She refused to make a pitying spectacle of herself in front of the other guests. Here was a man offering her genuine regard when she needed it, there was no reason not to accept.

She slid her hand over his arm and stood confidently beside him. 'Yes, Lord Kingston, you may.'

The clang of the gong echoed up from the main hall and pulled her away from the sweet memory and back into the reality of the present. It was time to go down for dinner and Alfred wasn't here to walk with her tonight. She must face whatever awaited her alone and deal with it as best she could. It made her wish she had packed up and gone back to Winsome.

No. I won't be so weak. She took the gloves that Mary held out to her, cursing the tremor in her hands while she tugged them on. She shouldn't be this nervous. Hugh meant nothing to her and what had happened was a long time ago. Except he did mean something, he represented everything Clara had been before she'd become a marchioness, an ill-at-ease girl who, despite a respectable inheritance, had been unable to catch or hold a gentleman's attention long enough to secure a proposal. She was no longer that woman, but echoes of that girl dogged her steps as she escorted Anne out of her room and down the hall towards the stairs.

The old awkwardness was especially potent when they spied the end of the line of people waiting to queue up for dinner. A number of them smiled and nodded appreciatively, but it wasn't them that Clara fixed on, but Lord Westbook and Lady Fulton. They stood one step apart, with Lord Fulton too engrossed in conversation with Lord Worth above him to care if his wife spent her time whispering to Lord Westbook. Lady Fulton's small eyes widened at the sight of Clara, and Lord Westbook stopped his incessant talking to take Clara in.

Clara's awkwardness melted away and she held her head high and strode forward with purpose, thankful Anne had suggested she change. Clara hadn't forgotten Lady Fulton's derisive remarks about her six years ago and the way they'd revealed her true opinion of Clara. She was not a girl in a simple dress and wearing her jewellery as if it were nothing better than an old chandelier chain that she'd decided to drape around her neck. Clara's gown might be muted, but it was fine, and the emeralds she wore spoke of her increased status. She was no longer a plain country mouse, but a refined lady.

'Lady Kingston, there you are. Come now, you must take your place beside Lord Delamare so we may all go in,' Lady Tillman called out, moving up through the parting guests to reach Clara and take her by the hand.

Clara did her best to concentrate on the stairs and not trip over Lady Tillman's short train as her hostess pulled her down the stairs. Around her, the line had gone silent and she could almost hear people wondering if they would be treated to the same show of courting and rejection that they'd witnessed six years ago. They would not enjoy any sort of amusement from her, assuming Hugh decided to behave with dignity when she reached him. If he wished to give a little of what he'd got from her in the library, this was a perfect opportunity to do it. She didn't think him so petty, but after what she'd heard of him in London, it was a possibility. It made her want to twist out of Lady Tillman's grip and run back to her room, but she would not look like a coward in front of the other guests, especially Lady Fulton. Instead, she would sit next to Hugh at dinner with all the bearing and dignity of a marchioness and everyone else could get their entertainment elsewhere.

Lady Tillman and Clara finally reached the bottom of the stairs and Clara stopped before Hugh, her heart racing from both the quick descent and her nerves. If Clara's attire had changed in six years, then so had Hugh's. He was taller than the gentlemen on the step above him and his broad shoulders did more credit to the wool covering them than the talents of his Jermyn Street tailor. His dark trousers hugged his trim middle and thighs, and he wore his hair combed back off his strong face, the knot of his white cravat tucked neatly beneath his square chin. If she hadn't heard the rumours, she would have thought he'd spent the last three years at Everburgh riding and engaging in other sports, not in debauchery at the theatres and clubs of London.

'Good evening, Lord Delamare,' she greeted, trying to convince everyone, including herself, that it made no difference to her if she was seated next to him and that she could be gracious and friendly to an old flame with the poise expected of a woman of her standing.

'Good evening, Lady Kingston. You look lovely tonight.' His unstudied words raised Clara's confidence higher than when she'd approached Lady Fulton at the top of the stairs and allowed her to breathe again. She hadn't known what to expect when she'd descended, but she hadn't expected this compliment and it almost rattled her surety, especially when Lady Tillman laid Clara's hand on Hugh's arm.

The sight of her satin-covered fingers against the black fabric of his coat brought back a hundred memories. They were of Alfred escorting her into dinner or a ballroom, the two of them chatting and laughing while they walked. It'd been two years since she'd stood beside a man like this and loneliness and loss overwhelmed her. It should be Alfred beside her, but it wasn't and it never would be again.

'Are you all right, Lady Kingston?' Hugh laid his hand comfortingly over hers.

She raised her face to his, having forgotten for a moment to keep her chin up. She offered him a weak smile, trying to be regain her composure, but it was difficult with his warm hand covering hers. If she could let down her guard long enough to tell him the truth, she would, but she couldn't, not here and certainly not with him. 'Yes, only sometimes I find it difficult at this time of year.'

It was the most she could say.

'I understand.' He squeezed her fingers, his thumb lightly brushing hers, the steady motion soothing her. There was nothing calculated in the gesture or his words, only a desire to ease her pain in a way very few had tried to do since the weeks surrounding the funeral.

'Are you ready to lead them in?' Lady Tillman asked, drawing Clara's attention away from Hugh.

'Yes, of course,' Clara stammered, everything she'd intended to do tonight from walking regally like a queen to ignoring Hugh thrown into confusion. For a long time, her grief had been hers alone to bear, expected by all to grow fainter as time passed, but he'd seen it and for a moment he'd helped her to

shoulder it. This was a greater comfort to her than
all the showing up of Lady Fulton and Lord Westbook, and it stunned her that it should come from
him. After the way she'd spoken to him in the library, she'd expected derision instead of kindness.

They started off down the hall and she raised her
head high, concentrating on the pearls woven in their
hostess's coiffure and not Hugh's steady steps or the
shift of his arm beneath her palm. His hand remained
covering hers, the pressure of his fingers distracting. She wished he'd acted like a rake instead of a
gentleman. It would make it so much easier to decide how to behave with him tonight. While his kind
words were appreciated, it didn't change their past
or her opinion of him and this unfortunate seating
arrangement.

They all strolled into the dining room. The table
was bereft of treats and laid out in its splendid china
and silver which glistened in the high polish of the
table's finish. Everything about this room was sumptuous with the walls done in a deep red wallpaper
covered with numerous gilded frames of hunting
portraits and the English countryside. Along the
edges of the room, the guests moved past fine burled
oak sideboards with marble tops and elaborate can-
delabras, vases and other adornments. At the other
end, a large fire roared in a hearth decorated by white
moulding similar in shape to the classical front of
Stonedown Manor. Clara pitied Lord Tillman who
would sit with his back to the blaze and likely roast

as much as the meat course. If he did mind the heat, he never said anything, enduring it so the guests at Clara's end of the table would not shiver through the meal.

Despite the formality of the setting, everyone except those newest to the party approached their seats in leisure as if they were in their own homes. When they reached their places, Hugh finally let go of Clara and she took her place beside Lady Tillman, conscious of every move Hugh made when he sat down on her right. With Lord Worth on Lady Tillman's other side and dominating her attention with conversation, Clara realised she would either have to slurp her soup in silence or find a way to speak with Hugh. She didn't wish to converse with him at all, but to be alone and think about what had just happened. He hadn't behaved at all as she'd expected and she'd been foolish enough to allow a touch of kindness to make her almost slip and reveal to him something of the lonely woman beneath the confident Marchioness. He didn't deserve to see that woman or to know the details of her heart, both good and bad. He deserved nothing but her disdain, but it was difficult to find the resolve to deride him so severely again.

Unable to decide what to do, she did nothing except remain silent and listen to the conversations around her while she ate. Hugh was in no hurry to break the stalemate either. Where he'd been quite free with his words in the library and then again on the stairs, he'd gone mute now, focusing on his plate as if it was the most important thing in the room. He didn't even make an effort to speak to Lady Pariston who sat on his other side. The manners her mother had instilled in her urged Clara to at least mention the weather, but she couldn't bring herself to do even that. She didn't want to appear like an overeager debutante and force him into a conversation he clearly didn't want. Instead, she continued to eat her soup, thankful that with the balls and other events, there wouldn't be too many similar dinners to endure this week.

Clara swirled her soup with her spoon, leaving a quickly disappearing trail in the thick, pale green surface, the tension between them ruining the taste of her food. This was not at all how she'd imagined this week unfolding and she wondered, if she chose to go with Anne and Adam to London, if that experience would be any better. There had been moments of delight during her first Season in London, but they'd quickly faded while she'd stood against the wall at dances or watched her mother send yet another young man with a pile of debts in search of a rich wife packing. Returning to London as the wife of a peer in the House of Lords had been so much better. She'd been proud of Alfred's accomplishments and had done her best to help him by hosting dinners for his political friends and attending balls. She hadn't returned to town since his death, not wanting to face all its pitfalls alone. She would have to face it if she wanted to find a new life, for the society of the country was very limited if Hugh's presence was any indication. Lady Tillman must be hard up for guests to have invited him.

She glanced past Hugh to thin Lady Pariston with her lace shawl and tweedy-coloured dress, the weight of the large diamond necklace she wore making her hunched posture more pronounced. While Clara used to enjoy sitting with Lady Pariston by the fire in the evenings and listening to her tales of Stonedown Manner in the old days, she wondered if becoming a similar little old lady was to be her fate. She was a dowager, too, and glancing around the table, it was clear there would be no Alfred to rescue her this time from an ignoble future. It made her lose her appetite.

Then she caught Hugh's gaze and her heart made a little flutter. No, he wouldn't rescue her either, unless he deemed her purse large enough to make her more attractive. It would be up to her to find some other way of moving on long after this party concluded, but, touching her gloved hand to where the imprint of Hugh's heaviness still lingered, it was difficult not to remember a previous Christmas that had been full of potential, until it hadn't been.

Hugh set down his soup spoon and sat back against the chair, allowing the footman to take away the half-eaten dish and replace it with the next course. Beside him, Clara began to eat her fish, her gloved hand moving the silver fork elegantly back and forth from the plate to her full red lips. Every now and then she'd lean forward in her seat, lengthening the line of her back, her pert chin pressed out a touch above the long line of her neck to where it curved down to her supple chest. The whiteness of her skin was a stark contrast to the deep green of her gown. The colour matched the richness of the emeralds in her necklace and the jewels sparkled with each of her movements. The cut of her bodice, although modest, still revealed a touch of the soft creaminess of her chest. She was finely attired even if it whispered of mourning, but the heavier material flattered her more than the wispy gowns of the women who'd come up from London for the house party. The gown added grace to her once-awkward movements and told him that she had grown a great deal since the last time he'd seen her.

She set down her fork and frowned a touch when she could not catch all the words of Lord Worth's conversation with Lady Missington from across the table. That Clara longed to be sitting next to him and taking in every story about the last session of Parliament instead of beside Hugh was clear. If it were in his power to release her to do so, he would, but they sat where precedence dictated and they were beholden to it, and to each other to make conversation, except they had yet to make any.

Hugh poked at his fish and the white sauce covering it. He'd spoken to Clara twice today. The first time, she'd sneered at him and his reputation and accused him of being in search of money, leaving him in no doubt about her opinion of him. The next time, with her standing beside him, her hair swept off her neck and done in ringlets at the back of her head that shivered with each of her delicate movements, she'd lost her sneer and the veil of courage she'd worn when she'd descended the stairs to reveal the grieving woman beneath. Without thinking, he'd laid his hand on hers, recognising her hurt and longing to crush it like a walnut shell. She didn't deserve to suffer, but to enjoy her youth and the merry season. He'd succeeded for a quick moment in easing a pain he knew all too well, but his comfort hadn't lasted. Nor had it been enough to change her mind about him, even a little. She remained determined to think the worst of him and make him endure her silence because of it.

He cast Clara another sideways glance and she paused in her eating, conscious of his scrutiny and quickly meeting his curious gaze before she returned to her fish. He let her go, but not without a great deal of guilt. He'd ruined her Christmas once before by being too open and easy with her when he should have been more guarded and reserved, reminding him of how much she'd changed since they'd last sat at this table together. Back then, she'd been further down the line of precedence and across from him, hindering any chance he might have had to speak with her despite their eagerness to converse. They'd spoken instead through longing glances, smiles and coquettish looks tossed across the table, not careful or caring if anyone else saw them, and it had in-creased her embarrassment in the end.

People would whisper again, but this time it would be about the stony silence between them, the one that had already garnered a number of small frowns from Lady Exton from where she sat next to her husband. Once in a while she would comment to Adam who would glance up at Clara and Hugh. He didn't silently urge Hugh to speak to his sister, but simply offered a few words to his wife before returning to his meal. Hugh set down his fork and picked up the punch he'd requested from the footman. The sweetness nearly made him gag. His failed courtship of Clara had al-most cost him his friendship with Adam, he didn't wish to risk it again by mistaking the brief moment at the bottom of the stairs for something more than a genuine thank you for his having been kind. This silence was intolerable, but he would endure it to keep the peace between himself and Adam and to spare Clara from any derision that his previous lack of discretion had caused her. He had no one but him-self to blame for her poor opinion of him and again he cursed his actions of the last three years.

Hugh took in the other guests who were too en-gaged in discussion with those around them to no-tice him, but he caught a few curious looks thrown in his direction now and then. It was clear in the way that many regarded him with sidelong glances that they'd heard the stories about him and continued to wonder if they were true. He would show them they

weren't through his actions and defy all their low
expectations, even Clara's. He was here to begin the
slow process of undoing his mistakes in London after
Hermione's death, to rebuild the good name he'd
once prided himself on holding, the one he'd carelessly tossed away in his grief. No whiff of scandal
could touch him, especially while Lord Westbook
was here and no doubt watching for any more stories to entertain other hostesses with. Everything
Hugh did this week, especially in regards to Clara,
must be above board and if it meant sitting here in
silence beside Clara until she chose to break it, then
so be it. He'd endured worse things in his duty to the
Delamare name. He could endure this even while
he wished there was some way he could change it.

At the end of the meal, Lady Tillman led the ladies out of the room while Lord Tillman called for
the brandy. The men rose from their places of prec-
edent and took up more informal seats at Lord Tillman's end of the table. Hugh chose the chair beside
Sir Nathaniel, eager to talk to the man who, before
his ennoblement, had been a celebrated barrister and
who understood the vagaries of the law better than
most titled men. The letter informing Hugh that a
lawsuit for possession of Everburgh had been filed
had forced him out of London as much as his disgust
with himself. He might have turned away from duty
and responsibility for a while, but he hadn't given
up on it entirely because it wasn't an easy thing to

set aside, nor could he abandon trying to accomplish everything that his father and even Hermione had sacrificed their lives to help him achieve. It might mean more struggle and difficulties, but he would see this through and seize every advantage available to him, including setting his pride aside and asking for help from Sir Nathaniel, Lord Tillman and Adam.

To Hugh's dismay, Lord Westbook took the chair on Hugh's opposite side. He gave the man no notice as he leaned in towards Sir Nathaniel. 'I understand you once handled a case concerning the signing over of an estate when the signee was in no position to make such a decision and succeeded in having the contract voided.'

'I did.' Sir Nathaniel leaned forward with his elbows against the table to give them some privacy in their discussion. The rest of the gentlemen sat back, savouring their drinks and the conversation, while Lord Westbook sat ramrod straight in his chair, no doubt watching and listening to everything. Let him hear what Sir Nathaniel had to say, his opinion and all his stupid little stories meant nothing to Hugh. Besides, the pending case was already well known in London and another of the many tales already attached to his name. 'And I'm familiar with your case.'

'What do you think of it?'

'I think you have a solid one against the enforcement of the contract, should the Scotsman ever produce it. Who's representing you?'

'No one, yet.' He couldn't afford any long, drawn-out payments to solicitors. Everburgh might be clear of debts, but the harvest had not sufficiently recovered enough to provide a robust income. Hugh must continue to economise and endure a few more lean years before he and his estate workers could at last breathe easy, assuming Everburgh wasn't stolen out from under him. 'I was thinking of engaging Featherton and Associates.'

'A good firm, but not the one for something like this. You need Allenton and Associates, one of their best barristers used to work for me, I trained him up. He knows the case you're referring to and has handled other matters dealing with questionable contacts. He's the best for you.'

And expensive, Hugh thought, but in a matter like this he could not afford to be stingy. He would find a way to obtain the money to pay for their services, he had no choice. 'I'll be certain to engage them.'

The footman tried to set a snifter of brandy before Hugh, but he waved it away.

'Is there another spirit I can offer you, Lord Delamare?' the footman asked, eager like his employer to make the guests happy.

'None, thank you.'

'Nothing to warm the soul on a cold night?' Sir Nathaniel asked, taking up his drink.

'I warmed my soul one too many times on both cold and hot nights to realise I need to return to simpler more noble pursuits, such as my estate.'

'An admirable choice a number of gentlemen would do well to make.' Sir Nathaniel regarded him with an appraising look, the kind Hugh usually saw in mamas sizing him up at balls as a potential catch before they wrinkled their noses in displeasure and moved on to greener and less tarnished pastures. Hugh waited for Sir Nathaniel to do the same, but instead he took a deep sip of his drink and set it down, more admiration in his expression than reprimand.

'If you'd like, I can write to Allenton and Associates to recommend you to them so you receive their best service,' Sir Nathaniel offered.

'I'd like that very much.' This raised his spirits more than brandy ever could. This was not the usual reaction he received from those who'd appraised him of late, especially those with whom he was not well acquainted. There was no reason for Sir Nathaniel to assist him, but Hugh was glad of his kindness and generosity and would do all he could to deserve it.

It was then Lord Westbook sat forward, his long and narrow face punctuated by a too snake-like smile. 'I'm sure your turn towards temperance in this and other pursuits will help you a great deal in your case, Lord Delamare.'

Hugh pinned the man with a hard stare, in no mood to share any of his personal matters with this weasel. 'My behaviour has no bearing on the enforcement of the law.'

'Behaviour always has a bearing on cases for judges are men like any other and, given your opponent's spotless reputation, a judge might look upon him more favourably than he does you.'

'Careful how you call my reputation into question, Lord Westbook, or I may find a way to revive it in your eyes with a more formal challenge,' Hugh growled in a low voice. Thankfully, Mr Alton asked Sir Nathaniel a question, drawing his attention away from the less-than-civil turn in Hugh and Lord Westbook's conversation.

Lord Westbook went pale beneath his ruddy complexion, his spine not so stiff when faced with a challenge more formidable than making society ladies titter with delight at scandalous tales in order to secure an invitation to yet another party.

Hugh rather hoped Lord Westbook was man enough to force his hand, but Hugh didn't wish to be rude to their host or to lose Sir Nathaniel's newfound respect by calling out a fellow guest. Nor did he appreciate the kernel of truth in Lord Westbook's nasty words. Hugh might not have done more than most lords in London, but he'd been careless in keeping it discreet. Lord Westbook was right. If his matter came before the wrong judge, Hugh's past behaviour might be taken into account. It made his need to be impeccable and avoid any whiff of scandal from here on out far more pressing.

'Lady Kingston, we haven't had a chance to speak since you arrived.' Lady Fulton squeezed in between Clara and Lady Pariston where they sat on the sofa, enjoying the fire and a great deal of catching up. Anne had been forced to leave the women directly after dinner to help take care of poor Lillie who'd eaten too many sweets and become sick in the nursery where the rest of the children dined. From across the new arrival, Lady Pariston threw Clara a sympathetic and curious look, both of them wondering what in the world Lady Fulton could possibly have to speak with Clara about. Lord Fulton was an agreeable man, but his considerably younger wife, who'd possessed more mercantile money than lineage before becoming Lady Fulton, wasn't such a charming delight. She was tall and slender, and although her bloom had faded she was still attractive. However, her constant sneer did a great deal to temper it. 'I must say, your necklace is gorgeous. Was it your mother's?'

'No, it was a Christmas present from my late husband,' Clara answered coolly, irked by the woman's uninvited intrusion and her ignoring Lady Pariston.

'He had exquisite taste in jewellery,' she purred with a covetousness to make Clara think she meant Alfred had more taste in baubles than he did ladies, but she smiled and accepted the compliment with far more graciousness than Lady Fulton deserved. 'It's a pity precedence has forced you to waste this display of finery on a man like Lord Delamare. One would think after what happened the last time the two of you were here together that he would have had the decency to stay away. I'm surprised, given

his reputation in town, that he was even invited.'
She raised her hand to speak from the back of it as
if she and Clara were sharing some great intimacy.
'As much as I adore Lady Tillman, I've always questioned her selection of guests. Sometimes they can
be so common.'

Her gaze flicked over Clara, who was certain that
Lady Fulton was including her in that collection.
Clara's title might garner her respect, but not from
everyone, especially someone like Lady Fulton who,
despite the fashionableness of her dark blue evening
dress, and the gaudy gold jewellery she wore, could
not completely hide her more humble roots.

'I believe a wide variety of guests always lends a
touch of surprise to any gathering. One never knows
who one might meet here, isn't that right, Lady Pariston?'

'It is,' the grand dame concurred, too old to be
ruffled by a parvenu like Lady Fulton. 'Who knows
what might come of new friendships.'

'But they aren't all new, are they?' Lady Fulton
leaned closer to Clara, her look of affected concern
as sickening as her overly sweet perfume. 'It can't
be easy for you to see him again.'

Clara sat up straighter so she could peer down her
nose at the rude woman. Whatever impression she'd
made on Lady Fulton in the hallway before dinner
had worn off. It was time to assert herself again. 'I
find it as easy to see him as I do to see those who

overstep the bounds of propriety by speaking too intimately to their betters.'

Lady Fulton jerked back and pressed her thin lips tight together at having been put in her place and by Clara of all people. Clearly she hadn't expected this show of spirit and if she hadn't risen at that moment to seek out other companionship, she would have tasted a great deal more of it. Clara almost wished she had stayed for, with her hackles raised and the tension still lingering from dinner, a little tiff would help her sit much easier on the sofa while they waited for the men to join them.

'Well done, Lady Kingston,' Lady Pariston congratulated, patting her on the knee. 'You stood up to her as you should.'

'I wish it hadn't been necessary to do so.' But Lady Fulton had been the one to strike the first blow. Who was she to cast any aspersions on Clara or even Hugh? Yet she'd felt bold enough to do it simply because of Hugh's presence and their unfortunate seating at the dinner table. 'With any luck, that will put an end to any of her other observations about me, at least in public.'

She could not control what they said in private any more than she could command Hugh to leave. She could only hope that nothing else happened this weekend to give that vile woman or anyone else more cause to look down their noses at her or to insist on seeing her as nothing more than the awkward young girl she'd once been. She would not be made to feel inconsequential again, not by Lady Fulton and certainly not by Hugh.

'Care less what others think and you'll be happier, I promise,' Lady Pariston instructed, as if able to hear her doubts about herself and this week. 'Besides, the way Lord Delamare regarded you tonight won't silence anyone's tongues and if they're going to whisper then you might as well give them something worth whispering about. A house party is as good a place as any to do it.'

'Lady Pariston!' Clara could not believe she was having this conversation with a woman who could be her grandmother or that Lady Pariston was suggesting that Hugh had regarded her with a great deal of interest. The only thing he was probably interested in was her money.

'Oh, don't look so shocked. You'd be surprised by what all these ladies get up to, but you won't hear about it because they're discreet. I was discreet, too, and oh, I did have my fun, not when I was married, mind you, but on a number of occasions afterwards.' She laid a wrinkled and bejewelled hand on her chest and smiled with winsome pride. 'With a little discretion you could get up to a little trouble with that fine specimen of a marquess yourself.'

First Anne, now Lady Pariston. There were times when Clara seemed like the only one who cared about the blemishes of Hugh's past. 'I've already had enough trouble with Lord Delamare and, judging by what I've heard of him, he's had a fair amount of his own trouble.'

'Good, it means he knows his way around a woman.' Lady Pariston winked at her before throwing back her head and laughing. Clara's cheeks began to burn as people turned to view them before returning to their amusement. Then Lady Pariston sobered and faced her again. 'Seriously, my dear, you have been placed in this position at far too young an age and now you must make the best of it. Don't work so hard to please others, only yourself, and if that pleasure should include the young man, then so be it.'

Clara waved her hand in front of her face against the heat of the fire. 'I assure you, what I want does not include Lord Delamare.'

'Don't be so set against it. It does no good for a woman to be alone, especially when there is a man willing to keep her company.' Lady Pariston sat back, regarding her out of the corner of her eyes as if she didn't believe for a moment what Clara had said.

Clara laid her hand in her lap with a sigh. She could insist it was true but there was no point. Lady Pariston was right, people would believe what they wanted and Clara should not be guided by a desire to try to control it. All she could control was how she responded to everyone, including Hugh, but she had no energy to do any more of that tonight. Rising, she offered the ladies goodnight and took her leave, unwilling to wait for the arrival of the men.

It would be a pleasure to be alone in her room

where no one expected more of her than blowing out her candle before she fell asleep and she didn't need to deal with the issue of Hugh and how to handle him while she was here. She wasn't about to follow Lady Pariston's advice, but she was at a loss for her own ideas about what to do. She needed her rest if she was going to face more of it tomorrow. Heaven knew this was not how she'd expected this week to be.

Chapter Three

'You and Lord Delamare were quite silent at dinner last night,' Anne remarked, taking the empty seat beside Clara in the sitting room where all the guests were gathering for the traditional partnering for the week's activities. The ladies wore their sturdy pelisses and shoes and held their leather gloves in anticipation of an outside game. The weather had remained pleasant if not cold and everyone was sure the Tillmans would take advantage of it to amuse their guests. The men were equally bundled up in heavier coats and redingotes, but everyone had undone the top few buttons to keep from sweltering in the warm sitting room.

'We weren't completely silent,' Clara explained matter of factly. 'I asked him to pass the salt and he was most obliging.'

'Yes, quite the conversation.' Anne rolled her eyes.

'I wonder who we'll be paired with,' Clara mused, eager to change the subject as she glanced around

at the motley collection of titled and untitled guests
scattered about the room. She rather hoped it would
be with eighteen-year-old Lord Wortley so she could
help set him at ease. She remembered what it was
like to be without one's parents at his age and how
awkward it'd been. Thankfully, Hugh wasn't here.
With any luck he would continue to stay away and
she would be spared his presence for the better part
of the day. Sadly, there was still tonight's dinner to
endure.

'I'm sure it will be exciting no matter who is chosen for you.'

'I hope so.' The festive activities here had always been one of Clara's favourite parts of the annual house party.

Lord Tillman sat in an armchair next to the fireplace, entertaining James, Lillie and a number of
other children with a sleight-of-hand card trick. If
Lord Tillman weren't such an honourable and forth-
right gentleman, he could make a great deal of money
at the tables with such tricks, but, recognising his
talent, he often refused to play unless it was for fun
or small stakes. He would make the cards disappear
as if by magic, eliciting from the children oohs of
amazement before he made the card reappear from
behind one of their ears, sending the children into fits
of laughter. Their delight both warmed and saddened
Clara. There wasn't a child of hers among them to
marvel at Lord Tillman's sleight of hand.

The curtain of melancholy threatened to fall over

her again, but its descent was halted by the arrival of Hugh. With him standing on the threshold taking in the guests before his attention alighted on her, the last thing she wanted was to appear glum or to risk losing a single tear. He'd humiliated her enough in front of most of these people once before. She didn't need her private sorrows, no matter how much they seared her heart, leaving her in a crying puddle to be pitied. Determined to appear at ease, she touched the combs in the back of her coiffure, pretending as if Hugh's arrival made no difference to her.

He soon looked away from her and strode up to Sir Nathaniel and began to chat with him. As if aware that she was watching him, he tossed her a quick glance that made her drop her gaze to her feet and the sturdy boots she wore. She wasn't sure how long he regarded her, but no matter where she looked or how much she concentrated on the view through the window she could not forget that he stood only the length of the room away from her. Outside, the snow that had threatened yesterday had not fallen, but the clouds lingered to blot out the sunshine and cast a grey pall over the countryside. Very soon, or so everyone had discussed at breakfast, they expected to see snow. It would be a great delight for the children and the guests since the Tillmans owned a sleigh that they placed at their guests' disposal for rides. Clara and Hugh had taken advantage of the Tillmans' generosity with the sleigh many times during their last visit, with Hugh expertly handling the ribbons as he'd guided the sturdy plough horse over the gently sloping hills and wide fields. Clara would sit close beside him, her hips pressed against his and the lap blanket spread across both their thighs to keep them warm. During the rides, he'd talked endlessly about his hopes for Everburgh and how his inheritance sat heavy on his shoulders. He'd explained to her all his ideas for improving the manor lands to increase the crops and the profits derived from them, and she'd encouraged every one of them, convinced that he would succeed in making Everburgh as magnificent as it had once been. As she'd held tight to his arm, sometimes leaning her head on his shoulder, she'd imaged herself beside him, helping him overcome all the difficulties that he'd endured over the years until they were firmly set in the past. Clara had understood what it was like to struggle under the weight of a title for she'd watched Adam assume the earldom and all responsibility for Winsome after their father had died. She knew how difficult it was to make the transition and how much more so it was for Hugh. Winsome had been well managed and smoothly run with nothing like the troubles that had plagued Everburgh. While Hugh had spoken, the breath of the horses driving the sleigh had risen like clouds over their heads and Clara had dreamed of helping him make his dreams for the manor come true.

Clara flicked a piece of fluff off the skirt of her pelisse, missing that old easiness with Hugh. There'd been none of it last night and when she turned from the window and her eyes caught his again, all the stiff awkwardness returned. Not even when Hugh had been nothing more than Adam's friend and she a pest of a little sister had his mere presence in the same house as her been so unpleasant. At least back then, when they were little more than children, he'd held some genuine regard for her.

'Don't stare too much, Clara, or people will talk,' Anne teasingly warned.

'I wasn't staring, I was simply marvelling at how well he conceals the meaner side of his personality.' He'd hidden it from Clara, her parents and even Adam, so much so, her brother still pretended these traits didn't exist. Adam approached Hugh who offered her brother the first smile she'd seen since his arrival, even if it was a shallow one that faded fast. She wished she could be so at ease with him.

'It isn't as mean as you wish to believe. He was grieving, Clara, like you and chose to deal with it in his own way,' Anne insisted, but Clara wasn't convinced.

'By acting like his grandfather and dallying with half the actresses in London?'

'Lord Delamare isn't the awful man you think he is and if you simply spoke to him I think you would see that.'

Clara wondered at Anne's continued defence of the man and if Anne knew something about Hugh's situation that Clara was not privy to, but there was no time to ask for Lady Tillman entered the room carrying an old hat. A ripple of excitement spread through the still as she joined Lord Tillman at the fireplace.

'Welcome, everyone, and thank you so much for joining us again. It warms the heart to have my family and all my old friends and their children near at this special time of year,' Lady Tillman announced.

'Hear, hear.' A rousing cheer went up from the men while the women offered polite applause. The children were shooed out of the room by their nurses and governesses while Lord Tillman explained about the hat and the pairing for those new to the group. Lady Tillman would draw a woman's name from her hat and then Lord Tillman would draw a man's name from his hat. Those two people would then be paired together for each activity that Lord and Lady Tillman had devised for the week. It was one of the rituals that had been taking place here for so many years and would, if fate allowed, continue for many more to come.

When at last the Tillmans were done thanking and welcoming and explaining, a footman came forward to hold the two hats. Lady Tillman drew the first lady's name.

'Lady Pariston.'

The Dowager nodded from where she sat wrapped in a large shawl.

Lord Tillman reached his hand into his hat and pulled out a name. 'Lord Wortley.'

The room applauded the strange pairing, while Lord Wortley rose to join his new partner. Clara almost slumped her shoulders in disappointment before the announcement of the next pairing drew her back into the excitement of the morning, one tinged with a touch of anxiety at Hugh's continued presence. She did her best to ignore it and to enjoy instead the anticipation and laughter that met each new announced pair. Family members and strangers were brought together or separated in the spirit of the Christmas festivities and Clara waited, wondering who she would end up with for a partner when at last Lady Tillman drew out her name.

'Lady Kingston,' she announced.

'And what lucky man will be paired with what I can only describe as the loveliest of ladies and the most eligible?' Lord Tillman teased while he dipped his hand into the hat and rustled the paper. Then at last he drew out a small slip and opened it. Clara balled her hands over her legs and waited as if she were receiving a Christmas morning present.

Lord Tillman's eyebrows rose a touch before he showed the slip to his wife, who giggled like a young girl before the both of them turned to face Clara.

Lord Tillman's clear voice rang out. 'Lord Delamare.'

Clara nearly fell out of her chair. No, no, no, this wasn't possible.

A quick intake of surprise almost sucked the smoke from the chimney as all eyes turned to either her or Hugh. Both Clara and Hugh knew what was expected of them, they should rise and, in a fit of laughter and smiles, pair up on a sofa or in the matched chairs near the window, but neither of them moved. Clara didn't so much as look at him as she struggled to smile, to breathe, to do anything except sit there like a startled rabbit.

It was Anne who broke the ice, clapping and laughing as was expected of the guests after each announcement. Slowly, the rest of the room joined in. Clara shot Anne a stiff smile, hoping her sister-in-law would catch the panic just beneath. She had no desire to be paired with Hugh for dinner much less for every activity of the entire week, but it was either speak up and insist that Lord Tillman draw again and be rude to their host and cause even more unnecessary whispering or rise and take her place beside Hugh. Not wishing to make more of a spectacle of herself than she feared she already was, she had no choice but to get up and join him.

Why in heaven's name had she allowed Anne to talk her into coming to this house party?

Clara stood slowly, putting on her best party face as she turned to greet Hugh in the centre of the room. He wore a similarly false and overly wide smile, pretending like her that this was not a very unexpected and unwanted turn of events. Her heart raced, not with excitement like it had six years ago, but with the painful realisation that everyone was watching them. Not even Lord and Lady Tillman had moved on to form the next couple—they, like the rest of their guests, were waiting for Hugh and Clara to move aside. Not one to prolong the awkward moment, Clara made for an open seat near the window and Hugh followed her. They said nothing about the imposed partnership, but sat through the rest of the pairings, clapping as stiffly at each announcement as they had during the four words they'd exchanged at dinner last night.

Adam and Anne, by chance again, were paired up to their mutual delight while Lord Westbook found himself with Lady Fulton. Lord Fulton was left to join with Lady Worth while Sir Nathaniel was paired with Mrs Alton. Clara thought Lord Westbook and Lady Fulton a good match for they were both overly fond of gossip and would have a great deal to discuss while they were together, unlike she and Hugh. Heaven knew what catty remarks that pair of busybodies would make about Clara this time.

No, I shouldn't care. Lady Pariston's suggestion to ignore people's whispering came back to her, but Clara found it difficult to shrug off her concern. She didn't like being the subject of gossip, good or bad, and here she was at the centre of it again and it was all Hugh's fault.

Finally, the pairing complete, Lord and Lady Tillman had the footman take away the hats and set to explaining the first activity.

'It's a scavenger hunt,' Lady Tillman announced, sending another wave of excitement through the crowd. 'There are ten things on the grounds of Stonedown you must find and visit. The footman is hand-

ing out the papers with the clues and each numbered
clue has a corresponding number on the item it de-
scribes. Work out the clues and go to the objects to
see if you are correct, then you will return here, write
out your answers and give them to us. The pair with
the most correct answers will receive a fine bottle
of brandy to share between them.'

Lord Tillman held up the brandy which made the
bored husbands sit up and take notice. 'You will have
two hours to find all the objects. In the event of a
tie, we will ask questions about the object you saw
so pay attention to what you are seeing. A shot will
sound when you have fifteen minutes left and then
another will tell you when it is time to return. Good
luck, everyone, and happy hunting.'

Couples who already had their clues set off in
search of their described objects. While Clara and
Hugh waited for their copy of the clues, Clara tried
to appear pleased and relaxed, but inside she silently
sighed. At least the first activity wasn't a sleigh ride,
the lack of snow having put paid to any chance of
that. Snow or no snow didn't change the fact that
she must spend the following two hours combing
the Stonedown grounds for landmarks with Hugh.
At last, the footman handed her a copy of the clues
and Clara pretended to concentrate on them so she
wouldn't have to look at Hugh. Lady Fulton strolled
by with a swagger that made Clara look up from the
parchment.

'It will be an interesting game, won't it, Lady

Kingston?' she said, as if this were ample revenge for their exchange of words last night.

'They always are,' Clara responded as calmly as she could, as though this were just another event here and not the second most shocking and uncomfortable experience of her life.

'Well, perhaps you can share in our brandy after we win it, because we will win, won't we, Lord Westbook?'

'We have as good a chance as anyone.' He held out his arm to her and she took it before both of them stepped out into the frosty countryside air.

After that challenge, Clara could no longer stare at the parchment or ignore Hugh. She rose, trying to be polite and gracious even while she wanted to ball up the clues and lob them at the back of Lady Fulton's elegant hat. 'Shall we?'

'Lead the way.' He waved his arm towards the French door left ajar by the last couple who'd passed through it in search of brandy and glory.

Securing the buttons on her gloves against the cold air outside, she stepped on to the stone portico following the line of the house. Just beyond it was the brown lawn leading out towards a copse of trees. The grass, brittle with frost and cold, crunched beneath their boots while they walked, the harsh noise seeming to echo the chill between them.

The heavy silence that had enveloped them at dinner hung over them again like the clouds did the countryside, the weight of it just as oppressive. All around them, Clara could hear the excited chatter and laughter of the other guests enjoying themselves as they struck out in search of their treasures. She glanced at him as they walked side by side in no particular direction, having discussed none of the clues or where they would begin. His face was passive with no hint of disappointment at this unfortunate circumstance, except Clara was tired of disappointment and worry and the constant tension. She didn't wish to spend another Christmas in this state and Hugh Delamare be damned. She would not allow this awkwardness to dominate the week or ruin yet another merry season. He was the past, a very brief moment of it, and she would no longer permit it to command the present.

'I assume you know where we are going?' Hugh asked.

'Just there.' She pointed to the line of trees at the edge of the lawn, eager to be out of sight of the house and far enough away from the other guests to give Hugh a clue of a very different kind. She led him into the shadow of the trees where the temperature noticeably dropped, adding a deeper chill to the already biting air. She was glad for it because it stiffened her resolve even while she clutched her arms around her to stave off the cold. 'We must speak before we can discuss the clues.'

'About what?' Hugh asked, the cold appearing not to trouble him.

She rubbed her arms, fighting off the desire to

take the easy path and let him be the one to speak first or to keep pretending that all was well, even when it wasn't. She would not sacrifice a chance at a pleasant Christmas merely to protect her ego from the possibility that she was about to make a bigger fool of herself now than she had with him six years ago, but the matter had to be settled.

'It seems there is some tension between us, if dinner last night is any indication,' she announced with all the directness of her and Adam's old tutor. 'We needn't rehash why this may be, but I hate to ignore it either. What happened between us the last time we were here together was regrettable, but that was a long time ago and a great deal has happened to us both since. I would hate for either of us to have the rest of the week ruined because of it. I'm not asking that we be friends, but that we put the past behind us and be to each other as we would if we'd been paired with anyone else. There's no reason to feel awkward together or ruin a good house party. I hope you agree.'

Clara set her shoulders, waiting to see what reaction this would provoke. She was amazed to see admiration slowly replace his shock.

Hugh stared down at Clara, who spoke to him with the same directness his man of affairs employed whenever he had to deliver bad news about the estate. He admired her ability to be so straightforward. It was a trait he rarely witnessed in any woman, especially not in his last mistress, Lady Frances. Even at the end of the relationship when they'd clearly been together out of habit and not affection, she hadn't possessed the same strength of character as Clara, leaving it to Hugh to end things between them. It had been a relief to both his pocket and his conscience. Other high-born men might dally with one young lady after another and think nothing of the consequences, but having a mistress was something he'd never been comfortable with. A good amount of late nights and cheap brandy had helped to quell his conscience, but it hadn't silenced it completely.

He was glad to see Clara possessed more fortitude than to allow this tension to linger between them and he regretted not being the one to say it first. She was right, their time together six years ago had been brief and although he had cared a great deal for her, far deeper than even he had been able to believe in so short an amount of time, he had made his decision and both of them had gone on to live other lives. Now they were together again and she was calling a halt to the unease that had dominated dinner last night, the one that would continue to annoy them if they didn't face this square on.

'I agree, Lady Kingston. I suspect that we've both come to Stonedown with similar purposes, to enjoy a Christmas of brightness after a few years of dark ones. I don't wish for my presence to prevent you from having what would otherwise be a wonderful holiday. We must put the past behind us and do our best to have fun during the brief time here.' He held out his hand for her to shake.

She stared at it a moment, clearly as aghast by his frankness as he'd been by hers. Hugh's fingers twitched while he waited for her to take his hand and he wondered if she would. Despite the moment at the base of the stairs last night when he'd comforted her, she hadn't been open or kind to him since their reunion. Even her proposal had been all business. There was nothing to say that this agreement between them would do anything more than thaw a touch of the ice surrounding them and things wouldn't continue on as they had since last night, except with a little more conversation.

He was about to pull back his hand and admit the futility of trying to reach out to her when she slowly stretched out her hand and finally took his.

The coldness of the trees overhead seemed to vanish as he stared into her eyes, the clouds of their breath meeting in the space between them. This gesture should have been nothing more than the sealing of a bargain, but it wasn't. While he held on to her, the time that had passed and all the heartache that had filled it between today and six years ago disappeared. She was simply young Clara again and he was taking the first tentative steps towards making her so much more. If he could draw her to him and slide his arm around her waist and bend her into the curve of his body to taste her full lips, he would. He wanted to make her wide eyes close with a sigh while he clasped her small body against his. If he could touch her so intimately, then maybe he could touch the Hugh he used to be, the one not corrupted by disappointment and his own failings, but a man she'd at one time admired and craved.

Instead, he let go of her and lowered his hand, the delicate imprint of her fingers on the back of his as vivid as her pale skin against the darker tones of her hair. They would never again mean what they had to each other back then, but at least the painful stiffness between them and her low opinion of him might change. If he could redeem himself in her eyes and receive her forgiveness, he could redeem himself in everyone's eyes and perhaps forgive himself. It was a goal he longed to obtain.

Clara let go of Hugh, but she didn't step away from him. Instead, she continued to stare at him, doing all she could to hide how stunned she was by his ready agreement and how easily she might have fallen into his arms and repeated all her prior mistakes when his hand had touched hers. When she'd spoken, she'd braced herself, expecting him to laugh off or dismiss her concerns as nothing more than an overactive imagination such as the one she'd employed when she'd thought that he would propose. She hadn't expected this ready agreement or the heat in his eyes that had threatened to melt the icicles hanging on the branches above them. If she had stepped closer to him, tilted back her head in invitation, she was certain he would have taken her in his arms and kissed her, and she wouldn't have stopped him. It was madness and she smoothed her hand over the front of her pelisse, trying to shake the feel of his fingers wrapped around hers, relieved the moment had passed.

I've spent too much time listening to Lady Pariston and Anne and it has muddled my thoughts.

Their tenuous truce would never hold if she fawned on him as she had six years ago. Besides, it was plain that their time together, for whatever it was worth, was long gone and while she might be lonely since Alfred's passing, she wasn't so lonely as to mistake Hugh for a man capable of easing it with both discretion and genuine affection. With a shaking hand she raised the crumpled parchment to read it, thinking they'd better get on with the hunt and stop dallying around before they found themselves in who knew what trouble. 'We should read the clues and see where to go before we run out of time and have no objects to our credit.'

'We can't have that.'

'Imagine how thrilled Lord Westbook and Lady Fulton would be to brag about besting a marquess and a marchioness in something as simple as a game.' She was certain that after the way Lady Fulton had approached her last night and at the start of the game, the woman would continue to do all she could to try to knock Clara down a peg or two. This odd pairing gave her more ammunition to do it with.

'Judging by the way she spoke to you at the start of the hunt, I see you've suffered the privilege of being the topic of one of Lord Westbook's stories or on the receiving end of Lady Fulton's sharp tongue.'

'More than once. I understand Lord Westbook, but I can't see why Lady Fulton has to be so difficult.'

'Because she's jealous of you.'

'Jealous?' It didn't seem possible.

'By belittling you, she hopes to raise herself up. You have a kindness and beauty that she lacks and where she bargained her money for a title, you achieved yours through love.'

'I'd never considered it that way.' Strange it should be Hugh who pointed it out and called her beautiful. She clasped the sides of the parchment tight against the compliment, afraid to read too much into it. It was his way of honouring the truce and nothing more. 'We can't let them beat us.'

'Then read the clue and let's win this game.'

She cleared her throat and read out the first clue. 'A thing with no hands that helps a man.'

He came to stand behind her, looking over her shoulder at Lady Tillman's fine Italian script. The strong scent of his sandalwood shaving soap made more potent by the crisp morning air took her by surprise. She shook off the temptation to tilt her head back against his shoulder and inhale by reading the words again. She could forgive him for what had happened but it didn't mean she should forget it or what he'd made of himself since. His prior behav-

iour told her more about him than any of his compliments ever could and she must believe this above all
other things. 'What do you think the clue means?'

'Hmmm, something helpful, but with no hands.'
Thankfully, he stepped away from her to ponder it,
stroking the fine line of his jaw with his fingers, his
eyes raised to the sky as if the answer were written
in the grey and white clouds passing overhead. In
this stance, he reminded her of the boy who used to
come to Winsome Manor to study with Adam during holidays, not the wastrel Marquess he'd become.
If only he could have held on to that innocence and
sense of youth, but, as Clara well knew, mourning
had a way of ageing a person. 'A tool, perhaps, something in the carpenter's shed?'

Clara shook her head. 'Lady Tillman may not
stand on convention, but she wouldn't send her
guests there. No, it has to be something closer to
the house.'

Across the lawn and somewhere beyond the trees,
they heard other guests talking and laughing while
they puzzled out different clues or moved on to a
new one.

'We'd better figure it out soon or we'll be the only
ones who don't find anything.'

Clara snapped her fingers, her gloves muffling
the sound. 'I know what it is. It's a sundial.'

'A clock with no hands and a clock is helpful to
man,' Hugh mused. 'Well done, Clara, but where's a

sundial? I didn't notice one in the garden when I was out there walking yesterday.'

She ignored his use of her familiar name, guiltily enjoying how it sounded in the deep tones of his voice. She shouldn't allow him to be so familiar with her, but if she chided him for it then the truce might end and the awkwardness she dreaded would return. 'It isn't in the garden, but at the top of a rise in a clearing overlooking the lake.'

'Then lead the way.'

Chapter Four

Clara and Hugh raced along the crushed gravel path that meandered through the trees to where it opened on to the lake near the bottom of a gently sloping hill. Along the bank of the lake, the path continued, disappearing up into a thick patch of trees that sat on a small hill overlooking the water.

'There's the path,' Clara announced when they were out in the open. Taking up the hem of her skirt, she made for it and Hugh followed close beside her. Their progress slowed a touch when the ground began to rise, the pace of their breathing increasing as each step became a little harder.

'Are you sure there's anything up there?' Hugh asked, not nearly as winded as Clara during the climb. Through the thick branches, they could barely see the lake or believe that this tangle of leafless ash and oak trees would ever break into something open.

'Yes, I'm certain it's there, but the area around the path has grown up so much I think most people who were aware of it have forgotten the way. The rest probably don't know it's here.'

'What makes you remember it so well?'

She raised her hem a little higher to step over a fallen branch. 'My mother and I used to walk here during our visits with Father for the hunting season. The view of Stonedown from the top is magnificent.' The closer they drew to the crest the quicker Clara moved despite the exertion of the climb and the constant dodging of rocks and dead branches. For a moment this was more than a scavenger hunt, but a brief chance to touch a part of her past that was as painful as the loss of her husband. With the stone sundial coming into view, the memory of her and her mother racing out from the line of the trees to see who could reach it first overcame her. She'd always win and her mother would laugh before standing with her arm around Clara to take in the view of Stonedown. Clara didn't race to the sundial this morning, but approached it with solemn reverence, the happy memory bittersweet. She was tired of mourning, of losing and regretting, and yet here she stood at this once-meaningful site with Hugh, one of the most potent regrets she'd ever endured.

She touched the sundial, running her hand along the front of it. So many times she'd tried to puzzle out the time, but reading the sundial, unlike retaining some Latin, was a skill she'd never mastered no matter how many times her mother had demonstrated how to do it. With no sun out today, there wasn't even

the chance to try. She missed her mother and father
and the happy days as a family with them at Winsome before their passing had left her with an inheritance and all the insecurities of a young woman
without a mother to guide her through the pitfalls
of society. If her mother had lived, perhaps Clara
wouldn't have stumbled with Hugh, or been left to
find her own way when it came to dresses and carrying herself and dealing with people like Lady Fulton.

Clara's melancholy turn must have shown on her
face for Hugh came up on the opposite side of the
sundial and rested his big hands on the solid surface.

'Are you all right?' he asked.

Clara thought of some flippant answer she could
give him about being winded from their walk, but,
like the real concern he'd shown her on the stairs last
night, it was clear by the grave tone of his voice that
he genuinely wanted to know. She owed his kindness a touch of truth untainted by any past bitterness. 'I was thinking of my mother and how much
I miss her and my father at this time of year. Some
days it feels as if I've spent too many Christmases
mourning loved ones.'

'I know.' He tapped one carved Roman numeral
with his fingers. 'Three Christmases before we…'
The rest of the sentence drifted away with the breeze.
Clara nodded to tell him he didn't need to speak the
words because, like him, she knew the story, too. He
said nothing more about the incident as he continued. 'I lost my father. It was difficult that first sea-

son to look around the table and realise someone so important was missing and how much that loss had changed me and everything. Then, after Hermione and my mother, every year has grown harder to bear. It's a lonely table now.'

'I know. Loss changes so much,' Clara whispered, once again struck by how strange it was that she could talk with him about her grief without shame or embarrassment. She shouldn't do so, but after keeping it bottled up for so long, afraid people would tire of listening to it or tell her that she should move past it, it was nice to speak with someone who genuinely understood, even if that someone was Hugh.

Hugh peered out over the water, the rippled surface of which had turned silver with the grey clouds covering the sky above it. Loss had changed him a great deal, far more than he cared to dwell on either silently or with Clara. He'd gone from the son of a marquess who'd been willing to set aside the desires of his own heart to do his duty to his family to a wastrel in London, cursing duty and determined to blot out the pain and guilt of his wife's loss through wine and women. He'd done everything asked of him and it still hadn't mattered and yet, in turning his back on his responsibilities, he'd made the pain even worse.

'You miss your wife?' Clara's sweet voice drew him away from the torment of his mistakes and back to her and the stunning countryside surrounding them.

'You seem surprised,' Hugh countered, but not in accusation. Hers had been a soft question of surprise and Hugh wasn't upset by Clara asking it. Everyone had known that his and Hermione's marriage had not been a love match.

'The last three years might indicate otherwise.'

'My exploits in London were greatly exaggerated.'

'All the actresses, you mean?'

'Yes. There were one or two, but their company is not as enjoyable as that of a woman of quality.' Hugh swallowed hard, sick again at the kind of man he'd become. He only hoped it wasn't too late to redeem himself and become again the honourable and noble man he'd once been.

'But still you dallied.'

'There are many reasons a man seeks out diversions in London, sometimes it's to be reckless and sometimes it's to forget. Hermione and I may not have gone to the altar in love, but we came to love one another through our work to finish what my father and mother had started at Everburgh. She shared my desire and willingness to do whatever it took to rebuild it and to make sacrifices to see that it, and the line, endured.'

He balled his fists against the pain, not sure why he was telling Clara this. They were not intimates or confidants, but in the soft, patient manner with which she regarded him, he couldn't hold back. In London, there had been many people willing to drink and carouse with him, but none eager to listen to or ease the

grief he carried, the one he'd tried to ignore and forget with one more glass of brandy or one more evening with Lady Frances. When he'd run into Adam
in London last Season, he'd thought his old friend
someone he could confide in, but Adam and Anne
were too happily married and certain of the solid-
ness of their life together for Adam to do more than
listen with sympathy. He couldn't understand Hugh's
pain the way Clara did. 'The day I lost Hermione was
one of the most difficult of my life. She'd been with
child, but lost it early. All should have been well and
we should have gone on to have more chances and
time together but the midwife, and later the doctor,
couldn't stop the bleeding. When I pressed them for
answers, all they could say was that sometimes this
happens and they didn't know why. That night, I sat
with her, encouraging and willing her to live, but
the weaker she grew, the less she heard me until she
was gone. I should have known she wasn't meant to
have children and been more cautious with her, but
she wanted so much to do her duty as a marchioness
and give me a son that she hid the true depth of her
weakness from me and everyone.'

'You aren't to blame for what happened.' Clara
reached out and covered his hand with hers, the motion impulsive and uncalculated, just as she'd always
been. 'Sadly, it's all too common even with the strongest of women.'

'But she died for nothing. I married her for money.
I admit that, but I didn't do it out of greed. I did it to

preserve everything my parents spent their lives trying to achieve. Although I came to love her, even her dowry wasn't enough to make Everburgh completely safe or free from worry. Despite every sacrifice that I and Hermione made, I'm still dealing with problems and on the verge of losing everything again. It's the reason I turned my back on duty when I was in London, for I did my duty and Hermione tried to do hers, and what did it gain us? Nothing.' Hugh wanted to smash the sundial to pieces until the pain inside him was smashed, too. Duty had once been the noblest reason for anyone to act, but it had become a chain that could kill the people bound to him, including his parents and his wife. He took a deep breath and unclenched his hand, refusing to allow the dark hate and anger that had nearly trampled him in London to claim him once again. 'Without her I was lost and a lost man is apt to lose his way in other regards.'

'I'm sure you'll soon find your way again.' Clara's grip on his hand tightened and she leaned towards him with a conviction to admire. 'I'm trying to find my way, too.'

'You don't seem as if you've lost your head.' He turned his hand over in hers and held it tight. Their gloves separated their flesh, but not the warmth between them and he clung to it and her, drawing comfort from both.

'I have in my own way. After Alfred's death, I cloistered myself at Winsome, avoiding the world and thinking that in doing so I could stop the pain, but it only made it worse. I can't live like that, without hope or prospect of a better future, nor would Alfred have wanted me to.'

'You don't deserve to be unhappy, but to enjoy life here or wherever you choose.'

'Some day we'll both be happy and all this awful business will be behind us, not entirely forgotten, but not so present and troubling.' She smiled and the sight of it swept the chill off Hugh in a way nothing else in the last three years, not all the brandy or his time with his mistress or anything, ever had.

'Yes, we will.' He gently squeezed her hand, eager to hold on to her and the contentment surrounding them for as long as he could, but it didn't last. From somewhere in the trees behind them, the voices of a man and woman made the birds stop twittering and Clara let go of Hugh.

'This way, I tell you it's here. I used to come here with my mother,' Adam's voice declared as he tugged Anne out of the line of the trees and into the clearing. They held hands, laughing and smiling, the love and ease between them obvious and admirable. There were few among their class who could claim such joy in their union, but Anne and Adam's marriage had been a love match, one for any couple to admire and emulate. Hugh hoped very much that he and Clara might soon meet people who would allow them to join their ranks. The fleeting thought that they could find such happiness together whispered through his mind before he pushed it aside.

Adam and Anne jerked to a halt, but the laughing smiles on their faces only grew wider. They exchanged a knowing look and Hugh could practically feel the heat of Clara's blush from across the sundial. Thankfully they hadn't caught Hugh and Clara holding hands. Their gesture of comfort was innocent enough, but Hugh knew other people wouldn't take it that way. Thankfully, it was Anne and Adam who'd stumbled on them. They would be more discreet than someone like Lord Westbook, but how the two of them felt about what some might view as Hugh dallying with Clara again remained to be seen. Blaming it on the spirit of the game would only go so far and like society and Sir Nathaniel's good opinion, Adam's was one that Hugh didn't wish to lose.

'I see you figured this out, too, Clara,' Adam called to his sister, striding forward, his wife's hand in his, the bliss between them and their freedom to revel in it enviable.

'It wasn't too difficult. How many other clues have you worked out?' Clara recovered herself with admiration, but there was no missing that the red colour of her cheeks was from more than the cold.

'Five, we're halfway done. How about you two? What have you worked out so far?'

'Just the one.' Clara limply motioned to the sundial and the number one affixed to it.

'Then we'd better stop dawdling over the view and get on with it, shouldn't we, Lady Kingston?' Hugh suggested. He wasn't about to give Adam and Anne any more to talk about by acting like a schoolboy caught skipping lessons.

This snapped Clara out of her shock and the blush disappeared from her cheeks as she faced her brother and sister-in-law. 'Yes, we must, because we're determined to win, aren't we, Lord Delamare?'

'Indeed we are.' He threw Anne and Adam a wave, ignoring the shock that decorated their faces at this change in Clara's attitude towards Hugh as he and Clara set off for the path. 'Good luck to you both.'

'And good luck to you,' Anne sang after them, but Hugh ushered Clara away before she could singe her delicate cheeks with any more blushes.

Clara hurried down the hill faster than she'd raced up it, needing the quick activity to shake off the unease of Anne and Adam having almost happened upon them in the clearing and the confusion created by her conversation with Hugh. If her brother and sister-in-law had stepped out of the trees sooner or without warning, they would've caught Clara and Hugh in a most compromising position, one Clara still couldn't believe she'd stumbled into. She hadn't intended to touch Hugh out of comfort or any other emotion, but she'd been unable to help herself. No one deserved to suffer the loss of their cherished spouse. For all the wrong Hugh had done her, she wouldn't wish that sorrow on her worst enemy and she couldn't ignore it when it was in front of her either. His pain was so similar to what she'd endured these last two years and she'd wanted to drive it away as Anne and Adam had done so many times for her. It had also surprised her.

Despite the dubious beginning of his union with Lady Hermione, whose family's shipping wealth had given them more money than hers could ever have hoped to possess, Clara was glad the woman had garnered his love. During the Seasons that Clara had been in London with Alfred, she'd seen more than one arranged marriage falter from the start, leaving each person wishing for the passing of the other in order to free them. That Hugh and Lady Hermione had come to love one another, and that his reasons for marrying her had been guided by duty to his family and not simply greed, altered so much of what she'd come to believe about Hugh. For so long, she'd been unable to see anything except the calculating bargain that Hugh had struck at her expense but, as Adam had once tried to tell her, there had been a great deal more to his decision.

However, for all the comfort they'd offered one another and the relief and calm it had given them, and for all the ways his words had begun to change her opinion of him, a small warning continued to play in the back of her mind. It'd sounded when they'd touched across the stone and it continued to assert itself while she walked beside him. She should be more cautious with her feelings and his and better mind her emotions in his presence, but in the face of his tender questions she'd been helpless to resist being open with him. She hoped he didn't make her regret it as he had before for there were a number of days left in the house party and, as she'd learned with him last time, his preference for her could change at a moment's whim. He might have had honourable reasons for leaving her, but in the end he had still chosen someone else over her and she must remember this and the kind of man he'd become since. His motives for doing what he'd done in London didn't excuse it and the fact that a man with his privileges who could have chosen any distraction had selected the basest ones seemed to say more about him than what he'd told her. She would do well to heed the warning and to not allow her opinion of him to soften so much that she forgot herself again with him. They could be friendly with one another, but not friends and certainly not, as Lady Pariston had suggested last night, more.

At last, Hugh and Clara reached the beginning of the path that led back to the house and the rest of the clues and stopped to catch their breath.

'Where do we go next?' Hugh asked, his voice steady as if nothing on the rise had happened, or it hadn't meant as much or been as confusing to him as it had been to Clara. This was probably closer to the truth than anything else Clara wished to believe.

Clara read the second clue, determined to be as aloof and unruffled by what had happened as Hugh. 'Holiday sweets are made sweeter and brighter by

me, the fruit of this tree, round like a globe and dis-
liking the cold.'

'Nothing but apples and plums grow in this part
of England and they can tolerate the cold,' Hugh
mused, remaining a polite distance away from Clara,
seemingly aware of how close they'd come to trouble at the sundial and unwilling to have it happen
again. With them at the bottom of the rise near the
lake, anyone in search of the first object could happen upon them. After having inadvertently thrown
caution to the wind at the sundial, Clara appreciated his caution here, even if all this restraint and
the constant shifting of emotions where Hugh was
concerned was beginning to wear on her. Being so
serious was not what she'd come to Stonedown to
do. She did enough of that at home.

Clara read the clue twice more. On the third reading, the answer came to her. 'Oranges. The clue is
oranges.'

Hugh looked sceptical. 'They don't grow here in
the winter.'

'They do in the orangery near the stables. Lord
Tillman has a fine specimen and it's always laden
with fruit at this time of year. As children, Adam and
I loved the treat.' She couldn't wait to see it again.

'Then that must be it.'

'There's only one way to know.'

'I'll race you to it,' Hugh challenged with a
rogue's wink that Clara couldn't help but answer.
Despite the cold it was a beautiful day and the sun

cutting through the clouds and the naked branches of the trees couldn't help but infect her soul. It was difficult to remain morose or introspective in the middle of such gorgeous countryside, especially with Hugh teasing her into a race. It'd been a long time since she'd run like a girl in short dresses and she missed the freedom of it.

'Ready. Set. Go.' She took off before she was even done speaking, darting out ahead of Hugh like she used to do with Adam whenever they would race as children.

Behind her she could hear the fast fall of Hugh's feet when he set off after her, his long stride allowing him to quickly pass her before they even reached the turn in the trees where they'd called their truce. He glanced over his shoulder and, seeing her far behind, slowed down until she caught up to him.

She raced past him, forcing him to catch up, but this time he didn't pass her, but kept pace, the two of them flying down the path, his delight in running matching hers.

Then the glass roof of the orangery and the weathervane on the stables came into view over the tops of the trees. The closer they drew the stronger the earthy scent of horses grew and Clara's excitement increased. The crush of the gravel beneath her feet and the sharp breeze stinging her cheeks was the way it used to be when she and Adam had run along these paths with her parents. The joy of those carefree days filled her, lightening her steps and her heart. It amazed her that such a marvellous time should be had with Hugh, but it didn't matter, nor did the past or the future or her opinions, nothing except this did. It was exactly what she'd come to Stonedown to find.

They continued their quick pace until they turned the bend in the path and almost collided with Sir Nathaniel and Mrs Alton. Jerking to a halt, they couldn't help but laugh through their winded apologies for the near miss.

'I see you two are getting on well,' Sir Nathaniel observed with a smile as wide as Hugh's. His round nose was so red from the cold it was almost the same shade as his maroon redingote. 'With all this hurrying you must have solved many clues.'

'Not at all. We're racing to catch up.' Clara laughed through her hard breath, her joy spreading to Mrs Alton who flashed Clara and Hugh a friendly smile.

'Then I wish you great success.' Sir Nathaniel turned to Hugh. 'Before you go, Lord Delamare, I want you to know I sent a letter to the solicitor I recommended this morning. You should hear from him shortly. I told him that I know you and instructed him to give your matter his full attention. I don't do that for everyone, only those I like.'

'Thank you, Sir Nathaniel.' Hugh sobered, taking the man's hand and giving it a firm shake. 'Your support and regard mean a great deal to me.'

'Now off you go so Mrs Alton and I may venture

on to our next destination.' With a raise of his bea-
ver hat, Sir Nathaniel bid them goodbye and escorted
the quiet Mrs Alton away.

'Come on, we're losing time.' Hugh took hold of
Clara's hand and pulled her along the path.

Everything inside Clara told her to let go of him,
but she held on tight, too afraid to open her fingers and be sent whirling from the many shocks of
today, including the one Sir Nathaniel had lobbed
at her. She'd known the man for years. He was well
regarded by many, but it often took a great deal for
him to regard others well. That he'd looked on Hugh
with respect and offered to help him was amazing.
At the sundial, she'd assured Hugh that he would
find his way back to a more respectful life and it
was clear from Sir Nathaniel's regard that he was already on that road. It called into question once again
all Clara's opinions of him, ones she didn't wish to
think of right now for fear they would mar her enjoyment of the day.

They approached the glass dome of the orangery
and the riot of greenery and flowers inside. The vivid
colours were a sharp contrast to the grey and brown
landscape outside the glass and iron door. Hugh let
go of her and pulled it open. Clara flexed her fingers as she stepped inside, the heat and warmth hitting her as hard as the loss of Hugh's grasp. They
shouldn't have held hands, especially when they'd
passed the stables and the stable hands inside attending to the horses that stood snorting and neighing

in their stalls. She remembered how fast the maids had informed Lord Westbook of Hugh's engagement last time. They didn't need the grooms whispering anything to their aristocratic riders, but the gesture had been so much in the spirit of the game that she didn't mind. It was the loss of their joy she would mind more if she chided him for being so familiar so she said nothing.

'This wasn't here when I last visited.' Hugh studied the ornate and sweet-smelling flowers lined up in pots on trestle tables along the glass walls.

'It was, but a hail storm had damaged it that autumn. Lord Tillman worked hard to save the tree, but he lost almost everything else,' Clara explained as they moved towards the orange tree in the centre. It rose out of a large hole in the stone floor, the slick green leaves dotted here and there with sumptuous round oranges. 'He's spent the last six years reviving it. Isn't it amazing?'

'It is.'

Hugh felt a little like the greenery around him and the tree, as though he'd been torn down and ruined and was fighting to rebuild. He'd gained Sir Nathaniel's regard and hopefully with it an advantage with his case and he was, in this small way, proving to Clara that he wasn't the cad she believed him to be. He, like the tree with the oranges he reached up to touch, wasn't beyond saving and apparently others beside Adam were capable of seeing it.

'There's the number two.' Hugh pointed to the paper number tied with a ribbon around the tree's trunk. 'What's our next clue?'

'I almost hate to leave here.' Clara sighed. 'It's so cold outside.'

'We'll lose if we stay and then we'll have to endure all Lady Fulton's bragging if she and Lord Westbook win.'

'I suppose you're right.' Clara didn't look at the parchment, but continued to take in the tree, tilting her head in thought to one side and making the curls at the back of her head brush her pink cheeks. She found contentment beneath the tree, one he hadn't witnessed either on the stairs, at dinner, or even at the sundial. He'd only seen it grace her face once before, six years ago when they'd stood beneath another bit of greenery, the flush of their first kiss making her cheeks as ruddy as they were today. He tapped his fingers together, almost able to feel the mistletoe berry he'd plucked from the branch, Clara still in his arms, the taste of her lingering on his lips.

Hugh opened the top button of his black redingote to give him some ease from the heat of the orangery and continued to watch her, captivated by the delicate line of her jaw above the raised collar of her pelisse and the flush of heat that gave colour to her skin. When he'd glanced over his shoulder to see her running so far behind him, smiling like she used to do when they'd ridden together in the sleigh six years ago, he'd wanted to turn and take her in his arms, to sweep her off her feet and spin her in a circle until her laughter silenced all the birds in the forest.

He and their time together had brought that smile to her face and he didn't want to lose it. Not even when they'd come upon Sir Nathaniel had her exuberance dimmed. She hadn't looked on Hugh like some pariah, but had smiled and laughed with an infectious ease that had cast a spell over him until he'd been able to forget himself and everything and just be with her. Even now he should be urging them to continue with the scavenger hunt so he could return to the men and Sir Nathaniel and work to secure their help in ending the threat to Everburgh, but he couldn't tear himself away from Clara and this moment. It would mean losing the ability to regard her unobserved and force him to act as if each time their hands touched or her voice rang out in the clear crisp air that she didn't enchant him.

He turned away from her to view the tree, resisting this captivation and the desire to be anything more than friendly with her. He'd had good reasons for giving her up six years ago, a commitment to honour and duty that had cost Hermione her life and Hugh a piece of his soul. But he could no more go back and change what had happened between him and Clara than he could bring back Hermione and, until he was certain again of the solidity of those old beliefs and what they meant to him and his life, he could be certain of little else. Besides, after her greeting in the library yesterday, anything more than friendship would be viewed with nothing but distrust, especially with Everburgh still in needs of funds to battle the pending court challenge.

With a great deal of reluctance, he did up the top button of his coat, determined to focus on the hunt. He was required to be her partner, not to pester her by wailing about his miseries or what had happened before. They would have fun and they would win and that's all they'd have between them. 'What's the next clue?'

The following two hours were a joy for Clara as she and Hugh hurried from one part of Stonedown to another. The clues led them inside the large house and then back out to the garden and many other places of note. They passed numerous other guests during their travels and each couple smiled and waved to the other while teasing them that they were going to win the brandy. The good-natured teasing didn't hide the surprise that decorated many faces at the sight of Clara and Hugh so easy in one another's company, especially after their noticeable silence at dinner last night. Clara could almost hear people whispering in amazement about it as they left them, but she didn't care. Let them say what they liked about her and Hugh. She was enjoying herself in a way she hadn't done in a very long time and she wouldn't allow anyone or anything to ruin it.

At last, with the pale sunlight hidden behind the

clouds beginning to dim enough to tell them that their time for the search was drawing to a close and that the early evening darkness of winter would soon force all but the stoutest of souls back inside, she and Hugh studied the last clue.

'Pages of sparkling gold and red easy to ignore in its progress through the year but standing ever ready for those who care to notice,' Clara read again.

Hugh slipped the parchment out from between her gloved fingertips and read it again. 'What do you think it is?'

'I can't say. The other clues seemed so obvious once we really thought about them, but not this one.'

'You're to thank for that. Without your knowledge of Stonedown, we never would have deciphered most of the clues.'

'But you guessed the peacock bench in the garden.'

He glanced up at her from across the paper. 'Only because that wasn't one of Lady Tillman's more difficult clues, but this is.'

He furrowed his brow as he considered the last clue, concentrating on it as if it were a faro table and he was waiting for his ball to land on his number, except of all the stories she'd heard of him in London, gambling had never been one of them. He hadn't been known for his outrageous bets or nights spent at the tables losing far more than he could afford. His stories had involved fast carriage rides down Rotten Row with questionable company beside him during the fashionable hour and at least one duel that he'd won without doing more damage to his opponent than sending a ball through his fine wool coat. Some said he'd deliberately aimed wide to spare his opponent and that if he hadn't his lethal aim would have split the man's skull. Clara shivered from more than the cold, finding it hard to reconcile the London Hugh with the one before her who'd shown so much delight in this simple game and so much tenderness with her at the sundial. Part of her wanted to ask him about the incident, but she held her tongue, unwilling to end the good will between them with questions about his curious past.

In the distance, from the direction of the house, the warning shot sounded.

'We only have fifteen more minutes.'

I should have been concentrating on the clue and not Hugh.

She hated to think that their missing this last item might mean the difference between them and Lord Westbook and Lady Fulton winning. She wasn't sure how they'd done in the game for they'd only passed them once, but they'd both seemed very sure of their progress.

'Then we must think and fast.'

Clara peered over his forearm at the wrinkled and torn paper, for he was too tall for her to look over his shoulder. It brought her cheek close to his arm and, if this had been six years ago, she could have laid her head on his chest and let him wrap his arm around her shoulder while they struggled to figure out Lady Tillman's clue. But this wasn't six years ago and, for all the holding of hands on the way to the orangery, they hadn't touched since. She had no desire to make this awkward by reaching out to him again.

'I know what it is.' Hugh jerked up straight, his face brightening with realisation that made Clara bounce a little on her toes. 'It's the illuminated manuscript.'

'Of course,' Clara exclaimed. 'The ink is red and gold and it follows the liturgical year.'

'Let's go and make certain.'

She followed him around the side of the house and up the back stairs of the portico, certain that when they reached the library the number ten hanging on the bookstand would confirm that he was right. Victory was only one room in Stonedown away and she couldn't wait to seize it. From across the different areas of the estate she could see people trickling in together to form small groups and discuss the hunt. Hugh pulled open the French doors leading into a small sitting room off the back of the house. They both sighed with relief and delight at the heat that greeted them and began to remove their gloves and open the buttons of their thick coats as they crossed the room and stepped into the hall leading to the library.

There, on one of the benches lining the long wall, sat Lady Pariston and Lord Wortley. It was an odd but charming pairing that one who didn't know better might mistake for a grandmother and her grandson, but there was no mistaking the defeat making their shoulders slump.

'Lady Pariston, Lord Wortley, how did you fair?' Clara hated to see them looking so dejected.

'Not well I'm afraid, Lady Kingston.' Lord Wortley stood and bowed, his manners perfect, but his voice, like his frame, not having reached its full potential. 'Lady Pariston was unable to walk the grounds.'

'My hips hate the cold,' Lady Pariston explained with more unhappy regret than elderly complaint.

'We've been trying to work out the clues without actually visiting them but I'm afraid we haven't fared well for I don't know the estate, but I believe Lady Pariston did an excellent job guessing many of the items, even if we couldn't prove it.' To his credit, the young man demonstrated no bitterness about being held back from activities by his aged partner who appeared more sorry than he did at having been unable to fully partake in the festivities.

'I told the young man to go ahead without me and have fun, but he wouldn't leave me. I think it was very kind of him to sit here and keep an old lady company.' She patted him tenderly on the arm. 'Even if it means we don't have a shot at winning that brandy and I so love a small taste of it now and again. It helps with my rheumatism.'

'What answers do you have?' Hugh motioned to

see their paper. Being in the house, they'd been able to write down their answers.

Lord Wortley gave it to Hugh and he and Clara studied it.

'You have done remarkably well,' Hugh complimented.

They were only missing the last two.

'I'm sure if I'd had more time, I could have come to the correct answers.' Lady Pariston sighed. 'But my memory, like my hips, isn't what it used to be.'

Instead of giving the paper back to them, Hugh slipped their answers behind his, then offered Lady Pariston his arm. 'May I escort you into the sitting room?'

His offer brought the smile back to her aged face. 'Yes, I would like that very much.'

He and Lord Wortley helped her to her feet. With one hand grasping her walking stick tight and the other firmly fixed on Hugh's arm, she allowed him to lead her into the sitting room.

'May I, Lady Kingston?' Lord Wortley offered Clara his slender arm, his chest puffed out in pride at being able to escort her.

'Yes, you may.' She took hold of his arm and they followed Hugh and Lady Pariston down the hall, through the main entrance hall and into the sitting room.

While they walked, Lord Wortley commented on the weather, the food at dinner last night and all the other polite topics required by the conventions of conversation.

Clara didn't hear much of what Lord Wortley said for she was too busy watching Hugh and Lady Pariston. Hugh's tenderness with the Dowager Countess, his easy way with her and his ability to elicit more than one smile or laugh from her touched Clara. Lady Pariston had appeared so downtrodden in the hallway, but now she looked as if this had been her best scavenger hunt ever. Hugh had no reason to be cordial and kind to her but he was, just as he'd been with Clara. It surprised her and left her wondering. Today, he'd acted like the Hugh she'd known as a girl and nothing like the London rake she'd heard so many stories about. Perhaps this was all for show, but his movements and words seemed so natural that it was hard to believe that he was this good a charlatan. Maybe this was the Hugh that Adam and Anne were able to see and Clara should give him the benefit of the doubt as her brother and sister-in-law did. No, it couldn't be or he wouldn't have so many sordid stories attached to his name.

A wave of conversation met them when they entered the front sitting room where the other teams had gathered to exchange stories about the scavenger hunt and how well they had or hadn't done. A group of gentlemen stood around the writing table where a number of quills and inkstands had been set out so the players could write down their answers before handing their papers to Lord Tillman. Hugh escorted

Lady Pariston to the comfiest of the two armchairs flanking the fire and helped her to sit.

'If you three wish to stay here and warm yourselves, I will turn in the answers,' Hugh offered and, with a bow, made for the writing desk. He was stopped halfway across the room by Lord Westbook who held up his own sheet, seeming to gloat over his and Lady Fulton's progress. Hugh said nothing in reply, but bent over the table, took up a quill and wrote out their answers. He then handed both pieces of parchment to Lord Tillman. Hugh did not immediately return to Clara, enticed into conversation by Sir Nathaniel instead.

Disappointment dogged Clara at Hugh remaining across the room, but she tried to shake it off. He'd been in her company for the past two hours. She wasn't surprised he wanted someone new to talk to, especially a man like Sir Nathaniel who was going to help him with his case. Clara knew very little of the legal matter facing Hugh, having avoided bringing it up during their hunt in an effort to not ruin their good time, but she knew it had something to do with Everburgh and its future ownership. She would have to ask Anne about it for she always seemed to hear everything about everyone, especially where Hugh's details were concerned. Unlike Lord Westbook, she was far more discreet with her knowledge.

As if hearing Clara thinking about her, Anne appeared at her elbow. Taking hold of Clara's arm, Anne drew her to the other side of the large marble

mantel and away from Lord Wortley and Lady Pariston. Mischief burned in her green eyes as bright as
the candles scattered about the room to add additional light on this cloudy day.

'Did you and Lord Delamare enjoy the scavenger
hunt?' Anne asked, certain she and Adam had stumbled upon something more than a deep conversation
about mourning.

'Yes, we did.' Clara hoped a direct answer would
put an end to this line of questioning. It didn't.

'Did you, now?' Anne prodded.

Clara tilted her head and pinned her with a chas-
tising look. 'Nothing happened between us and nothing is going to happen between us.'

Anne ignored what should have been a silencing glare. 'That's not what it looked like when we
saw you.'

'Whatever you have in mind you can go ahead
and dismiss it. We are simply enjoying ourselves
and that is all.'

'Be sure to enjoy yourself a little bit more while
we're here,' Anne suggested 'You never know what
might happen.'

Anne made off to join Adam, leaving Clara to
shake her head at her sister-in-law's insinuation. It
seemed being in the country was more boring for
Anne than it was for Clara if she was willing to make
up all kinds of fanciful notions about other people,
especially Clara. Thankfully, there had been no single male visitors to Winsome of late or who knew

what other possible romances Anne might have concocted for Clara.

Once everyone had turned in their answers, Lord and Lady Tillman spent another few moments examining them before Lord Tillman placed one on top of the stack and raised a silencing hand. 'We have our winners.'

The chattering died out as everyone waited to hear who it was. Clara exchanged a triumphant glance with Hugh, certain they would be among those caught in a tie, if not the outright winners. Unfortunately, Lord Westbook and Lady Fulton appeared just as smug from where they sat on an overstuffed ottoman. Clara hoped she and Hugh had bested them. They deserved a little harmless comeuppance for all their arrogant love of gossip and belittling.

'In the past, people have accused me and Lady Tillman of writing clues that were too easy,' Lord Tillman explained, leaving them in suspense a little longer.

A few heads nodded in agreement.

'Judging by the results this year, I think we've greatly improved. In fact, there was only one team that got all the answers correct.'

Speculation swept through the room and Clara exchanged an excited glance with Hugh, knowing they'd found everything. He met her eyes with a humility she couldn't fathom. Whatever the reason for his look, there was no time to consider it as Lord Tillman announced the winners.

'The team with all the correct answers is…' He paused, causing everyone who was sitting to perch on the edge of their seats.

'Get on with it, man,' Mr Alton urged and everyone laughed.

'Lady Pariston and Lord Wortley.'

The surprise on Lord Wortley and Lady Pariston's faces was equal to that of the enthusiastic clapping that greeted the announcement. Lord Wortley looked back and forth from Hugh to Clara, as amazed and perplexed as she was. He opened his mouth to protest the proclamation, but Hugh crossed the room and clapped the young lord vigorously on the back in congratulation.

'You and Lady Pariston deserve this honour more than anyone else.' Hugh's heavy-handed congratulation made Lord Wortley stumble a bit and stopped him from saying whatever he'd intended to say. 'I hope you very much enjoy the proceeds of your winnings.'

Lord Tillman stepped forward with the brandy and presented it to Lady Pariston who smiled as brightly as she had when Hugh had escorted her into the sitting room. No more was said about the paper not being theirs as they held up the bottle in triumph together and received the congratulations of the entire room.

Hugh stepped away from them and came over to join Clara.

'I assume you didn't accidentally mistake the papers when you set our names to them?' Clara asked in a low voice, the rousing chatter in the room covering their conversation.

'No, I didn't. I hope you don't mind, but I thought they deserved a little joy and triumph more than we did.'

'I don't mind at all.' It was worth their losing to see the delight making Lady Pariston beam and Lord Wortley stand a foot taller, and to realise that Hugh had given up their victory for no other reason than kindness. It made her wonder again whether she'd judged Hugh too harshly, for in one afternoon he'd made it very hard for her to hold on to her poor opinion of him and to forget that he was a man not to be trusted. Except she wouldn't trust him, not entirely, until she could figure out who was the real Hugh, the man she'd spent time with today or the London rake.

Chapter Five

Clara stood in front of the full-length mirror in her bedroom, turning from side to side to admire the fourth dress she's tried on in the last fifteen minutes. Last night she'd attempted to not give a great deal of attention to her attire until Anne had commented on it. Tonight, what she wore seemed to take on too much importance. She longed to appear at her best without looking too contrived in her efforts, all the while lamenting the overly simple styles of her dresses.

Only because I wish to show Lady Fulton that I am not a dowdy mouse, she tried to tell herself, but deep down she knew this was a lie. She cared about her attire because she would be beside Hugh again.

She'd greeted him this morning with very low expectations and he'd defied every one of them, leaving her unsure what to think about him, and all of Anne's teasing didn't help. Under the spell of the scavenger hunt, he'd been the old Hugh she used to admire, but when she was alone with nothing but her past slights and memories it was hard to hold on to this view of him. Hugh could be tricking everyone about his change, using his friendliness and charming personality to draw them in, or it could be real. Unlike the steady grip of his hand against hers today, she couldn't be sure. She twisted the ring on her finger as she took in her reflection, wishing her mother were here. She would be able to ferret out the truth about Hugh, for Clara didn't know what to think, but her mother wasn't here and Clara must decide for herself. If she were thinking clearly, and not battered by old memories of Alfred, her parents and past times at Stonedown, she might be better able to see the truth, but it was so difficult at present.

She dropped her hands to her sides and stood up straight, getting a hold of herself.

There's no need to lose your mind or waffle like a chicken with its head cut off.

There was no reason to rush to form any opinion about Hugh or to be crystal clear about anything except that she must be friendly with him. There was nothing more to it. During her and Hugh's last visit here, the desire to unite their lives had seized them so quickly that she hadn't stopped to think about consequences or difficulties and it had cost her a great deal. It wasn't the case this time. Perhaps, during dinner and the rest of the activities, she might better observe him and uncover more of the man worthy of Adam's friendship, the one she'd caught glimpses of during the scavenger hunt. If so, then she would change her opinion of him. If not, then so be it. There was nothing more to it, certainly not enough for her to fret and worry, except there was.

A small part of her, the one that had taken comfort in his presence last night at the foot of the stairs and again at the sundial, the one that had laughed so easily with him during the hunt, wanted the changes in him to be real. If they were, then maybe the joy she'd experienced with him today could be hers again and she could finally stop worrying about their past and simply enjoy the present.

In the meantime, she must finish dressing for dinner and look the part of the Marchioness of Kingston.

'What do you think, Mary? This one or the dark blue one?' Clara asked the maid who stood patiently nearby, waiting for instructions to either do up the buttons or to choose another dress from the dwindling selection of gowns.

'This one suits you the best, my lady. The gold embroidery on the sleeves makes your necklace sparkle and gives your skin such a nice hue.'

Clara wanted to believe her, but wondered if the maid simply wanted to end this torturous routine and go downstairs to join the servants for supper. Clara would summon Anne for her opinion if she thought it wouldn't garner more teasing about Clara and Hugh. It was another decision she must make on her own.

Taking one last look in the mirror and knowing

the dinner gong would soon ring, Clara decided to trust Mary's opinion. 'I believe this dress will do, but I wonder about the others. Lady Exton is right, everything I have is so dark.'

It was difficult to impress people like Lady Fulton when one dressed like a wraith.

'Some of your older dresses are much cheerier in style. Perhaps you would like me to send to Winsome to have a number of them fetched?' Mary suggested.

Such a ridiculous use of time and effort by the servants would normally have made Clara decline, but the more she thought of the pink, yellow and light green dresses she hadn't worn since before Alfred's passing, the ones she'd purchased in London, the more the idea appealed to her. 'It probably wouldn't hurt to have them here. After all, I don't know what other events Lady Tillman has planned and I wouldn't want to appear too dour or wear the same dress twice.'

That was something only a simple country mouse did.

'I'll see to it at once, my lady.' Mary dipped a curtsy that hid her smile, as if she'd known this would be the answer and didn't believe for a second Clara's practical reason for sending for the dresses.

The dinner gong sounded as Mary finished fastening the clasp on Clara's bracelet and Clara froze. It was time to join the others and Hugh for dinner. Every doubt she'd ever had about stepping away from the wall at balls during her Season rushed back to

her, making her want to undress and plead a headache to avoid going down. Except she couldn't be so
cowardly. Whatever awaited her at dinner tonight she
must face with the same fortitude as she'd met other
difficulties. She threw one last look at herself in the
mirror, determined to be again a woman worthy of
notice by everyone, especially Hugh.

Hugh stood at the bottom of the stairs while the
other guests formed up on the steps behind him. He
adjusted his cravat and his shirtsleeves for the hundredth time since coming downstairs. After he'd
taken leave of Clara at the end of the scavenger hunt,
Hugh had done everything he could to distract himself from thinking about her. He'd sought out Lord
Tillman to ask his advice about the case facing Everburgh. He'd played billiards with Lord Missington
and accepted Lord Wortley's effusive thanks for
the brandy which, judging by the high flush on the
youth's cheeks, he and Lady Pariston had decided to
enjoy the moment the scavenger-hunt party had dis-
persed. Hugh had then gone to his room to correspond
with his man of affairs about Sir Nathaniel's referral
and the suggestions Lord Tillman had made. All these
things had distracted Hugh for a while, but none of
them had kept thoughts of Clara completely at bay.

During the hunt, she'd lived up to her promise to
enjoy herself with him, casting no more disparaging
remarks at him and even looking on him with admiration when he'd admitted to giving the win to Lady

Pariston. That look had meant more to Hugh than the sultry pouts of any of the actresses he'd ever had on his arm, any race he'd ever made in Rotten Row and even the winning shot in the duel with Lord Cecil. It had told him that he could change, that he could be a better man again because she was beginning to see him as one. It hadn't been his goal in giving the win to Lady Pariston to garner Clara's admiration. He'd simply wanted to make an old woman and a young lord who deserved to enjoy the season as much as anyone happy. He knew what it was like to be left behind and forgotten because of poverty or a myriad of other reasons. It's why he'd always liked Adam and his family. Whenever he'd stayed with the Extons during school holidays, they'd never made him feel poor or pitied for his predicament of coming from a distinguished line and not having a pot to piss in. He'd wanted to return a measure of the kindness he'd received where he could. Until this weekend, chances had eluded him, as had the look of admiration Clara had offered him. For a moment, it had taken him back six years, before Lord Matthews's letter had arrived, before his mistakes in London, when every possibility of being happy with Clara had still been real and obtainable. The glimmer that it might be again had lingered in her proud smile and the feeling had been difficult to shake. It was also a dangerous one to entertain.

There couldn't be more between them, especially not while they were under the same roof. Everyone here probably knew about his relationship with Lady Frances and they probably looked on Clara as soon sharing the same predicament, but she wouldn't. She would be no man's mistress, especially not Hugh's, for he wouldn't blot her reputation in such a way nor would he leave this party with her an object of pity like he had before. She didn't deserve such shabby treatment or a tarnished man like Hugh. Even if, like Adam, she could look past all his faults, the past still stood between them, along with Hugh's current financial difficulties. Affection could not bloom beneath the weight of doubts about him and his motives for pursuing her.

The shuffling of feet on the stairs behind him drew Hugh out of his thoughts and he turned to see the guests parting as Clara descended. The earrings dangling from her ears sparkled in the candlelight of the entrance-hall chandelier and glistened against the smooth skin of her neck above the round mounds of her breasts. The rich, deep red silk of her dress heightened the paleness of her skin and brought out the darker tones in her hair. She held her head high with a self-possession to make his chest and other places constrict and nodded like a queen to everyone who greeted her. He couldn't take his eyes off her, especially when she turned her smile on him and she appeared to glow even brighter. Last night, she'd viewed being beside him with all the derision that he'd thrown at duty after Hermione's death, but not tonight. More than one of the gentlemen she passed admired her figure and Hugh's chest filled with pride. She was coming to stand beside him and lead them into the dining room.

Except she wasn't his Marchioness and she carried another man's name.

Regret gripped him as hard as desire. If things had been different six years ago, then she would be here tonight as his wife, with their children in the nursery, the two of them free to enjoy one another's company at dinner and for as many hours afterwards as they wished in the darkness of his room, but that wasn't the way things had ended. Hugh had made another choice and it had cost him any chance of ever having her.

He let out a long breath when she stepped down off the final step and came to stand beside him and laid her gloved hand on his arm. Her touch was light but powerful, making the manor and the other guests fade away. He was proud to give her the sturdiness of his support even if she didn't need it. It was, as the glittering diamonds encircling her neck and rising and falling with each of her long breaths reminded him, the only thing he could offer her. He could not adorn her with dresses and jewellery or even provide her with a house to manage that wasn't plagued by troubles or threatened with ruin. He couldn't even offer her a title. Where precedence and the fate of the name drawing had brought her close to him, reality placed her far beyond his reach. He cursed again his weak and debauched grandfather and all the troubles he'd left for Hugh to correct. The most he could do was enjoy this moment and the brief time that Clara was in his presence.

'You look stunning tonight.' He laid his other hand on top of hers, encasing it in warmth against the chilliness of the main hall. A blush spread across the bridge of her nose and the spattering of freckles marring the fine white skin, adding to her loveliness more than any of the jewels or even the fancy combs in her hair. It reminded him that she was still, in many ways, the Clara he'd first fallen in love with even if he was no longer the Hugh who had captured her heart.

'You're quite striking, too.' She tilted her head a touch to look at him from the corner of her eyes, a teasing smile drawing up the fullness of her cheeks. 'I think your London tailor suits you very well.'

London was not a place he wished to think of right now. 'This isn't from London, but from a local man in the village. I do my best to give him as much work as I can. With Everburgh slowly recovering, I must share with those on my estate what little prosperity we've enjoyed these last few years.'

'But isn't it the fashion to shop in Jermyn Street? You wouldn't want society to consider you unfashionable,' she teased, but there was admiration behind her merriment and he wanted more of it than even the prosperity of his manor, to believe that there might be something more potent between them than this tenuous friendship, a chance to reclaim not just his past reputation but his worthiness to pursue her.

'I don't care what society thinks of me as long as I'm helping those in my care to thrive.'

'Is that really the only time you don't care?' she asked with disbelief.

He could almost hear her thinking the same thing so many matrons did when they spied him—a cross between wanting to protect their daughters from the rumours they'd heard about him and their desire to believe that they weren't true because it better suited their pursuit of a marquess. Except it wasn't a title or his lands that Clara sought, but a man of trustworthiness and honesty. Not for the first time in the last few months he cursed having been so flippant with his reputation. 'It is.'

'What about at the gambling tables?' she asked with a much prettier tone of reprimand than his mother used to employ. She used to scold him like the devil whenever he saw her, afraid he was going down the same path as his grandfather and wanting to stop him, but she hadn't been able to. That decision had needed to come from Hugh. That it had come too late for his mother to witness was another regret to add to the pile.

'I don't gamble.' It was the one vice not even he, in his disgust with the world and fate, could not lower himself to indulge in. He was angry at duty and how all the things he'd been taught to believe in had failed him, but he wasn't a sadistic fool. He wouldn't allow that weakness to erode the few gains that doing his duty had provided or prove beyond a doubt to everyone, and especially himself, that he was as bad a wastrel as his grandfather. Even in his darkest moments he'd held on to the pride of knowing that he was nothing like that man.

'Then when you enjoy your claret at the club?' she prodded.

Sadly, this hit a touch too close to the mark for he'd out drunk more than one lord, winning a considerable sum in a challenge once for being able to remain upright long after his opponent had collapsed on to the floor. It was another victory in which Hugh had taken no real pride, especially when his opponent had become so sick there were fears he would expire from his excesses. Guilt and shame washed over Hugh. For a time, he'd been an ugly man, but he couldn't change it, he could only strive to redeem himself. 'At one time I indulged at my club, but not any more. I've given up drink. I've seen the damage it can do and no longer have a taste for it.'

'Then I commend you for your admirable changes.'

She wouldn't commend him if she knew half of what he'd done, but she didn't and for the moment he could enjoy her tender smile and bask in her approval, no matter how brief it might be.

The invitation to proceed into the dining room was made and Clara tightened her hold on Hugh's arm, conscious of the thickness of the muscle beneath his fine wool coat. Together they strode into the red-wallpapered room, the walk giving her a chance to consider everything he'd told her. She wanted to believe in the good in Hugh, to trust what she'd seen of him today, but it was hard. During her first and only Season in London, she'd learned that what a man said wasn't as important as what he did. Hugh might speak well of helping those he cared about, but he'd all but turned his back on those in his care when he'd gone dissolute in London. He might have been on the verge once of asking for her hand, but he'd walked away in an instant to marry a richer woman. These actions spoke louder than any of his words, and yet with each strong stride he took beside her, the patient way he waited for her to take the seat next to him before taking his, and the many smiles he brushed her with that she couldn't help but meet, she grew more and more confused about what to think of him.

She flicked out her napkin and set it over her lap while the footman slid in between them and filled her wine glass before moving on to fill Hugh's. Clara watched Hugh out of the corner of her eye, wondering if he would ignore the drink or if his having sworn off spirits had been a lie intended to bring him further into her good graces. She shouldn't be watching him or concerning herself with his habits. They were none of her business, but she couldn't help herself. Life in the country had become very boring indeed if, in the middle of a lively dinner, this was how she chose to amuse herself.

When Lord Tillman gave a toast to Lord Wortley and Lady Pariston, Clara raised her glass, unable to stop herself from checking to see if Hugh reached for his. He didn't take up the wine, but chose instead the orange juice that had also been provided. Even after the footmen took away the fish and set down the meat, then went around the table with the red wine, leaning past Hugh to fill his glass, it remained on the table in front of him to turn to vinegar in the same way the white had been left. He didn't even appear to notice nor reach for it before jerking back his hand in remembrance of what he'd told her about abstaining.

When Lord Wortley, obviously under the influence of the brandy he'd won and the wine served at dinner, made a toast to their host, everyone took up their glasses again. Clara watched Hugh, waiting to see if he would slip, but again he raised his orange juice glass and, feeling her watching him, furrowed his brow at her in curiosity.

Clara smiled nervously, guilty about trying to catch him out. She shouldn't be so petty and want him to fail, but wish for him to succeed in bettering himself in the same way she was trying to improve herself. He had a great many sins to atone for, but at least he was trying.

'Are you enjoying your orange juice?' she asked.

'I am.' He tilted his glass to her. 'Are you not having any?'

'I will have some, along with a little bit of a confession.' She dropped her voice so as not to be heard by the others.

'I'm listening.' He set down his orange juice and took up his knife and fork, listing a touch towards her to hear what she had to say while he cut his mutton. 'What sins have you committed that I need to hear about?'

She pushed her meat through the gravy on her plate, certain he wouldn't care to listen to her sins as much as she would like to hear some of his. They were probably more interesting and a touch less embarrassing, at least for her. She was only revealing this because she wanted to stop herself from being so petty and for acting like a woman who had nothing more to occupy her time than chewing over old slights. It was the sort of thing a country mouse would do. 'I've been wrong in regards to my opinion of you.'

He paused in the cutting of his mutton and stared at his plate for what felt like ages before he finished slicing through his meat. She waited for him to turn hard eyes on her and for the stony silence that had settled between them last night to return, but it didn't.

'Wrong in what regards?' It was the same tone her mother used to employ when waiting for Clara to tell her the truth about why a particular vase was broken or one of the slices of cake was missing at tea time.

Clara took a deep breath, hesitant to be so honest, but it was more for herself than him, a way to finally let go. 'About the man I thought you'd become since the last time we knew one another. I have not been entirely correct in my assumptions about you.'

He slipped a piece of mutton into his mouth and chewed it for a long while, leaving her to wonder about his response. If someone had frankly told her about their low opinion of her she wouldn't react with this much patience, but snarl at them the way she had Lady Fulton. Hugh did neither, but set down his knife and fork and fingered the stem of his orange-juice glass before finally answering. 'No, you weren't wrong. I was that man deserving of your low opinion. I still am for the way I behaved in London and with you.'

'Why did you court me when you knew you couldn't?' Clara asked without thinking, wanting the answer to the old question, the one that had cast her value as a desired woman into doubt, despite even Alfred's attention and love. She would not live with that lingering doubt any longer.

Hugh glanced down the table to where Anne watched them before a question from Lord Tillman drew her attention away. His voice was barely above a whisper when he answered. 'I never thought the negotiations with Lord Matthews would come to anything. I thought I was free to follow my heart, but I wasn't.'

'Yes, you were, until you decided you weren't.' She checked her irritation, lowering her voice to match his and keep the conversation discreet between them. She shouldn't be looking back or allowing the old wound to smart so much, but with

Hugh and the truth laid out before her like the table settings it was difficult not to confront.

Hugh smoothed his napkin over his lap. 'I've never been free, Clara, not in the way you and Adam are, unaware of what it's like to struggle, to wonder if there will be food on the table, heat or even a roof over your head, to watch your parents ruin their health while they work to free themselves and the estate of crippling debt and court cases.'

'But I had money.'

'Not enough and the debts would have taken it all. I would have dragged you down into poverty with me, ensuring that the suffering and hardship my family endured for twenty years would be visited upon you and our children. I don't want my sons growing up with a great title and threadbare clothes like I did, to see them cold in the winter and hungry every time the harvest failed, to have everything their station should allow them to enjoy sit just beyond their reach and me unable to do anything about it. I saw what that regret did to my parents and I couldn't do that to you or to any future children.' He took a deep breath, staring at the delicate check pattern in the tablecloth while he continued. 'My parents made so many sacrifices for me that when I inherited the estate, I wanted nothing more than to give my mother an easier life free from worry so that her last years would be a comfort instead of a struggle. With a single church ceremony, I was able to do that. You're right. I shouldn't have courted you, but I was young and inexperienced in the way of things and while we were here together I couldn't see the potential consequences, only you and how happy we were together.'

Clara studied him, his face soft with his sincerity and the unspoken desire for her to understand. In his eyes, she caught the faint reflection of the moment he'd stood across from her in the library six years ago. She'd expected a marriage proposal and he'd told her that he was leaving to marry another. The memory didn't burn like it used to because she finally understood why he'd behaved as he had. With her, he'd enjoyed a respite from his crushing responsibilities in the same way she'd enjoyed one from her crippling shyness. Reality had stepped in to end it like it sometimes does. The blame she'd held against him so long finally eased. Adam was right, Hugh had possessed good reasons for marrying another. 'If I'd been in your shoes and seen my mother suffering the way yours had, I would have done the same thing.'

'I appreciate your graciousness. It is a quality most people don't possess.'

'Then it's a good thing you're sitting beside me and not Lady Fulton.' She smiled at him, easing the tension and seriousness between them.

'It is a good thing indeed.' He leaned close to her again, the tang of his shaving soap as tantalising as the glimpse of his thigh clad in tan breeches just beneath the white tablecloth edge. 'Do you remember when Adam and I hid a frog under the silver serving cover for the cook to bring in?'

Clara giggled, trying not to draw attention to them. She'd quite forgotten about that prank and was surprised he'd remembered it. Adam and Hugh had been so young, then, and she even smaller. It was a delight to have someone besides Adam to remember what it had been like at Winsome when her parents had been alive and she'd been a child. 'It was your first visit with us. I was certain Father would never allow Adam to ask you back, but I was wrong. Do you remember when the three of us stole into the kitchen to sneak slices of the plum pudding, the special one our cook had made for the vicar's visit?'

'I do, especially the stern lecture about stealing we got from the vicar after dinner. The man could talk up a storm, couldn't he?'

'He still can. I once caught him warning James and Lillie and a few of their friends with that tale. We are legends in the parish.'

Hugh stifled a large laugh with the back of his hand and Clara was sorry he did. She wanted to hear him laugh like he used to and not appear so trodden on by the world but light and full of hope as he'd been six Christmases ago.

'Do you think your niece and nephew will be able to accomplish such legendary mischief?'

'They try every day to outdo us. One of these days I'm sure they will succeed.'

'I hope not in too many regards, but something worthy of giving your vicar a new story to tell.'

'You will have to help them devise something the next time you come to visit.'

He set down his knife and fork and turned to her. 'Do you think I will be invited to Winsome again?'

There was no mistaking the hope in his question, one she felt deep inside herself. 'Adam likes you, I'm sure you can expect an invitation.'

He straightened one of the forks beside his plate so it matched the other one. 'And would you welcome me to your home?'

Clara took up her wine and indulged in a bracing sip. He cared about whether or not she wanted him at Winsome and, at this moment, she did want him there. It would be like old times with her, Hugh and Adam and it would bring a touch of gaiety to what were sometimes much too serious days. 'I would be happy to have you visit again.'

If Hugh could have taken her hand and pressed his lips to it to convey his gratitude in the most potent way possible he would have, but in the presence of the others he showed restraint. In Clara's words there hadn't been the all-encompassing forgiveness Hugh had been searching for since leaving London, but it was a start. If Clara could absolve him enough to imagine spending more time with him at Winsome, especially after his great mistake with her the last time they were here, there was hope in a complete transformation of himself and his reputation.

'And what will you do now that you've officially

returned to society?' Hugh asked, eager for the light conversation they'd enjoyed before, the one that had lifted his spirits. He was also curious about Clara. At one time he'd known her so well, but they'd since become strangers and he no longer wanted it to be like that. He'd experienced and collected enough of those types of people in his life in London. He wanted another real and true friend.

'I don't know.' She cut her meat, her interest in the food fading as she pondered how to answer. 'That's a question I've both considered and avoided for some time. I've never cared much for London.'

'You're right not to.'

'But it's where people are and I need to be around more people, not alone in the country. Perhaps then I might find someone like Alfred, a good decent man and with him my own place in the world again. I'm too young to be a dowager.'

Hugh tightened his hand on his fork, the jealousy rising up in him at the mention of this unnamed man she sought taking him by surprise. The confidence she'd gained in the last six years added to her beauty more than the inherited jewels or her fine London attire. With such a striking combination, it would only be a matter of time before some man took notice of her and won her hand. Hugh didn't look forward to that day any more than he'd enjoyed hearing of her engagement to Lord Kingston in the months before his own wedding. Back then there'd been the slightest hope of things not working out with Hermione.

He'd imagined returning to Clara to try to win her back, but her marriage had put paid to that fantasy. It could happen again and this troubled him more than it should have. 'You won't find a man like him in London.'

'Surely a few gentlemen of quality must venture to town to take up their places in the House of Lords. Perhaps if I haunt those halls I might find one.'

'Or find yourself installed in a seat and voting for a bill,' he teased, releasing his grip on the silverware. At present there was no other man, simply her and him together at this table. 'If you're especially talented at haunting, no one will even notice that you're there.'

Clara laughed. 'I think my choice of clothing might give me away.'

'Not if you sit high up in the back benches where the less civic-minded lords sleep and simply call out "yea" or "nay" when required. Of course you will have to deepen your voice a touch to make it convincing and not call out too loudly and wake the snoring lord beside you. If you do, smile prettily at him and tell him that you've lost your way to the ladies' gallery.'

'If I startle a lord awake and dazzle him with a look or two, maybe I'll catch a husband.'

He leaned even closer to her, wishing he'd taken his duties in the House of Lord a touch more seriously. 'You wouldn't be the first to do so.'

'Are you saying you've woken up in the House of Lords beside a charming woman before?'

'Not me, but Lord Missington.' He nodded down the table to where the baron and his wife sat together. Lord Missington was a good many years older than the pretty young Lady Missington, but judging by the way they spoke to one another while they ate, appearing quite content in one another's presence, it was obviously a happy marriage.

'Really?' Clara didn't bother to hide her interest in this harmless bit of gossip.

'Yes, except it wasn't in the House of Lords, but at the theatre. He fell asleep in his box and she happened in and sat down, thinking it the box of a friend. When he woke she introduced herself and they have not been parted since.'

She took a sip of her wine, smiling around the edges of the glass at this charming story. 'Then I will definitely keep my eye out for a napping lord or two.'

'In your presence he would have to be napping to miss your beauty.'

She froze halfway to placing the glass back on the table and Hugh braced himself, waiting for a silent or vocal rebuke for being so forward, but she recovered her mirth and set down her wine. 'Then I shall have no trouble succeeding in London.'

He didn't doubt she would. Any man who couldn't see her charm or who didn't pursue her for more reasons than his pocket wasn't worthy of her. If he hadn't taken himself out of the running with all his past mistakes he might be the man to win her, but while he believed in second chances he knew better than to expect too many. At present, her friendship and good regard would have to be enough.

'The next time you return to London, you must be certain to stay awake so some crafty lady doesn't ensnare you.' She nodded past him to Lady Pariston who watched him with interest, then winked at him when he turned to her.

He took Lady Pariston's small, frail hand in his and raised it to his lips. 'She has already enchanted me.'

'Liar.' Lady Pariston batted her other hand at him, but there was no mistaking the twinkle in her aged blue eyes. 'But you may continue to kiss my hand.'

Clara, Hugh and Lady Pariston laughed, drawing the attention of the entire table.

'What is so amusing, Lord Delamare? You must tell us,' Lady Tillman insisted.

Carla stiffened in her chair, waiting with the others to hear what Hugh had to say and curious about how much he would reveal. Certainly Hugh would have the decency to keep their conversation about her sneaking up on a sleeping lord to ensnare him to himself. She didn't wish to appear so desperate for a second husband as to resort to such ridiculous antics.

'I was telling Lady Pariston how taken I am with her.' He raised the older woman's hand in the air between them with a graciousness that made the ladies at the table sigh.

'But I told him he's too old for me and I've decided on a much younger husband instead.' Lady Pariston flashed doe eyes across the table at Lord Wortley, who turned as red as his wine.

To his credit, the young man, despite his embarrassment, recovered himself quickly. 'When I reach my majority, Lady Pariston, I shall be yours.'

The table erupted in laughter and Clara relaxed, joining in the gaiety and marvelling at how easily Hugh did the same, turning a roguish smile on all the ladies as they called back and forth across the table, claiming their future intendeds. Clara didn't join in, but watched until Lord Tillman noticed that no one was claiming Clara and called across the table to her.

'What do you say, Lady Kingston? Would you be willing to move down the line of precedence for an old man like me?'

She could think of nothing as witty as Lady Pariston had offered, but raised her glass to her host. 'It would be an honour, my lord.'

'No, I think I'll keep her by my side,' Hugh announced. Clara stiffened at the bold declaration that made the entire table go quiet. He'd dared to compliment her beauty before with a sincerity that had touched Clara to the core. She was sure this announcement was only him teasing her like he used to do when he came for visits with Adam, but suddenly she wasn't so sure. Seeming to sense he'd become too serious, he turned back to Lady Pariston. 'But only if Lady Pariston allows it.'

'She can be the wife. I'll be the mistress.' Lady Pariston threw back her head and laughed.

Everyone laughed, too, but there was a noticeable hesitancy to it this time and Clara wasn't certain if it was for the mention of her as Hugh's wife or Lady Pariston's blatant acknowledgement that some men kept mistresses. It was one thing to know about it and quite another to say it out loud at dinner when people might be planning to slip down the corridors tonight. It was a practice Clara didn't approve of for it left a woman open to ruin while the man risked almost nothing. However, given Lady Pariston's age and experience, she was allowed to be bold and daring with her words.

When the awkward laughter died down, Lady Tillman gently shifted the conversation away from matrimony and adultery and to the ball at Holyfield taking place tomorrow night. They would all attend, just as the Holyfield guests would come to Stonedown on Christmas Eve to enjoy the Tillmans' annual ball. While the ladies eagerly discussed what they would wear and the men surmised what refreshment might be served, Hugh leaned close to Clara once again.

'I hope I didn't offend you with my jokes, but I enjoy us being at the top of the stairs. It gives Lady Fulton a much better view of your diamonds.'

'I agree.' She accepted his kind words the way Lady Pariston had accepted his teasing, doing her best to take it for nothing more than good fun despite the way it made her heart flutter. She'd intended to be friendly with him, but she hadn't imagined sharing more confidences, laughing so easily or enjoying herself this much with him. She could kid herself all night about not caring about him, but she did. It was difficult not to after everything he'd told her and all that they'd shared.

'Good, because you deserve to be at the head of the line where everyone can see you instead of hidden in the middle where you used to be. Don't allow anyone to make you feel inferior.'

Clara sobered and studied his intense brown eyes. There was nothing dishonest about the comment, but a genuine willingness to build her up as she'd tried to do with him at the sundial. It was the same way he'd spoken to her six years ago, helping her to feel more like the daughter and sister of a viscount instead of the country mouse Lady Fulton wanted her to be. She wasn't that woman any more, nor was he the heartless rogue she'd believed him to be. He was Hugh Almstead, Marquess of Delamare, her and her brother's friend. 'Thank you for your appreciation of my place.'

The seriousness between them passed as quickly as it had come and his expression changed to one of delightful enjoyment tinged with humbleness. 'And thank you for putting up with my jokes and for being my partner. I realise I probably wasn't your first choice.'

'If I'd known you were going to give away the brandy, you wouldn't have been.'

He smiled even wider, increasing the quick pace of her heart. Yes, she regretted being paired with him not because of the past and what had happened, but because of the real risk to her heart and her wits. If she reacted so easily to his smiles and tender words, then she was very much in danger of offering Hugh more than her friendship in another moment of honesty between them. Surprisingly, she didn't care. At present, she wanted to be bold like Lady Pariston and less like the reserved Lady Clara Kingston, to laugh and enjoy herself, especially with Hugh.

The men didn't linger long after dinner over their brandy, choosing instead to join the women much sooner. Hugh was glad, for his mood was buoyant after his time with Clara at dinner. He craved more of her fresh humour, the lilting notes of her voice and the optimism in her manner. It was something that had been sorely lacking in the ladies of London, especially with Lady Frances and the hours he'd wiled away with her more out of boredom than desire.

The moment he entered the sitting room, he spied Clara on the sofa near the fireplace. Unlike many of the other women who were at the tables playing cards, she sat alone, watching the logs burn, the warm firelight caressing her face. She'd chosen to stay up tonight instead of retreating to her room as she had last night and he knew that she was waiting for him.

Hugh fought the urge to rush over and sit beside her, choking on the formality required by all the people gathered here. While he made his way slowly around the room, he remained as aware of Clara's presence as he was certain she was of his. Many of the men took places at the card tables, but Hugh didn't despite the numerous invitations to join various games. Instead, he stopped here and there to watch others play and to help poor Lord Wortley to win a hand by pointing out that he had four eights.

Finally, when he reached the table closest to hers, he extricated himself from Lady Fulton's desire to hear some news of London and sat beside Clara.

'I thought for sure Lady Fulton would trap you at the table and make you tell her every detail of the last theatre performance you attended.' Clara peered up at him through her lashes, the gesture as beguiling as her unashamed confession that she'd followed his progress around the room. With her rich eyes fixed on his and the rainbows from her gems splashing over her neck and cheeks, his reservation and reasons against pursuing her began to vanish. Could they start over?

Hugh shifted on the sofa, the question pricking him like an errant feather from the down cushions. At one time he'd wanted nothing more than to win her back, but that time had passed after her marriage and his. Yet here they were, choosing to sit together and speak the same way they'd done six years ago, as easy with one another as they'd been during all his visits to Winsome. 'She isn't charming enough to trap me and the last play I saw wasn't good enough to relate in detail to anyone, including the audience.'

'Do you intend to give up the temping delights of London for good?' Clara asked, her pretty voice as warming as the fire in the grate.

'I had planned to avoid town for a couple of Seasons, but with this new matter facing Everburgh, I'll have to return with the opening of Parliament in the spring. It will stop me from fulfilling my vow to give up less reputable establishments.'

Her smile faltered a touch. 'You mean clubs and other places?'

He tilted towards her, her full lips slightly parted as enticing as her sweet perfume. 'I mean the House of Lords and most government offices.'

She laughed, the sound as charming as the sight of Lord and Lady Missington together in the window seat, still smitten with each other after a number of years of marriage. 'Adam never makes sitting in the House of Lords sound so delicious.'

'Then press him to tell you better stories than whatever he's telling you now.'

'I must. It also gives me even more reason to return to London with him and Anne in the spring. I want to see all of these things you've described tonight.'

'I only hope I haven't built them up so much that you find them disappointing.'

'After the quiet of the country, any spectacle in

London, no matter how disappointing, will be a nice change.'

Hugh tapped his knee, considering his words before he spoke. 'Perhaps I can join you on a few of these excursions? I imagine this Season's theatre bill must be better than last Season's and I'd hate to disappoint the next person who asks me to describe a performance.'

'I think, given your and Adam's friendship, it's very likely you will accompany us,' she answered, as non-committal as he was hesitant. 'You must tell me what other dens of vice to visit, such as the Royal Academy and the British Museum.'

'The British Museum is the worse. You shouldn't go there. More people meet scandalously in the Greek Gallery than at the theatre. It's awful.' He shook his head in mock disapproval, this chance to deride London as pleasurable as strolling beside her and listening to the silk of her dress rustle against her legs. She was lovely here beside him, back straight, shoulders firm, and her gems adding to her beauty instead of making up for a lack of it. She didn't need them or any fancy airs to be stunning, but he enjoyed them all the same.

'And what of Vauxhall? I've heard wicked things about what takes place along the dark paths there.'

'It's a nunnery compared to Hookham's. The people perusing their prints will taint any respectable woman.'

She crossed her hands in her laps in decision.

'Then I must go there for I'm in desperate need of a new novel to read.'

'Make sure it is a very bad one for you want to keep up with the latest fashion.'

'I'll make sure it is one of the worst,' she assured him with a wink.

It was then Hugh happened to notice the interest that Lord Westbook took in their conversation. He sat on the far side of the card table closest to them, deep in conversation with Lady Fulton who sat on his left. While they spoke, Lord Westbook took in Hugh with a scrutiny that Hugh would have demanded Lord Westbook explain if they were in his club in St. James's. Here, he allowed the overly curious and condemning look to stand, not wanting to create any more trouble for Clara than he might have already caused by sitting beside her longer than precedence and dinner demanded.

If she was aware of Lord Westbook's interest in them, she made no indication of it, taking in instead the selection of rich desserts laid out on the table in front of them by a footman in the Tillmans' blue and gold livery. One could always count on indulging at Stonedown.

'You're not having any?' Clara noticed he didn't make a move for the food while she selected a plate along with a few tempting treats.

Hugh glanced at her, then the assortment and then Lord Westbook, catching him and Lady Fulton watching both Hugh and Clara from the corners of their eyes. As much as he wished to stay here and enjoy a custard along with more of Clara, he suspected it was time for him to leave. They'd made a great deal of progress today. He was loath to have a bunch of busybodies ruin it.

'I don't think I will. In fact, it's time for me to retire.'

'Already?' She gasped with no small amount of genuine surprise. 'What would people in London say if they saw you going to bed before midnight?'

'That I'm preparing for a dawn duel.' This made her smile again, the sight of it warming him more than the raging fire in the grate. 'Goodnight, Lady Kingston.'

To his silent delight, disappointment at losing his company whispered across her face. 'Goodnight, Lord Delamare.'

He didn't rise, but continued to regard her as she did him, and the room and all the people surrounding them seemed to disappear. If he touched his lips to hers, she would raise her hand to his cheek, press herself against him and surrender to the need flooding them both. It was there in her wide eyes and parted lips, in the way she leaned forward on the one hand, resting on the brocade between them, and tilted her head up to him, inviting him to come closer. If he did, she would be his again. All he need do was slide over and press his hip against hers as he slid his arm around her back. He laid his hand on the cushion, his fingertips achingly close to hers, every muscle in his body tight with the desire to touch her, but he didn't move. He couldn't. They weren't alone.

Instead, he pulled his hand away and rose, offering her a bow, a temporary farewell before turning and denying himself the sight of her. With each step that carried him away from her, he fought the urge to return by reminding himself that there was tomorrow and more time. He would not make the same mistake as before and rush at her like some starstruck boy. Instead, he would employ patience like a proper gentleman. With her taking her first steps back into society after the seclusion of her widowhood, he didn't wish to command all her attention, but to give her a chance to decide and choose, and himself a chance to prove that he deserved her affection and attention. The spark of something had flared between them and there was plenty of time to coax it into roaring fire, assuming it didn't find a reason to flare out.

Clara watched Hugh go, missing his humour and companionship before he'd even stepped out of the door. For a little while tonight, the boy she'd known at Winsome, the one she'd fallen in love with at Stonedown had been beside her. With him, she'd felt a little more like the carefree young woman she'd once been and not the mourning matron. Without him, the unease that his conversation and teasing had kept at bay slowly began to return. She glanced at the cushion and the imprint of his hand lingering there and traced it with one finger, making the feathers beneath the fabric shift until the outline and the warmth of him began to fade. What remained was the craving for Hugh that had enveloped her when they'd sat so close. There'd been more than friendship in his eyes when she'd thought he would lean forward and take her hand and kiss her.

Kiss me, indeed. She smoothed what remained of the imprint out of the cushion and sat up straight. He wasn't about to be so bold in a room full of people, nor would she have allowed it, except she would have. Apparently, she'd been without a man for too long if she were so eager to kiss the first one who showed any interest in her. Lady Pariston would say there was only one remedy for it, but Clara feared the cure would be worse than the illness and she wasn't about to throw away any chance of proving that she'd changed by potentially making the same mistake twice. Only she wondered if the mistake was in letting Hugh go.

She looked at the door where he'd disappeared through, tempted to rise and go after him when movement along the edge of her vision made her turn. Anne, who couldn't hide her delight behind her hand of cards, was watching her, as was Lady Pariston, who nodded with approval. However, it was Lady Fulton's smug smile and Lord Westbook's scrutiny that jerked Clara out of her daydreams and back into the sitting room.

She was doing it again, being careless in her regard for Hugh in front of everyone and risking another public humiliation.

He wouldn't do that to me again, or would he?
She didn't know. Whoever he'd been in London, that man was not the one she'd been with during the scavenger hunt or at dinner or just now, but the London one remained behind him like a shadow, clouding her view of him.

There's no reason to rush into any decision, either for or against him, she reminded herself, rising to join one of the card games and to stop everyone from staring at her and speculating. She would keep her before-dinner vow to be careful and watch and observe him, to have the patience to draw out the truth about Hugh, good or bad. Her mind hoped it would be bad and then she could walk away proud of herself for having avoided any pitfalls, but her heart had other ideas, ones she was afraid to admit even to herself.

Chapter Six

Thick shafts of morning sunlight streamed in through the large windows lining the upstairs hall of Stonedown Manor. Clara moved through each of these warm patches, ignoring the magnificent views of the winter countryside surrounding the manor outside. She held on tight to the banister while she descended the stairs, far more awake than expected after a night spent tossing and turning while she worked to untangle the mess of thoughts she held about Hugh until, exhausted by the effort, she'd finally fallen asleep. The bliss of unconsciousness had been short lived and she'd awakened long before sunrise to mull over again all the things discussed yesterday. She'd forced herself to stay in bed until the sun had at last peeked through the heavy curtains and the maid had entered to light the fire. Then she'd taken her time dressing, all the while trying to pretend that she didn't want to hurry downstairs and see Hugh again. She'd dreaded her first morning here and encountering him. This morning, she longed for more laughter and jokes and the excitement of whatever the Tillmans had planned. This wasn't at all how she wished to be. She wanted to be rational and calm, cool headed and logical where Hugh was concerned, and she was being everything but. Even now when it should make no difference to her whether he was below stairs or still in his room she had to struggle not to race to the dining room and see if he was there and how things might be between them today.

As she approached the dining room, she forced her racing heart to still with each step that drew her closer to breakfast and possibly Hugh. She didn't wish to walk in and beam at him like the smitten ten-year-old who'd followed him around Winsome during his first visit, her head full of fanciful dreams that he might notice her. She was too refined a lady to behave like that, although at times last night she'd wondered if she was as refined as she believed. When he'd sat with her on the sofa she'd felt very much like that smitten ten-year-old and had almost behaved like one.

Blast all this nonsense. She paused at the dining-room door, pushed back her shoulders and strode in like a marchioness.

The instant she crossed the threshold she realised how futile worrying about Hugh had been. He wasn't there. None of the men were present except for Lord Westbook, who sat at the far end of the table beside Lady Fulton enjoying his eggs and ham. It was a stark reminder of why Clara shouldn't allow herself to be carried away when it came to Hugh. If he was half as excited to see her as she'd been to see him he would have been here waiting for her.

Shoving down her disappointment, Clara offered greetings to those seated at the table before making her way to the sideboard, far more reserved in her movements than she'd been before she'd entered, but no less agitated. She looked over the selection of food in the chafing dishes, but her stomach was too knotted for her to choose more than a slice of toast. She should be glad that Hugh wasn't here for it spared her the effort of being in the same room with him and pretending at indifference. She wished she really was indifferent. She was tired of her emotions bouncing around like an overeager puppy.

'Ah, Lady Kingston, good morning.' Lord Westbook stepped up beside her at the sideboard and refilled his plate. It was amazing he was so slender given how much food he ate. 'Come and sit with me for a while. It's been ages since we've spoken.'

He wasn't exactly the man she wished to speak to this morning, or any morning for that matter, and she cast him a sideways glance, wondering why he was suddenly so interested in her and why he was the only man in the dining room. 'Where are the rest of the gentlemen?'

She could guess why he was interested in her.

'They decided to take advantage of the morning sun to enjoy a ride. Most don't think the good weather will last and we'll have snow by Christmas. Not being much of a rider myself, I decided to remain indoors.'

This gave Clara a touch of hope as she set her plate at an empty seat at the table and waited for the footman to pull out her chair. If all the gentlemen were eager to ride, Hugh couldn't have been expected to remain behind with the ladies like Lord Westbook. She would see him again shortly, for the men were sure to return before the end of breakfast to fortify themselves for whatever event Lord and Lady Tillman had planned next. Clara sat down, amazed when Lord Westbook took the open place beside her. Lady Fulton was still at the table and would make him a better dining partner than Clara.

'How are you finding Lord Delamare? Is your pairing successful?' he asked, leaning too far over the arm of the chair and taking much more interest in her answer than politeness dictated.

'It is going well.' She scraped some butter over her toast, littering the china with crumbs. 'And your pairing with Lady Fulton?'

'Splendid, of course.' He flicked his hand as if waving away a fly, making it clear it was not his pairing he wished to discuss when he lowered his hand to the arm of his chair and leaned closer, dropping his voice. 'But I'm concerned about you.'

'Are you now?' she answered between bites of her toast, wishing he'd go away.

'I was here during that awful business between

the two of you last time when we all thought he would declare for you. How embarrassing it must have been when he left so abruptly and then announced his engagement to Lady Hermione.'

She worked to choke down the dry toast. His desire to make sure she remembered her embarrassment was irritating, especially with Lady Fulton watching them. She resisted the urge to dump her plate of crumbs in his lap and tell him a thing or two about his manners. Instead, she took another bite of toast with all the dainty disregard for him and his comment that she could muster. 'That was a long time ago, Lord Westbook, and I've quite forgotten most of it.'

'Yes, but I fear Lord Delamare may be up to his old games.'

His sugary caring, so different from Hugh's genuine concern, made her stomach twist. 'You have nothing to worry about on my account.'

'But I do. I've known you too long not to be worried, especially with you being a widow—my condolences on your loss.' He laid a long-fingered hand over his heart, his signet ring clinking against one of the buttons on his waistcoat. Clara offered a terse nod in acceptance which gave him leave to continue in his present vein while she tried to contrive some way to politely extricate herself from this conversation.

She glanced across the table to Anne, who'd come in and taken a seat and who watched their exchange with incredulous curiosity. Clara knew the minute she shook free of this troublesome man, Anne would sweep her away to find out what he'd wanted. Good, for she needed a distraction both from thinking of Hugh and fuming over Lord Westbook's insolence.

'I realise that things are more permissible than a number of years ago,' Lord Westbook continued, 'but I want to warn you about indulging in all the delights of a house party. Lord and Lady Tillman, like most hosts, are quite tolerant of, how shall I say it, unorganised nocturnal activities, but it doesn't mean everyone else is.'

Clara dropped the half-eaten toast on her plate, unwilling to endure any more of this insufferable man and all his unwanted and lewd suggestions. 'Lord Westbook, we are not on familiar enough terms for my delight in a house party to be any of your affair.'

She moved to rise, but he placed a staying hand on her arm. 'I don't mean to be rude, Lady Kingston, but if you'd heard the things I have about Lord Delamare, you would be far less congenial to him than you are at present.'

Clara said nothing, curiosity getting the better of her and keeping her in her seat.

Lord Westbook glanced around to make sure no one was listening before he spoke in a low voice, taking her silence for an invitation to continue. 'For a number of months, Lord Delamare was involved with Lady Frances, a young window much like yourself who is well known in London. Despite a great deal of speculation, no marriage proposal was forthcoming when both were free to take their pleasures legally, as one might say, and to protect the future, of, how shall I put it, any consequences of their liaison. He didn't, but broke with her six months ago, casting a serious shadow on her reputation. His reputation did not suffer for with his carrying on with more than a few actresses, much like his grandfather used to do, his behaviour was nothing more than what people expected of him. His one saving grace is not having gone into debt which ruins so many men, but this one admirable trait does not make up for the rest.'

Clara wasn't sure which disgusted her more, hearing his frank discussion of other people's intimate lives or the unpleasant details that Lord Westbook provided about Hugh. She'd heard a number of stories about Hugh, but nothing about him having a mistress. It wouldn't be difficult to discreetly learn whether or not everything he'd told her about Hugh and Lady Frances was real or one of Lord Westbook's exaggerations. Sadly, the sinking in the pit of her stomach practically answered the question for her. She'd left Hugh last night with a greatly raised opinion of him, but it was wilting fast in the face of Lord Westbook's story. It lifted the veil from her eyes and helped her to see the situation as it was not as she wanted it to be. His actions were defining him more than any of his words ever could.

'I'm sorry if what I said upsets you, but I remember your parents with great fondness and I'd hate to see you fall prey again to a man like Lord Delamare,' Lord Westbook explained.

Whatever Lord Westbook's motives for speaking to her, she couldn't remain here, not with Lady Fulton watching them and making heaven knew what of it. Clara could well imagine. She thought Hugh's absence had spared her any difficulties this morning, but instead it had made them far worse.

She set her napkin on the table beside her meagre and half-eaten breakfast, careful to show nothing of the turmoil inside of her as she faced him. 'Thank you for your concern, Lord Westbook, but I assure you I am quite adept at fending off false offers of friendship.'

She rose and this time he didn't stop her. In a daze, she left the room, but instead of going up, she wandered to the library, needing time to think over what he'd said and how she would deal with it. The Hugh that Lord Westbook had described was not the man who'd been with her at the sundial or the one who'd sat beside her at dinner and afterwards and who'd looked on her with an admiration she hadn't seen since she'd walked down the aisle to meet Alfred. He was a gentleman who'd cared only for his own pleasures and concerns in London, heedless of the damage it did to the woman he was with. If she were not careful she might become like that woman, for if Hugh had seen no reason to marry Lady Frances after dallying with her so that all of London was aware of it, then he wasn't likely to offer for Clara should anything develop between them.

Nothing will develop between us, especially not after hearing this news. She had more self-respect than to lower herself in such a manner, especially when Hugh would be free to walk away from her again, especially if any consequences should arise from their liaison. She longed for a child of her own, but she would not make it a bastard.

She paced back and forth across the large rug in the centre of the room, annoyed that her holiday should be plagued by this nonsense. Hugh wasn't why she was here. She wanted to have fun and enjoy herself, not be bogged down in all this fretting and worrying. She'd done enough of that in the days leading up to Alfred's death and afterwards when she'd been bereft of a husband, a place, all her dreams for a family of her own and lost and lonely. Except Hugh had lifted a great deal of that loneliness yesterday and she couldn't help but want more of it, but not if it meant becoming another Lady Frances.

Clara sat down on the leather sofa, the coldness of the material seeping through her gown along with a growing weariness. She should never have allowed Anne to talk her into coming here.

'Clara, are you all right?' Anne entered the library and peered about as if she'd never been in this room before. 'You left breakfast so quickly.'

'I'm fine, only Lord Westbook was making a nuisance of himself.'

'Isn't he always?'

'He outdid himself this morning by warning me to be a little more careful where Lord Delamare was concerned, as if how the two of us regard one another is any of his business. Then he told me something quite shocking.'

'About Lady Frances?'

Clara jumped to her feet in shock. 'You know about her, too, and didn't think to warn me?'

'His past relationship with her has no bearing on the present situation.'

'Of course it does. How am I to form a true opinion of him if I don't have all the facts?' Her sister-in-law could be as bad as Lord Westbook when it came to indulging in other people's affairs, especially Clara's, except this time she hadn't stepped in when it would have been to Clara's advantage for her to do so. She needed to have a conversation with her sister-in-law about sharing *all* the gossip with her, not just some of it.

Anne crossed her arms and slid Clara a sly look. 'A proper opinion? Is that what you're forming with Lord Delamare?'

Clara went to the nearest bookshelf and pulled out a book to flip through, not really caring what it was about. 'There is nothing between us. We were paired up and we are being cordial and friendly with one another.'

'Is that what they call it now?'

'That is exactly what it's called.' Clara shoved the

book back into the hole in the bookcase. 'Besides, what am I supposed to do, ignore him?'

'I must be very right for you to be so cross with me.'

'I'm not cross, I simply hate for people to think there is more to it when there isn't.' And there wasn't, or so she continued to say, but it was clear she wasn't fooling anyone, especially not herself. If he had tried to kiss her last night, she would have allowed it and this troubled her as much as trying to work out Hugh's real character. Oh, but the man was frustratingly perplexing. 'Why are you so interested in me and Lord Delamare? Surely there are better, more eligible men that you and Adam could throw in my path.'

'Not this week, there isn't,' Anne answered as if this were not a very grave subject.

Clara huffed in frustration, forcing Anne to take this discussion a touch more seriously.

She approached Clara with an earnestness that was not very convincing. 'Clara, we are at a house party in the country during Christmas. Other than partaking in the events, speculating about what other guests are up to is almost all there is to do here. You would be doing it, too, if you weren't at the centre of that very speculation.'

Clara took a deep breath. Anne was right. Clara and her mother had attended a number of house parties after her coming out where they'd spent a great deal of time wondering who was pairing with whom.

She never thought to be standing here wondering about herself.

'Why not enjoy the attention and the fun?' Anne suggested. 'After all, isn't that's what you came here to do?'

'No, I mean, yes, but not with Hugh.'

Anne cocked a curious eyebrow. 'Hugh?'

'Lord Delamare.' Clara balled her hands in frustration at her slip for it gave a great deal of credence to all Anne's insinuations. 'What do you know of him and Lady Frances?'

This dulled Anne's amusement. 'I've heard that Lord Delamare, like a great number of gentlemen in London, does have something of a past, which as a matron you are allowed to hear about.'

'And the fact that he wouldn't marry her? Am I allowed to hear about that?'

'Lord Westbook has been busy, hasn't he?'

'And he's right, isn't he?'

'I'm sure there's a good reason why Lord Delamare didn't marry Lady Frances although I'm not privy to it. Don't assume the worst of him, Clara. He's had a rough time of things and, like you, he needs friends.'

It wasn't a friend Clara needed, but someone who would cherish her the way she wished to be cherished, to be there for her when she was hurting and to make her smile and laugh and to give her hope. She had her doubts about that man being Hugh.

'Come, we must dress for the next activity,' Anne said.

'Fine.' Clara yanked a book off the shelf without looking at the title, tired of wading through all these roaring thoughts. She followed Anne out into the hallway, not caring what book she carried. She wouldn't be surprised if she climbed into bed tonight to see she'd chosen a tome on the subject of irrigating crops. Oh, well, at least she would learn something.

Anne and Clara were not two feet out of the office when Lady Tillman approached with her hand on a young man's arm. He was new to the party and to Clara, and tall, not as tall as Hugh, but impressive enough with sandy blond hair and light brown eyes. His chin was sharper and not as strong as Hugh's, nor was his chest so well developed beneath his finely tailored suit. The cut of his coat reminded her more of those men whose tailors were firmly established in London than Hugh's and she sensed at once this was no country gentleman.

'Lady Kingston, Lady Exton, allow me to introduce you to Lord Stanhope. He's a friend of my cousin and is joining us for the remainder of the week. It's his first Christmas house party here at Stonedown.'

'Or any manor, truth be told,' he offered with appealing graciousness.

'Then you're in for a treat, for no one hosts a party so well as Lord and Lady Tillman and you're sure to enjoy tonight's ball at Holyfield. It isn't as good as Lady Tillman's Christmas Eve one, but I'm sure you'll find everyone very welcoming and in good spirits,' Anne offered, doing her best to make the man feel welcome, but with his easy stance and air of confidence, Clara suspected he needed no encouragement to step straight in to any group or festivities and make himself at home.

'The country ladies will be thrilled to have a new dance partner,' Clara added, not as clearheaded as Anne to think of something more witty or interesting to say.

'Might I be so bold as to ask for your first dance, Lady Kingston, before the country ladies overwhelm me?' He shifted the full focus of his charm from Anne to her and, if Clara was not mistaken, it radiated a little brighter for her than it had for her sister-in-law. Over his shoulder, Anne widened her eyes at Clara as if to say there was now someone besides Hugh to be thrown in Clara's path. Clara ignored her, thinking her sister-in-law was the worst matchmaker she'd ever encountered.

Instead, she kept her eyes fixed on Lord Stanhope's, standing up a touch straighter when he dropped his gaze down to take in the length of her before raising it once again to meet hers. 'Yes, it would be a pleasure to enjoy the first dance with you, Lord Stanhope.'

If Hugh had been given half the warnings she'd received today from so-called well-meaning people like Lord Westbook, then he wasn't likely to ask her to dance with him. Good. She didn't need to give anyone any additional reasons to keep speculating on whether or not she would become the next Lady Frances. There was someone new here that they could whisper about, one with no past connection to her and whose presence by her side would cause a great deal less whispering and speculations. Dancing with Lord Stanhope might not have been what she'd imagined for this evening, but he would be a refreshing change from the last day.

'Until tonight, Lady Kingston.' Lord Stanhope offered her a bow worthy of an audience with the King and then allowed Lady Tillman to lead him off to make more introductions, but not before tossing Clara one last look over his shoulder, his smile as strong as his stride.

'I suspect Lord Delamare might have some competition,' Anne joked.

'Lord Delamare doesn't need to worry. His past behaviour has already knocked him out of the running.'

'Clara, don't underestimate the power of a good apology from a man. I have gained some of my best jewellery from Adam this way.' Anne laughed, for she and Adam rarely fought.

'It is probably my jewels more than me he's after.'

'Really, Clara…'

'No, I won't be tricked by him again. Let him woo some other widow, I will see what other men there are in the world.' He wasn't the only one worth having.

* * *

Hugh and Adam walked back from the stables, the musky scent of horses and leather saddles clinging to them as much as the cold morning air. When Adam, Sir Nathaniel and some of the others had asked him to ride this morning, he'd quickly agreed. The stinging air and the demands of commanding a horse had been a welcome distraction after a night spent lying on his back, staring up at the ceiling and thinking of Clara. She'd dominated his thoughts more so than even six years ago until he could think of nothing but her, not even the dangers facing Everburgh. It was wrong, but he'd been powerless to stop it. When he and Clara had laughed and reminisced about their past at Winsome, his current troubles had lessened their hold over him. She'd been the girl who'd once captured his heart because she hadn't derided him for having a grand title and no money. When they'd ridden together over the grounds of Stonedown in the sleigh, she'd listened to all his dreams for Everburgh and had believed that they would come true. He hadn't realised he would have to let her go in order for his dreams to be realised. But it was no longer six years ago and his reasons for not pursuing Clara were beginning to fade as quickly as the frost on the grass.

It was how he would win her that had remained as elusive as sleep. The truth was he hadn't had to work for her heart before, their love had simply blossomed. Now a great many obstacles stood between them and he would have to clear each one if he wished to make her his.

'I'm glad to see you and Clara getting along so well,' Adam remarked from beside him as they walked from the stables to the main house.

'We are, surprisingly well.' Hugh's breath formed small clouds above his head before the wind carried them off. 'She told me she's considering venturing to London for the Season.'

'Good. I very much want to see her back out in the world again. It will help for her to have another friend in London.'

'I'd be more than happy to escort her when required, if you and she are amenable to the idea.' Hugh wondered how far he might venture with Clara and if Adam would disapprove or not. Adam knew more about Hugh's past than most and, despite remaining his friend, Hugh wondered if Adam would see him as a suitable match for his sister. She might not need her brother's permission to marry, but her family was important to her and he refused to cause strife between them. Even if Adam did approve, if fate contrived to separate Hugh and Clara again and she was hurt, he was sure Adam would finally discard him and Hugh's quiet re-introduction to society would end. His title might gain him a certain admiration and invitation, but he no longer wished to be a titled face at a ball and to return at night to a silent house. He would rather not be invited to a hundred balls and have one good and true friend and the real love of a wife than to strut about in society with his station and a gaggle of hangers-on who would disappear the moment they got wind of any trouble or difficulty.

'Are you quite free to serve as Clara's escort?' It was a probing question, the kind the father of a potential fiancée might ask.

'I'm entirely free and under no obligations to anyone. Lady Frances and I broke with one another six months ago. I have not spoken to her since nor has she made any effort to contact me.' It'd been a mutual parting with neither of them suffering when the end had finally come. They'd never been in love, merely a convenience. Lady Frances was a shrewd woman who'd been married to a much older man before he'd died and had delighted in the attention of a man her age. She understood the way of the world and was not full of enough dreams and whimsy to wish to bind herself to a lord with a great deal of hard work ahead of him.

'I'm glad to hear it.' Adam clapped Hugh on the back as they climb the stairs to the doors of Stonedown.

Adam and Hugh spoke of possible hunting in the autumn before they parted at the top of the main staircase to go to their rooms to dress. While Hugh prepared for the day, he thought about Clara and how much he wanted to see her again. Whether she was as elated by the prospect of being with him remained to be seen. She'd been friendly and tempted by him last night and it gave him hope, but the light of day and a night to think things over could change things. Either way, he would not be as serious or melancholy with her as he'd been yesterday. Not every connection between them could be about mourning or past troubles, for he was certain there were other, more enjoyable things to draw them together and make the holiday much brighter for both of them.

Chapter Seven

Hugh stood at the back of the guests assembled in small groups and scattered about the main staircase of Stonedown Manor. It'd taken him longer than he would have liked to dress, making him the last to join the group and hear what Lord and Lady Tillman had planned for today.

Hugh peered over everyone's heads, searching for Clara. He spied her on the far side of the group standing beside Lady Exton. The sunlight illuminating the room from the windows flanking the front door played in the wisps of hair escaping from the loose curls at the back of Clara's head. She did not wear the elaborate jewellery that had adorned her last night, but had chosen instead simple pieces of gold with smaller gems that highlighted the lighter colour of her deep yellow gown. Her bright dress was a stark contrast to the more muted colours that she had worn for the last two days and the warmer shade lightened her face, which would have shone even more if she'd worn a smile instead of her strangely strained look.

Her lips were pressed tight together and there was no trace of the ease with which she'd sat beside him last night, nor did she appear as excited about the forthcoming game as the others. In fact, she looked as thrilled as she had when she'd come downstairs on the first night to stand beside him. She also didn't hazard a glance at him although he was certain she was aware that he was here. She was purposely ignoring him the same way she'd done when she'd sat beside him at the first dinner.

Worry crept into Hugh, pushing out the excitement and hope that he'd experienced during the early hours of dawn and in the time since. Something had happened between last night and this morning and it had changed her opinion of him. Then he caught Lord Westbook's eye and the answer seemed to make itself clear in the superior arch of his brow before he turned back to listen to Lord Tillman.

As if unable to avoid Hugh's searching stare, Clara finally glanced in his direction. He smiled and nodded at her, conscious of the thrill that gripped him at capturing this small bit of her attention. The feeling evaporated when she did not return the smile or do anything more than turn back to Lord and Lady Tillman, deliberately snubbing Hugh. If he could have pressed his way through the guests and come to her side and drawn her into another room where they could speak privately he would have, but he wasn't about to make a scene, especially while Lord and Lady Tillman were explaining the next activity.

'With the weather a great deal colder today and with everyone in need of a free afternoon to prepare for the Holyfield ball tonight, we've decided on a game of hide and seek.'

'Rather scandalous, don't you think, Lord Tillman?' Sir Nathaniel called out, as amused as he was serious in his question.

'Given our present pairings, I don't believe we have a reason to worry or to suspect that anyone will be doing too much dallying while the searcher seeks out his quarry.'

A number of people turned to look at either Hugh or Clara and Hugh inwardly groaned. This would not help him make his case against whatever had turned Clara against him this morning.

'Speak for yourself, Lord Tillman.' Lady Pariston laughed, grabbing on tight to Lord Wortley's arm and making everyone laugh, except Clara.

This did not bode well for a pleasant afternoon with her.

'Who will be searching?' Mrs Alton asked.

'Lord Stanhope. Being the newest member of our party, he is without a partner and has graciously agreed to be our searcher.' Lady Tillman motioned to Lord Stanhope who stood off to one side with an air of languid superiority on his square face. Hugh didn't know much of the man, but he didn't like the way he glanced up the stairs at Clara, flashing her a very inviting smile that, to his chagrin, she returned. He wished the Tillmans would hurry up and get on with the game, then he could speak to Clara and find out what was the matter.

'When the gong rings, you'll have five minutes to hide. Then the gong will sound again and Lord Stanhope will begin his search. There is nowhere on this floor in Stonedown that you may not venture, but you are not to go upstairs. The butler is going to stand here to make sure you don't. The prize today will be to lead the first dance at the Holyfield ball tonight.' Lady Tillman motioned to the butler who stood up on the landing with the gong. He rang it and Lady Tillman clapped her hands together before announcing, 'To your hiding places.'

The room quickly emptied as everyone grabbed their partner and set out in search of the perfect place to conceal themselves. Hugh strode through the confusion of people to reach Clara, who appeared in no hurry to set out or to be alone with him.

'Where do you suggest we hide? You know this house better than many and must be privy to all its secret chambers and rooms,' Hugh said, trying to inject some of the spirit of the game into the tense air between them.

'I don't have as intimate a knowledge of the house as you believe so you may choose where we hide.' Her flat tone made it clear that the last thing she wished to do this morning was hide with Hugh waiting for who knew how long to be discovered.

He'd been eager to reach her before, but now he wasn't so certain he wanted to be alone with her and risk her sharp words but he had no choice. He must find out why she'd changed her attitude to him since he'd seen her last night and this was the best way to do it without danger of anyone whispering about them are overhearing. 'I have an idea. Follow me.'

He raised his hand to take hers and then thought better of it. He turned on his heels and led her away from the entrance hall. She followed in silence, as dour as if this was nothing more than another duty that had to be done before she could continue with the rest of her day.

The deeper they walked into the house, the less they heard other people, with the occasional door closing or a muffled giggle to alert them that there were a few souls around them.

'Where are you going?' Clara asked.

'The large cupboard near the billiards room.' Hugh reached the door set in the panelling in the wall just beyond the billiards room, the last one along the long corridor before the large window at the end. He pulled it open to reveal old trays of billiard balls and stands holding extra sticks waiting to be used if a number of guests wished to play at the same time. It was a small, musty room, but wide enough for two people to secrete themselves away for a little while. 'Quick, in here.'

Hugh turned to find Clara standing halfway down the hall.

'You want us to hide in a cupboard?' She threw him a dubious look that he was certain had more to do with the confines of the space and how close they would be forced to stand rather than the actual hiding place itself.

'Lord Stanhope isn't familiar with the house and, if nothing else, it will take him some time to search the other rooms. With any luck, by the time the gong rings he won't have come this far and we'll still be hidden.'

'I don't know if I'd call that lucky,' Clara murmured and Hugh questioned the wisdom of stepping into such tight quarters with this little tiger. He was apt to be bit, but if he didn't take the chance he might not discover what was troubling her.

Thankfully, the deep sound of the gong marking the start of the game made her dart into the small space faster than any words he could think of to convince her to join him. He followed her inside, closing the door behind him.

While Hugh's eyes adjusted to the dim light filtering in from beneath the door, he listened to Clara's quick breaths, noting how they slowed as she settled herself in the darkness and waited with him to either be found or to have to reveal themselves at the end of the game. Hugh guessed she was praying they would be discovered quickly, for there were no words about winning and becoming the lead couple in the first dance and showing up people like Lady Fulton and Lord Westbook. There was only a silence as tortuous as her rose perfume. The scent of it was more potent than the dust covering the equipment and he longed to break the tension between them by reaching out and slipping his arm around her waist. He could draw her to him and bury his face in the curve of her neck and inhale the sweet warmth of her skin, leave small kisses in the hollow of her throat and make her sigh with a pleasure to drive out all her objections to him, but Hugh didn't move. He could see in the faint light slipping beneath the door that she was standing as far away from him as she could without knocking over the stand of cue sticks behind her. It was not an inviting pose and the whole house was likely to hear her slap him if he dared to touch her so intimately. Last night she might've accepted his kisses, but not today.

'What's wrong, Clara?' Hugh ventured in a low voice, keeping an ear out for any footsteps in the hallway. This wasn't a particularly clever hiding place but in his eagerness to be alone with her it had seemed like the best choice.

'What makes you think there's anything wrong?' Clara crossed her arms over her chest, her stance less welcoming than it had been in the entry hall.

'After yesterday, I thought you'd enjoy this kind of game.'

'Then you guessed wrong.' She trilled her fingers on her bare upper arm, her fingertips brushing the smooth creaminess he wished he could caress.

'What happened since we parted last night? You weren't this sharp or callous with me yesterday.'

His directness made her lips form an enticing *O* of shock before she regained her voice. 'I heard a very enthralling story at breakfast, one that involves you and a certain widow in London. It appears you have a fondness for intimate friendships with widows.'

'What do you mean?' He didn't defend himself for there was no defence against the truth. He thought she'd already heard that story, but apparently she hadn't. However, if she were bold enough to throw his past relationship in his face, one that had nothing to do with her, then he would see how much bolder she was in pursuing this line of discussion.

'Lady Frances. I understand she and you were…' She stopped, too embarrassed to say the word. She didn't need to say it because he did.

'Lovers. Yes, we were.' She wanted the truth and he would give it to her and prove that he was still the honest man she once believed in despite his questionable past.

Clara struggled to keep her jaw from dropping at his blunt answer. She hadn't expected him to so readily admit his sins and yet he'd confessed with all the frankness of a grocer telling her the price of apples. 'I don't know whether to forgive you for your honesty or lecture you about your vices.'

'My past vices,' he corrected, his words much tighter than they'd been when he'd led her to this hiding place. 'And you needn't lecture me. My mother did enough of that when she was alive. Trust me, she was no more thrilled by my time in London than you are.'

'I don't blame her.' No doubt he'd hoped by coming here to do something more pleasurable than discuss his mistress while they'd hid. She was glad to disappoint him. 'Is your time with Lady Frances really over?'

'It is and it never should have happened, but things were different for me then, and like you she was free to make her own decisions.'

'I'm nothing like her.'

'No, you're not.'

'Are you disappointed?'

'Not at all.'

This took the angry wind out of her sails, but it didn't settle the anxiety that had forced her to speak. 'Lord Westbook said you weren't willing to marry her.'

'Did he?' He ground his jaw, his shoulders and neck stiff, so unlike the Hugh who'd charmed her into almost making her forget herself in front of everyone last night.

'He did.' She never would have believed that she would be quoting Lord Westbook of all people. She couldn't stand the pompous man and yet she'd been all too willing to listen and believe him this morning, except what he'd said was true, at least the part about Lady Frances being Hugh's mistress. The rest she still wondered about.

'Then allow me to tell you what he doesn't know.

A few months into our relationship, I offered to make Lady Frances an honest woman. She turned me down. My title was grand enough for her, but not my income. It was the beginning of the end of our rather weak relationship.'

His unwillingness to mince words forced Clara back into silence. She should be glad that someone who'd been all too willing to marry a woman for money had discovered what it was like to be rejected because he didn't have enough of it, but she wasn't. Instead she was left once again to try to reconcile the things he told her with what she knew of him and decide whether to believe his words or his actions. Deep down, she should trust her instincts and not the whisperings of a well-known gossip monger like Lord Westbook or the doubt he'd tried to plant in her, but her instincts had been wrong about Hugh before. If she chose to believe he was a scoundrel, then turning away from Hugh would be easier. Admitting he wasn't meant admitting to so many other things that terrified her, including how afraid she was of being wronged and humiliated again and how much the longing in Hugh's eyes matched the one in her heart.

Every bit of common sense and the awful lesson she'd learned from her previous experience with him screamed against this insanity, but still she could not dismiss it. All his supposed honesty could be nothing more than a ruse to gain her trust and then deceive her again. With troubles still facing Everburgh, he could be pursuing her simply because of her wealth, or because he did genuinely care for her. She didn't know which and she was tired of this ambiguity. 'What is it you want from me, Hugh?'

'The faith you showed in me yesterday and last night.'

'Why?'

'Because if you can believe in me again, then the man I used to be and wish to be again is not lost.'

Clara fingered the cold, smooth top of a cue ball sitting in a tray beside her, unsure how to respond. He was giving her opinion of him far more importance than it merited. 'Surely there are other people who can better offer you what you seek.'

'None with heartfelt honesty like yours. You don't play games, Clara, or ever leave me in doubt about your true feelings.'

'Or perhaps it's simply because I'm here and convenient, a single mistake from your past you can easily remedy on your way home in order to clear your conscience.'

'Is that all you think you are to me?'

'I don't know what I am to you. I never have.' He'd given her so many reasons for why he'd done the things he'd done, but he'd never admitted to loving her. She wanted this more than any apology or excuse, but her pride wouldn't allow her to ask for it. She'd stood in front of him, waiting for him to ask her to be his wife, and instead he'd told her the honour would go to another. She wasn't about stand here and demand his heart and listen to him give her a thousand reasons why it couldn't be hers, all of them very noble. She wasn't so hard up for love as to do this to herself.

'You're so much more than you realise.' He stepped up to her, towering over her in the semi-darkness of the small space. She stared at him, the shadows beneath his eyes darkening his brow while the light from beneath the door highlighted the angle of his chin. Beneath the musty smell of old equipment and dust, she caught the faint scent of his shaving soap and the earthier smell of horse and sweat from his morning ride. It was an enticing scent that took her back to Winsome and the many days spent with him and Adam running through the garden, before their time under the mistletoe had ruined the charm of those memories. She'd come here to set the past aside and claim a new future, and so had he, yet here they were together with everything that had passed between them still hanging in the air like the fine dust they'd disturbed.

She didn't know how to settle it, especially the quiet part of her that remembered what it was like to love him, to experience hope and possibility in his arms. If she reached out her hand and laid it on the side of his face, she could touch it all again, not the misery but the happiness, but fear kept her hands firmly at her sides. His sudden care for her might be nothing more than his old regard for her family and Adam and have little to do with the true preferences of his heart. Except the way he looked at her was more than admiration for her family, but the desire of a man to cross the darkness and take her in his arms.

Clara took a step closer to Hugh, then stopped, unwilling to give way completely to the temptation urging them closer together. If he made the first move and crossed the short distance that seemed like miles, then she would take a chance and go against every logical thought she had about him and follow him, but he must be the one to make his intentions clear in his touch, to tell her in his kiss that he truly meant everything he said to her, that it wasn't simply the heat of the moment like it had been before and when the clouds of infatuation cleared he would walk away from her again. She held her breath as she waited for him to lean down and press his lips to hers, to reveal the truth of his intentions in his kiss. He moved slowly, closing his eyes as she closed hers, his mouth so close she could almost taste him.

Suddenly, light spilled into the room, making Clara and Hugh flinch and raise their hands to cover their eyes. They stepped back from one another, the moment lost.

'It looks like I've found two more.' Lord Stanhope stood with the door open, smiling in triumph at them. 'At this rate the game will be over long before the gong rings.'

Clara stumbled past him and into the hallway, her heart pounding as she blinked against the shock of the light. Near misses with Hugh were quickly becoming the rule instead of the exception and if Lord Stanhope had been a moment later, he would have had quite a story for the breakfast table. There'd been nothing sordid about the encounter, no furtive clawing at one another or adjusting of clothes but there was no mistaking that Lord Stanhope's arrival had interrupted something. It wouldn't take much for him to guess what and for the story to be all over the house by the time the ball started, assuming he wasn't a discreet man. She didn't know enough about him to say if he was discreet or not. Clara pressed her hand to her chest, trying to work out the tightness sitting there. She should have known better than to have tempted Hugh and fate and yet once again she'd ignored her better senses and thrown off caution, to her detriment. It seemed like she would never learn.

She slowly turned to face Hugh and Lord Stanhope, smoothing the front of her dress with her hands while she composed herself. She tried to appear as if nothing untoward had been taking place in the cupboard, but for all her fear at their near miss, there was regret, too. If she and Hugh had kissed, her lingering questions about him might have been answered. Instead, what remained was confusion and the possibility for more humiliation.

'Lord Stanhope,' Hugh greeted their finder with little enthusiasm, as troubled by the interruption as her.

'Lord Delamare. It's been a while, but you appear well, certainly better than the last time I saw you.

Where was it? Ah, yes, I remember.' He snapped his fingers. 'The field outside London. You'd winged Lord Cecil and secured your honour. What was it he'd called you?'

'I don't recall.' Hugh glanced back and forth between Clara and Lord Stanhope, clearly not appreciating this reminiscence so close on the heels of the one he'd been forced to endure about Lady Frances.

'I wish I could be so cavalier about a duel.' Lord Stanhope chuckled. 'Not that I've ever fought one.'

'Shall I call you out for finding us?'

Lord Stanhope held up his hands up in mock defence. 'I'm only doing my hostess's bidding.'

'And we can't fault him for that, can we, Lord Delamare?' Clara added, drawing his attention away from Hugh and the discomfort marring the moment. 'We surrender and wish you luck with the rest of your search.'

'Thank you, Lady Kingston, yours is the most gracious concession I've encountered this morning.' Lord Stanhope took her hand and raised it to his lips, his eyes never leaving hers and making her swallow hard. He was a potent reminder of everything that might be waiting for her if she stopped looking back and chose instead to move forward.

'I'm happy to be such a good sportsman.' Clara glanced over his shoulder to see Hugh watching them, his eyes clouded with irritation.

He's jealous. Clara inwardly smiled in triumphant delight, for she wanted him to see that she wasn't a simple girl new to love who could be wooed away from her better sense by a gentleman capable of over-awing her, but a mature woman whose good opinion he must work to secure. She also wanted him to know that he was not the only one capable of claiming her attention.

Following the line of her gaze, Lord Stanhope let go of her and turned to Hugh, his smile dimming to a more humble grin. 'Off you both go to the dining room. Lady Tillman instructed me to tell all the people I find that the noon repast is served. It seems we are to be treated to a theatrical performance by the children this afternoon.'

With a bow, Lord Stanhope turned and wandered off down the hall in search of more guests.

'Shall we go to lunch?' Clara asked when they were alone again, not sure what else to say.

'You go. I have some business to attend to before this afternoon.'

She didn't try to convince him to accompany her. They needed time apart after the confines of cupboard and everything they'd discussed, especially with them swinging from being at each other's throats to almost venturing into a place she wasn't certain either of them was ready to travel.

She wandered down the hall towards the dining room, glad there wasn't anyone else about. It allowed her to compose herself before she faced the others. For the second time in less than a day she'd been tempted by Hugh and almost too weak to resist. She hoped he didn't knock on her bedroom door tonight for she was beginning to doubt her ability to send him away. A little space to breathe was a very necessary thing.

Hugh watched Clara go, her yellow dress swaying about her legs and brushing her hips as she walked. His gaze remained fixed on her until she turned a corner and was out of sight, and then the regret rushed in. In an effort to be close to her, to answer the questions she'd asked him and the temptation he'd seen in her eyes, he'd nearly kissed her. In doing so, he'd almost opened her up to more gossip.

Except it wasn't just his mistakes that ate at him as he made his way to the study to try to distract himself with correspondence, but Lord Stanhope. He knew little about Lord Stanhope despite having seen him on more than one occasion at the theatre or his club, but there was no missing his obvious interest in Clara. Nor had Hugh failed to notice how willing she'd been to return his smiles, reminding Hugh again of the challenges he faced where it came to her. She had every right to show interest in a man who hadn't already wronged her and didn't bear a rake's reputation, at least not one he was aware of. If Hugh were willing to tolerate Lord Westbook for more than a second or two, he might sit down with the man and discover what he knew about Lord Stanhope, but he could imagine how that would set tongues wagging about Hugh sizing up the competition.

The more the image of Lord Stanhope bowing over Clara's hand and her basking in his attention tortured him, the more the patience he'd vowed to employ with her last night began to desert him. He'd lost her quickly once before when, after leaving Stonedown, she'd met Lord Kingston and then married him in a matter of months. If Hugh left her at the end of the party without a clear understanding of his future intentions, he might lose her again. When she'd stepped close to him in the closet, as eager for his touch as she'd been last night, he'd realised there was still hope for them to be together. Like all his opportunities to save Everburgh he must seize it. He might have lost his way for a while, but he wasn't a man to give up and he would not give up on a chance with Clara. It would mean risking his heart, but if it meant capturing hers and having her stand beside him in the struggles facing him, to remember what it was like to enjoy life the way he had last night and during the hunt yesterday, then it was worth the risk.

Chapter Eight

Dark clouds moved in to cover the blue sky in the hours after lunch, casting Stonedown deep into early winter darkness. Footmen lit the candles and chandeliers in the hallways and common rooms to drive back the encroaching gloom. Everyone was gathered in the sitting room to enjoy the children's theatrical performance. At the far end, a small stage had been erected and thick curtains hung on ropes draped either side of the boards.

Clara entered the impromptu theatre late, having spent the time after lunch in her bedroom enjoying the solitude and the chance to think uninterrupted about what had happened between her and Hugh in the closet. His past with Lady Frances was what she should focus on and how it was another in a long line of reasons why she should have nothing more to do with Hugh, except the incident didn't trouble her as much as she thought it would. While she hadn't liked finding out about his relationship with Lady Frances, he'd been honest with her instead of trying to hide behind lies or excuses. He didn't pretend, like everyone had when Lady Pariston had called attention to it, that such things didn't happen between men and women.

It was what had nearly happened before Lord Stanhope had stumbled in on them that troubled Clara far more than Hugh's previous dalliance. For the second time in as many days she'd almost kissed him. The man she'd vowed to be nothing more than friends with had almost become…what? She didn't know. She refused to be like Lady Frances and yet she'd almost fallen into Hugh's arms the moment he'd barely reached out to her. It shocked and scared her how willing she'd been to do so. She shouldn't want him or have him mean anything more to her than a regrettable part of her past and perhaps as a future acquaintance, yet every time they were alone together they kept inching towards a line she'd never wanted drawn in the first place.

She longed to call it foolish weakness, but it was a great deal more. When he spoke of his troubles it was as if she was hearing herself speak. When he admitted his failings and weaknesses she could see her own and how the grief that had changed her had done the same to him. Outwardly, they seemed so different in how they had dealt with hardship, but inside they were very much alike and she could speak with him about it all because he understood. Even in the moments when she doubted his integrity, he offered her every reason why she shouldn't, undercutting all of her arguments against him and every advice about judging a man by his actions that her mother had ever given her. There was more to what he told her about his past than false words, but truth, reason, honour and grief. Then when he looked at her, as he had in the closet, it was as if she was the most precious thing in the world.

Her feelings about Hugh continued to baffle her, especially the closer she drew to the sitting room. She had no idea how she would greet Hugh or how to behave. It was wrong, but the more time she spent with him the harder it was to ignore logic and not listen to her heart. In his way, he was trying to help her put the pieces of it back together and she couldn't help but yearn for him.

Thankfully, Hugh wasn't in the sitting room and Clara let out a small sigh of relief. She took one of the empty chairs near the door, unnoticed by all the other guests who were enthralled with talk of their children and the upcoming joy of watching their little ones perform. The one good thing about worrying over Hugh was that it had distracted her from thinking about the play and her lack of a little player to watch. In the semi-shadows of the back of the room, the old pain rushed back to her, especially with the parents sitting in delight at the front where they deserved to be. As a marchioness, Clara might take precedence over all these people, but she would gladly trade that privilege to be sitting at the front row and waiting for a child of her own to step on to the boards. She turned her wedding band around on her finger, tired of waiting and mourning. At times this week when she'd been with Hugh, her losses hadn't hurt so much because he understood what it was like to lose one's future and dreams. With Hugh beside her she'd had someone to talk to whose care and concern gave her hope. Without him here, it was difficult to keep the sadness at bay.

Her private moment was short-lived as Lord Stanhope entered the room. He stopped on the threshold, taking in the guests and the available seats before spying the empty one beside her. Flashing a wide smile, he made directly for her. She should be flattered that he wished to sit with her, but something in the way he regarded her that didn't quite liven his eyes, so unlike Hugh with his natural admiration, made her wish he would chose a different seat. He appeared to be a pleasant enough man, but there was an exaggerated aspect to his pleasantness that was difficult for Clara to put into words or to dismiss.

'Good afternoon, Lady Kingston. May I?' He pointed to the chair.

Clara was about to tell him to sit when Hugh came up behind Lord Stanhope, stepped around him and took the empty seat. 'Excuse me, Lord Stanhope, but this is my place.'

Clara gaped at Hugh while Lord Stanhope's charming smile went stiff about the sides. If Clara was not mistaken, distaste for Hugh flashed through his eyes before he covered it with a bow of defeat. 'Of course, Lord Delamare.'

Lord Stanhope made for the opposite side of the room and the empty chair beside Lord Worth.

'Rather forward of you, don't you think?' Clara asked, more charmed than annoyed by the little tiff over who had the right to sit beside her. It was the first time in her life that two men had vied for her attention and, far from being annoyed with Hugh's heavy-handed deciding of the matter, she was flattered.

'Not at all. I outrank him.' Hugh tilted up his head in mock arrogance. 'Can't have these lower men thinking too much of themselves, now, can we?'

'No, not at all.' Clara stifled a giggle. 'To think that a mere…um… What is he?'

'The Second Baron Stanhope.'

'That a baron, and only a second one at that, can sit next to a marchioness is outrageous.'

'If I'd allowed his impertinence to stand, who knows what might have happened. Viscounts could challenge earls and then there would be no end to the chaos in line before dinner.'

This time Clara didn't hold back her laughter, glad to enjoy herself and their jokes instead of enduring the tension of her accusations and his defence and her loss. She slid a sideways glance at Hugh, taking in the tight cut of his breeches against his firm thighs, the close fit of his waistcoat about his trim middle and the strength of him that called to her more than she cared to admit. It could happen between her and Hugh if she wanted it to, as Anne and Lady Pariston had suggested. All she need do was slip down the dark hall tonight to his room, but she wouldn't. It was an entanglement some women could indulge in without risk to their hearts, but not her. She wanted a man's whole life, not simply the sordid pieces hidden by the dark and not spoken of in polite society. If he could give her this, then she would be his, but he had to offer it, to make it clear to her and everyone that this time his affection for her was real and his promises to her would be kept.

'What play do you think we will be treated to today?' Hugh asked, his breath brushing the side of her cheek and making the desire swirling inside her to go to his room tonight even stronger.

'I don't know, but I'm sure it will be a riveting production,' Clara whispered, fighting to control this silly temptation. Thankfully, the performance began and Clara clapped with the rest of the audience as the youngest of the children took to the stage amidst a great deal of oohs and ahhs from the parents.

The sons and daughters of the guests, the littlest being about four years old and the oldest not quite out of the nursery performed a Christmas play about the Lord of Misrule and some of the antics he got up to during a Christmas house party.

Clara watched the performers, but it was difficult to concentrate on even the scenes with her niece and nephew with Hugh sitting so close. More than once, his thigh brushed the skirt of her dress when he moved, making the soft fabric caress her bare skin beneath.

'They're fun to watch, aren't they?' Hugh asked when James and another boy, both of them dressed as knights, began a mock battle on stage.

'Yes, they are,' Clara answered in a weak voice, trying to retain her smile as the all-too-familiar pain began to well inside her. Despite the joy of watching little James, the presence of Hugh and the jokes they'd shared before the start of the performance, she couldn't hold back the sadness. If things had been different, Clara would be in the front of the room beside Adam and Anne, clapping enthusiastically for a well-delivered line and beaming with the same pride that decorated the few faces she could see from where she sat.

The longer the performance went, the more thoughts of Hugh beside her faded, replaced by an emptiness that made her chest ache until she could no longer sit still. Without making her excuses to Hugh, she rose and fled the room, doing all she could to not draw attention to herself. She didn't wish to dull anyone else's enthusiasm for they had the right to enjoy their children's performance without her pain ruining it.

In the shadows of the hallway where the voices of the little mites were muted by the distance, Clara stopped. Wrapping her hands about her waist, she took a few deep breaths, doing her best to calm herself and regain control. It was one thing to cry in her room alone and quite another to do it where anyone might happen upon her. It also angered her. She thought she'd got over these fits of melancholy ages ago, but she hadn't. They weren't as frequent as they used to be, but they still hurt and she was helpless to do anything but endure them until they passed. They were something she did not speak about, not even to Anne, not wanting to be pitied. There was no one else to talk to because everyone else expected her to have moved past it, to forget. She wished it was so easy to forget, but it wasn't.

'Are you all right, Clara?' Hugh asked, his voice soothing and comforting in the dim light of the hall.

Clara turned to face him, glad it was he and not someone else who'd stumbled on her. The closer he came, the more she wanted to throw herself in his arms and wet the wool of his coat with her tears. She wanted him to hold her and tell her that she wasn't alone in her grief and that all was well and that, in time, everything would be all right, but she didn't move. She longed to be brave as she always was in front of everyone, but she couldn't lie to him either. She was tired of enduring the isolating grief that swathed her in moments like this, helpless to do more than let it wash over her until it passed. Perhaps if she gave it words it might release its hold on her and she could once again enjoy such simple delights as children performing at Christmas without the threat of tears.

'Sometimes it's difficult to see what others have and be reminded that it's not a joy I share. I don't wish them ill or that they go without like I do, but it hurts to not have a little one of my own.'

'Some day you will applaud as enthusiastically for your child delivering their stilted lines as much as Adam and Anne,' Hugh assured her in a gentle voice, coming to stand in front of her.

'I want to believe that, but it's so difficult.' During her marriage, Clara had consulted the midwife who, finding nothing wrong with her, had said it must be Alfred. He'd suffered from an awful bout of scarlet fever as a child and the midwife had heard stories of men fathering no more children after such illnesses. Given that he and his first wife had not been blessed, this had seemed right, but Clara had always held out hope that time might have proven the old woman wrong, but there hadn't been enough of it. 'I wish with all my heart that I had something more than a title and a widow's portion to remind me of my former life.' The one that had ended too soon, the memories of which were fading more and more every day.

'You will find love again and have a child some day.'

In the background, the high voices of the children delivering their lines rang out in the room along with the occasional chuckles and ahhs of their parents.

'That's what everyone says.' She turned away from him and stared up at the portrait of some past Lady Tillman in her heavy velvet dress and wide, ruffled-lace collar. She stood with her hand on the shoulder of her son, both of them looking out from the canvas in confidence. 'But it's difficult to believe sometimes. What if I never meet anyone else?'

'You will, I promise you.' He came up behind her and laid his hands comfortingly on her shoulders, their weight stronger than the melancholy draping her. 'Don't give up, Clara.'

His low voice in her ear was as soothing as it was warm against her skin. Six years ago, when she'd been hurting, Alfred had come to her and helped her. Now she was hurting in a different way and here was Hugh doing the same. She leaned into him, his comfort meaning more to her than anyone else's because he'd experienced this, too. His spouse and every dream he'd had of a child with her had been stolen from him, leaving him, like Clara, to find his way to whatever the future held for him.

'Sometimes I find it hard not to give up.'

'We've both tried giving up before, you with Winsome, me in London and it didn't help either of us.' He tightened his arms round her, his chin close to her temple as he held her and spoke. 'If we give up, then we will lose and we'll really have nothing. I don't want to have nothing. That's a pain I can't live with, more than mourning or anything. It's why I'm here, to try to make things better.'

She closed her eyes, the resolution in his words giving her strength. With his firm arms around her she could believe that some day it would be her in a portrait with her children or her clapping for her child's performance. Behind her his chest rose and fell with each of his long breaths, his arms tight against her chest. She raised her hands to rest them on the soft wool of his coat, revelling in the safety and contentment of his embrace. He pressed a kiss to her temple, his tenderness making her sigh. In his embrace there was more than comfort or need, but the answer to the questions she'd asked in the cupboard and the truth she'd sought all last night and most of today. She opened her eyes and looked up at the copper flecks in his brown eyes as he watched her. He hadn't sought her out because of money or boredom, but because he truly did care for her as much as she did him and it would all be different this time.

She could have stood within the security of his arms for hours, but applause thundered out of the sitting room accompanied by shouts of 'Bravo'.

'I think the performance is over.' Clara reluctantly straightened and Hugh let go of her. Despite what had happened between them, they stood where anyone leaving the sitting room could see them. 'James and Lillie will expect me to be there to congratulate them.'

'Then let's not disappoint them.'

Clara walked beside Hugh back into the sitting room, the quiet between them more comfortable than words. The awkwardness of the cupboard, of their first dinner and all the near misses vanished like the smoke from the candles, as did Clara's doubts about him. She'd come downstairs this morning eager for clarity about Hugh and in his arms in the hallway she'd found it. He wasn't the schemer who would break her heart, but a man she could reveal her fears and weaknesses to without worrying that he would laugh or make her regret being so open.

They entered the sitting room and were met by the sight of proud parents hugging their little players, fathers holding up their sons and mothers cuddling their daughters. While they watched the parents congratulate their children, no one, not even Lord Westbook or Lady Fulton, noticed them in back so far from the candle footlights. In the semi-darkness, Hugh stretched out his hand to touch hers. Clara didn't pull away but turned her hand to accept his caresses. In his touch was the promise that their turn to be this happy and content with children and families and estates would come, too. Some day, she would return to Stonedown filled with the love of a husband and the joy of children. She had no idea when it might happen, but under the influence of Hugh's encouragement and the pressure of his touch she believed that she was a little closer to claiming it. She would not give up or allow grief and isolation to keep her from gaining the things she craved. She would strive on, as Hugh urged, and succeed.

Chapter Nine

Clara entered the Holyfield ballroom beside Anne, pausing a moment on the threshold to search for Hugh. Among the dresses that had arrived from Winsome had been a light pink one with a flowing silk skirt and a bodice of rich velvet embroidered with silver thread that sparkled when she walked like the sapphires around her neck. The jewels had been her mother's and in the family for three generations, but she wore them tonight as if they were hers and no one else's. A number of people on both the dance floor and the crowd around it turned to take her in, eyes wide with amazement or with smiles of approval. However, it wasn't for them that she'd chosen this dress and necklace, but for Hugh.

After the play, convention had forced them apart and the demands of preparing for tonight had left them without another chance to speak, but the unspoken promises that had passed between them in the hallway, and again when he'd taken her hand, had been enough to carry her through the rest of the day. All the doubt that Lord Westbook and others had tried to sow in her, and all the second guessing she'd done since the beginning of the party, were over. Whoever Hugh had been in London, he was no longer that man, he never had been, but like her he'd been lost and hurting. Except when they were together the pain could not touch them. She'd leaned in to him today without thinking and he'd offered her the support of his body and his experiences to comfort and hold her. She couldn't throw that away out of fear of what people might think or out of her own worries that the past might repeat itself. Neither of those things was important any more. Hugh had reminded her that what had happened before was gone and only the present and the future mattered, and she wanted him to be a part of both and for that life to begin tonight. She could love him again and she felt certain that his heart was hers already.

The shifting forward of the receiving line forced Clara to stop searching the room and greet Lord and Lady Elmswood, the owners of Holyfield. The arrival of guests from Stonedown had been slowed by the snow that had begun to fall at sunset and the many carriages needed to convey everyone to the ball. Thankfully, the snow had not come down hard enough to block the roads and prevent anyone from reaching this Tudor wood and plaster house with the magnificent wood-beamed great room. The numer-

ous rafters were decorated with garlands of evergreens that infused the air with the scent of pine.
Clara did her best to concentrate on Lady Elmswood
while they spoke, careful not to keep looking about
in search of Hugh. She didn't know which carriage
he'd ridden in or if he was here already or waiting to
arrive. He might be in the card room, watching the
play or enjoying refreshment from the Elmwoods'
generous outlay.

No, if he was here, he would be waiting for me.

Clara flexed her hand where a few hours before
Hugh had touched his bare skin to hers. The impression of it had lingered long after the parents leaving
the sitting room had forced them apart. She wanted
to see him again, to dance and be with him and experience once more the optimism and hope of his presence. When he was near, she felt as if anything was
possible and it was a feeling she was loath to lose.

'Searching for someone?' Anne nudged Clara
with her elbow as they made their way along the edge
of the dance floor after leaving Lady Elmswood.

'Perhaps I am?' Clara answered in a sing-song
voice, not irritated by Anne's continued interest in
Clara and Hugh. Soon everyone would be aware
of it and it didn't matter. She didn't care what they
thought of her or Hugh or what they said about them
being together. From here on out, no one's opinion
but her own would guide her or hold so much importance.

'I'm glad to hear it.' Anne snapped open her fan

and waved in front of her face, making the ruby earrings dangling from her small ears swing with the slight breeze. 'I wouldn't mind if you two renewed your former friendship.'

'Is friendship all you're interested in seeing between us?' Clara enjoyed torturing Anne as Anne had enjoyed doing it with her.

Except Anne suddenly turned serious. 'I want to see you well settled again, Clara, and despite what happened before, I do believe that Lord Delaware could make you happy if you gave him a chance.'

Clara clasped her fan in front of her, tempted to tell Anne that the chance had already been taken, but she didn't. This was no place to explain to her that she had changed her mind or why. She wasn't sure she could explain it in a manner that anyone, even Anne, could understand. She barely understood it herself.

'You needn't make any decisions yet,' Anne assured, pointing over Clara's shoulder. 'For look who's coming to join us.'

Clara's heart began to race and she stood up straight, careful to maintain the grace and confidence that she'd carried with her into Holyfield. Slowly she turned around, waiting for the moment when Hugh saw her and she could bask in his attention.

Lord Stanhope approached her with the stealth of a tiger. All Clara's excitement vanished at the sight of him and she struggled to maintain her smile and her manners. 'Lady Kingston, I'm so glad you've arrived for I haven't forgotten your promise.'

'My promise?' She could barely remember having spoken to the man today much less making him any promises. It was Hugh who had commanded her attention when present and who continued to do so even while they were apart.

'To give me your first dance.'

'Oh, yes.' She had promised this and with Hugh having yet to arrive, she had no choice but to place her hand in Lord Stanhope's and allow him to lead her out on to the dance floor.

While they walked, there was no fluttering in her chest like there was whenever she touched Hugh. She marvelled at this for Lord Stanhope was very handsome with manners to charm the teeth out of a snake. The two of them walking together garnered a number of looks. They weren't the looks of amazed curiosity that had startled so many at the Holyfield ball six years ago when people must have wondered what it was that the Marquess of Delamare had seen in the quiet and shy Exton girl, but genuine awe at a bejewelled marchioness being escorted by a handsome lord to her rightful place on the dance floor. Clara should have revelled in the moment, but everyone's admiration paled against her desire to be beside Hugh.

The musicians struck the first notes and she and Lord Stanhope began the dance, hands touching and raised in the air between to make the required turns.

'You are quite stunning tonight,' Lord Stanhope complimented, this one, like all his others, too exuberant and almost studied for Clara to take seriously.

'Thank you, but as we have not met before, how do you know I'm not this stunning every night?' Clara enjoyed this flirting and the power she felt in it—it was a prelude to everything she hoped to enjoy with Hugh.

'I'm sure you are this stunning every night, as I'm certain to discover during the rest of my time at Stonedown.'

He was very much overestimating how much time the two of them would spend together if he thought so.

'What brings you to Stonedown, Lord Stanhope?' Clara searched the people watching them, but still did not see Hugh. She wondered if he'd decided at the last minute not to come. No, he had to be here, to want to see and be with her as much as she longed to be with him. The snow must have delayed his arrival. All would be well, just like he'd promised. She was certain of it.

'The promise of charming company is the reason I'm here.' Lord Stanhope made the turn around her this time, his eyes never leaving hers, their intensity almost laughable if it weren't for the seriousness of his look. 'What other reason could there be?'

'There must be plenty of charming company in London.' Most of whom would enjoy his constant flattery and charm more than her.

'I find the company of the country far more lively and refreshing than what's available in town. Unless you decide to venture there next spring?'

'I have not decided.' She had no desire to make him any more promises.

He raised her hand again and held it while she made a turn. As she came around him, facing out to the audience, she finally spied Hugh across the room standing with Sir Nathaniel and Adam. A small muscle along the side of his jaw twitched while he watched Lord Stanhope place his arm around her to promenade. She didn't feel Lord Stanhope's touch, but longed instead to be in Hugh's arms.

She endured many more of these turns and promenades, catching Hugh's eye during each one. It took all her strength to remain beside Lord Stanhope and not dart off to join Hugh, for the dance lasted much longer than she remembered. During it all, she was polite and cordial as expected of a woman of her rank, but her heart was across the room with Hugh.

Finally, the musicians brought the piece to an end and Lord Stanhope offered her the most gallant of bows before escorting her off the dance floor. Once they were back in the crowd, he turned to her as if he was about to ask for another dance when Hugh appeared beside him.

'Lady Kingston.' Hugh held out his hand for her to take, ignoring Lord Stanhope and making clear to him, and Clara, that he was not to expect any more dances for Hugh would be her partner.

She pressed her gloved palm to his and he closed his fingers over hers, claiming her as she wished to be claimed.

At the far end of the room, the musicians began the slow melody of a waltz. A murmur of excitement raced through the room with everyone amazed that Lady Elmswood would sanction such a dubious dance. It didn't stop them from choosing their partners and hurrying out to the dance floor to delight in this near-scandalous endeavour.

'Shall we?' Hugh asked, his voice as husky as if he were leading her into his bedroom.

'Yes, please.' She was eager for him to place his hand at her waist and to clasp his other around hers. As much as she needed a good country dance with a great deal of sashaying to help quell the energy building inside her at being this close to Hugh, she was glad for the intimacy of the waltz. She could be alone with him in this small way, free to speak and enjoy the strong lines of his face, his deep voice and pleasant smile without censure.

He led her to the centre of the dance floor and turned her to face him, laying his strong hand on her waist and taking her hand with the other. Then he stepped close, towering over her with his wide shoulders and solid chest, his heady cologne mixing with the pine fragrance filling the room. She took a deep breath as much to savour the nearness of him as to steady herself. Then he set them both into motion in time to the slow melody. Her skirt whispered against his legs with each sure step and his fingers tightened against her middle as he led her in the dance. Clara held tight to his shoulder, wishing she could stretch out her fingers and caress the smooth skin of his neck. Once in a while, his thigh brushed against hers, the tease of it almost making her knees buckle, but he held her in the sturdy circle of his arms and she didn't falter. With his gaze riveted to hers, the ballroom and everyone in it seemed to fade away until it was just the two of them and the music. She surrendered to his lead, allowing him to sweep her along and deeper in to him.

'You look stunning tonight, Clara.' Hugh's compliment was unstudied in a way that Lord Stanhope's had not been. It'd been too long since she'd received such sincere praise, especially from someone who mattered.

'Thank you.'

'What were you and Lord Stanhope discussing?'

'London and whether I will venture there for the Season.'

'And will you?'

She tilted her head to gaze up at him through her eyelashes. 'Is there a reason for me to go there beyond trying to catch a napping lord?'

'I will be there.' He pulled her a touch closer, his coat brushing her waist when they moved.

She shifted her hand on his shoulder a bit closer to his neck and allowed one finger to brush his skin. 'Then that is a good reason for me to go.'

He turned his head enough to make his chin graze the back of her hand, his lips so close to her skin, he could almost kiss her. Her entire body tingled with anticipation, but they couldn't be so intimate, not here in front of everyone. Someone might be watching, but if they were Clara didn't notice. She could only see Hugh and all the possibility for their future in his eyes.

At the end of the room, the musicians brought the dance to a close. Hugh stopped, but didn't let go of her until holding on made them stand out and he at last removed his hand from her back, but not his hold on her hand. He raised it to his lips as he bowed to her, viewing her from beneath his brow with a look to take her breath away. 'I think we have a spectacular new year to look forward to.'

'I think we do.'

With the couples around them shifting off the floor and quickly being replaced by new dancers, Hugh tucked her arm into the crook of his elbow and escorted her into the crowd. They didn't stop, but continued towards the back of the room and to a hallway leading off the ballroom. It was quiet here and far from the glare of the chandeliers illuminating the beam-ceilinged great room. Paintings of horses and dogs sprinting across the landscape dotted the hallway along with a generous sprig of mistletoe that hung from the small chandelier in the centre. Hugh guided her beneath the sprig and together they stared up at the single berry clinging to the stem. The kiss it conferred on them could be theirs if Hugh leaned forward and touched his lips to hers. Clara very much hoped that he would, defying the small voice in the back of her mind that said she shouldn't be standing here with him where anyone who wandered by would see them together. That voice was blotted out by the longing to be free and to not care. She was a widow and for all the heartache it'd foisted on her, Lady Pariston was right, it also gave her more leniency to do as she pleased in a way she never could have enjoyed as an unmarried woman. She would use it to be brave with Hugh and to not doubt herself or him or this Christmas. It would be the first of what was sure to be many happy ones to come.

'It seems a pity to leave it hanging there, all alone.' He flicked a glance up to the mistletoe and the single berry still clinging to its stem. 'To think of it being burned with the rest of the greenery when the Christmas season is over and never fulfilling its duty to those standing beneath it.'

Clara's heart began to race and she tilted her head back a touch to flash him an amused and inviting look, enjoying this rush of boldness. 'We can't have that, now can we?'

'Not at all.' He stepped forward and took Clara's hands, towering over her in strength, but with a tenderness to touch her heart. He leaned forward, his gaze never leaving hers until she closed her eyes, waiting for their lips to meet.

When they did, every part of her came alive. She

inhaled his breath and the subtle scent of his sandal-wood shaving soap made more potent by the sweat from their last dance. Raising her hands, she laid them on his shoulders, holding on tight to him to steady herself against the thrill making her tremble. She revelled in the press of his lips and the soft weight of her in his arms around her waist and his breath caressing his face. There were a hundred reasons why she shouldn't be here alone with his mouth claiming hers and his tongue drawing out hers to savour the taste of him, but none of them mattered. This was no mere groping or illicit stolen moment, but something more. It was there in the light way he held her, in the restraint in his lips and the promise she'd seen in his eyes before they'd kissed.

Hugh savoured the sweet taste of Clara as the lively notes of the musicians' stringed instruments accompanied by the steady murmur and laughter of voices carrying out of the ballroom swirled around them. When he'd stepped into the ballroom and seen her dancing with Lord Stanhope, smiling and laughing at the gentleman as if he were the most charming man in the room, every fear he'd had about losing her by holding back had seized him. Then he'd approached her and the widening of her smile that had made her beam like the mirrors reflecting the candle-light told him that he couldn't lose her for she was already his. All he need do was pick up where they had left off six years ago, before duty and responsibilities had forced him away from her. Those things might still be with him, but so was Clara, as free to be his as he was to be hers. With her by his side, he would strive to finally secure Everburgh and make it everything he and his family had wanted it to be, and to make her his Marchioness.

The tempting rise and fall of her chest against his made his pulse pound in his ears. Beneath the fine fabric of her dress he could feel the subtle boning of her stays and the curve of her hips below a small waist. With her firm body beneath his palms he longed for the freedom to be with her, the one denied to him six years ago and the one he would deny himself again until she could be truly and legally his.

He slid one hand up the curve of her waist and along the length of her bare arm above her glove to cup her cheek. She willingly fell deeper into his embrace and opened her lips to take in the gentle sweep of his tongue against hers. In the air between them, her rosewater perfume blotted out the fresh fragrances of the pines and evergreens heralding the approach of Christmas. All too soon the kiss was over and he leaned back, leaving his arms around her to steady himself against the rush of feeling making him want to clasp her to him again. He brushed a wisp off hair off of her cheek and tucked it behind her ear. Her skin was warm and soft against his palm and she looked up at him, her eyes sparkling like the jewels adorning her neck. 'I'll be sorry to see the party end.'

'Me, too, but there are still a few days left.'

And many more chances to speak and be with Clara, to slip into dark corners and enjoy more of her kisses and her touch until the Christmas house party ended and they parted for the remainder of winter. Spring and the opening of Parliament couldn't come soon enough. He wouldn't avoid London this year, but join Clara for the Season and make it her last as an unmarried widow. The end of the Christmas season would not be the end of things between them, but the beginning of many wonderful years to come and all of them spent with Clara.

Hugh bent down, ready to claim her mouth once more when an all-too-familiar female voice purred in disgust, making Hugh freeze.

'Hugh, it's good to see you haven't changed.'

Clara jumped back out of Hugh's embrace, her heart racing at the starling interruption. Hugh didn't move so fast, slowly lowering his arms and straightening as he stiffly turned to take in the woman watching them at the entrance to the hall.

She was a stunning blonde, much taller than Clara with a certain poise that whispered of a London polish. Her dress was of the newest fashion and cut far lower than Clara would have ever dared, revealing an enviable bust. She wore nothing more than a gold chain against her luminous skin and small white flowers in the elaborate curls of her hair.

She barely spared a glance for Clara, taking in

nothing more than her large diamond and sapphire necklace which Clara was glad she'd worn. She almost felt gaudy in it beside this woman, but her inclination to cover it with her fan ended at the annoyed curl of the woman's lips. Whoever this woman was, she was not happy to see Hugh with Clara and this set Clara on edge.

'Who is she?' Clara whispered to Hugh.

'Lady Elizabeth Frances,' Hugh said through clenched teeth.

Clara's jaw dropped as low as Lady Fulton's and Lord Westbook's who'd stepped into the hall just in time to witness this scene, curse the busybodies. Both of their eyes widened in amazement before Lady Fulton narrowed hers with relish at what appeared to be the makings of a good tale, and a chance to best Clara.

'What are you doing here?' Hugh demanded of Lady Frances.

'I'm a guest of Lady Tillman's,' she answered before Clara could warn her that they were not alone. 'My cousin is acquainted with her and applied to her for invitation.'

Lady Frances glided towards Hugh like a boat on calm water, the wispy fabric of her skirt clinging a little too much to her slender legs. She came so close to him she crowded out Clara, who had no choice but to step aside or be struck by the woman's enviable bosom. Lord Westbook and Lady Fulton took the opportunity to shift closer, too, stopping Lord and Lady Missington when they passed and encouraging them to watch. Clara was too stunned by all of this to reprimand any of them for so blatantly intruding on what was clearly a private conversation. 'London can be so cold and lonely this time of year, especially for a young widow.'

Hugh didn't answer, staring down at her not with the hot look one might expect for so finely built a woman, but with a disdain Clara felt creeping up her spine. His silence encouraged the woman to carry on.

'Ever since I arrived this evening I've been searching for you.' Her words sucked what remained of Clara's cheer out of the hallway the way the flue did the smoke from a fireplace.

'Now you've found me. What do you want?' His brusque question at last wiped the simpering smile off the woman's face.

Clara wanted to know, too, fearing that this ball was about to turn from the most magical into one as heartbreaking as the holiday six years ago.

Lady Frances stepped back, the same disgust filling Hugh's eyes making her blue eyes hard. 'To tell you I'm carrying your child.'

Chapter Ten

'Impossible, I tell you, it's impossible. We haven't seen each other for six months,' Hugh railed, storming the length of Adam's bedroom at Stonedown. Adam stood across from Hugh, listening to him rant. His friend already knew what had happened in the hallway at the ball beneath the mistletoe. Hugh was beginning to curse that damned plant.

After Elizabeth's none-too-subtle announcement, Clara had bolted from Hugh as fast as if he'd come down with the plague. Hugh had left soon after, not about to stand there and discuss so delicate a topic in such a public place. He'd returned to Stonedown, glad to see that Anne and Adam had possessed the clarity of mind to remove Clara from Holyfield and that Adam was still willing to speak with him. Hugh needed to explain the situation to the one man he could trust to listen without too much judgement. He would not lose this friendship because of a lying woman. 'She doesn't even look pregnant. Did you think she looked pregnant?'

'With the current style of gown it's difficult to tell. All ladies look as if they are a few months gone. I made the mistake of asking Anne if she was expecting once when she showed me a new gown. The look she gave me could have burned bread.'

'I tell you, Lady Frances is lying.' At a moment like this he wished he hadn't given up drinking, but he need a clear head to handle this situation. One fogged up with spirits was how he'd landed himself in this mess.

'I've heard no rumours of her taking up with another man and let's be honest, Hugh, she wasn't exactly discreet with you.'

'Well, she's either lying about the child or she's become far more discreet. Either way, she obviously came here to make a spectacle out of herself and trap me in marriage. It makes her claim even more dubious.'

'I agree that her method of approaching you was poorly planned and I have heard some rumours about her in London, especially in regards to debts.'

'There are richer and more gullible men she could trap without resorting to tricks or theatrics.' Suddenly the joke about Clara approaching sleeping lords and startling them into jumping to the altar didn't seem so amusing any more. Nor was the look of horror that had crossed her face before she'd left him. The trust and affection he'd spent hours working to gain over these last few days had been wrecked in a matter of moments and by the one person he'd never expected to see in the country. Lady Elizabeth Frances wasn't the country type.

'There are richer men,' Adam concurred, 'but, for whatever reason, she's chosen you.'

'You must believe me; the child isn't mine.' He couldn't even remember the last time he and Elizabeth had been intimate before they'd parted.

Adam picked up a silver comb off the dresser and tapped it against his palm. 'If the child is yours, will you do right by it?'

Hugh took a deep breath as the chains of duty tightened around him and for the second time Clara would be the one to suffer because of it. By morning the entire countryside would know about what had happened at Holyfield and in a few days all their friends would learn of it by letter. He could practically hear the people in the adjoining rooms scribbling on the parchment in delight about this scandalous new tale. It was everything he hadn't wanted, every complication he'd sought to avoid when it came to Clara. When he'd decided to pursue her a second time it'd been with the intention of acting honourably and safeguarding her heart and her trust in him. In one quick moment, everything he'd achieved with her had been destroyed. Heaven knew what Hugh would face when he saw Elizabeth again for she was sure to press her suit as pub-

licly here at Stonedown as she'd done at Holyfield.
With all the people eavesdropping on them at Holyfield, there hadn't been time to speak privately to
Elizabeth. Hopefully she'd returned to Stonedown
as quickly as Clara for Hugh needed to resolve this
with her as soon, and as discreetly, as possible. Until
then, too much hung in the balance. 'I must find a
way to make her confess the truth.'

'And if what she's saying is the truth?'

'I tell you it isn't.' Hugh brought his fist down
hard on the top of the mantel, making the porcelain
figures decorating it rattle. 'And I won't lose Clara
again because of some lying woman.'

'After Lady Frances's display tonight, I don't
think Clara would have you even if Lady Frances
stood in the middle of Rotten Row and declared some
other man the father.'

Hugh dug his fists into his hips and stared at a
scuff on the floor, the truth in Adam's words as difficult to hear as what Elizabeth had said. He'd seen
Clara's cheeks flush with embarrassment and horror after Elizabeth's announcement. Then he'd heard
the gasp of shock from Lady Fulton and Lord Westbook. Hugh, without meaning to, had humiliated her
in front of the worst two people possible. No, she
wasn't likely to speak to him again. 'It's never been
my intention to hurt her, but always things appear
so far beyond my control.'

Before, there'd been the threat of an engagement
to Lady Hermione to temper his excitement with

Clara, but this impediment had come at him out of nowhere. Hugh rested his elbow on the mantel and pressed his fingers against his forehead. Like the last challenge to Everburgh, no matter how hard he worked to free himself from debt and lawsuits and marriages of convenience, they sought him out like a hound does a fox and this time they were succeeding in bringing him down. 'I can only ask a woman to forgive me so many times before she runs out of patience and understanding.'

'Her brother, too. I'm afraid I must ask you not to come to Winsome in the New Year.'

Hugh lowered his hand and flexed his fingers before bringing them to rest on the cool marble. 'I understand and I'm sorry, Adam.'

He truly was for the pain he'd caused his friend and Clara, and for all the mistakes he'd made that had led them to this moment. During the meagreness of his childhood, his visits to Winsome had always been a chance to forget the hardships and deprivation at home, to enjoy being a boy without worrying about food or bills or the darkness of the manor. He'd hoped to find there with his oldest friend that same comfort again and yet by his own mistakes he'd ruined his ability to enjoy that kind of peace ever again. It tore at him as much as having lost Clara for a second time.

'I'm not the one you should apologise to,' Adam suggested.

'I will speak with her.' He didn't know when or

how, for she wasn't likely to see him again, much less allow him to say the words, none of which would make this awful situation any better or repair the damage Elizabeth's scene had caused to Clara's opinion of Hugh and to his future. Once more, he'd been on the verge of finding love with Clara and it was being torn away from him. It made him doubt ever having left London, swearing off drink and devoting himself anew to duty. The desire to ring for a footman and demand a bottle of brandy or wine made his palms itch, but he held back, unable to go back on his promise to himself. He'd vowed to see all his troubles through and make a better life for himself and it was a vow he would damn well keep, one way or another. He wouldn't lose his head and falter, but remain strong and dignified as expected of a marquess. He would not be like his grandfather.

'How could he do such a thing?' Clara stormed back and forth across Anne's bedroom at Stonedown Manor, going over for the hundredth time what had happened. She'd found Anne moments after leaving the hallway, Lady Frances's announcement ringing in her ears as if she'd stood too close to a church bell during matins. Worse than that had been the glee decorating Lady Fulton's face and the realisation that Clara was no different than she'd been six years ago, and now everyone knew it. It made fresh tears spring to her eyes. 'How could I have been foolish enough to fall for his tricks a second time?'

'I saw him with you. I don't think they were tricks, Clara, not this time or the last.'

'Then why am I here crying with you and not at Holyfield dancing with Hugh? I can't believe this is happening again.' She wiped her cheeks with the back of her hands, the pain and humiliation cutting so deep she could barely breathe. All her hopes and dreams for this week, and her desires to prove to everyone that she'd changed, were lying in ruins at Holyfield.

'Perhaps Lady Tillman will rescind Lord Delamare and Lady Frances's invitation and the two of them will leave and take this awful situation away with them,' Anne offered with more hope than Clara possessed.

'Lady Tillman isn't likely to send anyone off in this weather. You saw how much harder the snow was coming down on our way home. By tomorrow morning the roads will be difficult to pass.' Clara wished the snow had come a few days sooner and stopped Lady Frances from arriving at all. However, all it would have done was postpone the inevitable, perhaps after Clara and Hugh had given more to each other than a kiss beneath the mistletoe. 'The snow means I won't be able to leave either.'

How she would escape from this house party with what remained of her dignity she didn't know. Half the countryside had probably heard the tale by now thanks to Lord Westbook and Lady Fulton, who'd sprinted away after Lady Frances's announcement as if to inform the entire manor that the house was on fire. Clara walked to the mantel and stared at her reflection in the gilded mirror hanging over it. She still wore her ball gown and jewels, but, for all the diamonds, fine silk, and title, she was nothing more than a woman to be pitied because she had poor judgement when it came to matters of the heart. How Lord Westbook and Lady Fulton must be laughing at her now.

'Lady Tillman will be polite enough not to draw attention to it, but it shall be up to the three of you to resolve the matter as discreetly as possible.'

'All opportunity for discretion ended the moment Lady Frances opened her mouth.' Clara rubbed at the tightness in the back of her neck. It was bad enough she must face Lord Westbook and risk an 'I told you so' from him, but to have to face the rest of the guests after tonight's farce made her sick to her stomach. 'Besides, there's nothing to resolve. She has the prior claim on him and she's welcome to it. He's nothing to me any more and I want nothing more to do with him.'

'Except you're his partner and precedence demands that you sit beside him.'

'Curse precedence, his new fiancée can sit beside him. I'll sit with Lord Wortley.' Clara plunked down hard on the ottoman in front of the fire, the warmth of the flames heating her back, but doing little to drive away the iciness surrounding her heart. She'd loved Hugh once and in their time together he'd rekindled it. For a moment beneath the mistletoe all the possibilities for a bright future that he'd promised her in the last two days had almost come true. Except it wasn't true, but a nasty, awful lie, and this time she couldn't even mourn her loss in private, but must do it in front of everyone here. Curse Hugh and curse her for being so gullible. 'I wish we could go home and leave them to each other. I wish I'd stayed at Winsome.'

The pain of her loneliness was easier to bear than this.

Anne came and knelt before her and took Clara's hands in hers. 'I'm so sorry, Clara, for everything that's happened. This is never how I imagined or wanted it to end.'

'It's not your fault.'

Anne bit one lip and cringed a touch away from Clara. 'I'm afraid it is.'

Clara sat up a straighter. 'What do you mean?'

'I knew he'd be here and I didn't tell you, and then I arranged with Lord Tillman for your name and his to be drawn out of the hat at the pairing.'

Clara stared at Anne, unable to believe what she was saying. She jerked her hands out of her sister-in-law's and jumped to her feet. 'You did what?'

'You know how clever Lord Tillman is with palming cards?'

'Every child here knows that.' He wasn't shy with his tricks.

'Well, I spoke with Lady Tillman about you and

Hugh and how much I think the two of you would suit one another. She, being quite the romantic, spoke to Lord Tillman and he palmed your name and Hugh's during the drawing to make sure that you would be together.'

'I can't believe you'd do such a thing.'

'I didn't think it would end like this. None of us did.'

'None of us who? Is everyone in on the collusion?'

'Just Adam and I, and Lord and Lady Tillman.'

'Adam, too?' Clara pressed her palms against her forehead, wanting to scream in frustration. This time everyone, including her own blood relation, had been plotting to throw her and Hugh together and she hadn't been smart enough to sniff out their plans. 'Why do you two always take his side against me?'

'We don't take his side, but because we're not involved, we can see things more clearly than either of you. He cares for you, very deeply, and if Lady Frances hadn't burst in to Holyfield tonight, he would still be there with you.'

'Of course he would be,' Clara sneered, crossing her arms over her chest as she faced Anne, unmoved by her argument in favour of Hugh. Anne might give Hugh the benefit of the doubt, but Clara wouldn't, not any longer. She hadn't been able to see things as they really were before, but she could tonight and it disgusted her. 'Hugh knew I would be here, didn't he? And he knew that I had more money now than even before and I'm free to marry again.'

'What are you suggesting?'

'Exactly what you think I'm suggesting. Everburgh is in trouble again with a potentially long and expensive court battle facing Hugh and a purse incapable of supporting it. I suppose I appeared quite attractive to him, didn't I?'

'You can't believe that he would be so dishonest.'

'After tonight I do. He said Lady Frances wouldn't marry him because he wasn't wealthy enough for her, but I think it was the other way around. She wasn't rich enough for him and he needs another wealthy wife if he wants to save his estate. I wonder if I shouldn't be thanking Lady Frances for exposing him before it was too late.' Clara shuddered. After all the years of avoiding fortune hunters and less reputable men, to think she'd almost fallen prey to one at a time when she should have been older and wiser disheartened her. In her grief and her desire for happiness, she'd been too blinded by the prospect of finding love to see the truth and it had almost trapped her in a marriage with a man who didn't truly care for her. After having known the joys of love it was awful to think she might have suffered for who knew how many years in a marriage devoid of anything but greed, all because she'd been too ready to believe in Hugh and all his lying words. If she could not sniff out the intention of a man like Hugh, she didn't know how she would guard herself against the many other men who would pursue her for no other reason than her wealth if she ever decided to go to London.

She wandered to the window and watched flurries of snowflakes stick to the panes and collect in the corners. Everything she'd hoped to accomplish this Christmas was slipping away and she wondered if she would ever find joy in this season again. Even the next few days would be a trial, for the trick wouldn't so much be facing the other guests as avoiding Hugh.

A knock on the door made both Anne and Clara turn. Adam entered, as shame-faced as Anne had been when she'd confessed to helping throw Hugh and Clara together. Clara crossed the room, about to confront her brother and berate him for his hand in this mess when Hugh stepped in behind Adam.

'What the devil is he doing here?' Clara demanded, ignoring the sharp intake of breath from both Adam and Anne for her language. They would hear a great many more curses if that man was allowed to remain in her room much longer. They might even find themselves paying for the replacement of a vase or a few candlesticks.

'Hugh would like to speak with you,' Adam explained, more apologetic than demanding.

Clara stared at Hugh with a look to drop a man. He didn't flinch, but met her gaze, as apologetic as Adam, yet unwilling to shirk or shrink under her hard stare. Oh, but the man was infuriating. Even when he was wrong beyond measure he didn't have the decency to behave like it. 'I have nothing to say to him.'

'Then Adam and I will leave you alone.' Anne

rushed to Adam, took him by the arm and pulled him from the room.

'No, wait,' Clara called, but it was too late. They were gone and the door shut behind them, leaving Clara to face Hugh alone. She would murder them when they were back at Winsome for continuing to be so troubling. She'd do it here, but she didn't wish their dead bodies to cause any more of a scandal than she was already embroiled in. She fixed on Hugh with an anger to make the fire burn brighter. 'What do you want?'

'To apologise and to explain myself.'

'You needn't explain for I've already heard enough tonight and so has the rest of the house by now, I'm sure.' He moved to protest, but she held up a silencing hand. 'You always have a convenient excuse for all your poor behaviour, don't you, and you expect me to believe it?'

'I never lied to you Clara, and I'm not lying now when I tell you the child isn't mine.'

'Stop. Stop with the lies and deceits and the pretences to caring about me.'

'I do care about you. I love you. I always have, ever since those days at Winsome when you used to sit across from me at dinner, unafraid to laugh at my stupid jokes or join in them with me. All those times you never looked down on me because I had a grand title and not one farthing to make it worth anything. Even back then when I was with you I could believe that there was a better future waiting for me, for us.

You were beautiful in your simple dresses with nothing but flowers or ribbons to adorn your hair and you've only become more stunning since. I was a fool to give you up six years ago, but I was bound by duty to choose another. I thought in coming here that I could have a second chance at life, to put behind me for ever the mistakes I'd made in London and become again the respected man who'd first courted you and who'd held the esteem of many good people. And then I saw you again and I wanted more than your esteem or redemption, I wanted you and your heart. You believed in me when few others did and with you I could be myself. You have not lost me. I will find a way out of this predicament and back to you and we will be together. I promise it.'

His unexpected pronouncement almost jolted Clara out of her anger. She lowered her hand to her sides, unable to do anything but stare at him in disbelief. He loved her, but that she should hear it now when all possibility of their happiness together was over infuriated her. She raised an accusing finger, not caring that it trembled with her rage and hurt. 'How dare you speak to me of love. You don't love me, you never have. I've never been anything to you except second best, a spare horse to keep in the running in case the one you're betting on to save Everburgh and your precious legacy falls and stumbles. I won't be taken advantage of like that ever again, do you hear me?'

'I do and you have every right to believe that of

me, but I swear to you by everything I have, my title
and my lands, that it isn't true. I love you.'

'No, don't say any more.' Clara turned away from
him, not wanting to hear these words while everything was crumbling, especially the façade he'd built
in front of him these last few days to shield the true
man beneath.

'If you will believe in me and stand beside me,
I will find a way to prove that the child is not mine
and we can be together.'

'No, I won't. I gave you a second chance, Hugh,
one I never should have extended and you ruined it.
You broke my heart tonight the same way you did
six years ago and I'm done with you. Go back to
Lady Frances and your child. They need you more
than I do.'

Hugh stared at Clara, her cheeks burning not with
the humble embarrassment of a compliment, but with
the fury of a woman who deserved to be angry. She
was right. She had given him a second chance and
he'd ruined it, not by what he'd done when they were
together, but because of the mistakes he'd made before. It was clear to him that no matter what he did,
no matter where he went or who he befriended, he
would never shake off the years in London he'd spent
frittering away his good name and reputation. With
it had gone every hope of he and Clara ever being
together. Of all the losses facing him this was the
hardest to bear. He could meet every trouble and

challenge that life lobbed at him, even the loss of Everburgh if she was by his side to support and help him, but she never would be and he had no one to blame but himself.

Hugh bowed to Clara, unable to tear his eyes away from her as he prepared to leave. 'I wish you all the love and happiness that you deserve. I hope you find it with a man who is truly worthy of you.'

His head held high against the crushing disappointment weighing down his heart, he strode out of the room, closing the door behind him and on every dream he'd ever had about Clara.

Outside the room, Adam and Anne stood together across the hallway, watching him, the pity on their faces as searing as the hate that had decorated Clara's. Without a word, he strode down the hall to his room, carrying with him what was left of his dignity. When he reached the stairs he met Sir Nathaniel coming up from below. Melting flakes of snow dusted the shoulders of his blue coat and the top of his dark shoes were wet from the weather. He stopped at the sight of Hugh, his lips drawing down in a disappointment that had become an all-too-familiar sight tonight.

'Bad show of things at Holyfield, Lady Frances making a scene like that,' Sir Nathaniel mumbled.

'Bad indeed.' The story was working its way through the guests faster than Hugh had anticipated if Sir Nathaniel had already heard it.

'That was no way to handle things, but of course,

a gentleman should know better than to find himself in such a situation.' Hugh wanted to protest that the child wasn't his and that he was being trapped, but he wasn't a gentleman to smear a lady's reputation, even if the lady deserved a thorough smearing. 'You will understand if I rescind my recommendation to the solicitors. I can't have my reputation or theirs entangled in such a sordid story.'

Hugh almost doubled over as if he'd been struck in the gut, but he forced himself to stand tall and to show this man no ill will for he was only doing what he thought best, like Adam, and heaven knew how many others. 'I understand and I thank you for your willingness to extend it. I wish I had been worthy of your continued support.'

With a terse nod, Sir Nathaniel made for his room, leaving Hugh alone in the darkness. If he could ride out for Everburgh tonight he would, but with Lady Frances's accusation still hanging in the air, he had to remain. If he left, everyone would think he was abandoning his duty before the matter had been settled and it would tarnish him more than her outrageous proclamation already had. He almost wished he had been a gambler—a monetary debt would be easier to deal with and would confer on him a touch more honour than this debt of the flesh.

With heavy steps, Hugh went to his room, eager to be alone where he could think in peace and concoct some way to get at the truth. There had to be a solution to all of this, there must be, just as there had been one for every trouble that had ever faced Everburgh. He only needed to find it and reveal it to everyone to reclaim his innocence, even if it was Clara he wished to prove it to more than society.

He pushed open the door to his room and stopped cold.

'Elizabeth, what are you doing in here?' He swung the door shut behind him. He wasn't ready to see her again. He needed time to collect his thoughts and her being here caught him on the back foot, a position he did not wish to be in for so important a matter.

'We must speak and now is the best time to do it.'

More than likely she'd crept in here hoping to make a grand exit when they were through and give even more credence to her claims about the child. He wouldn't be surprised if there was a footman or maid she'd paid to have them enter at the right moment and catch them. He would ask her to leave if he didn't think it would create even more of a scene, but she was right, they did need to speak.

'Whose child is it, Elizabeth?' Hugh demanded, turning to the offence, hoping to catch her off guard as she must have hoped to catch him.

'How can you say such a thing?' Elizabeth blanched, having the gall to appear insulted. 'You know it's yours.'

'Do I? You weren't willing to accept me when I asked you before. Suddenly, marriage to me looks very good. It makes me think I'm not so much the father as a convenient gentleman to save you from your mistake.' He curled his lip in disgust at how fast she'd changed her mind about marrying him when she was carrying some other man's bastard, but he couldn't prove it wasn't his. There wasn't a midwife in England who could tell him how far gone she really was or call the lady a liar when, during her travails, she named him as the father. Perhaps one of her maids could give evidence that there had been one or two courses or men since the last time Elizabeth and Hugh had been together. It was a stupid idea. He barely possessed the means to pay for solicitors to defend Everburgh, much less to engage the type of man who could slip a lady's maid a few pounds in exchange for what would be little more than nefarious gossip. He had done a great many things to help himself and the lineage, but he wasn't ready to stoop to such disgustingly low methods to free himself from this present entanglement.

'You're just as guilty as I am for what happened between us, don't think I will take all the blame for it, nor will I be humiliated in society and labelled a harlot for a situation that you helped create.'

Outside, the wind from the storm banged against the window in sharp whistles and whooshes. Hugh rolled his shoulders, the truth in her words as stinging as the cold night.

Her hard eyes softened and she twisted the ribbon on her pelisse between her fingers. 'I realise this is not the most ideal situation for either of us and perhaps I could have handled things a bit differently tonight, but when I saw you with Lady Kingston and I realised that I might be left to face the censure of society alone, and to have my child labelled a bastard, I lost my head.'

'And now you're all but forcing my hand, and you expect me to be glad of it?'

'You and I got along very well together for a time, we could again and it could be a splendid match for both of us.' She slid up to him and touched his arm, the rich perfume he'd once revelled in during the dark hours of night in London sickening today. She was a stunning woman, with her light hair and generous breasts, but in the six months since they'd last been together, whatever allure she held for him had faded. Their care for one another had been a shallow one more of convenience than of any deeper emotion and their time apart had killed it.

'A splendid match for you is what you mean. You'll gain a title much higher than the one you currently hold and your child, whosoever it is, will get a legacy and inheritance far above anything that he would enjoy at present.'

She snatched her hand off his arm, her smile twisting to a grimace. 'Yes, I would gain a better title, but one beset by nothing but problems. I know about the lawsuit and how if you're ruled against you'll lose everything. Do you really think I'd pursue you if the child wasn't yours simply to take on more troubles than I already have, to see myself sitting so high all the while knowing I have not a farthing to my name no matter how grand it might be? Do you really think that's something worth scheming for?'

Hugh peered down at her in disgust, his desire to do what was right and honourable tempered by her nasty words. If he made her a marchioness, she wouldn't stand by him through all his challenges, but sneer at and ridicule him for his failures while dismissing his successes as nothing more than something he should have already had. Unlike Clara, she would not help him to see that there was hope even in the darkest of times, nor would she be a pillar of strength for him to rely on when the strain of carrying on seemed like too much. She would be the shrew she was now and some day, if he couldn't give her what she believed was due a marchioness, she would come to hate him as much as Clara did. 'Such loving and comforting words from a woman so desperate to be my wife.'

She drew back, opening her mouth to offer some retort before seeming to think better of speaking and closing it again. She flashed him a simpering smile like the one that had first caught his notice in London. It no longer enticed him like it used to.

'I'm sorry, I don't mean to be so difficult or nasty, but a woman in my situation and condition is apt to not be herself.' She ran her hand over her stomach, but he could not tell through the thickness of her skirt whether there really was a child beneath it. Then she took hold of his arm again, leaning in to him and looking up at him with false tenderness.

'I'm sure that once this little issue with Everburgh is over, you will find a way to regain everything you need to be a proper marquess. You are so clever in that regard.'

Her false flattery didn't move him. 'I'm not certain that the lawsuit will be decided in my favour. Thanks to your outburst last night, I lost the support of a man who could help me. Who knows how many others will follow his lead?'

'Then we will do all we can as man and wife to regain their good opinion both here and in London. I know a number of men who can lend us the money we need to fight the lawsuit and who could help us entertain many influential men who can help us.'

'We aren't even married and already you want me to go into debt?'

'I want you to succeed.' She squeezed his arm to try to drive home the point and Hugh jerked it away from her.

'I need time to consider the matter.'

'There's nothing to consider. You can't leave me in this condition to face everyone's scrutiny alone, nor will I have you abandon me for that woman you were with tonight.'

'She, like many of the other allies I had in the lawsuit, is gone.'

'Good. I'm glad I could show her what kind of man you really are before she found herself in the same unenviable position as me.'

Hugh marvelled at the woman standing in front

of him, the one he'd never seen before who was both vindictive and nasty, but in some ways she was right. She was naming him as the father of her child and he was hesitating in his duty to do right by her, leaving her to wonder what the future held for her and the baby. It, and her condition, could allow Hugh to excuse some of what she'd said, but her hard words, more than his doubts about the child, still made him hesitate in asking her to marry him. She'd shown him what a future with her would be like and it made him recoil. This wasn't what he'd imagined for himself when he'd left drinking and London behind and yet it had followed him, like every other mistake he'd made in town.

Hugh raked his fingers through his hair, unable to believe he was faced again with the decision of whether or not to marry a woman he did not love. For all the time he and Elizabeth had spent together, the word had never passed between them because both of them had recognised that it hadn't existed. It had been there with Clara. He hadn't intended to tell her tonight with her shooting daggers at him, but he hadn't been able to hold back. He'd wanted Clara to hear the truth even if she didn't believe it, to comfort her with the peace of knowing that he had genuinely cared for her even if his sins had risen up to consume him. It was a peace he hadn't been able to offer her last time and one she'd rejected tonight and all because of a lying woman.

Now he must do his duty as a gentleman and do

what was both right and expected of him. Perhaps, as with Hermione, he and Elizabeth would come to really care for each other. She might mature into a woman who could stand beside him, if not out of concern for him, but out of necessity for herself, for she'd already proven she was willing to work hard in that regard. When his troubles became hers perhaps she would find the strength of will to support him as he needed and to leave this waspish woman before him behind. It was the best he could hope for.

He took Elizabeth's hand and raised it to his chest. She didn't clutch him as Clara had or eye him with the same anticipation and hope. Instead, there was a covetousness in her eyes that made him want to wince and let go, but he held on even while the words were rising up in his throat to choke him. He wanted the love he'd experienced with Clara, the one he'd seen between his parents, the sure thing that would support and carry him through these trying times, not the promise of what might be with another woman, a promise that he doubted would ever be realised. Once again, the desires of his heart no longer mattered. The only thing that mattered was what was best for Everburgh and the Delamare line although he was not certain the child was his. In offering for her, he was taking the chance that another man's child would become the heir to Everburgh and that that man's blood and not Hugh's would benefit from every sacrifice and accomplishment he and his parents had ever made. He was glad his mother was not here to see it, for it did make him as bad as his grandfather.

No, I am nothing like that man.

They'd entered into their relationship freely and parted on amiable terms. If he left her like this, she would suffer far more than he would for their indiscretion. He might not wish to marry her, but he wasn't cruel enough to destroy her completely. He would do his duty and the honourable thing.

'Elizabeth, will you marry me?'

A wide smile of triumph spread across Elizabeth's face and Hugh wished he could take back the words, but he didn't. He might not have Sir Nathaniel or Clara's regard, but he had his honour and he would damn well hang on to both even while he was losing everything else.

Chapter Eleven

Clara left her bedroom and walked down the Stonedown Manor hallway with heavy feet. She'd remained in her room for as long as possible this morning, lingering not so much over her dressing, but the dark circles beneath her eyes from a night spent crying. If she could've avoided coming down altogether she would have, but it wasn't possible. To linger in her room would be to admit defeat and she wasn't about to lower herself any further in the eyes of all the guests more than Hugh's actions had already done. She'd left her jewels behind in her room and decided against wearing one of her new dresses in favour of an older one. There was no point putting on airs now that everything she'd come here to accomplish had been shattered.

At the turn to the stairs, she slowed her steps. Lord Westbook and Lady Fulton walked together a number of paces before her, their backs to her, heads bowed together, their voices low, but not low enough for Clara to miss what they said. They were so involved in their conversation that they didn't notice Clara descending behind them.

'I pity the girl,' Lord Westbook tutted. 'Despite her lineage and wealth this is the second time she's failed to catch a poor marquess.'

'What do you expect from a plain mouse? She might dress herself up in London fashion and Kingston jewels, but she is no better than that country girl who didn't even have the sense to employ a London modiste all those years ago. She might be well off, but she can't compare to a woman of sophistication like Lady Frances and men search for such qualities in a wife.'

At the bottom of the stairs, they made for the back of the house instead of the dining room and their nasty words faded away.

Clara wanted to climb the stairs and return to her room, to lock the door and crawl beneath the covers and stay there until Boxing Day, but instead she forced herself to continue towards the dining room. She had no choice but to put on a good show and make the best of things, to try to reclaim what remained of her dignity. Except she didn't feel dignified, but lonely and hurt and eager for this day and this house party to be over.

With reluctant steps she approached the dining room and paused just outside it to listen to the mix of voices as the other guests chatted with excitement about the ball last night and no doubt about what happened between Clara, Lady Frances and Hugh. Unable to linger here all day and unwilling to have anyone catch her skulking in the hallway, she took a deep breath, composing herself in a manner that would have made her parents proud, and strode inside.

Her suspicion about being the topic of every conversation was confirmed when she appeared and all the voices settled to awkward looks and stares punctuated by an occasional whisper. She didn't chide anyone for speaking about her, but made her way to the sideboard to try to eat breakfast even if she had no appetite for the food. She had to carry on as if everything was not falling apart, just as she'd been forced to do on that Christmas six years ago. Christmas Eve and the annual Christmas Eve ball at Stonedown Manor would be tomorrow night. The next morning would be Christmas and then the morning after that she could safely leave without drawing any more attention to herself than events had already done. She only had to get through the next two days and then she could go home and nurse her broken heart in private and decide what to do next. With the silence behind her growing to fill the entire room, she sensed it would be a very long two days.

'Lady Kingston, it's a pleasure to see you.' Lord Stanhope stepped up beside her, standing much closer than she would have preferred, but having the decency to keep his voice low while the conversation behind them slowly resumed. 'I admire your fortitude in coming down this morning. There are many London ladies who, after having endured what you did last night, would've taken to their beds. I'm glad to see you're made of sterner stuff.'

'Thank you, Lord Stanhope, for your faith in me.' At least there was someone here who appreciated her better qualities far more than Hugh ever really had. Strange it should be Lord Stanhope.

'You are most welcome, Lady Kingston, for I hate to see someone as nice as you subjected to such an awful thing.' When she finished dropping a small spoonful of eggs on to her plate, he took it from her hands and carried it along with his to the table. 'Please let me know if I may be of some assistance to you for the remainder of our time here. Your new activity partner, perhaps, for I doubt very much that Lord Delamare will have the wherewithal to participate.'

'No, I suppose he will have other matters to attend to.'

Such as arranging for the announcement of his engagement in the London newspapers.

Clara closed her hands into fists at her sides, making her nails bite into her palms before she forced them to relax.

'And if he is so bold to try to come and ruin your good time, I will be sure to call him out and teach him a lesson.'

Lord Stanhope's willingness to serve as her champion brought a small smile to Clara's face. As he set her plate down on the table in front of her before taking his own seat a little of the gloom that had covered her this morning began to lift. Hugh was not the only man in the world and if Clara had the strength to get through this, then in the spring she might have the temerity to endure London, to risk again the chance that she might find love or disappointment. With Lord Stanhope beside her, she felt a little better, but not nearly as hopeful as when Hugh had been with her.

After breakfast, Lord Stanhope's prediction that Hugh would not turn up for the games or insist on remaining Clara's partner was proven correct. Everyone gathered in the sitting room, waiting for the game of charades to begin and Lady Frances and Hugh were nowhere to be seen. In many ways Clara was glad, for it spared her the awkwardness of facing the two of them together since last night in front of all the guests. However, his absence also pointed out once again that she'd been thrown over in favour of a previous lover. It left Clara to sit on the sofa where she'd once enjoyed his attention and bear the many sympathetic looks being tossed her way. Except not all the looks were sympathetic. Lady Fulton stood with Lord Westbook by the window whispering behind her fan. The craven delight brightening her eyes every time her gaze landed on Clara made Clara want to walk over and knock the silken slats away from her and call her out. However, Clara was not a man to defend her honour in such a way, instead all she could do was keep her back ramrod straight, determined not to crumble or to allow any of the nasty woman's whispering to undermine what remained of her confidence. She must pretend all was well and endure everything alone once again.

To her relief, Lord Stanhope came to stand over her. He wore a fine fawn-coloured coat that contrasted well with his dark waistcoat and added to his debonair air. 'Might I assume by your former partner's absence that I will have the privilege of stepping into his place?'

'I think you may make that assumption, Lord Stanhope, and I appreciate very much your willingness to make such a sacrifice on my part.'

He flipped up the tail of his coat and sat down beside her, stretching out his legs and the highly polished boots covering them up to his knees. 'I assure you it's no sacrifice. Pretending to be a swan or a rose or whatever other object Lord Tillman has selected for us to draw for this game of charades will be much more pleasant with you here to cheer me on.'

'I hope I'm enthusiastic enough to secure your victory.' Clara wondered where she would find the resolve to care enough about this game. It was already taking so much effort to appear before everyone as though her heart was not breaking.

'With you behind me, I'm sure I cannot fail in this endeavour.' Lord Stanhope took her hand and raised it to his lips. He glanced up at her from beneath his eyelashes, the look beguiling and for some reason, at the same time, uncomfortable.

'What have I done to be so worthy of your belief in me?' She withdrew her hand as politely as possible. Although everything he said should turn her head, his touch and his words did not affect her in the same way that Hugh's had. Perhaps it was simply her disappointment in her misplaced faith in Hugh and what it had cost her that kept her from enjoying Lord Stanhope's attention, or maybe it was something else. With her emotions and thoughts in such disarray it was difficult to tell. She was growing weary of all this confusion about men. It made her wish once again that she'd never left Winsome.

'Your mere beauty and charm make you worthy.' He laid his hand on his heart, the gesture drawing her attention to his cravat pin in the shape of a family crest.

'That is a unique cravat pin. Did you have it made in London?' she asked, eager to turn his attention away from his over-exuberant fawning to something more mundane.

'No, it was left to me by my father. One of the men on our estate made it for him. Usually I wouldn't bother with the simple work of country craftsmen, but the man who did this one was quite good.'

'You don't seek to better those who reside on your land?'

'They're hardly worth the effort when it comes to trying to better them. They resist all opportunities to do so, nor can they possibly hope to compete with London craftsmen.'

'But surely your concern for their welfare is one of your top priorities?'

'They must look to their own welfare and work as their station in life dictates. Whether they succeed or not is up to them,' he dismissed, almost regarding her as if what she'd said was to point out that he had two heads instead of one.

Clara laced her fingers in her lap and shifted away from him a touch, his attitude towards those in his care so much different from Hugh's.

He isn't a man I should be holding up as an example.

In the end, Hugh had proved himself to be far less noble than she'd once believed. Perhaps Lord Stanhope was the better man, although at this moment his dismissive words put him in close competition with Hugh. 'I think it very necessary for a landowner to be concerned with the welfare of those on his estate, for if they don't prosper then neither will he. It's something my father always instilled in me.'

As if seeming to realise his mistake in being so flippant about those employed by his estate, Lord Stanhope tilted his head in contrition. 'Yes, of course you're right, I shouldn't sound so callous about their welfare, but I've had great difficulty with them. Many are lazy and refuse to do the work necessary to make sure the estate prospers. They don't care if the harvest is good or not and it's caused me no end of difficulties.'

Clara wondered if their lack of concern was because their landowner didn't care about them, but there was no time to pursue the matter. Lord and Lady Tillman entered the room with the hat full of slips of paper with objects to be used for charades. It was time for yet another game to begin.

A new energy surged through the room, but it didn't touch Clara. She was tired of games, especially ones where she had to guess again and again at what something really was. She forced herself to sit through this one, laughing and clapping as required even while her heart wasn't in it. She wished she could be anywhere but in this room, but especially back at Winsome.

At last the game ended and Clara applauded Mrs Alton and her partner Sir Nathaniel along with everybody else.

'Would you care to join me in a walk to the orangery?' Lord Stanhope offered as she rose with the others to take her leave.

'No, I think I'll return to my room to rest and read. I want to finish the story before the end of our trip here.'

'I hope you enjoy your book and your time in bed,' Lord Stanhope said through a sly smile.

Any other time Clara would've laughed at his attempt at innuendo, but all she could offer him was a wan smile and mumble her excuses, leaving before he or anyone else could think of some reason why she should remain.

Clara went upstairs to her room and sat down near the window with her book, trying to read, but the story held little interest for her. Where she'd craved quiet in the midst of the charades game, it overwhelmed her here and she found herself unable to sit still. Setting the book aside, she wandered from one part of the room to the other, unable to shake the nervous energy building inside her, the one that threatened to bring back all the thoughts about Hugh that had kept her up last night and made her want to burst into tears. Not content to spend another moment alone crying, she went downstairs in search of company. Except when she heard the laughter of the people in the rooms around her, the desire for solitude swept over her again. She wandered down the hall to the library and the illuminated manuscript. She wasn't sure what it was that drew her to this book, but she longed to enjoy the beauty of the words and the serenity of the figures painted on the vellum.

She was not two feet into the room when she regretted coming here. Hugh stood over the book, flipping slowly through the pages. He stopped reading at the sound of someone behind him and turned, the regret in his eyes as powerful as the one in her heart. Whatever it was that had happened last night, it was clear that he was genuinely sorry, but Clara hardened her heart against him. Once again he'd dallied with her when he had not been entirely free to do so and for the second time it was she who would be left without.

'I'm sorry to intrude. I'll leave you to your reading.' Claire began to back out of the room, but he raised his hand to stop her.

'No, please stay.'

'Why?' He wasn't likely to tell her that he'd proven that Lady Frances's child wasn't his and that there was some way for them to be together. It was ridiculous to even think he would. He'd never once fought to be with her, but always followed duty into the arms of another. If she weren't so upset she might even admire him for it, but she couldn't, not today.

'I wish to speak to you.' He stood with his hands behind his back and with all the formality and deference he used to show her parents whenever he would stay at Winsome Manor in between school terms. There was no trace of the swooning lord from last night, no twinkle of humour in his eyes and no hint of his charming smile. Instead, his expression was distant and apologetic, the way the doctor's had been when he'd informed her and Adam that their mother would not recover from her illness and soon follow her father to the grave. It was the same way he'd looked before he'd told her he was going to marry Lady Hermione.

'I think we said all we needed to say to one another last night. There's nothing further to discuss.' Just as before, no questions had been asked or accepted and no promises between them had been made. There was nothing holding them together, no obligations and no reason for her to stay here and endure any more of Hugh and his lies and disappointment. She'd been jilted before she'd even had a chance to accept him and during the Christmas season of all times.

'I want you to be the first to know that I've asked Lady Frances to marry me,' he stated before she could object or leave, his announcement dropping like a piece of stale plum pudding between them. From somewhere down the hall, Lord Westbook's and Lady Fulton's voices carried through the still. Clara couldn't understand what they said. All she could do was focus on Hugh and the disappointment filling her.

The strength she'd employed to face the other guest this morning began to crumble as whatever small hope she'd held that this would turn out all right, as he'd promised, was crushed beneath his announcement. 'Just like last time.'

'This isn't how I wanted things to end between us.'

'And yet it is.' Her words struggled to find their way out of her throat and through the tight air of the room.

'I would give up my title and Everburgh if I could take us back to the moment last night beneath the mistletoe and see it through, to make you my Marchioness instead of her.'

'But you can't.'

'No.' He shook his head. 'Once again duty compels me to wed someone else instead of where my heart is.'

'Stop, Hugh, please, I don't wish to hear it or to know that your love for me is never strong enough for you to fight for us to be together, that your duty to Everburgh or the Delamare line or anything else never includes me.'

'I can't treat her so shabbily, Clara, surely you must see that. I would be less of a man if I did and you know it. If the situation was reversed and it was you instead of Lady Frances carrying a child, you would want to know that I'd do right by you and not cast you aside.'

He moved closer to her, standing over her with the same conviction that she'd faced him with the first day of the house party. Back then she'd intended to dislike him for good and to do nothing more than endure his unfortunate presence. Instead she'd grown to see beyond her prejudices and the London rumours to a man she'd thought was honourable and worth a second chance. It would be easier to forget him if she could continue hating him, but he was right and she hadn't been entirely wrong about him. He was willing to do what was required of him even at the expense of his own desires and happiness. That it also kept being at her expense rankled. She didn't want to listen to his reasons or any other excuses, but wanted him to hurt as much as she did, to experience even a small amount of the pain and humiliation flooding her. 'Yes, I realise you must do the honourable thing. I only wish for once that it was me you were willing to uphold duty and honour to win instead of being cast aside because of it.'

'So do I.' He reached for her hand before remembering himself and pulling back. 'Seeing you that first night here was like experiencing all the hope and optimism we'd shared six years ago. It's a gift I will always treasure and call on to give me strength when things are dark.'

Clara swallowed hard, forcing back the tears stinging her eyes. He'd given her the same gift and then taken it away. 'I'm sure Lady Frances will offer you similar comfort and support.'

The stricken look on his face told her he didn't agree, but to his credit he did not disparage the woman who was to be his wife, the one who'd stolen him from Clara. For the first time since the debacle at Holyfield she pitied him. In doing his duty and being the honourable gentleman, he was entering into a union that might bring him more misery than joy. It was a fate she would not wish on any man or woman. If she was capable of freeing him from this bond she would, but his life was no longer her concern. He must make his own way now and so must she.

'I wish you all the happiness you deserve and I hope you can find the same contentment with Lady Frances that you offered me during our time here.' Unable to trust her voice or the tears she held back any longer, she turned and left the room, refusing to allow her back to bend or her shoulders to droop with any of the disappointment draping her like the greens did the banister in the entrance hall.

Hugh watched her leave. There was nothing he could do but let her go. In time she would find love again, he didn't doubt it, and he would have to relive once more the agony of reading about her betrothal in the paper and learning about her marriage from friends. What the future held for him he could not say. He would marry a woman he neither loved nor trusted and face a lawsuit in which he might lose everything. The most he could hope for was that the child he would come to love was his and that he could make its future better and its life much easier than his had ever been. This is what would carry him through the dark nights and lonely days facing him, the ones he'd once dreamed that with Clara beside him he could finally end.

Hugh left the library and made for his room, ready to instruct the man assigned to serve as his valet to pack Hugh's things. The snow had abated overnight and the moment the roads were passable, he would leave. It'd been awkward enough this morning inside Stonedown when he'd passed the other guests, enduring their sideways glances of disapproval and whispering. He had no desire to subject himself to any more of it. He'd come here specifically to rebuild his reputation and that goal had failed miserably. There was also no point in staying and causing more discomfort and trouble for either Clara or himself. Word of his engagement to Elizabeth would soon make the rounds, most likely because of her desire to spread the news, and it meant no one could accuse him of shirking his duty to the child. He also had no intention of going downstairs tonight for dinner and putting himself and Clara through the torture of sitting beside each other and pretending that the entire house wasn't whispering or watching them. It hadn't mattered during the last two days when their whispers had been little more than amused speculation about what might happen between them. Since everyone was currently aware of their unfortunate situation, his presence would serve no purpose but to further inflict insult where he'd already caused injury. He also had more difficult matters to consider and attend to. With Sir Nathaniel's help gone, Hugh needed to write letters to other men who had enough of their own skeletons in their closets to not look askance at Hugh's. He hoped they could help him expose the Scotsman for the fraud he was and grant Hugh a reprieve from this last threat facing Everburgh.

Hugh left the library and made his way down the hall towards the main staircase, running over in his mind who in London might help him when a voice interrupted his thoughts.

'A moment of your time, if I may, Lord Delamare?' Lord Westbook stepped out of one of the small sitting rooms, bringing Hugh to a halt.

'What could we possibly have to discuss?' He wanted to throttle the man for spreading the story of him and Lady Frances. If he hadn't been so free with his tongue, the matter might have remained private, but instead he'd made sure that it was fodder to delight the entire countryside.

'Your future and the future of the Delamare line. I couldn't help but overhear that you and Lady Frances are to be married.'

'Do you never tire of listening in doorways to matters that don't concern you?'

'I know you don't think well of me, Lord Delamare, and I don't blame you.' Lord Westbook stepped back into the sitting room and motioned for Hugh to join him. 'But I wish you to know that I sympathise with your situation more than you realise.'

Against his better judgement he followed the man, closing the door behind him so no one else might overhear their conversation. 'You had a solid hand in making the situation worse.'

Lord Westbook fingered his watch chain. 'I do not enjoy a generous income, Lord Delamare, a situation I am sure you can relate to.'

Hugh said nothing.

'I must make myself amiable to people, for if I do not live off the generosity of hosts at many houses during the year then I very often find myself with nowhere to live.'

Hugh unclenched his hands at his sides. For all his dislike of Lord Westbook, he understood the strangling constraints of poverty and the depths one had to sink to in order to survive. For Lord Westbook it was spreading tales that made him a much sought-after guest. For Hugh, it was marrying first for money and waiting for the love to come later.

'I see you do comprehend my predicament. I wish you to know that what I do is never personal, simply a necessary requirement for my welfare.'

'And what does this have to do with me?' Hugh could sympathise with Lord Westbook, but it didn't mean he had to condone his vicious tongue or his hurtful gossip.

'Lady Frances is not the wronged woman she seems.'

This made Hugh a great deal more interested in the man. 'What do you know about Lady Frances?'

'The one thing you need to free you from your present difficulty.'

Hugh stared at him. Was it possible that there was a way out of this? 'Tell me.'

'I will, but first we must come to an understanding.'

Hugh curled up his lip in disgust. 'I won't pay you if that's what you're after.'

'I'm not after money, but a tale. I will provide you with the proof you seek to extricate yourself from your present difficulty if you ensure that I'm privy to everything that happens. A story like this will ensure me a great many invitations and I am in need of them.'

'You want me to sell out a woman to save my own hide?' He should punch the man in his smug face for thinking Hugh so low a man.

'I want to stop Lady Frances from deceiving you and you from breaking Lady Kingston's heart.'

'I don't believe you're this noble.'

'I'm not, but I knew Lady Kingston's parents. They were good people and I was sorry to see them pass. The many times that I've been a guest here have allowed me to watch Lady Kingston overcome a great many sorrows to become a woman worthy of carrying the title Marchioness. Lady Frances is not. I should hate to see her usurp the title from a much more deserving woman.'

Hugh studied Lord Westbook, the sincerity in his small eyes one he'd never seen there before. For whatever else the man was, at present he was honest and his care for Clara real. Hugh must make a decision, but it wasn't a palatable one. Despite having inadvertently done it to Clara more than once, he didn't have it in him to knowingly make a woman the centre of gossip, but if Lord Westbook was right and could confirm Hugh's suspicions about Elizabeth's child, he could reveal her scheming to everyone and regain his reputation and the freedom to marry where his heart dictated. Everyone would see that he was the innocent party and he could do for the first time the one thing Clara wished he'd do— uphold duty and honour to win her instead of having it force him to cast her aside. 'Tell me what you know about Lady Frances and her child and then I'll decide if we have a deal.'

Chapter Twelve

'I thought dinner would never end,' Clara complained, sitting at the foot of Anne's bed. On the table beside Anne, who laid against the headboard, the small clock announced the eleven o'clock hour, the little notes of the chimes singing out in the room.

'I have to say that it was the strangest dinner I have ever endured here. The two most interesting people in the house party were missing and at the very moment when everyone wanted a good look at them.'

'At least they had me there to amuse them.' The last three hours had been as torturous as they'd been the first night when she'd sat beside Hugh. His chair had been empty along with two others at the table tonight. Hugh had sent his excuses to Lady Tillman for why he did not appear with her at the front of the line. Neither Lady Frances nor Lord Stanhope had been there either, both of them pleading headaches to remain above stairs.

'I wonder why Lord Stanhope didn't come down to dinner.' As insincere as she guessed his flattery of her was, she wouldn't have minded a little of it to lift her spirits. Instead, she'd gone without it, slurping her soup in silence like Lady Pariston.

'He probably had something or someone else to keep him in his bedroom,' Anne mused, arching one knowing eyebrow at Clara and making her suspicious.

'What do you mean?'

'Don't you think it's rather odd that Lady Frances and Lord Stanhope arrived on the same day and that they both had some obliging cousin who could recommend them to Lady Tillman?'

'Are you suggesting that Lady Frances really came here to see Lord Stanhope and not Hugh?' Clara didn't put much credence in this speculation, not wanting it to offer her a sliver of hope that Hugh somehow might be freed from his obligation. She didn't care if he was or not, he no longer mattered to her or so she tried to tell herself. After leaving him in the library, she'd done nothing but think about him, lamenting the peace of his presence. He'd been so quick to ease her heartache yesterday and the day before, and now he was the cause of it.

'Perhaps they are conspiring together, especially given that they're both suddenly suffering from same malady preventing them from enjoying the hospitality their cousin went to so much trouble to arrange for them?'

'I doubt that's what it is for I can well imagine why Lady Frances stayed in her room.' There were very few who approved of her way of going about declaring Hugh the father and they hadn't been shy in telling Clara so. It hadn't mitigated Clara's embarrassment, but it had helped to know that people were on her side, except this wasn't a battle because she and Hugh had already surrendered to being apart.

'What if Lady Frances isn't alone in her room? It would be easy enough to find out.' Anne looked up at the ceiling in a gesture Clara knew well. It was the same one she employed whenever she plotted a surprise party for Adam or some secret amusement for James and Lillie.

'You can't possibly be suggesting that we barge in on Lady Frances to see if she and Lord Stanhope are together.' There was no doubting that Anne had gone mad and Clara, too, for even sitting here and listening to this insane idea.

'It would be easy. We simply throw open the door and say we made a mistake in looking for Lady Pariston's room. If she is alone with a wet towel on her head, then we'll know I'm wrong, but if she is alone with more than a towel, think what this could mean.'

That Hugh was right when he said the child wasn't his. No, this was preposterous.

'We'll look like fools if we're wrong.' The whole situation had already left her humiliated enough. Hugh had never been willing to fight for her or risk public embarrassment on her behalf. There was no reason for her to do the same to try to clear his name, except that Anne's suggestion was tempting. No, it wasn't. 'It isn't our affair to meddle in.'

'It involves you as much as anyone else.' Anne rose and slipped on her shoes, indicating she was indeed very serious about this.

'Then it isn't right.'

'Neither is trapping a man into marriage. It's one thing for a widow to dally here and there discreetly and quite another for her to have a child out of wedlock. If Lady Frances is indeed with child, then she is in a very bad situation and will do anything she can to get out of it.'

'Then why doesn't she marry Lord Stanhope if they are involved, as you say.'

'Because he has even less money than Lord Delamare. I heard so from Lord Westbook after dinner when he came in with the men and he's as reliable a source as any. Besides, if I've learned anything from all his stories, it's that most unmarried ladies who find themselves in difficulties by one man who won't marry them won't hesitate to trap another into doing it, especially one whose estate, with a little more effort and time, is likely to recover and become prosperous again. The prospect of being a marchioness, even a poor one, is a great deal more attractive than a scorned woman.'

It all made sense and yet it still sounded so unbelievable, as did Anne's continued faith in Hugh which continued to defy expectation. 'So once again you're taking Hugh's side, believing him despite all evidence to the contrary.'

'Yes, and you should, too.'

'Not after what he's done to me.'

'He did nothing to you, Clara, at least not purposely. His relationship with her was well before you and he truly believed it was over and done until she arrived with her outrageous claim.'

'Why do you and Adam always believe the best of him? Why can you not stand with me for once instead of him?'

'I am standing with you, that's why I'm suggesting this. I saw you at the Holyfield ball with him and at dinner the second night and even during the scavenger hunt and a hundred other times when you were laughing at his jokes and smiling in a way I haven't seen in a very long time. He makes you happy, Clara, and brings back the joy in your eyes. I don't want you to lose that or throw it away because of some London whore making an outrageous claim.'

Clara started. If Anne was using such salty language, then she must really believe what she was telling Clara, but still Clara didn't step off the bed and put on her shoes. She'd already placed so much faith in Hugh and look what it had got her, nothing but grief. If she raised her hopes again and followed Anne in this ridiculous notion, it might bring her more trouble. No, it was better to sit here and let Hugh go, to imagine that out there somewhere was another man worthy of her heart and life, one who wouldn't keep disappointing her and who might be to her everything Hugh had been during the few happy hours they'd enjoyed before reality had stolen him. She only had to go to London and endure a hundred balls, dinners and outings, to weed through fortune hunters and other questionable men to find him. Clara sighed. Perhaps being an unmarried dowager wasn't so bad.

Anne came to the bed and rested her hands on the coverlet, leaning in close to Clara as if they were about to sneak into the Tower and steal the Crown Jewels. 'All we have to do is open Lady Frances's bedroom door and then we'll know, one way or another, if I'm right and Lord Delamare is being trapped or you're right and he's a rotten scoundrel.'

'I don't need to sneak into a room to know he's a scoundrel.' Clara couldn't believe Anne's tenacity or the way it piqued her curiosity. What did Anne know this time that Clara didn't? 'Besides, what makes you so certain that this is the time to check?'

'Let's call it a woman's intuition.'

Clara's intuition said nothing of the sort, but the sense that another name was being palmed and that there was more to this than Anne simply wanting to get up to mischief made her slide off the bed and put on her shoes. Oh, but she would look like an idiot if Anne was wrong and the increase to her current humiliation almost made her scoff at Anne and make for her own room. But if Anne was right?

She didn't know, but the urge to take the risk of

further embarrassment to learn if everything Hugh had told her about loving her and longing to be with her was true was too powerful. It would ease her broken heart to know that he had wanted her and that she hadn't been duped. That it was she and Anne instead of Hugh contriving to find this out saddened her. He should be the one fighting to prove himself to her, not her working to clear his name. It wouldn't change things between them but, if nothing else, perhaps by the time they were done the house would have something else to talk about besides her being jilted. 'All right, I'll go with you.'

Anne and Clara crept down the dimly lit hallway, the sound of snoring coming from behind more than one of the bedroom doors. The rest of the guests were still awake, the light of their candles slipping out from beneath their doors to illuminate the hallway enough for Clara and Anne to find their way. Clara walked along the carpet on the balls of her feet, Anne clinging to her arm as if at any moment they would be discovered and sent like children back to their rooms. Clara's heart raced and a small bead of perspiration dotted her temples when the door to Lady Frances's room came into view. It was near the end of the hall, across from Lady Pariston's. There was no light beneath the old Dowager's door, but one flickered from beneath Lady Frances's.

The closer they came to the door, the slower Clara walked until she finally came to a halt.

'What's wrong?' Anne whispered.

'We shouldn't do this.' It was as bad an idea as coming to Stonedown in the first place.

'Of course we should.' Anne started to pull her towards the door, but Clara dug in her heels.

'What if you're wrong?'

Anne took her by the upper arms, the seriousness in her eyes, even in the low light, unmistakable. 'Trust me, I'm not.'

'What do you know that I don't?'

'Why don't you go and find out?'

The resolve that Clara had almost lost came rushing back to her. Anne had been behind bringing Clara here and then having her paired with Hugh. The suspicion that there was another surprise waiting for Clara that was Anne's doing was too powerful to ignore.

Clara crept up to Lady Frances's door, but instead of taking the knob and throwing it open, she pressed her palms against the cool wood. Inside, the high notes of Lady Frances's voice were audible and it was clear she was speaking to someone. So far Anne was right. Lady Frances wasn't alone, but she could be giving instructions to her maid. Then a man's voice, certainly not Hugh's, made her press her ear to the wood to listen.

'You were perfect last night, darling. You captured him and gave him no way out. Well done,' Lord Stanhope said, his voice muffled by the wood, but not enough to stop Clara from hearing his words. She bit her thumbnail to keep from making a squeak of surprise before her wide-eyed gaze met Anne's who had come around to the other side to listen, too.

'Since I've ruined him in Lady Kingston's eyes, she will be much more amenable to your charms.' Lady Frances laughed with wincing triumph. 'You can soothe her broken heart all the way down the aisle and straight into her sizeable annual income.'

'Once I have her money, you and our child, the future Marquess, will want for nothing,' Lord Stanhope promised. 'Thankfully, she's such a simpleton she'll fall for any man who is kind to her.'

Clara gripped the doorknob and, having heard all she needed to hear, threw open the door and stormed in. 'Is that so? I wonder if you have the courage to say such things to my face, you lying cheat.'

They had been lounging in bed, the sheets covering their entwined bodies. At the sight of Clara bearing down on them, Anne following close behind, they jumped apart and, in a frenzy of pulled-up coverlets and the quick donning of garments, tried to cover themselves.

'How dare you barge in here?' Lord Stanhope dropped all pretence to the manners and politeness he'd formerly lavished on Clara as he tugged on his breeches.

Lady Frances sat in the bed, her face buried in her hands in shame.

'How dare you think you can trick me into turning my money over to you or that you could pass off your child as Lord Delamare's.'

'We didn't do anything,' he protested, stuffing the long end of his shirt into his breeches. 'Lady Frances wasn't feeling well and I stepped in here to assist her.'

'With your clothes off?'

'There's no point lying any more for you've both been revealed for the snakes you really are.' Hugh's voice boomed out from behind them. Clara whirled around to see him stride into the room, Lord Westbook and Adam on his heels. 'You thought to trap each of us into a marriage beneficial to you both, one to gain enough money to cover your sizeable debts, money I could not provide Lady Frances, the other to raise up your child sired out of wedlock. Afterwards, you intended to carry on as you are behind our backs and at our expense. Did you really think you could fool us?'

'Yes, they did,' Clara spat, crossing her arms and pinning Lady Frances with a stern look. 'They thought we were simpletons who wouldn't figure out their scheme, but we aren't and now she doesn't even have the courage to look me in the face.'

Lady Frances didn't, turning to one side to avoid Clara's fury as she hugged the sheets up tight to cover her naked body. Lord Stanhope wasn't quite so timid, standing squarely in defiance of Clara until Hugh stormed up on him.

He hustled back, but not fast enough to avoid Hugh who rammed his fist into the man's face. Lady Frances let out a scream as Lord Stanhope went flying backwards, the chair against the wall stopping him hitting the plaster. He slumped to the floor, gripping his jaw. Hugh stood over him, shoulders tight, hands balled at his sides with barely concealed restraint. 'I demand satisfaction for this insult, not to my honour, but to Lady Kingston's. A woman of her forthrightness and genuine love and care for others does not deserve to be treated so poorly by the likes of you.'

Clara clapped her hands over her mouth. Hugh was demanding that Lord Stanhope face him at dawn and risking being hit by a musket ball and dying to see the humiliation heaped on her by their plot righted. It wasn't his honour he cared about, but hers, and he was willing to place himself in jeopardy to see it restored. He was upholding honour and duty for her, at last.

Rustling near the door drew Clara's attention to the shocked faces of numerous other guests, including Sir Nathaniel, Lady Fulton and Lady Pariston who, having been roused from their rooms by the commotion, watched what was unfolding with as much interest as Lord Westbook.

Lord Stanhope looked back and forth between Hugh and everyone crowded in the doorway.

'What do you say, sir, will you meet me?' Hugh demanded. 'Will you answer for your insult against Lady Kingston?'

Lord Stanhope pushed himself to his feet, cradling his bruised jaw with one hand.

Clara gripped her hands tight together, waiting

for him to accept Hugh's challenge, but he did not possess Hugh's conviction.

'If I apologise, will that satisfy you?' Lord Stanhope limply asked, his shoulders slumping in defeat.

'Ask Lady Kingston,' Hugh commanded, the tightness in his body easing at his victory.

Lord Stanhope turned to her, more chastened than Clara had ever seen any child who'd been reprimanded. 'I'm sorry, Lady Kingston, for the insult to your honour. I humbly apologise and ask for your forgiveness.'

'Is it enough, Lady Kingston?' Hugh asked.

Clara paused, making Lord Stanhope shift on his feet in nervous anticipation. She should refuse his apology and force him to meet Hugh with pistols, but she knew the outcome of a duel wasn't certain and that it could be Hugh and not Lord Stanhope who might be killed. To imagine him lost to her for good was more than she could bear and she nodded. 'Yes, your apology is enough.'

'Then we are both satisfied,' Hugh announced. 'We'll leave you alone for you deserve one another.'

Hugh ushered Anne and Clara and the others out into the hallway that was now illuminated with the many candles carried by many guests tempted out of their room by the noise. The latecomers demanded to know what had happened and Lord Westbook was more than willing to tell them a tale that made their eyes widen in surprise.

'What is going on?' Lady Tillman demanded,

coming down the hall from her bedroom, her hair in a long plait over her shoulder, Lord Tillman beside her in his dressing gown.

'We are righting a number of wrongs, including every one done to Lady Kingston by Lord Stanhope, Lady Frances and me.' Hugh took Clara's hand and she gasped, the shock of everything including his touch making her tremble. She tried to pull back, but Hugh's grip remained tight, especially when he brought it up to his chest. It gave everyone something else besides Lord Westbook to focus on. 'Before all these people, I want you to know, Clara, that I love you and I don't want anything to ever come between us again. I was a fool to almost allow evil people to try to separate us once more, but I swear to you that it will never happen again.'

A collective gasp of surprise whipped through everyone gathered, but Clara didn't care. Let them whisper and talk, let them call her names and look down on her. It all no longer mattered. Hugh was risking the humiliation of her rejecting him in front of everyone to declare his feelings and he'd been the one to force the apology out of Lord Stanhope. At last, he was fighting for them to be together.

He dropped to his knee in front of Clara, his hands still tight on hers. 'I know I don't deserve you, but I will do everything in my power to be worthy of your love and your life. Clara, I make this vow to be yours always if you will have me.'

He did love her and he wanted her, not for her

wealth or anything else, but because of who she was and the joy they found together. In his eyes lingered the uncertainty caused by her silence. He was waiting, afraid she would reject him in front of all these people, but she couldn't. She loved him as much as he loved her. She laid her other hand on the side of his face, the faint stubble there rough against her skin.

'I was wrong about you, so many times, and I didn't believe in you when I should have. I fell for people's lies instead of trusting in what I'd seen for myself. I also placed my need to not be humiliated above the desires of my heart. I love you, too, Hugh and I will have you, assuming there is no one else out there that I don't know of who has some claim to you.'

'I promise you, there is no one.' Hugh breathed in relief.

'Well, perhaps one,' Lady Pariston announced, making everyone, including Hugh and Clara, gasp in surprise before she flashed them a wicked smile. 'But you can have him, Lady Kingston, since I know you prefer marquesses.'

'Indeed, I do.' She tugged Hugh to his feet.

He rose, his hand still tight around hers as he stood over her, admiring her as if she was the answer to every one of his prayers. 'Will you be my Marchioness?'

It was the question she'd longed to hear six years ago, finally being asked and in front of everyone who'd ever doubted how much they truly meant to one another. 'Yes, I will be your Marchioness.'

He clasped her in his arms and took her lips with his, the kiss, the future and everything they'd been denied at last theirs. Nothing could come between them after this and everything he'd promised her yesterday with his touch and the dance would come true. He loved her and she loved him and they would be happy together, meeting every challenge that faced them, confident in themselves and their care for one another. There would be children and many more magical Christmas seasons like this one. It was everything she'd come to Stonedown to find and it was here in Hugh's embrace.

Hugh slowly broke from her kiss, but held her tight, and Clara basked in the strength of his arms around her, her forehead resting against his. 'You must ask Adam for my hand, too, I want everything to be proper and right.'

'I already asked him this evening.'

Clara jerked back, but kept her hands on his shoulders and his arms around her waist, more things than their future becoming clear. 'Did you have something to do with Anne knowing that Lord Stanhope and Lady Frances were together?'

Clara spied Anne and Adam over his shoulder. They regarded her and Hugh with a smug certainness that Clara knew she would never live down.

'Yes. I asked her to help me by taking you to Lady Frances's room. I knew you had to see it for yourself and that everyone must know I was right in order to clear any doubt.'

'But how did you find out?'

'Lord Westbook told me.' He pulled her close again, his body firm against hers. 'I went to a great deal of trouble to arrange this.'

'I'm glad you did. Everyone will be talking about it and us tomorrow.'

'Do you mind?'

'Not at all.' She rose up on her toes and pressed her lips to his, not caring what anyone said or thought. She was with Hugh and that was all that mattered.

Epilogue

Stonedown—Christmas morning, 1807

Hugh watched Clara descend the stairs, the silk of her pale peach gown swirling around her legs as she walked with sure steps towards him. The Christmas morning sunlight from the windows at the top played in the lighter strands of her hair, making a halo around her like so many of the saints in the illuminated manuscript. Behind her, a gaggle of children ran by, racing through the halls and singing Christmas carols at the tops of their little voices to proclaim the arrival of the joyful morning.

Hugh barely heard them as he concentrated on Clara. She paused here and there to offer or accept a Happy Christmas from the footmen coming and going up the stairs, the festive green sprigs in their buttonholes adding to the merriment of the day. It'd been a year since Hugh had first seen her at the top

of the stairs in her green dress, an unwilling partner for dinner. There was no hesitancy in her steps
or stone-faced greeting this joyous morning, but a
quickness to be near him and a smile as bright as
the Christmas day. In her arms she carried their in-
fant son, who gurgled and cooed as he sucked on his
small fingers, his head just visible from out of the
top of the blanket.

'Merry Christmas, Hugh.'

'Merry Christmas, my love.' He swept her lips
with his and then rubbed his face against his son's
chubby cheek. 'And Merry Christmas to you, little
Hugh.'

The boy offered him a wide, toothless smile before making a large yawn, his eyes growing heavy
with sleep.

Upstairs, in the hallway outside the bedroom, the
other children ran past again, singing Christmas carols at the tops of their lungs and banging on the doors
of those still sleeping with cries of 'Happy Christmas' and startling little Hugh. 'Some day soon that
will be you, my son.'

'I can't wait for the day.' Clara kissed the sleepy
baby on the cheek, then handed him to his nurse.
She carried him back upstairs to his bed while Clara
took Hugh's arm and the two of them made for the
dining room and the sumptuous Christmas morning
breakfast waiting there.

'After church, I thought we could take a sleigh
ride before the Christmas banquet,' Hugh suggested,

the snow outside the front window white and glistening in the morning sun.

'That would be wonderful.'

'Do you like your present?' Hugh asked.

She touched the diamond pendant around her neck and smiled at him. 'I do and it wasn't necessary.'

'It was and some day the diamonds will be larger, just as you deserve.'

'You deserve it more than I do. If you and Sir Nathaniel hadn't fought the lawsuit so well and won, we might have found ourselves homeless.'

'My parents' dream has at last come true. The estate is safe and this year's harvest will make it once again worthy to support the Delamares.' The cold and sparse days of his childhood were long behind him, as was the lonely aimlessness of four years ago. He had a wife and child he loved, an estate to manage and purposefulness that made every day full and welcome.

They strolled into the dining room where Lady Pariston sat eating her eggs, Lord Wortley beside her once more, looking more mature than he had last year. Lady Fulton and Lord Westbook occupied their usual places and huddled together in conversation. Hugh offered Lord Westbook a respectful nod, glad to get one in return while Lady Fulton looked on Clara with a grudging respect that made Clara stand a little taller beside Hugh.

'There you are, Lady Delamare,' Lady Pariston called out at the sight of them. 'The Multiple Marchioness, as I've heard everyone call you.'

'Is that what they say?' Clara laughed as she sat down beside the old Dowager. Far from seeming embarrassed by the sobriquet, she tilted her head to one side to consider it. 'Well, it definitely has a certain ring to it.'

'So does Lady Wortley, but Lord Wortley still hasn't reached his majority,' Lady Pariston teased, making the young man turn as red as his waistcoat. 'But leave it to you to collect all the Marquesses and leave none for the rest of us, but I must compliment you for choosing the best of the lot.'

'Yes, I have.' She raised her hand to Hugh and he took it, bending over her supple skin to lay a soft kiss on the back of it. He was her Marquess and she his Marchioness and this was their happiest Christmas ever.

* * * * *

THE WALLFLOWER'S MISTLETOE WEDDING

AMANDA McCABE

To the memory of my grandmother,
Roberta McCabe, who loved
the magic of Christmas.

Prologue

Barton Park—summer 1820

'Oh, Rose! Doesn't the music just make you want to twirl and twirl and twirl?'

Rose Parker sat back on her heels and laughed as she watched her sister, Lily, spin in an exuberant circle, her new white lace and tulle skirts like a great cloud. The music from the party floated up to their chamber and it was indeed very twirly. 'You won't twirl for long if I don't finish that hem. It will come unravelled and you will trip and fall flat on your face—right in front of Mr Hewlitt.'

Lily came to an abrupt stop, stumbling on her satin slippers. 'Oh, no, Rose!' she cried, her pretty, heart-shaped face full of stark fear. 'I could never do such a thing. How he would despise me!'

Rose laughed again. She couldn't help it; her sister's adorable ways were always too funny. 'Lily, my dearest, Mr Hewlitt would never in a thousand years despise you for anything. In fact, stumbling and falling into his arms would probably only make him worship you more as his delicate angel.'

A tiny smile broke through Lily's pout. 'I—well, perhaps so. He is so terribly sweet.'

'And terribly sweet on you. Mama says he will surely ask you something very important indeed tonight,' Rose said. She did have to tease Lily just a bit, as she always had, even when her sister was a tiny, golden-curled cherub prone to blushing and shrieking when provoked. But she was serious, too. Mr Hewlitt had been stammering his way up to just such a moment for weeks and this ball at their cousins' home at Barton Park to celebrate midsummer seemed the perfect opportunity. It was true that he was a curate with only a middling income, yet everyone could see how good he was at his calling, so caring and energetic. Surely a bishopric waited for him one day!

And he adored Lily, as she did him. Together the two of them were as adorable as a box of new puppies.

Rose was happy for her sister, yet wistful, too. With just herself and their mother, their cottage would be much too quiet. Too lonely.

Rose sighed. She would have to procure a kitten, or mayhap a songbird. Wasn't that what useful spinsters did? Collect pets, especially cats, and

knit them little sweaters and such? It sounded rather
diverting.

'Come, dearest Lily, let me finish the hem,' she
said. 'Or the dancing will be over before Mr Hewlitt can find you.'

Lily climbed back on to the low stool, watching
in the mirror with a little frown as Rose plied her
needle through the delicate beaded tulle. 'Do you
really, truly think he will propose?'

'Of course he will.'

'Do—do you think I should accept, then? Right
away?'

Rose was surprised at her sister's suddenly unsure, quiet tone. She glanced up to see that Lily did
indeed look worried, something most uncharac-
teristic. She quickly thought back on Mr Hewlitt's
courtship: his visits to the cottage, his little gifts of
bouquets and books of poetry, his walks with Lily,
the way they stared at each other as if there was no
one else around at all. Had she missed something?
'Do you have doubts, dearest? Has he done something—ungentlemanly?' She couldn't quite imagine that, but then again one never really knew with
men. Look how their own father had concealed his
debts, his terrible gambling habits, from his wife
and daughters until he died and they were cast out
of their home.

Surely Mr Hewlitt would never do that. If he
dared to hurt Lily in any way, Rose would murder him.

'Oh, no, not at all! It's just—' Lily broke off, biting her lip. 'Well, what will you and Mama do?'

'Oh, Lily.' Rose gave her the most reassuring smile she could manage. Was that not the very same question she had asked herself since Father died? 'You must not worry about that, dearest. We will be absolutely fine. Indeed, I'm quite looking forward to making your chamber into my very own sitting room. The mind reels at the thought of so much space! I will be just like a duchess with my own suite.'

Lily laughed, as well she would. Their cottage was approximately the size of a thimble, even with Lily's extra little chamber they had built at the back. 'And you will visit me very often, won't you? I won't be far away.'

'So often you will be heartily sick of me.'

'Promise?'

'Just try to keep me away.' Rose finished the last stitch in the hem and stood up to give her sister a hug, careful not to muss her ruffles and curls. Lily smelled of violet powder and sweetness, just as she had when she was a child, and Rose had held her dimpled little hands to help her walk. She laughed to keep from crying.

'You really should marry first, as the eldest daughter. That is the natural way,' Lily said.

Rose laughed again. 'Find me another Mr Hewlitt, then. Until I have just such a paragon, I would never be able to tolerate wifely duties.'

'He *is* out there, Rose, I just know it! The perfect man for you.' Lily drew back to stare most earnestly into Rose's eyes. 'You will find him when you least expect it, just as I did with Mr Hewlitt.'

'I haven't time for romance,' Rose said, tucking away her needle and thread in her workbox. It was quite true. When their father died so suddenly and they had to leave their home for the cottage, they'd had a very small income that would keep them from starving, but there would be no carriage or smart clothes or abundance of servants. Rose herself did much of the work: sweeping, sewing, looking after the chickens, taking care of their frail mother. She didn't mind very much; she actually quite liked the useful, busy feeling of tea to make and ironing of petticoats to finish. And her chickens were known to be the finest layers in the neighbourhood.

Their mother, however, *did* mind. Mrs Felicity Parker had grown up as gentry in a fine manor house, cousin to the ancient family of the Bancrofts of Barton Park, and expected more of the same from her marriage, only to be bitterly disappointed. She talked of it to anyone who would listen. All her hopes had long been pinned on the beautiful Lily marrying well. A poor curate had never been in her plans, no matter how kind and handsome he was, no matter how much he adored Lily. And Rose saw too clearly what happened when a woman had to trust in marriage, trust in a man. She wasn't sure she could do it.

Rose sighed. She very much feared her mother's plans might turn to herself now and this visit to Barton Park was part of them. As much as she enjoyed seeing the old house and meeting her cousins, she couldn't let her guard down.

'Are you quite well, Rose?' Lily asked, frowning in concern. 'You look as if you have the headache.'

Rose made herself smile and fluffed up the lace trim of her sister's sleeve. 'Not at all. It's just a bit stuffy in here, don't you think? We should make our way down to the party. Mr Hewlitt will surely arrive soon.'

With a squeal of excitement, Lily dashed out of the room, her gown floating and sparkling around her like angel's wings. Rose took a quick glance at herself in the glass before she followed, to make sure she looked presentable and tidy.

Presentable and *tidy* were about all she could hope for, she thought wryly. Unlike Lily, she had not inherited their mother's blond curls and pink cheeks, her petite plumpness. Rose was taller, thin to the point of sharpness, with light brown hair that refused to hold a curl no matter how long it was subjected to the tongs, and skin that had turned ever so slightly golden while working in the garden. Her eyes were not too bad, she thought, with a small spark of hopefulness. A green-hazel that looked emerald in some lights, when she did not have to wear the horrid spectacles. Sadly, those had become more and more necessary of late, especially when sitting up sewing in the lamplight.

She smoothed the sleeves of her gown and reached for her gloves. Unlike Lily's new dress, Rose had redone an old gown of their mother's for herself. The olive-gold satin, plain and lustrous with only a single row of gold embroidery at the hem, suited her much better than the current style for frothy pale muslins and ruffled sleeves, and her needle had managed to take in the fuller skirts and puff out the sleeves a bit, yet she feared it would attract whispers of 'unfashionableness' and pity for the poor Parkers.

'Ah, well,' she told herself. 'Fashion is something you could never really aspire to, Rose dear.'

She laughed, straightened the ivory comb in her upswept hair, slid her creamy Indian shawl over her shoulders and followed Lily out the door.

The party downstairs was just beginning, the first arrivals sweeping through the front doors and gathering in the marble-floored hall, leaving their wraps with the footmen, calling out merry greetings to each other.

Rose peeked over the gilded banister to the scene below. She had always loved Barton Park, the home of her mother's distant cousins, the Bancrofts, even though they so seldom got to visit. It was a beautiful house, not too small and not too grand, built on elegant, classic lines and filled with comfortable furnishings and plenty of books and art. A true family home for many generations, soaked through with stories and emotions and hopes. It had fallen into some disrepair for a few years, but under the care of the current owners, Jane, Countess of Ramsay, and her sister, Emma, it had found new life.

The gardens beyond the tall glass windows were equally lovely, especially on such a soft, warm summer's evening. Chinese lanterns shimmered in the trees, lighting up the pathways and the colourful tumble of the flowerbeds as carriages bounced along the gravel drive to the waiting doors.

Rose studied the crowd, a laughing, beautifully dressed throng gathered around Jane and her husband, the magnificently handsome Lord Ramsay. Jane looked as if she had belonged there at Barton Park for ever in her elegant dark blue gown, shimmering with lavender beads. She greeted each new arrival with a happy cry, sparkling with laughter before she passed them to her younger sister, Emma, a blonde angel much like Lily in her grey satin gown. Emma, too, smiled, though it was quieter, more unsure. When they were children, Emma had been quite the daredevil, but now she had returned to Barton as a young widow, trailing something of a scandal in her wake. Rose quite adored her, even as she worried for her.

The growing throng appeared a bit of a blur to Rose without her spectacles, but she glimpsed Lily near the open doors to the drawing room, where the music was drifting out above the hum of laughter.

Their mother stood beside her, the plumes of her striped turban nodding merrily as she laughed and chattered, but Lily didn't seem to be paying attention at all. She bounced on the toes of her dancing slippers, searching each face around her eagerly before falling back again.

Oh, dear, Rose thought. Mr Hewlitt had probably not made his appearance yet. She tiptoed down the stairs and slipped into the crowd, intending to make her way to Lily and their mother. She was stopped when Jane spotted her.

'Rose, my dear, do come and meet someone!' Jane said, grasping Rose's hand and drawing her forward. Jane was the kindest of women, but always most assiduous in her hostess duties. She would never just let a wallflower be a wallflower.

Rose flashed a quick smile at Emma, who smiled back uncomfortably. She looked as if she wanted to run for the safety of the comfortably shabby library as much as Rose did.

But then Rose turned to face Jane's newly arrived guests—and froze. All thoughts of fleeing, all thoughts at all, were quite gone.

A gentleman had just stepped through the front door and what a gentleman he was. He looked rather like something Rose would picture in one of the romantic French novels Lily liked to read aloud in the evenings—a man tall, dark and mysterious. His expression was quite solemn and wary as he studied the crowd, as if he was thinking of possible battle lines rather than dancing.

He certainly did have the bearing of a soldier, lean and ramrod-straight, his shoulders strong beneath the cut of his dark blue evening coat, his sun-darkened skin set off by a plain white cravat. His hair, so dark it was almost a blue-black, like a winter's night, waved back from his forehead, and his eyes were a velvet brown. He had a strange stillness, a perfect watchfulness, almost a—a menace about him, but one that was enticing rather than frightening. He was quite unlike anyone else she had ever seen.

'Harry, how delightful you could come tonight after all,' Jane was saying, once Rose could tear her attention away from the man's mesmerising handsomeness and hear the roar of the party again. 'We did hear you were off to battle in Sicily.'

'A soldier has to keep busy however he can.' The man smiled as he bowed over Jane's hand and it quite transformed him. He went from wary stillness to sunny charm in an instant, a dimple appearing in his sun-browned cheek that made Rose want to giggle like a schoolgirl. 'But it seems they don't need my assistance at this very moment. How could I resist the chance to see *you* again, Lady Ramsay? It's been much too long since you brightened the dull London ballrooms. Hayden is a beast to keep you away.'

Jane laughed and waved her lace fan at him.

'Silly flatterer. I know you are merely counting the seconds until you can escape to the library for a brandy with Hayden and a talk about your beastly battlefields. But it's lovely to see you again all the same, safe and sound. And you, Charles! Where on earth have you been keeping yourself?'

Rose was able to tear her gaze from the dark, poetic brooder for a moment to see another man standing just behind him. He was also tall, also handsome, with a cheerful smile and bright golden hair, and the same brown eyes as the first man. But though he was just as good looking, he did not have the same frightening magnetism.

'Nowhere as useful as my brother, I assure you, Lady Ramsay,' he said with a bow. 'But I haven't had a proper dance in ages and, unlike Harry, I miss it more than I can say.'

'That is one thing I can promise here. I hired the best orchestra from miles around.' Jane drew Rose and Emma forward. 'Emma, Rose, may I present two of our neighbours? Captain Henry St George, who was a great hero at Waterloo, and his brother, Mr Charles St George. Gentlemen, this my sister, Mrs Emma Carrington, and my cousin Miss Rose Parker.'

Charles was the first to bow to them, with grand courtly flourishes that made Rose laugh and even had Emma smiling. 'Ladies, I fear that unlike my dashing brother I am hero of very little except the billiards room, but I do claim some proficiency at waltzing, if you will do me the honour?'

Emma did laugh—the first time Rose had heard it since the young widow had returned to Barton— but Rose could still not find a way to tear her attention completely away from Captain St George. How very intriguing he looked, with his wry flash of a smile!

'Do you live near Barton, Miss Parker?' he asked, his voice low and deep, almost rough. He watched her closely, as if he listened only to her in the whole room.

'Oh,' Rose answered, and for an instant it was as if every word she had ever known flew out of her mind. She had to laugh at herself; it was quite unlike the sensible nature she usually prided herself on. Yet she comforted herself that no lady could surely be entirely immune from such a pair of eyes when they were focused so closely on oneself.

'Not too far,' she said. 'We used to visit often when we were children, my sister and I, and hunt for treasure with Jane and Emma.'

He smiled, his dark eyes crinkling at the corners. 'Treasure? That does sound intriguing.'

'Oh, it was!' she said, absurdly pleased to have 'intrigued' him. She found she wanted more than anything to make him smile that smile at her again. 'It is a wonderful old tale, about the lover of a Royalist soldier, Arabella Bancroft, hiding a royal fortune on the grounds of the estate, in the hope she and her love would one day be reunited to spend it together. Or something like that. We were quite hazy on the details when we were children.'

'And did you ever find it?'

'No, not even a farthing. It's just a legend, of course, but we did have some marvellous adventures digging for it in the woods. We would climb the trees and pretend we were the Royalists defending our fortress from Cromwell, with tree trunks for cannons...' She suddenly remembered he was a true captain, a hero of the terrible carnage at Waterloo, and felt her cheeks turn warm. 'Not at all like real battle, of course.'

A shadow flickered over his smile and he glanced away. 'Much more fun, though, I would wager. Real battle is all mud and noise, I fear, Miss Parker. But trees and branches as guns—just fun.'

Rose nervously twitched her skirts into place, feeling terrible at reminding him of such things when he was meant to be enjoying himself at Jane's party. Not for the first time, she wished she had some of Lily's gift of easy laughter and chatter. 'I am sure it was. I'm sorry for bringing up any bad memories, Captain.'

He gave her a wry smile. 'The memories are always there, Miss Parker, but they don't plague me on a night like this.' He paused to adjust a glove. 'And did they ever find each other again?'

'Find each other?' she said, confused.

'Arabella Bancroft and her Royalist.'

'Oh. No. He never came back. I think she married someone else in the end and abandoned Barton Park.'

'Then there is hope the treasure is still out there.'

'I never thought of it like that,' Rose exclaimed. 'Perhaps it is.'

Captain St George's brother suddenly turned towards them with a grin. 'Harry, I have just secured Mrs Carrington's promise for the first dance and Lady Ramsay tells me there are not yet enough couples for a proper set. You must find yourself a partner and do your bit for the party.'

'Charlie, you know I am hopeless dancer indeed,' the Captain protested.

'Of course you are not!' Charles said. 'Do not be an old stick in the mud again. Aren't you all about doing your duty? Well, being merry is your only duty tonight.'

Harry laughed, and turned back to Rose. 'Well, then, Miss Parker. Would you be brave enough to take me on for the first dance? With fair warning that grace is not my strong suit.'

Rose was not at all sure that could be true. He had such a lean, coiled stillness, she imagined that in motion he would be as elegant and lethal as a jungle cat. She longed to dance with him, more than she had ever longed for anything before, but she also feared he was asking only because she was the closest lady at the moment.

Not that it mattered. When would she ever be able to dance with such a man again?

'I—no, nor is it mine, Captain St George,' she answered. 'I do have a terrible tendency to trip over my own feet—my sister always hated sharing her dancing lessons with me. Perhaps we can figure it out together?'

He laughed and suddenly he looked so young, so carefree. Rose imagined perhaps he was like that all the time before he went to war and became so watchful. 'I am quite sure we can. The first dance, then, Miss Parker.'

'Yes, thank you, Captain,' she answered, and suddenly felt a hand on her arm. She turned to see Lily standing beside her, her sky-blue eyes wide.

'Oh, Rose!' she cried. 'He isn't here yet! What if he changed his mind?'

Before Rose could answer, the front doors flew open again as if in a stormy gale and a most fearsome figure appeared. As wide as she was tall, with iron-grey hair high-piled in the style of pre–Revolutionary France, and swathed in lace and satin, her dried-apple face was heavily rouged. Armed as she was with a carved walking stick with the head of a snarling dragon, she seemed the combination of Empress Maria Theresa and a Viking, combined with an ancient tree spirit.

'Aunt Sylvia,' Jane gasped. She hurried forward to try to help her, but the old lady impatiently pushed her away. 'How lovely to see you. We thought you could not attend tonight.'

Aunt Sylvia Pemberton. Rose stared at her in astonishment. She had thought the old lady, a sister of her own great-grandfather and Jane's and Emma's as well, was only some sort of legend, but now here she was before them. She lived in a vast house nearby, rich as Croesus and widowed for decades, but she never ventured beyond its gates. Even Captain St George seemed amazed by the sight, even after all he must have seen at Waterloo.

'I should never have ventured out indeed, Jane. A most disagreeable night and my rheumatism so terrible,' Aunt Sylvia growled. 'But I had to see what you have done with the old house, now that all your modern folderols have finished. You've quite ruined it, I must say. The windows are terrible and what kind of colour is that for walls?' She looked around, waving her stick as if the new pale blue paint was a personal affront.

'Ah,' she went on, 'and here is that disgraceful Emma, I see. And who is this? The Parker chits? How pale you are, girl. And the other one—too tall. Come here where I can see you better.'

Lily did indeed look quite white under such scrutiny and she clutched at Rose's hand. 'Must we?' Lily whispered.

Rose thought of the grandness of Aunt Sylvia's mansion and the tininess of their own cottage. She sighed. 'I think we must.' She glanced over her shoulder, but the Captain had quite vanished into the crowd. She could only fervently hope he remembered their dance.

'Don't worry, Lily dearest,' she whispered. 'We just have to say hello and then we can slip away. I am sure Mr Hewlitt will be here at any moment.'

'She might turn us into stone first,' Lily whispered back with a shiver.

Their mother suddenly appeared at Lily's other side, a smile on her face beneath the blond curls that peeked from her turban. 'Girls, be very nice indeed. We might need her help one day soon,' she hissed, before sailing forward to kiss Aunt Sylvia's cheek. 'Aunt Sylvia, how absolutely delightful to see you again after so long. You remember my dear daughters, Rose and Lily, I'm sure.'

'Hmmph,' Aunt Sylvia said with a thump of her stick. 'Still yours, are they? No husbands yet? How vexing for you, Felicity. I think we have much to talk about.'

As if he had been given a stage cue, Mr Hewlitt appeared in the doorway, looking handsome, but blushing and flustered in his curate's dark coat, his red hair rumpled. He lit up like the moon when he saw Lily, and hurried over to take her hand. 'Miss Parker, I am so sorry I was delayed! I have been so looking forward to—'

'And who are *you*, young man?' Aunt Sylvia boomed.

Poor Mr Hewlitt looked quite terrified, but much

to his credit he did not let go of Lily's hand. Indeed, he slid in front of her, as if to protect her. 'I am Mr Peter Hewlitt, curate of St Anne's, madam.'

Rose took the opportunity to slip away from the little scene and made her way through the crowd into the drawing room. The Aubusson rugs that usually lay over the polished parquet floors had been rolled away to make a dance floor, surrounded by conversational groupings of brocade sofas and armchairs, half-hidden by banks of palms and fragrant white flowers. The orchestra played on their dais, a soft song as dancers found their partners and footmen passed trays of champagne and claret punch. The windows were open to let in the soft summer breeze and everything was laughter and happiness for just a moment.

Rose smoothed her skirt again, hoping against hope Captain St George would find her—and just as frightened that he would. She didn't want to seem stammering and silly in his company, but she was sure she would. She seemed to quite forget everything else when she looked into his dark eyes.

'Miss Parker? Time for our dance, I think?' she heard his deep voice say behind her.

She spun around to face him and his easy smile made her feel instantly more at ease. 'Oh—of course. Thank you, Captain.'

As Rose took Captain St George's arm and walked with him across the crowded room, she felt something most distinctly—odd. Something she had never had an inkling of before. Parties and gowns and flirtations had never held much appeal for her, not compared to the pleasures of the piano or a good book by the fire. Parties were for her mother and sister, because watching their enjoyment made Rose happy, too. Mama and Lily had far less fun in their lives than they deserved.

Yet now, being with Captain St George, Rose found *she* could have fun as well. It was quite astonishing and rather delightful. They followed the lead couple into the steps of the lively dance, holding hands, their feet nearly touching as she skipped around him. They joined hands with two other couples, moving in an intricate star until they had to wait at the end of the line. It moved in a wonderful, bright blur, the greatest fun she had ever had in a dance!

'I'm sorry I'm not much of a dancer,' he said as he spun her around, making her laugh.

'I think you are quite grand at it,' she answered. 'But then I almost always have to practise with Lily and she does have a tendency to step on my toes rather more than I would like.'

'I'll try not to do that, then,' he answered, his smile widening. 'I don't have the chance to dance much, either.'

'I would think not, if you are always on the march. Do you have the chance to be in society a great deal?'

'Not a great deal, but for a time my regiment

was posted for training near Bath, which I admit I rather enjoyed.'

'I have never been there,' Rose answered with a sigh. 'And only once or twice to London. A large town must be delightful!'

'It's not so terrible,' he answered, his eyes crinkling at the corners in a most enticing way as he looked at her. 'But family parties are always the best.'

'Yes,' Rose answered, a bit out of breath as she looked up at him. 'Indeed they are.' And this one was turning out to be the best she could ever remember. 'I do like evenings at home, though Lily says they are dull. A book and a fine fire, a song at the piano.'

'It sounds quite perfect, Miss Parker. Exactly what I would want one day. Some music in the winter evenings, a welcoming fire after a walk in the garden...'

'Exactly so,' Rose said. For just an instant she had an image in her mind, a picture of herself and the Captain walking down a path arm in arm, the doors of a manor house open behind them to spill out welcoming golden light. Something like what her family had when she was a child, before her father died and they found out it was all a deception, before she realised having her own family, her own secure home, was not to be. But with this man, she could imagine it all, even if it was only for a moment.

They took their turn once more in the set and Captain St George almost lifted her from her feet as they swirled around, making her laugh again. She actually felt delicate in his strong arms, like a lady in a novel, small and dainty next to her hero. They spun, breathless, and ended in a low bow and curtsy.

But the dance ended much too soon and she had to let go of his hand. They made their way to the edge of the crowd and Rose glimpsed her mother standing near the open tall windows with Emma Carrington and Charles St George. They were laughing and Rose had to smile to see her mother's enjoyment. It *was* all going rather well, better than she could have expected when they set out from their cottage that evening.

Then she saw the lady standing beside Charles St George, smiling languidly at the mirth of the others. She seemed so beautiful as to be of some other world, even in the elegance of the Barton Park drawing room. Tall and willowy, she looked as if she should be posing as Athena in a draped gown and golden helmet, serenely smiling, above it all.

In reality, she wore a fashionable gown of blush-coloured silk, her red-gold hair piled high atop her head and fastened with a bandeau of cameos. She slowly waved her painted silk fan, her gaze skimming over the party.

Next to Rose, Captain St George's tall figure stiffened. Surprised, she glanced up at him and saw that his smile had faded. The man she had danced with, so easy and kind, had vanished. He looked darkly intent. Full of a night-like desire.

'St George, there you are at last,' Athena called and something inside of Rose, something soft and summer-like that had bloomed so unexpectedly, faded. She felt suddenly cold inside and she wanted to turn and run, to disappear back into the crowd. Why had she thought even for a moment she could be something besides plain, sensible Rose Parker?

Captain St George stepped away, not completely, not really, but he definitely withdrew in some ineffable way. He was not quite there any longer.

The lady glided towards them and took the Captain's arm in her silk-gloved hand. They looked intently into each other's eyes and her smile widened. 'I am terribly sorry I'm late,' she said. 'I do hope you were not too bored. I know you do hate such parties.'

'I am not much for crowds, of course,' he answered. 'But Barton Park is different.'

'So I see.' Her gaze slid to Rose and her smile turned down at the edges. She glanced up and down Rose's made-over gown and glanced away, obviously finding her to be of not much interest.

'Miss Helen Layton, may I present a cousin of the Bancrofts?' Captain St George said. 'Miss Rose Parker. Miss Parker, this is an old friend of my family, Miss Layton.'

'An old friend, my dear St George?' Miss Layton said with a creamy laugh. 'Surely more than that.

We have known each other since we were veritable babies. Charles says he expects an—well, an interesting announcement at any moment.'

An interesting announcement? Surely, Rose thought, that could only mean one thing. Captain St George and Miss Layton were a couple. She felt even colder, more foolish.

'It's a pleasure to meet you, Miss Layton,' she managed to say in a calm, steady voice.

'I think I just met your mother, Miss Parker,' Miss Layton said. She wafted her fan towards Rose's mother, who was still chatting with Emma and Charles St George. 'She says you live in a cottage nearby. How absolutely charming that sounds. Like Wordsworth, with roses round the door and sheep on the hills.'

Rose laughed, thinking of their smoking chimney and the vegetables she tried to grow in the kitchen garden mud, her chickens pecking around them. 'Something of the sort, I suppose, Miss Layton.'

'We must find something just the same when you get back from this silliness in Sicily,' Miss Layton said, her fingers curling around his sleeve.

He only gave her a tight smile and Rose could feel her cheeks turning warm as she longed even more to flee the whole uncomfortable scene.

'Rose! Rose!' she suddenly heard Lily cry and Rose had never been so relieved to see her sister. Rose spun around, away from the sight of the handsome Captain St George and the lovely Miss Layton, away from the foolish feelings that had come over her only moments ago.

Lily was running towards her, her face shining with happiness, utterly unconcerned with the impropriety of calling out and running at a ball. Mr Hewlitt followed her, just as glowing. Together they hurried towards Rose's mother, who was watching them avidly.

'Mrs Parker,' he said, trying so very hard to be solemn that it almost made Rose laugh. 'May I have the privilege of speaking to you for a moment? I know such things are not usually done at a dance…'

'Please, just follow me,' Emma said. 'You can use the library. It will surely be quiet there for a moment.'

As they hurried away, Lily held out her hand to Rose to display a small pearl ring. 'Oh, Rose! Isn't it the loveliest?'

Rose smiled, but she was afraid she might also start crying as well. The happiness of that moment, of her sister's dreams coming true just as her own fledgling, girlish ideas were nipped in the bud, was almost overwhelming. But she did the only thing she knew how to do. She laughed and hugged her sister tight.

'The loveliest, Lily. I know you will be so very happy.'

Over her sister's shoulder as Lily hugged her back, Rose glimpsed Captain St George, withdrawing to a quiet corner with his brother and Miss Layton. He gave her a small smile and it was so sad, so full of commiseration and understanding, that Rose nearly burst into tears. How perfect that one dance had been! Rose liked her life, her independence, but just for that moment she seemed to glimpse, far in the distance, the glimmer of something—more. A real home.

Miss Layton whispered something in the Captain's ear and the two of them turned away together, beautiful and perfect, leaving Rose in her ordinary world once more.

Oh, well, she thought, laughing at herself just a bit. Ordinary life was not so very bad after all.

'You will be a lovely bride, Lily dearest,' she said, squeezing her sister a little tighter before she let her go.

'And then it will be your turn, Rose, I vow it,' Lily said. 'I will find you someone just as handsome and sweet as my own Hewlitt.'

Rose closed her eyes, and saw, in the darkness of her mind, far away from the colour and noise of the party, Captain St George's all too brief smile. 'Oh, Lily. I don't think that would even be possible.'

The carriage was blessedly shadowed and silent as it jolted away from the lights of Barton Park and slid into the night. Harry leaned his head back against the leather cushions and closed his eyes, letting all the wondrous quiet wash over him.

Silence had become a precious commodity to him in the last few years. In Spain, and then at Waterloo, noise had been ever-present. The cacophony of military camps, drumbeats and shouted orders, and drunken laughter at night as men tried to forget their fears and loneliness around campfires. The explosion of shot and shell, the screams of people and horses as they fell, the sobbing afterward. No—quiet had no place in war.

Nor, it seemed, in a world after the war. Harry had returned to England thinking he was coming home to a world of green and rain and peace, the world he dreamed of in canvas tents at night. It had taken him years to return, but he had always been determined he would.

But it was not like that at all once he returned to London. There were parties all the time, dinners and teas and dances, with everyone clamouring for tales of the glorious heroics of war. He could hardly tell them the truth of it all, of the mud and blood and dying, so he said little at all. Charming social conversation had always been Charles's forte, not his.

Yet his silence only seemed to make him more sought out. Made more invitations arrive at his lodgings, more ladies want to sit beside him in drawing rooms or ride in the park. 'Like a corsair warrior in a poem,' he had once heard a lady whisper to her friend as they watched him at a musicale.

The memory made him laugh all over again. Him—a poetic corsair. If only they knew. He was just a rough army man, riding behind the drum, ever since he was a lad with his first commission. An army man with dreams of being a country farmer one day, of sitting by his own hearth after a day of watching his fields ripen and his sheep grow fat. A house where there was quiet all the time, except perhaps for a toddler's giggle or the sound of a lady playing at her pianoforte.

It was a dream that would have to be postponed again, at least for a time. His regiment had called on him once more, to go to sun-baked Sicily this time to put down a rebellion. There was only time for this one visit home, to his father's house at Hilltop Grange near Barton Park.

He hadn't wanted to go to the party at Barton. Yet more noise, more clamour, more stares. But Jane and Emma Bancroft were old neighbours, kind people, and he let Charles persuade him to attend. Now he was rather glad he had.

He closed his eyes and there he saw something most unexpected—the face of Miss Rose Parker. She had the sweetest smile he could remember ever seeing and even dancing, which he normally loathed, was a pleasure when he talked to her. She seemed almost like no lady, no person, he had ever met before. So calm, so serene—she made the very air seem to sigh with relief around her.

After so long in the rough world of war, he had almost given up ever glimpsing pure sweetness in anything again. Yet there it was, in Rose Parker's smile.

Until Helen appeared. Helen—one of his oldest friends, the daughter of his late mother's best friend, a lady of such beauty she was called in London The Incomparable. The lady everyone had always expected he would marry.

'How changeable you are tonight, Harry,' Charles said. 'Laughing, then scowling—one hardly knows what to expect next.'

Harry opened his eyes to study his brother, who lolled on the opposite seat. His golden hair gleamed in the moonlight from the open window, the perfect aquiline features that had always made him their late mother's copy, her darling, were outlined like a classical cameo. Charles was the perfect Apollo wherever he went to Harry's Hephaestus, always laughing and easy-tempered, making everyone around him feel easy as well. But now that the party was behind him, even Charles looked almost—sad, as he had rather often since Harry returned to England. Harry couldn't help but wonder what was plaguing his brother.

Perhaps it was because Charles had been left all those years to deal with Hilltop and their father while Harry was at war. And their father was not a kind man at the best of times. The house that had been their mother's pride, the glowing name she had loved, had been tarnished by him.

'I laugh because the party went better than I could have expected,' he said.

'Ha!' Charles answered. 'So you see I was right to make you attend. The Bancroft girls are always kindness itself.'

'They are hardly girls now, are they? Jane a countess, Emma a widow.'

'Poor Emma. Remember when Mother made us go to the children's tea parties at Barton and we all ended up climbing trees instead?' Charles said with a laugh. 'Father was never happy at all when we came home with our best new coats torn and muddy. He said Mother was raising monkeys.'

'And the switches would come out.' The switches so often came out with their father, especially after their mother died. 'But it was always worth it to visit Barton Park.'

'Wasn't it, though? Like a different world.'

Harry nodded. *A different world*. He thought of Miss Parker's tales of searching for lost Royalist treasures there at Barton and wondered why they had never crossed paths as children. What would it have been like if they had?

'La belle Helen was in fine looks tonight,' Charles said. 'If only we had a thousand ships that needed to be launched...'

Harry frowned at the reminder of Helen and her elegant face flashed in his mind, erasing Miss Parker's gentle smile. The weight of expectation, the weight of what had been and what was expected in the future, fell once again. 'Helen has always been lovely.'

'Did Miss Lily Parker's sweet little engagement not inspire you, Harry? No ring for Helen's pretty finger yet?'

Harry wasn't sure he liked something in Charles's tone, something dark and hard beneath his smile. 'Helen knows this is no time for an engagement. I am to re-join my regiment soon and I would not tie her down to someone like myself.'

'You may think that, but does she? The betting books in the London clubs were full of speculation about when she would snap you into the parson's mousetrap. Everyone's expected it since we were children.'

Harry frowned as he stared out the window, at the summer moon shining on the silent hedgerows. 'You have picked up some ridiculous slang in those clubs of yours, Charlie.'

'Well, a man has to find distractions, you know. Hilltop Grange is not exactly a haven of merriment. And everyone says you and Helen were made for each other. Any man would give his right arm to be in your position.'

Something in his brother's voice caught Harry's strict attention, something sharp and jagged that was quite unlike Charles. He swung around to face him, but Charles's face was hidden in the shadows.

'Made for each other?' Harry said. Perhaps it was so—they had been friends for so long, bound by the long ties of their families, by their mothers' wishes. He had thought of her when he was gone, dreamed of her, carried her miniature with him to inspire him. She was like a dream, just as all that green English quiet had been a reason to come home.

And by Jove but she *was* beautiful. The most beautiful lady in London, just as all those silly, betting-book dandies declared. For some reason, though, she seemed to prefer Harry to all those other men, at least for now.

But would Helen ever like that farm life he so envisioned? The quiet evenings, the small community? He was not at all sure. Perhaps that was what really held him back now.

Again he saw Miss Parker's sweet smile, felt her gentle touch on his hand, but he pushed such thoughts away.

'She agrees we should wait until I can resign my commission and we can see what happens next,' he said.

Charles shook his head, frowning. 'You should be careful, then, Harry. While you are gone on your adventures, someone else could easily pluck up such a prize. They do say that the Duke of Hamley, now that his time of mourning is at an end, seeks a new duchess.'

Harry laughed. Duchess—now there was a role that would suit Helen well. 'No one would make a better duchess than Helen.'

Charles was silent for a long, tense moment. 'I would never have taken you for a fool, Harry.'

Before Harry could answer, their carriage turned through the gates of Hilltop Grange and jolted up the winding old drive, past the overgrown forest that had once been a manicured garden under the careful eye of their mother.

Now, Hilltop looked nothing like the golden welcome of Barton Park, which had seemed to float above the night like a cloud of light. Hilltop had no light at all, save the glow of one lamp in the window of the library. Harry knew that once daylight came, the overgrown ivy on the grey stone walls, the crumbling chimneys, the covered windows, would all be too apparent. He felt again that deep pang of sadness, of guilt for following a different duty.

But that one light meant their father was still awake, or more likely fallen asleep next to his empty brandy bottle. He seldom left the library now.

'Our great inheritance,' Charles said, his tone quiet and bitter.

Harry gave a grim nod. 'I am sorry, Charles. I should have been here all along.'

Charles glanced at him, his expression startled. 'Oh, no, Harry, never. You are doing what you have to—your duty to King and Country as you are called to do. No one has been more dutiful than you, ever since we were children.'

He thought again of what their home had once been, what it was now. 'I don't know about that.'

'Well, I do. Whatever I face here with Father is as nothing compared to whatever you have faced all these years. Besides, I'm seldom here at Hilltop at all these days.' He grinned and that strange, solemn, thoughtful Charles vanished. The rakish, fun-loving young man everyone knew was back. 'London is much more diverting. Why would a man ever live anywhere else?'

'Diverting—and expensive,' Harry muttered, but he couldn't help laughing at Charles's devil-may-care smile. It was always thus with his younger brother, their mother's golden boy. While Charles was the fun one, Harry had indeed always been the responsible one. The quiet one.

Charles shrugged. 'What else can one do? I would be wretched in the army, worse than useless. The church would never have me.'

'What of your painting?' he asked, remembering the rare talent Charles once possessed with a brush, the way he could capture the mood of a landscape in a few deft strokes of paint.

Charles laughed. 'A boy's diversion. Not fit for a grown man, y'know.'

'According to who? Our father?' Harry asked quietly.

Rather than answer, Charles pushed open the carriage door as soon as they came to a full halt and jumped down. Harry followed him up the shallow stone steps into the echoing hall of Hilltop Grange. In the shadows, the portraits of their ancestors, including their golden-haired mother, watched them in silence. In the rooms beyond, the furniture was shrouded in canvas covers, like ghosts. Their mother's cherished pianoforte was silent.

For just an instant, Harry had such a different vision of the house, light gleaming on polished wood. The warmth of the fire, the scent of flowers from the gardens, the rush of small feet down the stairs, music. But the lady who turned from the keyboard to welcome him with a smile—her eyes were the sweet, soft hazel of Rose Parker.

'Father, wake up!' Charles shouted, banging on the library door with his fist. The dream was shattered, like the dust of Hilltop itself.

Chapter One

❦

Winter, three years later

*'Jouissons dans nos asiles, jouissons de biens tran-
quilles! Ah, peut-on être heureux, quand on forme
d'autres vouex?'*

'That's quite enough!' Aunt Sylvia shouted from
her armchair near the fire, where she was swathed
in shawls and a fur blanket. Her three lapdogs
shifted and barked. 'What a wretched song by that
horrid Rameau. Why would you play such a thing?'

Rose sighed and rested her wrists on the edge
of the keyboard as the last notes died away in the
overheated drawing room of Aunt Sylvia's vast
house. She would have laughed if she wasn't quite
so tired. She removed her spectacles and rubbed at
her eyes. In her years of working as Aunt Sylvia's
companion, she had come to learn no moment was
predictable. A favourite food one day, which had

to be ordered from London and fetched from the village shop, a two-mile walk, by Rose every day, would not be wanted once it arrived. An expensive pelisse would be dismissed as too itchy, then needed again. The wheeled Bath chair would have to be fetched for a walk in the garden, only to be greeted with shouts of 'What do you think I am, an old invalid? I shall walk! Give me your arm immediately, Rose. You cannot be rid of me so easily, you know, you silly girl.'

Rose did not want to be rid of Aunt Sylvia. She paid a wage that kept Rose's mother in her cottage, now that Lily and Mr Hewlitt had two children to take care of in their small vicarage and Mama's small income seemed even smaller than ever. Her mother deserved to stay in her own home and Rose had to work to make it so. But Rose *did* wish Aunt Sylvia would make up her mind for once.

'I thought you always enjoyed the old French songs, Aunt,' she said. 'Because they reminded you of your time at Versailles.'

In her youth, Aunt Sylvia had once waited upon Queen Marie Antoinette, before she married the wealthy Mr Pemberton and returned to England. She spoke of it all the time and definitely never let anyone forget it, with her grey hair piled high and panniers strangely paired with newer, higher waists and puffed sleeves.

'Why would I want to hear songs that remind me of such a terrible loss?' Aunt Sylvia said, thumping her walking stick on the floor. One of the dogs barked. 'You young people, you know nothing of such things. Nothing of how fortunate you all are.'

Rose suddenly remembered Captain St George and their dance at the midsummer party so long ago, the haunted look in his dark eyes as he mentioned battle and seemed to remember Waterloo. She had thought of him too often in the years since, especially in the long, quiet nights as she lay awake waiting for Aunt Sylvia to call her. Had he married the beautiful Miss Layton, had he come back from battle and found peace at last? She couldn't help but hope so.

She glanced out the window, out the slim rectangle of thick glass revealed between the heavy brocade curtains Aunt Sylvia kept closed all the time. It had started snowing, a light, lacy, delicate pattern of white against the night sky. It reminded her that it was nearly December, nearly the Christmas season, and she wondered what her mother, what Lily and her little family, were doing now.

Lily and her babies were surely decorating their small sitting room with greenery, baking plum cakes to carry to Mr Hewlitt's parishioners. Perhaps her mother was embroidering new little gowns to wrap up for her grandchildren's gifts.

She felt the familiar pang of sadness of missing them and she had to remind herself why she had to work in the first place.

'Perhaps I could play you a Christmas carol or two, Aunt Sylvia?' she said. 'It is nearly that season.'

'Christmas!' Aunt Sylvia cried. 'Don't even talk to me about the wretched thing. Play some Mozart. You know how I always like that.'

Except for when she called Mozart an overrated performing monkey of a boy. Rose smothered a laugh, and launched into the 'Allegro' from *Marriage of Figaro*. Just as she always could, she soon lost herself in the music, and the harsh world of Aunt Sylvia's house, her loneliness for her family, vanished. She floated in her own realm, above everything else.

One day, she thought with a happy smile, perhaps she would have her own home with her own pianoforte. Could play whatever she chose, while her family listened...

The piece ended and Rose felt as if she was pushed out of that magical, floating world into the stuffy drawing room. Suddenly all she could hear were the snores of her aunt, mixed with the softer snuffles of the dogs and the crackle of the flames as a log collapsed into ashes in the grate. She remembered how her childhood home had once collapsed, how such things were always dreams.

She peeked over her shoulder to find Aunt Sylvia had indeed fallen asleep, her head lolling back on her cushioned chair. Hardly daring to breathe, for fear she would awaken everyone and prolong the evening, Rose carefully lowered the lid of the pianoforte over the keys and slid off the stool. She cautiously tiptoed over to make sure Aunt Sylvia's shawls were still warmly tucked around her, and then crept out of the drawing room. She found Miss Powell, her aunt's long-suffering maid, waiting outside.

Rose gave her a nod, which Miss Powell tersely returned, and at last Rose could make her way up the stairs to her own chamber. It was not a large room at all, barely big enough for a narrow bed, a washstand and her trunk, and it looked down on the frost-covered kitchen gardens, but it was at least her own. In the cottage at home, she had shared with Lily until they could build on an extra room and her sister's feet at night were always freezing.

And then she missed her sister and mother all over again.

'Don't be such a goose,' she told herself sternly. Surely it was only the Christmas season making her feel so melancholy now, so homesick. She had too much to do to worry about Mama and Lily now. Aunt Sylvia would want her up early as usual, writing letters and walking the dogs.

As she dug around in her clothes trunk for her night chemise, hoping her sheets wouldn't be too chilled by the time she crawled between them, there was a knock at the door. Surprised anyone would be about at that hour—Aunt Sylvia dined early and only Miss Powell stayed up to help her retire—she hurried to answer it.

One of the young housemaids stood there, yawning into her apron. 'Beg your pardon, miss, but these came for you by the afternoon post, but I forgot to give them to you. We do get that busy with the tea things…'

Rose shuddered to remember the row with Aunt Sylvia and the undercooked almond cakes that afternoon. 'That is quite all right, thank you.' She took the letters eagerly as the maid hurried away.

One from Lily, she saw, recognising her sister's hurried scrawl. And one with a grander seal, pressed into fashionable green wax. *Barton Park*, the return address read.

A letter from Barton! Rose felt the warm touch of excitement, and not a little tinge of curiosity. She hadn't heard from Barton Park in quite some time. She knew Jane had been busy with having little heirs to the earldom, and Emma had recently married David Marton, one of their neighbours.

Rose quickly changed into her nightdress, carefully laying aside her sensible grey-silk gown, and climbed into bed to read the precious missives. She opened the one from Barton first. It was written in elegant dark green ink on thick, creamy stationery.

My dear Miss Parker—or may I call you Cousin Rose?

I am so sorry we have not met since Cousin Lily's wedding. We do miss your family so much and speak often of how your letters

*make us laugh. Your tales of being with Aunt
Sylvia—dear lady, but, well, she is Aunt Sylvia after all—are better than a comic novel
and cheer us to no end. You are a brave lady
indeed.*

*We also speak often of that lovely midsum-
mer ball when Lily and her vicar became en-
gaged. It seems so very long since Barton has
enjoyed such an evening.*

*Hayden has duties in the House of Lords
which often take him to London, and as you
know we now have four dear children—William, Eleanor, Emma and baby Edward.*

*Emma and David are also expecting a
happy occasion soon and Emma still has her
little bookshop in the village. She does insist
on scrambling up and down the library lad-
ders, frightening her husband no end, but she
declares she has never felt better in her life!*

*I do envy her. My own times bring nothing
but sleepiness. I often nod off by the fire quite
like Aunt Sylvia!*

Rose smiled at the image of Jane, nodding off by
the fire as her children dashed about. She pushed
away the hint of envy such an image gave her and
continued reading.

*In short, dear Cousin Rose, I have a great
favour to ask. Emma and I have decided to*

*revive our old Barton parties, this time for
the Christmas holidays. It has indeed been a
long time since we had such festivities here
and the children would so enjoy it.*

*Their governess, though, wishes to return
to her family for a few weeks and I am quite
overwhelmed. If Aunt Sylvia could spare you,
and if you think you could bear us and our
noise, would a position here suit you for a
time?*

*I remember how you loved music and my
own little Eleanor shows great talent at the
pianoforte and harp already. Aunt Sylvia is,
of course, invited as well, if she can ever leave
her own hearth. Fingers crossed that she is
quite comfortable in situ, though!*

*I do hope so, dear Rose, as we would
dearly love to see you again and have your
assistance with our little monsters. If you like
us, perhaps a longer stay here at Barton might
be possible?*

With much hope,

Your cousin, Jane Ramsay

Rose lowered the letter with a thoughtful frown.
She well remembered when they discovered the
disaster of her late father's debts, the wreck of her
mother's annuity and the near loss of their cottage.
Jane had been all that was kind at the time, offering assistance of every sort from financial gifts to

a new home at Barton. Yet Rose and her mother had been so loathe to take charity, even from family. The position with Aunt Sylvia was just that—a position, with wages for tasks and long hours. Not perfect, not merry or fun, but it got them by and let her mother stay in her home.

She wondered if Jane's offer now was also charity, carefully disguised as a temporary governess–music teacher position, but she found she didn't quite care. She closed her eyes and remembered Barton Park, how pretty it was, how welcoming, how full of fun. She remembered her dance there with Captain St George, the bright, hopeful way he had made her feel. Maybe she would find a spark of that again, there at Barton at Christmas?

She tucked the letter under her pillow, along with Lily's to save for a morning treat, and blew out her candle. She closed her eyes again and hoped to dream of music and mistletoe and dances with handsome partners…

'Jane, surely it is nearly midnight. Put that away and come to bed,' Hayden Fitzwalter, Earl of Ramsay, said, patting at the feather pillows next to him on their large, luxurious feather mattress.

Jane laughed, but she didn't look up from the pile of papers on her writing desk. She knew if she saw her gorgeous husband, his dark hair tousled, half-naked in their lovely warm bed, she would never finish her work at all. Even after years of marriage, those gorgeous blue eyes of his were too tempting indeed.

'I only have a few more invitations to write and they must go out with the morning post,' she said, her pen scratching over her creamy paper. 'We are going to have the grandest Christmas house party Barton Park has ever seen! We will have carols and wassail, and sleigh rides…'

Hayden laughed. 'Sleigh rides? What if there is no snow, my love?'

'Then we shall make some. It's the first Christmas we've all been together at Barton in ages.' They spent most of their time now in London, or at Hayden's earldom seat. But Barton, where her own parents had once been so happy and raised Emma and herself in a golden childhood, was always home. 'When Emma and I were children, our parents made the holidays so magical. Such games and music, and wonderful sweets on the tables. Green wreaths and dancing. I want it to be just like that now for the children.'

'And so it shall be, if *you* will it so. Everything you create in our lives is magic, my love.'

She looked over at him and smiled. 'Our lives *are* magical—now. If I can help someone else find the same thing…'

'Ah, I see.' His tone was full of smug satisfaction and he crossed his arms behind his head as he laid back on the pillows. 'Trying a bit of matchmaking, are you? Who do you and Emma have in mind now?'

Jane pursed her lips. 'No one at all, of course. If people just happen to meet at our party and just happen to like each other—well, how can that be a bad thing? Magical things *do* happen at Christmas.'

'So they do. Who are you inviting, then?'

Jane glanced over her list and named a few of their London friends she thought might enjoy Barton. Her old family house was small compared to Hayden's grand seat and there was not space for very many. There was definitely no space for Hayden's old rakish friends, from the dark days before they mended their marriage and started their family.

'Also, Mr and Mrs Hewlitt, though I'm not sure he can be spared from his clerical duties for the holiday,' she said.

'That is too bad. I remember when they became betrothed at Barton.'

'I know, wasn't it terribly sweet?' Jane said. 'I also asked her sister, Miss Rose Parker. I'm sure you remember her, too.'

'Of course. A most sensible and cheerful lady. Her performance of Beethoven at the pianoforte was impressive.'

'I hope she is still sensible and cheerful. She has been working as companion to Sylvia Pemberton.'

'Oh, that poor girl!' Hayden exclaimed. 'Will the kraken release its captive to come to Barton?'

'I am afraid I performed a bit of a subterfuge, since I know how proud Rose is and how their family has been brought so low of late. I told her we would need a governess for the children while Miss Essex is gone for the holidays and that Eleanor shows a proficiency for music, which she does.'

'Jane! You've just moved her from working for one monster to four.'

Jane laughed. 'Hayden! They are very well-behaved children, everyone says so.'

'Well behaved in public, maybe,' Hayden muttered, but Jane could hear the affectionate pride in his voice.

'The nursemaids will all still be here. I did have to lure Rose here somehow, or she wouldn't leave Aunt Sylvia and would have a miserable Christmas.' And there would be no chances for her to meet eligible young men if she didn't come to the party.

'Quite right. Who else have you invited, then?'

Jane hesitated as she looked down at the last invitation on her desk. 'The St George brothers, at Hilltop.'

'Is that quite wise? Harry has not been home long, and he has not received any visitors yet. He might not be quite—recovered.'

'When Dr Heath called last week, he told me he found Captain St George's health to be much improved last time he was at Hilltop, though not entirely as he once was, of course. A Christmas party might be just the chance to cheer him up! After all

he has been through—being wounded and losing
Miss Layton...'

'You mean Lady Fallon?' Hayden said quietly.

'The Dowager Lady Fallon now, not that it matters,' Jane answered. That sudden marriage, after
Captain St George left for Sicily, had surprised everyone. But if Jane had learned one thing in life, it
was that everyone had secrets they hid deep down
inside. Everyone deserved a second chance. 'If the
Captain does not yet feel like a party, he can always refuse. But I am inviting him, as well as his
brother, Charles, who I hear is back from the Continent now.' And Charles had always been such fun;
maybe Rose Parker could use a bit of that fun in
her life.

'You must do what you think best, my love. Yet
now it really *is* time to come to bed. It grows much
too late.'

'And much too cold, with you so far over there,'
she said with a laugh, thinking how lucky they were
indeed to have had their own second chance. Their
life together.

She sealed up the last invitation, the one bound
for Hilltop Grange, and snuffed out the candles before she hurried into the warm haven of her husband's loving arms.

Chapter Two

'Aye, 'tis a pity. Hilltop Grange was once so grand. Now look at it. Falling to bits.'

'Some who has it all haven't the sense to appreciate it. Fritter it all away. Shameful.'

'Oh, you two,' the barmaid tsked to the two old men as she plopped fresh pints down on their sticky, scarred table. 'Always grumbling 'bout something and not doing a thing about it. Now that the Captain is back…'

'Will he be any better than that brother of his? Or the father?' one old man muttered. 'Been gone for years, ain't he?'

'He has to care, doesn't he? Hilltop is his estate now,' the barmaid said as she turned away, wiping her hands on her apron. The two old men returned to the weather, to the threat of snow in the air.

None of them seemed to notice Harry sitting quietly in the darkest corner of the pub, the new owner of Hilltop Grange, nursing his ale and pondering what he had to do next.

He took a long drink from his tankard, but even that did not warm him. A few snowflakes drifted past the grimy windows, landing lightly on the cobbled streets of the village outside. A few people hurried past, stepping out of the greenery-bedecked shops, their arms laden with Christmas packages, laughing together in holiday cheer, brushing the snow off their cloaks and hats.

It wasn't the grey winter sky that made him feel so cold, or the joy in the coming holiday that he saw in others but barely remembered ever having himself. It was a numbness at his very core that had probably always been there, ever since Waterloo, when he realised the true ugliness of life.

No, he thought in sudden, startled remembrance. It hadn't *always* been thus. For one moment, long ago, it had lifted, like a tiny spark of sun through those clouds. When he held a hazel-eyed girl in his arms for a dance, and she laughed with him, those eyes shining with her enjoyment of the music and of all the life around them. He knew just for a small instant, with her, the sweetness he was really fighting for.

Miss Rose Parker. That was her name. And she'd looked like a rose, too, with the faint pink in her pale cheeks. Surely she was Mrs Rose Some-Other-Surname now, with a baby in her arms. Whoever he was—well, he was a lucky bloke indeed. Harry just hoped he appreciated what he had.

He touched the black patch over his lost eye, feeling the roughness of the skin around it, the scar that curved its way almost to his jaw. What would Rose Parker think if she saw him now? Would her smiles turn to startled fear, to quickly averted glances just like everyone else? Just like it had with Helen?

Harry gave a humourless little laugh. No, not Helen. She'd left long before the wounds; she'd left when someone with more to offer, with a title even, came around. Not that Harry could blame her, not a bit. Being a soldier's wife would never have suited Helen, no matter how much she once protested otherwise, how much their families wished otherwise. And now with Hilltop in the state it was…

Harry finished his tankard and pushed back his chair. Speaking of Hilltop, he knew he should be getting back there. He had lingered in the village too long after his visit to the lawyer Mr Wall. Hilltop would never have its roof and windows fixed by sitting around in taverns. The problem was—he wasn't sure yet how to fix it all. He knew the army, that was all. Now he had to learn how to be a landlord to a crumbled estate.

The barmaid appeared at his side. She looked at him with a twinge of pity in her eyes, but she didn't turn away.

'Another pint, then, Captain?' she said. 'Or maybe

some wine? We just got some bottles, special for the season.'

He gave her a smile. 'Not today, Nell, but next time. And it's just Mr now, not Captain.'

He left the tavern, striding past the grumbling old men without a word and out into the world. For an instant, his eye was dazzled by the bright grey glare of the light after the dim tavern. He pulled the brim of his hat lower and raised the collar of his greatcoat against the cold breeze. He was still trying to become accustomed to the way having sight in only one eye distorted the horizon.

The village was not a large one, but it was very busy at that time of day, as shoppers finished their last-minute errands before hurrying home to their warm fires. He knew every shop from when he was a child—the butcher, where Christmas geese and hams now waited in his window, the dressmaker, where his mother had had so many gowns sewn up, the confectioner, from whom he and Charles used to steal lemon drops.

All the doors were wreathed in greenery now, all the window displays decked in bows. The Christmas atmosphere of his home village was so very familiar, but so very alien at the same time. A dream world.

Harry turned towards the livery stable where he had left his horse. On the corner, an old man was selling bouquets of mistletoe and holly tied with red ribbon, and Harry impulsively bought one. He wasn't sure what he would do with it, but for a moment the red brightened his thoughts.

He passed by the bookshop that had once been owned by old Mr Lorne, but which he had heard now belonged to Emma Bancroft, or Lady Marton as she had become. He paused to examine the display in her bow window, the leather-bound volumes with their gilded lettering gleaming, the boxes of fine stationery. He remembered his mother going there every month for her new stock of novels from London.

The shop door swung open with a jangle of bells, and Emma Marton hurried out, nearly bumping into him. The young girl behind her, who must be her stepdaughter, the young Beatrice Marton, caught her as she stumbled and laughed. Emma looked as if she had not aged at all while he'd been gone, her blond curls still as sunny, her smile still dimpled. Like the village, she seemed to have stayed still while he felt centuries older.

But not everything had stayed the same. Under the folds of her green-velvet cloak, he could see the small bump of a child, one of the growing brood of Bancroft Park.

He remembered how once Barton had seemed as crumbling and lonely as Hilltop, and the Bancroft sisters had raised it back life. It gave him a spark of hope now to think of it.

'Oh, Harry!' Emma cried, her gaze flickering over his scarred face and then quickly away. 'How perfectly wonderful to see you home. We all so feared for your health when—well, when we heard what happened and…well—' Her words broke off and she blushed under the brim of her feathered bonnet.

He smiled down at her. 'I left one or two bits behind on the battlefield, but am now in good health, thank you, Emma. As I see are you. You are quite blooming.'

She laughed, turning even pinker. 'Oh, yes! In a few months, Bea here will be a sister again. You do remember Miss Beatrice Marton, my stepdaughter?'

The girl dropped a shy little curtsy as Harry bowed. She was a pretty thing, with dark hair smooth under her hood and sweet eyes; one day she would surely break hearts. 'Of course. How do you do, Miss Marton?'

'I am quite well, thank you, Captain St George.'

'I couldn't do without Bea's help at home and here at the shop,' Emma said proudly, taking Beatrice's hand. 'Especially now that Christmas is so near. I do hope we will see you at Barton.'

'I'm afraid there is still much to do at Hilltop,' he answered. Christmas was for family and good cheer, not for staring at wounded soldiers. He did not want to be the ghost at the feast.

'Oh, but you must,' Beatrice said warmly. 'There can surely be nothing merrier than the holiday Aunt

Jane has planned. Games and sleigh rides and plum pudding…'

'Oh, Bea, I'm sure Captain St George knows how he wants to spend his holiday,' Emma said, squeezing her stepdaughter's hand. 'But do know you are always most welcome at our homes, Harry, any time at all.'

'Thank you, Emma. That does mean much to me.' He impulsively handed her the bouquet of greenery he had bought. 'Happy Christmas.'

He turned and walked away, but when he glanced back Emma was watching him with a thoughtful frown. She quickly smiled and waved the bouquet, the red ribbon a banner of brightness against the grey day.

Unlike the village, Hilltop did not bustle with holiday preparations and cheer. The windows were blank in the gathering twilight as Harry rode up the overgrown lane; no smoke curled from the crumbling chimneys. There were, however, a few more fallen roof slates on the portico and in the tangled flowerbeds.

As Harry swung down from the saddle, he studied the house and for just an instant he remembered what it had been like in his mother's day, with the flowers blooming and bright against the pale grey walls, curtains elegant in every window. He could imagine a lady like Rose Parker in such a house, but not this one.

Then he blinked and the fantasy of a smiling lady welcoming him home was replaced with reality once more.

He left his horse with the young stable lad, one of the few servants left at Hilltop along with their ancient butler Jenkins, and hurried up the front steps into the darkening house. The doors to the drawing room and music room were firmly shut, the few pieces of furniture in the hall shrouded in dust cloths. Yet it was not quite as silent as he expected. The door to the library was half-open, and a bar of amber-gold spilled out. He heard the clink of heavy crystal, as if a decanter had just been plonked down on a table.

Curious, and not a little irritated that someone would break into his solitude uninvited, Harry tossed his hat and gloves on to the nearest canvas-covered table and strode towards the library.

The room was just as he had left it, half-empty and dusty, most of the books sold or packed away, but his brother, Charles, sat behind their father's desk. His dark gold hair was over-long and mussed, his buff travel coat dusty and a half-empty brandy bottle sat before him.

He looked up and Harry saw that his blue eyes were rimmed with red. He remembered the last time he'd seen Charles, when his brother was leaving for the Continent. To paint, he said, but more likely to get away from their father. 'My brother! The returning hero,' Charles called, raising his almost empty glass. 'Let me pour you a drink. You probably need it after meeting with old Mr Wall. That's where Jenkins said you were, anyway.'

Harry sat down across from him, stretching his long legs before him. He had learned long ago not to wonder about Charles's comings and goings. 'I've just come from the tavern and it looks as if you've already started the celebrating.'

Charles examined his glass. 'So I have. 'Tis the merry season, after all.'

'So everyone keeps telling me. Where have you been lately, Charlie?'

'Oh, here and there. Italy mostly. Then some German spa towns. Until I heard you were home.'

'Not doing your art, then?' Harry asked. Charles had always been a masterful artist, one who could be a professional in Harry's uneducated opinion, though their father had scoffed at it all.

Charles frowned. 'No, not really. Too busy with other matters.'

Harry nodded, but he said nothing. He didn't really want to know what those 'other matters' were.

Charles poured them each another measure. 'What did Wall say?'

Harry took a deep drink of the brandy. It was the last of their father's stock and not bad at all as it burned down his throat. 'About what you would expect he would say. Mother's money was spent long ago and there are debts on the estate.'

Charles sighed. 'I think there is only one solution, then, my dear brother.'

Harry laughed. 'Sell Hilltop and go back in the army? They don't want a one-eyed captain. Maybe you could get a job in the City?'

Charles shuddered. 'Lud, no. How appalling. I could never have a job, and I certainly don't want my brother nearly killed again.'

'I'm glad you care.' Harry thought of how it was when they were children, running together through the fields, jumping into the pond. And how far apart they were now.

''Course I do. You're the only brother I have. And I don't think we *can* sell Hilltop.'

'Indeed not. Even if it weren't entailed in the St George family, no one would want it.'

'Exactly. Ghastly old pile.'

'Then what is your solution?'

'Very simple. You must marry an heiress,' Charles said.

Harry laughed even harder. 'You always did have a fine way with a joke, Charlie.'

Charles scowled. 'I am absolutely serious. A lady, one with style and a fine dowry, would fix things in a trice.'

Harry shook his head. Even before he was wounded, his wooing skills had not been the greatest. To think of trying to win a fair, rich lady now— he laughed again. 'Who would you suggest, then?

Has a blind heiress come on to the market, perhaps? One who could tolerate a scarred old soldier?'

'You've always been far more handsome than you would admit, Harry. And now you're a wounded warrior. Ladies love that.' Charles paused to stare down into his glass. 'Helen Layton is recently widowed, you know. They say her husband left her well set-up indeed.'

Harry's smile faded and he swallowed the last of his drink. 'You know that was over long ago. I think *you* are the one who will have to find an heiress, Charlie. You always enjoyed society much more than me, anyway. You could take up painting again. Or you could go back to the Continent to look among the spas and casinos.'

'I doubt we would have to go so far. This came while you were out.' Charles slapped a letter down on the desk.

Harry gave it a suspicious glance. 'What is it? Another dunning letter?'

'Of course not. It's an invitation to a Christmas house party at Barton Park. Jane says there will be several ladies there, old friends and new.'

'Ah,' Harry muttered, pushing aside his glass. *Games and sleigh rides and plum pudding.* 'So that's what she meant.'

'She?'

'I saw Emma Marton in the village, she said something about Barton for the holiday. Thought it might be a good distraction.' And it might, he thought through the slight haze of the brandy as he studied the crumbling plaster of the ceiling. Anything would be better than looking at this room any longer.

'Well, I suppose somehow, some way, we have to try and save Hilltop,' Charles said. 'I know I've always been a useless wastrel, but...'

'No,' Harry said decisively. 'I am the eldest and this is indeed our family's home. We do have to save it and everyone who depends on it along with it. I will find a way.' *No matter what.*

Chapter Three

We are having a true, merry, family sort of holiday here at Barton Park, where we hope to see all our old friends.

We have not seen you seen you since Lord Fitzwalter attended Lord Fallon's funeral and we hope that your mourning will not deprive us of your company.

Her *mourning.* Helen, Dowager Lady Fallon, laughed as she dropped Jane Ramsay's letter at the side of the bathtub. She sank deeper into the rose-scented water and stared up at the painted tile ceiling of her bathing room in her London town house. Everyone had thought it so extravagant when she'd had it built on to her dressing room, with its marble walls and painted fireplace. But it was her favourite place, a small, cosy space where no one would bother her.

She had once thought being Lady Fallon would be a grand thing indeed, a life of ease and grandeur, full of pretty gowns and parties and fun. So different from her own family, their façade of liveliness and prosperity that hid a distinct lack of funds. She had given up Harry St George, so handsome and gallant, to marry a man thirty years older in order to get that life. But being Lady Fallon had not been what she'd expected.

It hadn't been worth it.

Helen sat up in the tub, the water frothing around her, and caught a glimpse of herself in her gilt-framed mirror. Her golden hair, curling with the damp air, her pink and white skin, it was all still youthful and beautiful. And she did have old Lord Fallon's money now, too. Surely it was not too late for her?

She reached for the letter again. *Old friends.* Did that mean Harry St George would be there? She had heard he had returned to England, more heroic than ever. What could she not do in society, with her new money and a war hero at her side?

Maybe a Christmas in the country was just what she needed.

Charles St George swirled the brandy in his glass and stared out into the darkness of the night. Winter clouds had lowered, extinguishing the stars and moonlight, but that was good. In the darkness, the shambles of the garden at Hilltop, the garden their mother had once so loved, that he had painted so many times, could not be seen. It was just a blank, like everything else.

It was quiet, a lot like the way he felt inside, Charles thought as he took another drink. As if he watched the world from a great distance, not caring particularly what happened one way or another.

That was the real reason why he had drifted around the Continent for so long. Their father had so often declared him useless, why not be so? Harry had escaped it all in the army. Charles had once tried to escape in art, which he loved but could not ultimately find fulfilling, and then in spa towns.

But now, back here at Hilltop with his brother again, he found he *did* care. And it ate at him. Harry had given so much; he deserved more than a wastrel brother and a falling-down house that had once been loved. He just wished to heaven he knew what to do.

Perhaps Christmas at Barton Park would be a good thing. A bit of merriment amongst other people, other families, away from the constant blankness.

'Fa-la-la-la-la...' he muttered and finished off his brandy.

Chapter Four

'Barton Park is just ahead, miss. Nearly there now,' the coachman called out as they slowed at the crest of a hill.

Rose leaned out the window, eager for a glimpse of the house of which she had such happy memories. It hadn't been an unpleasant journey, with a valise full of books to read and no Aunt Sylvia shouting out demands, but it *had* been a cold one. The winter wind did like to nip through her mended gloves and snatch at her cloak. Surely there would be a good fire waiting at Barton.

But she found she was a bit nervous as well. It had been years since she saw her cousins last—what were they like now? What would they think of her?

They passed through an open iron gate, beautifully wrought and crowned with a gilded B. The drive was a long, winding one, designed at the height of the craze for picturesque landscapes under Jane and Emma's scholarly father, and Rose was enchanted by the view. Even in winter, with all the trees bare and frost thick on the ground, it was lovely.

As the coach meandered past groves of trees and hedges, she glimpsed pale marble statues, like ghosts in the grey day. In the distance, she saw the *chinoiserie* peaks of an old summerhouse and the stone walls that marked off Rose Hill, Emma's husband's estate next door. She remembered playing on those grounds as child, looking for treasure in the medieval ruins of the cold castle.

Suddenly there was a fork in the lane and they turned off to find the house itself.

It was not a large house, but it was a romantic one, warm and welcoming with its time-mellowed red-brick walls, its grey stone front steps and inlaid stone patterns around the windows. Smoke curled from the chimney in fragrant, silvery plumes. The doors were decorated with green wreaths tied with golden bows and evergreen plants lined the portico in silver-stained pots.

Much to Rose's surprise, as the coach rolled to a stop the front doors opened and a veritable herd of children tumbled out. The two tallest were obviously the twins, William and Eleanor, and they led two smaller children, probably Emma and Edward, and Eleanor held a toddler by the hand whose golden curls looked like those of her mother, Emma Marton. They were bundled against the cold in a bright, jewel-like cluster of green- and blue-velvet coats and cloaks.

The coachman lowered the steps and helped Rose to alight, and as soon as her boots touched the gravel the children launched into song.

"'Good King Wenceslaus looked out, on the feast of Stephen! When the snow lay round about, deep and crisp and even...'"

Rose couldn't help but laugh in delight at the sweet sound of their voices, carried by the cold, clear air. It seemed to encourage them to sing even louder, until they reached the end on a long, carrying note.

"'...gath'ring winter fu-u-uel!'"

'Welcome to Barton,' the tallest girl said. She stepped forward with a little curtsy, presenting Rose with a mistletoe bouquet.

Rose curtsied back, charmed by the song—and, she admitted, a little relieved, after the stories some of her friends who were governesses told about wild children ransacking workboxes and setting loose mice.

'That was most beautifully sung,' she said. 'I am sure not even one of the royal princesses could expect a finer welcome.'

'Oh, we've been practising for days and days!' the oldest boy said. 'We have a different song for every guest. You're the first one to arrive. Would you like to hear another? Mother said you're very good at music.'

Jane appeared in the doorway and laid a gentle hand on her son's shoulder. She did not look like a grand countess, Rose thought, with her hair pinned up in loose curls and a soft Indian shawl wrapped over her muslin day dress. She looked like the cousin she always remembered. 'William, dearest, I am sure Miss Parker is weary from her journey and wants to come in from the cold.'

'Oh, of course!' young William cried and the children surrounded her to sweep her into the hall. It had the same air of elegant informality as the outside of the house, with its black and white tiled floor softened by bright rugs. The balustrade of the staircase that swept up to the next story seemed bright and newly gilded, lined with a blue and gold carpet runner, the blue silk-striped walls were lined with blue satin chairs tossed with red cushions. A marble-topped table held a large bouquet of holly and ivy, which cast their fresh, green scent into the warm air.

Jane kissed Rose's cheeks, clasping her hands in welcome. 'Rose, my dear, I cannot tell you how happy I am to see you again! And how grateful for your help. With a houseful of guests on the way, I would not know how to manage with this pack of ruffians.'

Rose untied and removed her grey bonnet, studying the smiling, rosy-cheeked children around them. 'They look civilised enough to me.'

Jane laughed. 'That's only because they are on

their best party behaviour at the moment. These are
my eldest, the twins, William and Eleanor, who is
quite the budding musician,' she said, as the children made their bows. 'And little Emma and my
baby Edward, who is not such a baby now. The littlest is Emma's girl Martha. Emma has gone into
the village with Beatrice, her lovely stepdaughter,
to see about her bookshop, but will be here for dinner with her husband later.'

Rose smiled as she watched them, remembering
their song and their promise of more. 'William said
guests will be arriving soon?'

'Oh, yes, most of them by teatime, I hope.
You are the first,' Jane said. She reached out and
straightened the vase of greenery. 'So you will have
plenty of time to rest before the merriment begins
in earnest! I told Hannah, our old housekeeper,
whom I am sure you remember, to make sure you
have a good fire and some tea in your room. Perhaps a warm bath? I do hope the journey was not
too chilling.'

Rose's head was whirling with all the information. 'I—not at all, Lady Ramsay.'

'Oh, Jane, please! We are family.'

'Jane,' Rose answered carefully. She remembered
Jane's letter, how it had asked for her help with the
children, especially in teaching them music, but it
felt like she was being welcomed at Barton as another guest. 'Are the children to make an appearance before dinner?'

'We have to do our songs!' William declared. 'We've been practising them so much, Mother.'

Jane laughed again, and ruffled her son's dark hair. 'I know, my darling, we have heard you. Yes, the children may come down for a while, and as a special treat William and Eleanor can dine with us tonight as it will be very informal. We have to choose the King of the Bean, after all.'

Eleanor clasped Rose's hand and whispered an explanation. 'The King of the Bean is the one who finds the bean in the special cake at dinner tonight and then they will rule over what we do for the rest of the festivities!'

'Oh, I see,' Rose answered. 'Like the Lord of Misrule?'

'Only not as wild, I hope,' Jane said.

'Well, I think it all sounds merry indeed,' said Rose. 'What time should I have them prepared to come downstairs, then, Jane?'

Jane waved her hand. 'The nursemaids will see to all that. Just come down with them when you're ready. We'll just be a small, cosy party tonight, with Emma and her family, and the vicar and his wife. Oh, and the St George brothers! I am sure you remember Harry and Charles. I was so happy to persuade them to join us this holiday, they seem intent on becoming hermits over at Hilltop.'

'The—the St Georges?' Rose whispered, feeling her cheeks turn warm as she was caught by surprise. Of course she had thought—feared—she might see Harry St George that holiday, as their home was so near Barton, but she hadn't expected to hear his name quite so soon, before she could prepare herself.

'You've gone all pink, Miss Parker,' Eleanor whispered.

'It—it must be warm in here,' she answered faintly.

Luckily, she was saved from answering further by the arrival of an older lady in stiff black silk, keys jangling at her waist from an old-fashioned chatelaine.

'This is Hannah, our dear housekeeper who has been at Barton for ever,' Jane said. 'She will see you to your room. You must take all the time you need to rest before you take on my wee monsters.'

'Mama!' Eleanor protested. 'Miss Parker will think we are most unruly.'

Rose laughed, pushing away thoughts of Harry as she tried to remember what she was really there for—the children and their music. 'Indeed I will not. You seem entirely ladylike to me, Lady Eleanor.'

'If you'll follow me, then, Miss Parker,' Hannah said, as Jane took her children's hands and led them into the drawing room. 'You've been given the yellow room, it's near to the nursery.'

'Of course.' Rose followed the housekeeper up the stairs and down a long corridor, past closed doors and a few open ones where maids bustled about preparing the rooms for their guests. Her own chamber was close to the end of the hall and when Hannah opened the door she saw it was small but lovely. The white-painted bed was covered with a yellow-satin counterpane and draped with pale yellow and green striped silk, as was the small dressing table where a maid was already laying out her toiletries. A fire burned merrily in the little white-marble grate and her trunk was placed near a small desk and yellow-cushioned chair.

'What a lovely space,' she exclaimed. She put down her bonnet as she studied the view out the window, a long landscape of drive and trees, the stone fountain and flowerbeds. She could see for miles; could see anyone making their approach to the house.

'Hmmph,' Hannah said, twitching the curtains into place. 'I will make sure hot water for washing and some tea is sent up. Be sure to let the maids know if you require anything else.'

'I don't think I could possibly need anything else, thank you, Hannah,' Rose answered. A chamber all to herself, with no Aunt Sylvia constantly ringing her summoning bell? It sounded most luxurious.

She glanced again out the window and remembered what Jane had said about the St Georges and their home nearby. She wondered whimsically if the chimneys she could barely glimpse in the distance belonged to them. Or maybe it was the ruins of the old castle where Arabella once hid her treasure, the story she had once shared with Harry, so long ago?

'Don't be so silly,' she told herself, and pulled the curtains closed. She was there to teach music and that was all. The silly, fanciful girl she had once allowed herself to be for one night so long ago had no place in the world any longer.

Chapter Five

'**W**ill you have some mulled cider, Miss Parker?
Lady Ramsay says it is most warming on a cold
day,' the stern housekeeper Hannah said as she
waited outside the drawing room, holding out a tray
laden with tiny crystal glasses filled with ruby-red
liquid. Rose had bathed and changed as quickly
as she could, but it seemed the party had already
begun. She could hear loud laughter from the room,
the clink of heavy crystal goblets.

Liquid courage—just what she needed, Rose
thought with a laugh. She needed to steel her nerves
to face the crowd, especially one that contained
Captain St George. 'Thank you very much.' She
gratefully took a glass. It was warm through her
glove and smelled of rich spices and fine red claret.
It smelled exactly like Christmas.

'Her ladyship and the other guests are in the

drawing room,' Hannah said, gesturing to the half-open door behind her.

The other guests? Including Harry St George? She hadn't been able to cease thinking about him since she heard he would be there. She could feel her cheeks turning warm again and worried that if they were too pink others would surely notice, as little Lady Eleanor had earlier.

'Am I the last to arrive?' she asked as she tried not to gulp down more of the wine. At Aunt Sylvia's house, the strongest drink was watered sherry and then only when the vicar called. She didn't want to get too giddy before she faced Captain St George again.

'No, Miss Parker. Several others are still dressing, I believe,' Hannah answered, with a disdainful sniff that revealed exactly what she thought of such laggards. 'Some have only just arrived and I believe the St George brothers are still above stairs as well.'

Rose smiled in relief. 'Thank you, Hannah. I will just join the guests, then.' She put her now-empty glass back on the tray and made her way towards the half-open doors of the drawing room. She could hear laughter and the hum of conversation, the faint strains of someone playing the harp, and it made her determined to enjoy her Christmas as well. It would all end much too soon.

Just like the hall and the bedrooms above stairs, the drawing room of Barton Park had been transformed under Jane's care into a space that was stylish, grand and cosy all at the same time. From the warmth of the white and yellow striped silk wallpaper to the flowered cushions of the deep chairs and sofas, to the fire that blazed in the white marble grate and the gold-framed landscape paintings, everything was warm and welcoming.

Rose marvelled, too, at the beautiful holiday decorations. Elaborate swags of greenery tied with red and green bows looped around the picture frames and formed into wreaths above the windows that looked out on to the chilly winter evening where snow was starting down in delicate, lacy flurries. Blue and white Chinese vases on their marble stands were filled with holly branches heavy with red berries and round kissing boughs of mistletoe and streamers hung in every doorway. The warm air smelled sweetly of cinnamon and cloves, spicy and sweet all at the same time.

The crowd gathered around the harp looked just as ready for the holiday spirit as the decorations were, a kaleidoscope of bright, jewel-like velvets and satins. They all sipped at the spiced wine, or sang along as Emma played the harp in an ever-so-slightly off-key version of 'I Saw Three Ships'.

Rose smiled at the scene, at the noise and happy chaos of it all. It had been so long since she saw such merriment around her. Yet it made her feel a bit nervous as well.

She smoothed the simple chignon of her hair, the skirt of her second-best grey silk dress, and hoped she would fit in with such a crowd. She also wished she had worn her spectacles, so faces wouldn't be *quite* so fuzzy. She narrowed her eyes to scan the figures around the harp and to her relief she saw that Hannah had been right—none of them seemed to be Captain St George.

'Rose! There you are,' Jane cried, rising from the sofa where she sat with two other guests. She wore a gown of deep forest-green satin, but Rose was happy to see the lines were simple, so she didn't feel quite so shabby. Jane's dark hair was tied back with a green and gold bandeau and her only jewellery was a pair of pearl drop earrings. She quickly fetched two glasses from a footman's tray, and hurried over to offer one to Rose. 'Hasn't the weather turned quite beastly? Almost everyone has already arrived, but I think we still expect a few others. I do hope they hurry, as the roads will be quite impassable soon.'

Rose sipped carefully at the wine, hoping it wouldn't go to her head like the last glass. She surveyed the crowd over the crystal rim, not sure how many others could possibly fit into Barton's cosy drawing room. 'Are you expecting very many more, Lady Ra—Jane?'

'Oh, just the Smythes, who are Emma's sister-in-law and her husband, and Lady Fallon. Perhaps you remember her as Miss Helen Layton? She is a widow now.'

Of course Rose remembered the beautiful Miss

Layton and how she took Captain St George's arm so intimately all those years ago. 'I—yes, of course.' She took another sip of wine. 'Barton does look so lovely dressed for the holiday. I can't remember a Christmas so festive.'

Jane laughed. 'Oh, I do hope it is. We're all in need of a lovely, old-fashioned Christmas. We'll have games later, of course, some snapdragon and hide-and-seek, and dancing. I've also arranged a Christmas Day ball and invited all the neighbours.'

The drawing room door opened again, and Rose turned with a smile—only to freeze when she saw it was Harry St George who stood there, along with his brother.

Charles St George was handsome, to be sure, and most fashionably dressed in a blue velvet coat and elaborately tied cravat, but it was Harry she could not look away from. She had heard he was wounded in battle, but not to what extent. He wore a patch over his left eye, and a long, raised reddish-purple scar arced down his cheek. It made Rose's heart ache to think of the pain he must have suffered with it all—and somehow it made him even more handsome than he had been the last time they met.

She swallowed hard and turned away, trying to compose herself before she had to speak to him. She did not want to make a fool of herself in front of him and on her very first day at Barton, too!

Jane came to her rescue. 'Rose, dear, could you

favour us with a song at the pianoforte? Nothing makes a holiday merrier than a fine carol!'

'Of course,' Rose said quickly. At the instrument, she could busy herself with the music, which was always a refuge. She hurried to the pianoforte and raised the lid as she tried to decide what to play. It was a very fine instrument indeed, better even than Aunt Sylvia's, and would make an excellent hiding place indeed.

She trailed her fingers over the keys and launched into 'The First Noel'. It was a good enough start to the holidays.

'I do hope I won't be sorry you persuaded me to come to this party, Charlie,' Harry muttered as he studied the crowd gathered in Jane's drawing room. He had avoided such noise since his return from battle, and the loud laughter almost made him want to go back to the silence of his room once more.

Charles laughed and snatched up two glasses of spicy-scented wine from the nearest tray. He handed one to Harry and tossed back the other. 'You agreed that a holiday away from Hilltop would do us both some good. Why not enjoy it, Brother?'

'Harry! Charlie! How lovely to see you,' he heard Jane call out. She emerged from the crowd, a vision of Christmas herself in forest-green and gold. She kissed their cheeks, smiling, and only a flicker of her lashes showed she noticed Harry's scars, his eye patch. 'I am so sorry I wasn't able to greet you when you arrived. I do hope your chambers are satisfactory?'

'When is your hospitality less than perfect, Jane?' Charles said.

'I do want people to be comfortable and, well, happy for the holidays.' She took their arms and led them to a nearby table, where a plan of the dining table was set with small white cards. Their backs were to the crowd, but nothing could disguise the loud singing, the beautiful playing of the piano-forte. Harry found it most distracting, and comforting, to have such familiar diversions. The song was lovely.

'You see, Charlie,' Jane said. 'You are quite near Mrs Anson, the lovely young widow who manages Emma's bookshop for her. She was asking about you just last week. She is also very interested in travel and I do think you have met once or twice before?'

Charles frowned. 'Mrs Anson?' He sounded rather confused. Harry wondered if this young, bookshop-managing widow did not quite fit into Charles's stated heiress scheme. 'I'm not sure I'm quite, er, interested in romance this holiday, Jane.'

'Are you not?' Jane said, teasingly nudging his shoulder. 'Are you sure you are feeling quite well?'

'If matchmaking is your aim for the holiday,' Charles said with a mischievous wink, 'you should turn your attention to my brother.'

'Really?' Jane looked up at Harry with far too

much intrigue and delight in her smile for his comfort.

'Jane,' he said warningly. 'Remember what a tease Charlie can be?'

'But ladies so love a war hero!' Jane studied her chart and nudged a card around. 'Lady Fallon is expected, you know, though I fear she has not yet arrived. I am sure you do remember her.'

Of course he remembered Helen and how she had married someone else—and was quite right to do so. They would never have suited in the end. 'Like my brother, I have no interest in romance this Christmas, Jane,' he said cautiously.

'Ah, well, just as you like,' she said with a bright smile. The door opened and Jane's children appeared, accompanied by their nurse and luckily distracting Jane from any matchmaking thoughts for the moment. 'Hello, my darlings! Have you come to sing for us?'

Harry was more relieved than he would have ever expected to see a group of carolling children. He reached for another glass of wine and looked for a quiet corner to retreat to. He turned—and found himself facing Miss Rose Parker, who had just got up from the pianoforte.

She was just as lovely as she had been all those years ago, slender and pale with a faint flush to her cheeks that brought to mind her name—Rose. Her brown hair was twisted up into a plain knot at the nape of her neck, held with a small silver comb that was her only adornment. It matched the light grey of her gown, enlivened only by a narrow edge of pink ribbon.

Her eyes sparkled and they widened as she glimpsed him there. She glanced over her shoulder, as if she would leave, but the crowd pressed too close.

He remembered their dance so long ago, as if it was in another life altogether, but one he could barely glimpse again, like a sunrise on the horizon. If she was not entirely repelled by his new looks.

'Miss Parker,' he said with a bow. 'How wonderful to see you again and looking so well.'

She dipped into a curtsy and as she rose she didn't quite met his gaze. Her gloved hands twitched at her skirts.

'And you, Captain St George,' she said. 'I'm happy you were able to join us for Christmas. Have you been home long?'

'Not long at all. I was in hospital in Italy for a time and the journey home was slower than I would have liked. All those muddy roads.'

Her eyes widened. 'Oh, no! It sounds quite appalling.'

Harry made himself laugh. He had to forget battle now, forget his lost friends. This was what he needed to focus on now. Being at home, doing his duty. 'Not at all. If one must be in hospital, Italy is the place to do it. The best wine and food far better than I've had in English camps. It was almost like a spa-town holiday.'

Rose shook her head, her lips twitching as if she tried not to laugh. She did look directly at him now and didn't seem to notice his patch, his scars at all. Her smile was just the same as it had been all those years ago. 'I'm not sure it was *quite* spa-like, but it does seem to have done wonders for your health.'

'So it has. I hope your own family is well, your mother and sister.'

'Oh, yes, very well. Mama is settled in her own cottage and Lily is married now, with two little ones.'

Harry suddenly wondered with a pang if Rose herself was also married, if her gloves hid a ring. 'And yourself, Miss Parker?'

'Me? I live with my aunt, Mrs Pemberton, as her companion. Jane asked if I could come here for the holiday to teach her children some music and I was glad to be able to visit Barton again.' One of the children cried out and a nursemaid appeared with a crowd of children. They were all clad in their Christmas best, taking in the crowd with wide eyes. 'I should go. Duty calls.'

'It was lovely to see you again, Miss Parker,' he said quickly, before she could run away.

She smiled in a way which seemed both shy and hopeful. Or maybe he was the one feeling hopeful in that moment. 'And you, Captain.'

She hurried off to lead the children to the pianoforte set near to the fireplace. Rose sat down on the bench again, her plain grey skirts draping gracefully around her. The children gathered close.

'What should we sing, then?' Rose asked cheerfully.

'What about "The Holly and the Ivy"?' Jane said, sorting through a stack of sheet music. 'We are all going on a greenery-gathering expedition tomorrow.'

'A very good choice indeed,' Rose said. She took off her gloves and tripped her fingertips lightly over the keys before she nodded at the children and launched into the song. Everyone else in the room gathered close to listen and Harry edged towards the door, out of the crowd.

But he couldn't escape yet. The door opened again to admit a latecomer. Harry was startled to see it was Helen Fallon, swathed in red velvet and glossy sables, rubies twinkling in her ears. Just like Miss Parker, she had not aged since Harry last saw her, perhaps seemed even younger. More glowing. So bright, in fact, she looked as if she would burn from it.

'Oh, dear, am I late?' she cried, handing her sable muff and velvet gloves to a footman and reaching for a glass of champagne on a tray. 'So bad of me, missing a party.' She glimpsed him over the edge of her glass and slowly lowered it. Her brilliant smile faded. 'Harry.'

'Hello, Helen,' he answered. How long he had

known her; how their childhoods were so entwined. Yet it felt like looking at a stranger. 'How beautiful you look.'

'Hardly aged a day,' Charles said, coming up behind them to take his own glass of wine. 'Here we all are again together. Just like old times, yes?'

The sound of the old carol sounded around them, a merry counterpoint to the sudden sense of unreality Harry felt.

'Just like,' Helen said wryly.

'Please, excuse me, Helen,' Harry said. 'I have an errand. I shall see you at dinner.'

'Yes, I want to hear all about what you've been doing,' she answered. 'All your adventures…'

Harry glanced at her fine pelisse. 'They can't have been as adventurous as your own life, I'm sure.'

Helen laughed. 'London? It's dull as tombs. At least here there is this lovely champagne.'

Harry bowed and made his way out of the drawing room. He heard the music swelling behind him and Charlie and Helen laughing together. But he knew that the past, the past they had once shared as children, was gone.

He only wished he could have spent more time talking with Miss Parker, standing in her gentle presence as the rest of the world swirled noisily around them.

Chapter Six

~~~~~~~~~

"'As I lay on Yoolis Night, Alone in my longynge, I thought I saw a well faire sight, A maid hir child rockynge.'"

'That was beautifully played, Eleanor,' Rose said with a smile as the girl finished her song at the pianoforte in the morning room. Rose had been most glad of the excuse of a music lesson to avoid breakfast with the other guests. She had seen the way Lady Fallon looked at Captain St George last night and it had made her feel strange and discombobulated, as if she wasn't quite supposed to be there. She wasn't sure she could face watching them at breakfast as well. And she was, after all, at Barton to teach music.

But the music lesson had proved most enjoyable. Rose had always been able to lose herself in a song, to pour out her emotions into the notes, and it seemed young Lady Eleanor was the same way.

Her sensitivity to the song, the easy way her small fingers played over the keys, was a delight.

Eleanor smiled shyly. 'Do you truly think so, Miss Parker? I always have such trouble here...'

'That is where you must change chords like this,' Rose said, showing her on the keyboard. 'It merely takes a bit of practice. But you have something much rarer—the ability to capture the very mood of a song.'

Eleanor nodded. 'So, when I am sad or frightened, I should play a happy song? To help me remember something lovely, like a warm summer's day?'

'Exactly so!' Rose exclaimed. 'I often do that myself.'

Eleanor gave her a long, questioning glance. 'Are you often unhappy, Miss Parker?'

'Not at all, my dear,' Rose answered gently. 'Music is a celebration at happy times as well as an escape at sad ones, you know. Just like now, at Christmas. We must rehearse more carols later this afternoon, something to dance to, perhaps?'

'Rehearsing!' William scoffed. He lay on his stomach on the pale blue carpet, pushing around a tiny carriage and horses. It seemed music did not interest him as much as it did his sister. 'That sounds very dull. We know the songs well enough. Who can sit still that long, singing one line over and over?'

Rose had to laugh; he sounded so much as Lily

had when they were children and she was too impatient to practise. 'What would you rather do, then, William? Read your geography lessons?'

'We could tell you about the treasure!' he said eagerly. His sat up, his carriage forgotten for the moment.

'The treasure?' Rose asked. She wondered if it was the same one that had entranced her and Lily when they were children.

'It's just an old story,' Eleanor said. 'Cousin Beatrice likes to tell us about how she went searching for it once, when she was our age. She hurt herself and Aunt Emma had to go find her. It's why we're not allowed near the old castle ruins on Uncle David's estate.'

'We would be much more careful if we were the ones searching!' William said. 'I'm sure it's there some place. It would make a splendid Christmas surprise for Mama and Aunt Emma if we found it.'

'Arabella's old treasure?' Rose said, falling into their enthusiasm. 'My sister and I used to like that tale, too.'

'Was Arabella the lady from a long time ago?' William asked.

'When Charles I was king and they wanted him to go,' Eleanor added. 'This lady was in love with one of the king's own knights…'

'And she hid a treasure for him in the old castle, so they could be together one day!' said William.

'But he died and she never returned for it, so it is
out there some place.'

'It does certainly sound romantic,' Rose said,
finding herself rather sorry for this long-ago couple,
kept apart by the cold realities of the world. 'But I
am sure your parents are quite right not to let you
go climbing about old ruins by yourself.'

'I do think it's terribly sad Arabella never got
to marry her true love,' Eleanor said with a sigh.
'I would only ever marry a man I loved madly, as
Mama and Aunt Emma have done.'

'Girls are so silly in that way,' William said.

Rose laughed. 'Why will *you* marry, then, William?'

'I don't know. Because I find a pretty girl some
day, I suppose. Her portrait will have to go in the
gallery of countesses, you know,' he said grandly.

Rose laughed even louder. She had known teaching children music would be better than serving
tea to Aunt Sylvia all day, but she hadn't realised
it would be quite so amusing. 'Very wise of you.'

Eleanor glanced up at her. 'Why have you not
married, Miss Parker? You are certainly pretty.'

Rose smiled at her and pushed her spectacles up
her nose. She remembered Lady Fallon, with her
beautiful gown and shining hair, everyone watching her as she laughed. Who would notice someone like Rose after that? And she knew marriage
didn't often turn out as well as it had for her sister

and her cousins. 'I haven't found someone to fall madly in love with yet.'

Eleanor gave a sad-looking frown and gently touched Rose's hand. 'I am sure you will, though, and very soon.'

'In the meantime, perhaps you might search for treasure with us?' William said hopefully.

Rose shook her head. 'I have been hired to teach you music, so I think we should go over these Christmas carols again. Something jolly, maybe— a dance?'

William reluctantly joined them at the pianoforte bench, but they had barely made it through their next song before there was a knock at the door. Jane hurried in, clad in a fur-trimmed pelisse and hat, a matching fur muff in her hand.

'Mama!' the children cried and ran to hug her.

'How is your lesson progressing, then, Rose?' Jane said as she hugged her children back. 'Are they prodigies yet?'

'They are excellent pupils,' Rose answered.

'Very good. I think that deserves a reward, then, don't you? We're all going out to collect more greenery in the park and since you have been such good children you may come with us,' Jane said. As the children cheered, she told them to go tell the nursemaid to fetch their coats.

William shouted out with happiness and dashed away, Eleanor following with one small, wistful glance behind her at the pianoforte. Rose started to tidy the musical sheets, already missing their company.

'You must come, too, Rose,' Jane said.

Go out—and see Harry St George again? 'Oh, no...'

'I absolutely insist! You are obviously a wonder with my children, I haven't seen them so well behaved in an age,' Jane said. 'And it's a lovely day outside; the sun is shining, though it's a bit chilly. I don't think we'll have many more days of such weather.'

Rose glanced out the window; she did have to agree it looked quite nice out, the pale sunlight shimmering on yesterday's dusting of snow. Surely there would be so many people there she wouldn't even find herself alone with Harry. She smiled and hurried off to find her pelisse and hat.

The rest of the party was already gathered in the front drive when Rose hurried to join them. Various carts and carriages waited, equipped with warm blankets, picnic baskets, as well as tools for cutting green boughs once they were found.

For a moment, she stood in the shadows of the doorway, just watching the bright scene before her. At Aunt Sylvia's house they seldom had company at all, except for the elderly vicar for tea, and at her mother's cottage they'd had no time or money for parties. This felt like a whole different world, the swirling brightness of velvet pelisses and caped greatcoats, the sound of laughter. She wasn't sure she belonged there.

She saw a quieter cart near the end of the row and started to turn towards it, to remain unobtrusive and watchful. But Emma Marton suddenly grabbed her hand and drew her into the very midst of the chattering throng, gathering her close.

'Miss Parker, I do believe there is a seat here,' she heard a deep, rich voice say, and turned to see Captain St George holding out his hand to her with a half-smile. In the sunlight, his scars looked more evident, yet that smile was as handsome as ever. *Too* handsome for her peace of mind.

Rose glanced around, but there was nowhere else to sit. *Don't be such a ninny,* she told herself sternly. Yes, he was an attractive man, and, yes, talking to him last night had made her feel things she never had before. Most confusing things, such as—a girlish desire to laugh. The exhilarating sense of being *seen*, of being heard, of being free of all the caution and responsibility, to be just a young lady talking to a handsome man, if only for a moment.

All those things *had* happened and it felt like a dream. Yet this was in the clear, cold light of day and she was a sensible, grown woman. A woman with many responsibilities. Surely she could not now make a giggling, silly fool out of herself.

He curled the outstretched fingers of his gloved hand and his smile widened, as if he could read her thoughts. His uncovered eye, so very blue, gleamed like a summer sky.

Oh, yes, she thought wryly. She could be a giggling, silly fool after all.

But she didn't have to show it to everyone. She smiled back and took his hand to let him help her on to the cart. She sat down beside him on the narrow bench, demurely arranging her skirts around herself. A few other people clambered up with them, and she glimpsed Lady Fallon climbing into the carriage ahead of theirs, helped by Charles St George. She watched Harry from under the brim of her fur-trimmed bonnet.

'I hope you slept well enough after last night's festivities, Miss Parker,' he said. 'I saw William racing through the hall this morning and he said he was late for your music lesson. I think he was stealing bacon from the dining-room sideboard.'

Rose laughed, more at ease with his light tone. 'Oh, yes, it all went quite well. Barton Park is very comfortable and the children most attentive to their lessons—once they are there. Lady Eleanor in particular is very talented.' She peeked up at him from beneath the brim of her plain grey bonnet. He smiled at her again and she suddenly felt so light, so wonderfully giddy.

'I remember from our last meeting, as well as last night, that you quite enjoy music, Miss Parker,' he said. 'Jane says that she's lucky to have a lady of your rare talent instructing her children.'

Rose felt her cheeks turn warm under his praise and looked away as the cart jolted in motion. 'I have no more talent than most ladies who are made to practise their pianoforte and harp from their childhood,' she said with a laugh. 'But, yes, I do enjoy it, very much. When I have the chance to play. My Aunt Sylvia does like things to be—quiet.'

The cart jolted around a corner, following the line of carriages before it in their jolly little caravan. Rose was not prepared for the sudden motion and fell against Harry's shoulder. He caught her against him and for an instant she felt all of herself pressed against him. She sat up straighter, feeling her cheeks grow embarrassingly warm again, and she was all too aware of his strength pressed so close to her.

In the open carriage ahead of theirs, Charles St George stood up and started to lead everyone in a rousing chorus of 'We Wish You a Merry Christmas'. The riders around Rose and Harry soon took up the tune and they were surrounded by the wondrous sounds of the season as they jolted and jounced over the frosty lanes into the wooded part of the park. Charles almost toppled over on to Lady Fallon.

'I do not think Barton could ever be described as *quiet*,' Harry remarked wryly.

Rose laughed. 'No, indeed. Aunt Sylvia would quite hate it. Your brother does seem to take his role as Lord of Misrule for the holiday most seriously.'

Harry smiled and Rose had the sense it was something rather rare for him, smiling. She found herself wanting to make him do it again, to laugh even. 'Charles would be King of the Revels all the time if he could.'

'He sounds like my sister, Lily. She does love a good party.'

'The curate's wife?' Harry said, his tone surprised.

Rose laughed again. 'You must not let that fool you. She does take her parish duties and her children very seriously, but she still loves a dance or a practical joke more than anyone I have ever known. When we were children, she would gallop up and down the stairs and pretend to be a pony whenever she could!'

'And you, Miss Parker? Did you concoct such games when you were a girl?'

Rose studied the scenery around them, the trees growing thicker, the shadows darker, as she thought about her girlhood with Lily, the sounds of music and laughter that had always echoed around their corridors—until their father died. She turned back to Harry to find him watching her intently, as if he could read her wistfulness.

'The world is different for an eldest child, is it not, Miss Parker?' he said.

'Is it, Captain?' She thought more of her childhood, of the times she had pulled Lily back from disaster. 'I had never thought of it thus, but so it seems. Someone must keep it all from falling to bits, I suppose.'

'Or put it back together when it does,' he answered, so softly she wasn't sure she'd heard him.

Before she could answer, could tell him of how things had fallen apart when her father died, the cart lurched to a halt in a large clearing surrounded by a circle of trees.

'Very well, everyone,' Charles cried, still Lord of Misrule, 'I command you all to go out and find as much greenery as possible to deck the halls of Barton tonight. The winner will have the first glass from the wassail bowl!'

A great cheer went up and everyone scattered into the woods like a flock of brightly coloured birds. Harry held out his hand to help Rose down, but when she stumbled on the step he swiftly caught her around the waist before she could fall. She gasped with surprise at the sparkling jolt of pleasure his touch gave her.

As he slowly lowered her to her feet, Rose wished she didn't have to let him go. Didn't have to keep her feet planted firmly on the plain, practical ground, as she always did. The Christmas spirit was taking her over.

'Th-thank you, Captain St George,' she said, wishing her voice did not sound quite so breathless. 'So clumsy of me.'

'Not at all. I'm afraid I must beg *your* assistance now, Miss Parker.'

'My assistance?'

'Yes. I see a patch of holly over there just begging to be a mantelpiece decoration, but my depth perception is not—quite what it was.' He gestured to the dark cloth over his eye.

'Oh, of course!' Rose cried, embarrassed she had forgotten his injuries. The truth was, after the first shock when they met again last night, she had barely noticed his scars. He was still much too attractive for her peace of mind. 'I am quite sure that between us we can defeat the holly and bring it home in triumph.'

As he offered her his arm, she glimpsed Lady Fallon's red pelisse through the trees, just ahead of them. She smiled up at Harry and took his arm to make their way between the thick wood, chattering easily about inconsequential matters such as the cold weather, favourite Christmas songs from their childhood holidays, and places they had seen— many for Harry, few for Rose. A chilly breeze swept around the bare branches, making the voices of the others a mere murmur, but pale sunlight struggled down on to their heads through the lacy patterns.

'And where else have you travelled, Captain St George?' she asked as she paused to clip a clump of low-hanging mistletoe, pearly with white berries.

'To Switzerland and Austria, many places in Italy,' he said, as casually as if he'd said Kent or Brighton.

'How lucky you are to have seen such things,' she said. 'I have never even been to Bath!'

He gave her a smile. 'Bath is overrated, I assure you, Miss Parker. As is Italy.'

Rose gazed around them at the quiet trees, the silent, pale sky. 'This must all seem so dull to you after all you have seen. A plain English country Christmas.'

He turned to study her for a moment, his gaze unreadable. She turned away with a blush. 'Oh, Miss Parker. An English country Christmas is one of the loveliest things imaginable. This quiet is astounding.'

'Of course it would be,' she answered softly. 'I have only read of battle and can barely imagine the noise and confusion of it all. I'm glad you have returned safely home.'

He smiled down at her warmly. 'I see you do understand, Miss Parker. So few do, even my brother. They think once it's over it is forgotten. And it's not a memory I wish to dwell upon, especially on such a lovely day.'

Rose nodded. 'Shall we conquer that holly, then? I see some with particularly luscious red berries right over there.'

She laughed and took his arm to make their way to the holly bush. It was indeed a lovely one, dark green against the frosty ground like diamonds and rubies. She held the branches high and still as he sawed them off to fill their baskets. She could hear the laughter of the others caught on the wind, could smell the crisp, warm scent of him against the cold snow and the greenery.

'This is quite nice,' she said. 'It does remind me of Christmases when I was a child and Lily and I would help our parents find decorations for the house. It smelled of evergreen then and we were always singing. My father would read us old holiday poems every night. How merry it was!'

He nodded, but he looked solemn as he finished gathering the last of the branches. 'It sounds delightful indeed.'

'Did you and your brother not do such things for Christmas at your house?'

'Christmas was not much celebrated at Hilltop, I'm afraid, so I'm learning it as I go this year. My father preferred quiet at all times and my mother usually went to visit friends in London, though she did like a bit of decoration around the house.'

'Oh,' Rose whispered, her heart suddenly aching for him. He smiled as he spoke, as if it was not a thing of much consequence, yet she heard the sombre touch of wistfulness behind the words. She couldn't help but picture two lonely little boys, left alone at the darkest time of the year without the Yule candles to brighten things. 'I am sorry.'

'Not at all. Charlie and I would be left alone to do naughty things like toast cheese by the fire, which we were never usually allowed to do.'

Rose laughed. 'Toasted cheese *is* a thing to look

forward to, I must say. Aunt Sylvia would never allow it.'

He studied her from beneath the brim of his hat. 'What is it like at your Aunt Sylvia's house?'

Rose thought about the drawing room, cluttered with old *objets* and closed around with heavy velvet curtains. 'Not so terrible, really. It's not as if I'm mining coal or some such thing. Mostly I read to her and fetch tea and shawls, and listen as she bemoans the ways of the world. We are apparently in quite a shocking state, you know, compared with how things were in her own youth.'

He laughed. 'So my father often said. I think I remember reading Plato saying the young people of his own day were becoming shockingly rude. By the time any nephews or nieces of mine are grown, who knows what horrors we shall face?'

Rose noticed he'd said 'nephews and nieces', not sons and daughters. Did he not hope for such things as a family, then? She wondered what horrors had taken such expectations from him and she wanted to touch his hand in sympathy, as Lady Eleanor had for her earlier that morning. But he gave her another smile, and in that smile, just for an instant, she glimpsed the man she had danced with all those years ago, in another life. The man whose kindness and handsome looks had fuelled her silly dreams for far too long. Whatever he'd seen and done in battle had carved the man with such sadness as well as outward scars, yet she saw the man she'd known was still inside somewhere.

'Well, I think I am about to do something shockingly naughty,' she whispered.

He leaned closer with a glint in his eye. 'I can't wait to see what that might be, Miss Parker.'

'I see a lovely little cluster of mistletoe up there and every house decorated for the holidays *must* have plenty of mistletoe for kissing boughs. I'm going to climb up there to fetch it.'

'Climb the tree?' he said doubtfully. 'Miss Parker, I don't think....'

Before he could stop her, Rose ran to the tree and found a foothold in the rough bark. She reached up and grabbed a thick branch. 'Lily and I used to climb trees all the time, when we were children. I'm sure I remember how.'

He frowned and rushed over to her, his arms out as if he was afraid she would fall. 'It could be dangerous.'

'Not as dangerous as riding into battle like you, Captain,' she answered and kept pulling herself upwards.

She felt a warm touch on her leg and looked down to find he was ready to catch her at an instant's notice. Somehow, just knowing he was there gave her more confidence.

She grabbed at the cluster of mistletoe and snapped it off. As she clambered back down, the toe of her boot caught on her hem and she felt herself falling with an instant of cold panic.

Before she could hit the frost-frozen ground, Harry caught her, holding her high for an instant above the rest of the world. Breathless, Rose held on to him and felt safer than she had in a very long time.

'Thank you, Captain,' she said. 'It seems you have saved me yet again.'

'I must find something useful to do in my new homebound life,' he answered. 'Rescuing fair maidens seems as fine a cause as any.'

Rose laughed as he lowered her to her feet. She found she didn't want to let him go at all; she had to make herself stand back and smile. 'You're quite good at it. And look at our mistletoe! Quite pretty, indeed, and not a single berry lost.'

She suddenly heard other voices, calling out and laughing, and she remembered they were not alone in the fairy-tale woods. Her small dream was shattered, like the icicles on the trees around them, and she stepped back from him.

'There you are, Rose,' Jane called. 'I think it's time for our luncheon, don't you? We've all been working much too hard! Oh, look at how much holly you've gathered, how marvellous.'

As Jane took her arm and led her away, still happily chattering, Rose glanced back at Harry.

Lady Fallon had gone to him and taken his arm, and he replied to whatever she had said to him.

Rose's throat tightened, but she made herself turn away and nod and smile at Jane. The day suddenly stretched very long before her.

Rose Parker sat the other end of the long luncheon table, with several laughing, chattering people between them, but Harry was aware of her at every moment. Aware of her soft smiles, the graceful movement of her hand as she raised her glass, and the quiet, sweet happiness that seemed to radiate around her like a pink, sunset cloud.

Yes—that was what she had, what he had never possessed—quiet sweetness, a pleasure in the moment. It was intoxicating after years of noise and chaos in the army.

He thought of that moment in the forest, with the snowy silence all around them and Rose looking up at him. He had wanted to take her into his arms more than he had ever wanted anything else, longed for it with a palpable hunger that took him entirely by surprise.

'...don't you think, Harry?' Helen, who was seated to his right, said. Her laughing voice pushed him out of his dream world and into the reality of the cold winter morning, of a footman pouring wine into his glass and Helen laying a light hand on his arm.

He glanced down into her smiling eyes, those beautiful sky-blue eyes of his old friend, the woman he'd even once thought of marrying. And all he could think of was Rose, her cheeks pink in the cold forest, her smile.

'*...should marry an heiress,*' he heard Charlie say in his mind. '*Do his duty—rescue Hilltop.*'

'I'm sorry, Helen, I fear I was wool-gathering,' he said.

She tilted her head, the feathers of her fashionable headpiece waving lightly. Her gaze flickered over his ruined face and then away. 'Charlie was just telling me about how Hilltop needs a lady's opinion on its furnishings. Perhaps I could advise you?'

Harry almost laughed as he thought of Hilltop, its roof slates crumbling, its floors cracking. Refurnishing was far down the list at the moment. 'I don't think it's quite ready for visitors.'

Helen laughed and reached for her wineglass. 'I am hardly a visitor. I remember being there so often as a child it almost seemed like a second home.'

Charles gave Harry a long, solemn glance over her head. 'We wouldn't know where to start without an educated opinion, would we, Harry?'

'I would so dearly love to see it again,' Helen said with a sigh. 'I am sure that whatever needs fixing there, it is nothing a lady's sure hand could not do. Your father was alone there for so long and a house is not a home without a mistress. A bit of merriment always helps as well.'

'And a new roof wouldn't hurt,' Charlie muttered.

'But such things are surely fixed in a trice!'

Helen said. 'Then a bit of redecorating, in modern colours, and it would be just like in our mothers' day. Tell me, Charlie dear, what are the French styles you saw while you were abroad?'

As Charles and Helen talked of colours and satins, Harry finished his wine and thought of that new roof. In Helen's world, such things happened as if by magic. For Hilltop and its tenants—well, it would take a bit more than the wave of a wand.

Chapter Seven

'The boar's head in hand bear I, bedecked in bays and rosemary!'

Rose applauded along with everyone else as the elaborate platter with the traditional boar's head—bright red apple in its mouth and wound with a holly garland—was paraded around the dining room with Charles St George leading the song in his Lord of Misrule role. It was a true traditional Christmas dinner, the table laden with plum cakes and silver wassail bowls, and everyone looked quite merry indeed.

She glanced across the table at Harry. He watched it all with a smile, but it seemed distant, as if he thought of something far away. She wanted to draw him closer, to bring him into their merriment so he forgot all else.

'Oh, Miss Parker, isn't it all so pretty?' Lady Eleanor, seated at Rose's left so she could be guided when it was time for her to sing, said as she watched the firelit scene with wide eyes. She reminded Rose of Lily when they were children, all curls and smiles, and it made her feel wistful to remember.

'Pretty indeed. Much like it must have been here years ago.'

'My father, as you know, was a scholar,' Jane said, listening to her daughter. 'And he always thought the old Christmas traditions were the best. Tonight we have singing, and the wassail bowl, and on Christmas Day and Boxing Day feasts and dancing.'

'And presents?' Eleanor asked.

Jane laughed. 'Small ones, perhaps.'

As plates of roasted boar and cinnamon-spiced apples were passed around the table, Rose thought of the Christmases she had known as a child, with her parents and Lily. They had not been grand, but there had always been singing around the pianoforte, special cakes at tea and her mother's embroidered handkerchiefs as gifts, wrapped around sweets and oranges.

Suddenly, the warm, crowded room seemed to vanish and she was swept up on a chilly wave of homesickness, of missing her mother and sister. She felt so alone in the midst of the noisy crowd and blinked hard to hold back the tears.

She glanced up and found Harry watching her from across the table. He gave her a small, understanding smile, as if he understood what she was thinking, and suddenly she did not feel so very alone.

'Christmas can be a difficult time to remember the past,' he said quietly. 'Whether it be scholarly, or in our own memories.'

'Then we must make new memories,' Jane said. 'William, Eleanor, would you like to sing for us now, my dears?'

The children looked to Rose and she nodded with a smile. No matter what, music, especially when shared with others, was a great refuge. They launched into another version of 'The Boar's Head', their small faces shining with pleasure. They made her forget, too, made her feel like just for a moment she was home again.

'Oh, well done, my dears!' Jane said, leading the applause. She exchanged proud glances with her husband. 'Rose, you have worked wonders with them.'

Rose was also most proud of her pupils and urged them to make another bow. 'The talent must be there to be worked with, I must say.'

'Will *you* sing something for us, Miss Parker?' Hayden said.

'Oh, yes, do!' Emma cried. 'No one sings as you do.'

Rose slowly stood up, wondering what she should sing, trying not to look at all the people watching her. She closed her eyes and remembered the sad old song her father once sang to her and her sister as they fell asleep at Christmastime.

'"*Lully, lullay, thou little tiny child, Bye-bye, lully, lullay. Lully, lullay, thou little tiny child, Bye-bye, lully, lullay,*'" she sang out.

As she made her way through the verses, a few voices joined her in sweet melancholy.

The words to the old song slowly faded away and Rose felt her homesickness grow in her heart again. Against her will, she found herself looking to Harry again, as if he could offer understanding, as he had earlier when they talked together about past holidays and seemed to be in perfect accord with each other.

He looked as startled as she felt, as if for an instant a mask had dropped away between them and a longing was laid bare. A flash of loneliness, comfort offered and accepted.

Then it was gone, his polite half-smile returned, and applause rang out for the song, breaking the sweet, sad stretch of silence.

'Will you sing for us again?' Jane asked.

Rose shook her head, afraid she would cry if she sang one of the old, familiar songs again. 'Perhaps someone else would grace us?' She glimpsed Lady Fallon from the corner of her eye, a scarlet-satin slipper tapping under her embroidered hem as Jane said,

'Lady Fallon, would you? Rose, perhaps you would join us for a hand of cards?'

Lady Fallon looked startled for an instant before she nodded. 'Oh, yes, of course, though I fear I am quite out of practice!'

Rose gave up the bench to Lady Fallon, who sorted through the music before she launched into a complicated Italian aria. As she sang, Rose sat down and examined her hand of cards, trying to remember how to play piquet. Aunt Sylvia rarely had enough company to make up a four-hand, so Rose's memory of the rules was rather faded. But Jane insisted she would do very well with herself, Emma and Emma's bookseller friend Mrs Anson at the table near the windows.

Lady Fallon's beringed hands flew over the pianoforte keys. Rose saw she was not well practised at her music, but she was very dramatic, drawing people near with her smiling, animated performance—including Harry and Charles, who gathered with the others near the instrument.

'It's quite delightful to see Lady Fallon and the St Georges together again,' Jane said, shuffling the cards. 'It's been too long.'

'Didn't I hear that they were once all great friends?' Mrs Anson asked.

'Oh, yes, their mothers were bosom bows,' Emma said. 'I think there were hopes of Helen and Harry making a match.'

'Really?' Mrs Anson said, her tone surprised. 'But Charles St George is so very handsome, and seems better suited to her—ebullience.'

Jane shrugged, dealing a new hand. 'It all became pointless when Harry went to battle and Lord Fallon came along with his great fortune. But now that Helen is a widow...'

'With all Lord Fallon's gold intact,' Emma said. 'What good such things could do at an estate like Hilltop! It would be lovely to see the old house come alive again.'

'Why?' Rose asked. 'What is amiss with it?'

'Old Mr St George was not the best steward,' Jane said. 'When his wife died, he quite lost all interest in the place. And with Harry and Charlie gone for so long—it was very sad.'

Emma glanced at the group around the pianoforte. 'Yet all can be well now!'

'Hopefully.' Jane glanced out the window, and let out a little glad cry. 'Oh, look, more snow! How delightful. Hayden has been wanting to try his hand at sledding again, as he did when he was a boy. Maybe we can all go tomorrow.'

Rose watched the snow drifting down, light and lacy, pale against the night sky. It was all so pretty, so peaceful. If only, she thought, all of life could be just that way.

Chapter Eight

How very strange it was, Rose thought, how very alone a person could really feel in a crowd. She felt steadier there, alone for a moment on the chilly terrace as everyone else took a moment from their games to find refreshments, than she had been surrounded by people and gossip about Captain St George and Lady Fallon. The light snowfall fell on her nose and made her laugh.

The glass doors opened behind her, the merest brush against the stone floor, and she turned to see a silhouetted figure against the night sky, the lights from the party behind him. His face was in shadow, but she knew it was Harry. No one else had quite his military bearing.

She felt her cheeks turning warm even in the chilly wind and looked away.

'Oh, I am sorry,' he said when he saw her there. 'I didn't know anyone was here. I was just looking for a—well, a bit of quiet. I'll leave you to your privacy.'

'It's quite all right, Captain,' she answered, hoping he wouldn't leave. 'I also needed some quiet for a moment, but I'm not averse to a bit of company, either.'

'Neither am I, especially when it's so amiable.' He came to stand beside her at the balustrade, leaning his palms on the cold marble. They stared together into the garden, all ghostly under the winter moon. 'Jane's party is very merry, but I'm not quite used to so very many people yet. My brother says I've become a growly old hermit.'

Rose studied him for a moment, his sharp profile against the snow, the sweep of his glossy hair back from his brow. 'I think you would have to grow a much longer beard to be a true hermit. You don't look nearly enough as if you lived in the woods.' They laughed together, and suddenly Rose felt entirely at ease for the first time that evening. 'I do know what you mean. It's so quiet at my aunt's house, I barely know how to make sense of all this noise. It's been a long time since I had a real family Christmas.'

He glanced at her, one brow arched in question. In the night, his scars were invisible. 'Were your childhood Christmases so very merry?'

'Not as grand as this. We usually visited my mother's relatives for New Year, but Christmas was just for us. My parents, my sister, Lily, and me. We would play games, do charades, eat too much pudding. We did have fun.'

'Your father has passed on?'

'Yes, years ago. My mother is still with us. She lives in a cottage near my sister and her family.' She hesitated for a moment, not accustomed to talking about her family. Yet somehow with him, there in the muffling quiet of the snowy night, she felt as if she could say anything. 'My father was something of a gentleman, you see, the grandson of a baron, a good match for my mother with her connection to the Bancrofts, and we had a lovely house with a very pretty garden. Lily and I used to play hide and seek for hours, or go into the attics to read and daydream. But when our father died, we found out he—well, he had debts.'

Harry frowned. 'And that is why you work as companion to your aunt?'

'Yes. Lily was already so fond of her curate and my mother's annuity is not large. Aunt Sylvia is always—interesting. I'm happy to be *here* for the festive season, though. Being with the children reminds me of those times.' She glanced back through the glass doors at the party, the glittering group gathered around the punch bowl, laughing together. Lady Fallon's jewels sparkled in the candlelight and Rose remembered the talk about her old understanding with Harry. 'You said before that yours were not so merry?'

'Not as fun as yours,' he answered with a laugh.

'Charlie and I made do, though. We would play our own games in the nursery and cajole the cook for extra gingersnaps. My father really *was* something of an old hermit, but my mother had a ball each year after New Year's Eve, when she returned from London. Charlie and I would sneak out to watch everyone arrive from the top of the stairs. My mother and her friends were so lovely, all laughing and shimmering in their holiday finery. I think it was the only time of year we really saw her laugh.'

Rose nodded, wondering if Lady Fallon reminded him of those days. 'Perhaps you can have Christmas balls at Hilltop again, now that you're home.'

He gave her a crooked smile. 'I wouldn't be as good at entertaining as Jane and Hayden.'

'But it wouldn't have to be just like this. It could be—family. And books and flowers, treats at breakfast, games after supper. Maybe gathering holly for a wreath or two. The important thing is sharing the holiday.'

His smile faded, but she thought he looked intrigued. 'The way your holidays were as a child?'

Rose nodded. 'Yes, indeed. Christmas can be whatever you want it to be. Whatever you need it to be.'

'I am sure you are quite right.'

She glanced through the doors again and glimpsed Eleanor and William dashing around the room, nearly running into a large vase of ivy and hothouse roses. 'Oh, no, they are meant to be in bed! I should go and gather them up, maybe make them sing another song if they have too much energy.'

To her surprise, he caught her hand in his as she turned away and raised her gloved fingers for a quick kiss. It felt warm and soft through the thin silk. 'Thank you for spending a few moments with me, Miss Parker. You've certainly brought back some memories for me.'

Flustered, Rose dropped a quick curtsy to him. 'Thank *you*, Captain, for keeping me company.'

She hurried back into the drawing room, trying not to look at him, to run back to him. As she slipped back into the party, it was like being dropped into another world entirely, full of noise and heat from the fire and the spicy scent of the wine punch.

Yet even in the warmth, she couldn't help wishing she was back on the chilly terrace, with him.

Chapter Nine

The cold wind snapped at Rose's cheeks and caught at her pelisse, and she laughed as she wondered if this was such a good idea after all. Sledding sounded like such a holiday fun sort of thing to do while cosy next to the fire in Barton, but the reality of it was quite cold indeed!

But Harry was there. She tucked her gloved hands deeper into her old velvet muff, watching him as he built a fire with his brother, Hayden and David Marton, the four of them competing to see who could pile the firewood higher.

He was a fine sight to see indeed, with his dark wool coat stretched taut over his wide shoulders as he stacked the wood. He had taken off his hat and his dark hair gleamed like ebony in the pale sunlight. He laughed at something Charles said, his bright smile breaking through his solemn demeanour. It made the cold day feel suddenly very—warm.

She was glad she had ventured out after all. The real world of daily worries seemed very far away.

She went and sat next to Jane and Emma, where they perched on a fallen log covered by an old blanket. At their feet was a hamper, overflowing with delicacies from the Barton kitchen. As the laughter of the children rang out from the nearby woods where they ran, Emma pulled out gingerbread and almond cakes and candied fruit tarts.

'Oh, sugared plums! And minced pies, salmon sandwiches, even some of the French wine,' Emma exclaimed. 'I have had such a craving for marzipan lately.'

'I feared I was stealing too much from the pantry, but I just had to grab whatever I saw. I dared not stay too long in the kitchen while they're working so hard to prepare for the ball,' Jane said. She poured out spiced wine into heavy pottery goblets. 'Here, Rose, have something fortifying to drink. The wine will warm us.'

'Thank you,' Rose said as she took the goblet. She felt the warmth of the wine through her glove and even better was the warmth of Jane and Emma's friendship. She hadn't realised quite how lonely and quiet her life had become after she left her mother and sister.

As she sipped at the rich, ruby-red drink, she went back to studying Harry. The men had finished building the fire and it snapped merrily as they stood back to watch it, congratulating each other on the fine job.

'Ha!' Jane said with a laugh. 'They act as if they were the first men to discover fire.'

'Better than letting us continue to shiver here,' Emma said.

'Quite right, my dear,' David Marton called to her. 'What would you do without our fire-making skills? Now, can you share some of that wine before we tote these sleds uphill for you?'

The ladies laughed and passed around the spiced wine before Hayden counted the sleds. 'We have enough for almost everyone to pair up, I think. Jane, my dear, shall I steer one for us?'

Jane laughed. 'I am not sure I entirely trust you not to send us into a tree!'

He put his arm around his wife, grinning. 'I have done all right so far, haven't I?'

In the confusion of dividing up the sleds, Rose somehow found herself with Harry. She glanced over her shoulder, half-fearing what she might feel if she was too near him, but everyone else was already making their way up the hill.

She turned back to Harry to find him smiling at her, offering his hand. 'Shall we, Miss Parker?' he said. 'I can't promise to steer us straight, my eyesight is not quite what it was, but I am sure we'll end up some place interesting.'

Rose laughed. Of that, she was quite sure. 'Thank you, Captain St George.' She took his hand

and let him help her up the slope of the hill, where he situated their sled to make the downward slide. She perched behind him, her arms around his waist, and closed her eyes as they launched into motion.

They coasted to a stop in a clearing at the bottom of the hill, Rose out of breath at the excitement of it all. She could hear the laughter of the others nearby, magnified by the cold wind, but it felt as if she was alone with Harry in the bower of winter trees. Frost hung from bare branches, sparkling like glass. It was quite magical, like a moment hovering out of time. She stared up at the diamond sparkle of it, dazzled.

'It's so beautiful, isn't it?' she whispered.

'Yes,' he answered, in a strangely hoarse voice.

Surprised, Rose glanced up to find he was staring not at the beauty around them, but at *her*. For an instant, all she could do was stare at him, captured by his gaze.

He gave her a rueful smile. 'When Charles and I were small, we had a nursemaid for a time who liked to read us fairy stories. One was about a winter queen, pale and shimmering in the snow. I haven't thought of it in years, until now.'

'Why now?'

'Because you look like her. A winter fairy queen in her ice palace. I had forgotten how beautiful it all could be.'

'Me? A fairy queen?' she whispered, amazed by such words. She knew she wasn't beautiful, that she was quite ordinary with her brown hair and her spectacles. Especially next to ladies such as her golden sister and her elegant cousin Jane. Yet she knew Harry was not a man to give compliments lightly, to say what he did not mean. He made her feel warm and glowing, all the way to her toes.

'Yes, with your pink cheeks and eyes glowing,' he said. 'And yet—' He broke off with a laugh, rubbing his hand over the back of his neck.

'Yet?' she whispered.

'Yet you, Rose, are real.' He suddenly took her gloved hand, holding it tightly in his. She curled her fingers around his, wondering at the feelings that came unbidden at his touch. 'Warm and real, not like an icy winter fairy at all. You have a—a kindness in you as warm as any fire.' He held her hand against his chest and through his thick wool coat she could feel the beat of his heart, flowing through her whole body.

'And so have you!' she cried, unable to hold back her words. 'A warmth, a kindness.'

He shook his head. 'Perhaps once. Long ago.'

Rose stared up at him, a bittersweet longing in her heart such as she had never known. She gave in to her feelings and leaned closer to him, letting her forehead rest on his shoulder. Suddenly she did not feel alone at all.

'What happened to it?' she said. 'What can bring it back?'

He was silent for a long moment, not looking at

her but out into the distance, as if he was very far away from her at that moment. 'When I was in the army, I became friends with a young man from a small farm not far from here. He had a young wife and a child, and he would talk to me about them in the evenings when we were all near the fire. The way he spoke about them—I quite envied him!'

'Envied him?' she said.

'Yes. Such love, so much to look forward to when he returned to England—a real home. A place where he belonged.'

Had Harry not felt as if he had a place to belong? Rose reached out to touch his hand, wanting so much to reassure him, to tell him he *could* have that, could have all he dreamed of. But she couldn't find the right words. 'And has he gone home now?'

Harry shook his head. 'He was killed in battle. I saw him, through the smoke and the terrible noise, the screams. I tried to save him, but—it was much too late. I went to see his wife after I returned, before she went back to her own parents. She was so brave, so kind, trying to reassure *me* when I was the one who owed her everything.' He gave Rose that crooked half-smile that always made her heart ache. 'She rather reminded me of you.'

'Of me?' Rose said hoarsely.

'Yes. So kind, so brave. I have never forgotten her or her husband. Nor have I forgotten the terrors of battle. Not until now. Is this not a peaceful place?'

Rose swallowed hard past her threatening tears and nodded. 'Yes,' she said. 'With the snow and silence—it is most peaceful indeed.'

They were quiet for a long moment and somehow in that still, perfect hush Rose felt closer to him that she ever had to anyone.

'Shall we take another turn down the hill before we have to leave?' he said finally. Rose nodded and in silence they made their way back up the hill. But it was not a heavy, uncomfortable silence. Indeed, Rose had not felt so utterly free of the chill of loneliness in a long time. And he still held her hand safely in his, leading her up the slippery slope.

At the top of the hill, she could see all the countryside around them, the fields laid out like an undulating blanket of grey and blue in the winter, the thicket of the woods, the sky stretching above them endlessly. 'How lovely it all is!' she exclaimed. 'At Aunt Sylvia's, I am indoors all the time. This is— is a wonderland!'

He smiled and it seemed brighter even than the light that broke through the clouds over their heads. 'We can even see Hilltop from here.'

'We can? Where?'

He pointed into the distance and Rose glimpsed a cluster of red brick and grey-stone chimneys in the distance. It looked like a castle in a fairy tale, just as he had said, with the last of the morning mist catching around its towers.

'It looks like something in your nursemaid's stories,' she said. 'A magical castle.'

The corner of his lips quirked in a half-smile. 'Perhaps you would come to visit Hilltop one day?'

Rose felt her cheeks turn warm in the cold breeze and she looked away. What could he mean by such an invitation? She certainly knew better than to hope anything at all, but she couldn't help the little nervous flutter deep inside. 'I—of course. I would enjoy that very much.'

'We can make a party of it soon,' he said, his smile widening. 'Once I can make certain the house is presentable. Parts of it are very old, but I admit it does not look like a fairy tale close up.'

Rose nodded. If he intended for the others to come, surely he meant nothing by such an invitation. Jane was his neighbour, of course he would invite her house party there. 'Yes, of course.'

'Come along, you two!' she heard Jane call. She turned to see Jane and her husband at the foot of the hill, waving at them. Rose hoped they couldn't see her silly blush from there. 'We shall be late for the assembly tonight if we don't get back to Barton soon.'

'Shall we, then?' Harry said, holding out his hand to help her back on to the sled.

She laughed and took his hand in hers again. She had to enjoy every bit of that freedom while she had it. He sat down behind her, his strong, warm body blocking the cold wind, and they launched down the hill. It felt as if her heart would soar free with it and she laughed in sheer delight.

Rose peeked curiously out the carriage window as they made their way along the Barton village street towards the assembly rooms. In the daylight, the building was a perfectly ordinary long, low, brick structure meant for meetings and gatherings. For a holiday evening, though, it was quite transformed. Golden light spilled from every window and doorway, covering all with a warm sparkle in the dark winter night. Laughter rose and fell from the revellers making their way inside, blending with the strains of music as the small orchestra tuned their instruments to prepare for the dancing.

As soon as they rolled to a stop, Jane had taken Hayden's arm and disappeared into the crowd, leaving Emma and her husband and Rose to follow them. The rest of the party emerged from the next carriage, without Lady Fallon, who had been rather late and promised to come after. Harry and his brother were also coming after. Rose tried not to look for him, tried not to wonder if he would ask her to dance when he arrived. Their moment alone in the woods seemed so far away here in the noisy crowd.

After their wraps were left with the attendants, the Barton party joined the stream of merrymakers making their way up the stairs to the ballroom itself. It was a long, narrow chamber, the walls painted a pale blue to match the heavy curtains at the windows where the light drifts of snow could be seen, but everything was made warm for the season with garlands and wreaths of greenery. Tables draped in snowy linens held punch bowls and plates of sandwiches and cakes, interspersed with silver vases of holly.

As Emma and the others melted into the crowds, Rose accepted a glass of wonderfully warm negus and found a quiet corner where she could watch it all. Everyone wore their holiday best, silks and muslins and velvets, the young people smiling shyly at each other as they found dance partners, Jane and a few others making up card tables near the fireplaces at either end of the room. It was a lovely scene, like a painting or something in a song of holiday cheer. Rose only wished she had something to wear besides her grey silk, especially as she saw Lady Fallon at last make her entrance, very glamorous in midnight-blue velvet and black tulle.

Oh, well, Rose thought ruefully as she sipped at her drink. Her grey silk was perfectly respectable and no one had asked her to play for the dancing yet, as she usually did on the few occasions she was at a dance. It was a rather nice evening. She had certainly become good at holding up walls and that was where she got the best view.

She pressed as close as she could to the wall behind her, feeling the smoothness of the blue paper through the old silk of her gown and sipping at the rest of her drink as she took the measure of the crowd. Every party was different, unpredictable, even when it was the same people going about the same activities of dancing and cards and gossip.

It was a surprisingly large crowd, considering the damp, chilly night it was outside, with a few drifts of snow lazily floating down from the sky. She thought she wouldn't completely mind being home by a large fire with a good book herself, but she realised with a sudden wistful pang that she wished it was her own house, her own fire, a book of her choosing and maybe, if she was truly to dream big, someone to read it with. To laugh with.

An image popped into her mind of Harry smiling in the snow, laughing with her as their sled flew down the hill. Rose blinked hard, trying to push away such an enticing and impossible vision.

But—he *had* invited her to visit Hilltop, albeit with their rest of the party. It was surely a mere spur-of-the-moment politeness which meant no more than that. What if, by some wondrous chance, though, it was something a bit—more?

Rose shook her head at herself and gulped down the last of her now cool drink. She had spent her whole life being the sensible one. She *had* to be, or her dear mother and sister would have been in even greater straits when her father died. Romantic dreams were luxuries. Luxuries she had always known couldn't be hers.

She glanced out the tall windows beyond the refreshment tables and saw that the snow was coming down a bit heavier, soft, sparkling flurries against the velvet night. Its wintry silence made the merriment indoors seem cosy and Rose couldn't help but wonder where Harry and his brother were. Surely they had not broken down on their journey to the village?

'Miss Parker,' she heard someone say and turned to see Emma Marton hurrying towards her, along with her husband and another lady, a tall, elegant woman in plain dark green velvet, who Rose recognised as Mrs Anson from their card game. 'Whatever are you doing here by yourself? And your glass is empty! David, dearest, could you fetch us some punch?'

David Marton, always such a kind and obliging, not to mention ridiculously handsome man, smiled and gallantly kissed his wife's hand before he disappeared in the crowds around the refreshment tables.

Emma turned back to Rose and said, 'You have met Mrs Anson, yes, who manages my bookstore for me? Rose Parker is our own cousin and loves books quite as much as we do, I'm happy to say.'

'I'm very glad to see you again, Miss Parker,' Mrs Anson said with a smile. Rose was drawn to her at once and not just because she also wore spectacles. 'It's always marvellous to meet friends of Emma's, especially a fellow reader. Have you by chance tried the new Mrs Radcliffe? I found it quite chilling.'

'I haven't, though I must say I have been dying to have a peek at it,' Rose answered. 'I'm working as companion to an aunt, you see, and while she does enjoy reading aloud, her tastes do tend to run to sermons and not horrid novels. I must sneak off at bedtime to read by myself in the candlelight, which makes such tales even more fearsome.'

Mrs Anson laughed. 'I do sympathise. After I lost my husband, I too had to live with some aunts, until this position in Emma's wonderful shop came about. Now I can read to my heart's content.'

'And I could not keep the store without her,' Emma said. 'I think books have certainly saved our sanity, if not our very lives, at times, have they not?'

Rose laughed and nodded as David Marton came back with their drinks. The orchestra, a group of local musicians who Emma said were more noted for their volume than their ability to stay in tune, launched into the first dance and couples started to form into sets on the narrow, crowded dance floor. At the same moment, the door opened to admit a party of latecomers. Among them were Harry and his brother at last.

Harry did look so handsome in his dark blue evening coat and stark white cravat, Rose thought. In the candlelight, his scars could barely be seen and his smile was open and friendly, if a bit cautious. Rose glanced away, feeling her cheeks grow warm again, only to find herself being watched by Lady Fallon. The lady's head was tilted to one side, as if she was curious about something, a small frown on her lips. When she saw Rose looking at her, she gave a jaunty smile and turned away.

'Harry, Charles!' Emma called, waving them over. 'There you are at last. We were beginning to think something dreadful had happened to you.'

Harry laughed and Rose was struck by how it lit his whole face. Indeed, he seemed altogether brighter that evening. It was quite enchanting. 'Only an emergency in which Charlie could not choose his cravat.'

'The right cravat is an essential element of one's attire,' Charles said chidingly. 'It must suit the party atmosphere.'

Rose glanced at the cravat in question, but to her it looked as all such things did—white and starched into ruffled folds. Mrs Anson laughed and said, 'Oh, it does indeed. I see you have chosen an emerald pin as well, very suited to Christmas.'

Emma glanced between them, a thoughtful expression on her elfin face. 'Such a cravat does deserve a proper showing, Charles. Perhaps on the dance floor?'

'Of course,' Charles said with a bow. 'My reeling skills are a bit rusty, but I would be honoured if you would be my partner, Lady Marton.'

Emma laughed and touched the small swell of her stomach under her velvet gown. 'Oh, no, I am not up to dancing tonight. I shall have to join my sister and the others for cards. But Mrs Anson does enjoy it so.'

Charles turned to Mrs Anson with a smile. 'Will you do me the honour, then, Mrs Anson? I promise not to tread on your slippers too much.'

Mrs Anson accepted with a smile and took Charles's arm to make her way into the set. Rose could feel Emma and Harry both looking at her and she fidgeted with her skirt to keep from blushing again.

'Shall we join them, Miss Parker?' Harry asked. She peeked up to find him smiling at her ruefully, as if he knew what she was thinking. 'My dancing skills have never been as fine as my brother's, but I'm sure we can learn together. It must be easier than guiding a sled.'

Rose laughed, put at her ease in an instant, as was always the case with him. 'It's been a long while for me as well, since Lily and I had girlhood lessons. I'm sure the dances we were taught then are most unfashionable by now, but perhaps if we just follow the others…'

'We danced well together before, did we not?' he said.

Rose smiled at the memory. 'Indeed we did.'

Harry offered her his arm and she slipped her gloved hand lightly on to his sleeve. His arm was warm and strong under her touch, reassuring as he led her through the crowd. She felt a strange, tingling sensation on the back of her neck, just under her heavy chignon of hair. Startled, she glanced back and found Lady Fallon watching her intently with narrowed eyes.

That look seemed—envious. Which was entirely ridiculous. Lady Fallon was a vivacious beauty, especially in her fashionable gown, ruby and diamond combs in her high-piled golden-red hair. Why would she look so at Rose, with her second-best, much-worn grey silk?

But then again—Rose did have Harry's arm at the moment, she realised. She remembered much too well the first time they had met, when everyone said surely Captain St George would marry the lovely Helen. He'd left with his regiment and she married the rich Lord Fallon, but all of that was changed now.

Rose glanced up at Harry, uncertain, and he smiled back at her. The candlelight, the music and the laughter, the sweet-spicy cinnamon smell of Christmas and above all the feeling of Harry at her side—surely it was something, one small moment, she could savour? It couldn't last long, but it made her feel a wondrous holiday glow all the same.

She vowed to forget Lady Fallon, to forget Aunt Sylvia and her cold house, to forget everything else just for a moment. She did have to be so careful in her life. She was with Harry now for just one dance. His arm felt so strong, so steady under her touch. Surely such a man would hold her strong and steady, never letting her fall in the confusing twirls and reversals of a dance that was too much like life.

Maybe, just maybe, he would give her another of those smiles again, too.

Rose Parker was a most unusual young lady indeed. Harry had known that from the first moment they met, at that party so long ago, and now he was sure of it. She *did* remind him of that fairy queen in his story, but warm and real and laughing. It had been hard to part from her at the end of their dance, to lead Helen into the figures for the next set. Rose had been led away to play at the pianoforte and he couldn't see her any longer.

As a line of dancers separated him from Helen, Harry tried to catch a glimpse of Rose over the heads of the crowd packed close around them, but she had vanished. He could only see the top of her light brown hair. He almost laughed at himself for the pang of disappointment he felt.

There was no use for it. He was too old, too damaged, too burdened with responsibilities now to think about a young lady like Rose Parker. She was too pretty, too kind—and too caught in the traps of responsibility to family, just as he was. They would not be good for one another, not situated as they both were in life.

Yet that disappointment *was* there, and no mistaking it. When Rose was near, she always intrigued him. What was she thinking about, behind those unfathomable eyes? She was always watchful, always with that small smile curving on her shell-pink lips, as if she saw all around her and found it amusing, delightful, despite the straits she found herself in with her poor curate's wife of a sister and working as a companion for an elderly aunt. But none of it seemed to have affected her sweetness, her pleasure in the Christmas festivities.

He had no place for someone like Rose in his life now, not with Hilltop depending on him, and she had no room for him. Long ago, when he went into the army after a too-wild time as a young man, when he had caused much pain and trouble for his family, he had vowed he would change. He would fight for what was right, for his country and his home, and now he had to fulfil that vow. However he could.

'Harry, darling,' Helen said merrily. 'You must pay attention!'

He snapped back into the real world, the noisy, crowded assembly, and saw that Helen smiled at him as she held out her hands. It was their turn to twirl down the line and the others watched them impatiently.

Helen laughed and clasped his hand to spin and skip in the elaborate steps he somehow remembered from childhood classes, when he and Helen and Charlie had been schooled by a stern French dancing master with other loud children.

'You do remember how to be a gentleman,' she said as they turned in allemande.

'Just barely,' he answered. 'It must be your elegant influence.'

'Oh, I don't know. You did very well partnering Miss Parker. I think you underestimate yourself, Harry,' she said. 'In so many ways.'

As she had underestimated him, leaving behind a possible future as a mere military wife to wed a lord? He almost asked her, but then he just laughed. All of that seemed so long ago. That Harry, and surely even that Helen, no longer existed. What did she want now?

What indeed did *he* want now? His life, a life that once was as regimented as a parade, was now like a grey cloud lowering over the horizon, obscuring all.

You need an heiress, he heard Charles say in his mind. And an heiress would indeed be an answer for Hilltop. He himself would admit that companionship, a partner, would be most welcome.

He looked down at Helen, at her brilliant smile, the flash of jewels in her hair, and for an instant he felt the tug of temptation towards a life that had never been his. A life of carefree glitter.

But then, over the swirl of the dancers, he glimpsed Rose Parker, laughing with the other musicians as her slender fingers lightly skipped over the keys. And he was drawn towards her soft warmth that was like a fire on a cold day, sustaining and sweet.

Rose deserved far more than what he had to offer, a wounded soldier whose house was falling down around him. That was one thing he did know for sure.

'Harry!' he heard Helen cry and suddenly realised he had once again lost the rhythm of the dance. Just like the reins of responsibility for Hilltop, he had to take them up again.

He took her hand and led her down the line again, Helen laughing as if it was all the greatest lark, as surely her life often was.

As they turned to circle the outside of the set, he glimpsed his brother standing on the sidelines, ignoring the elderly matron who chattered at his elbow. Charles grinned at Harry and raised his glass in salute.

Harry nodded back, but the delight in the party he had felt so briefly was gone.

'You see,' Jane said with a satisfied smile as she laid down her cards. Rather than dancing, she had decided another hand of whist with her husband and Emma and David was preferable, and now she was glad of it. From her seat at the table by the fire, she could observe the whole assembly. 'It is all coming off rather well.'

'What is?' Emma asked, frowning down at her hand of cards.

'My matchmaking, of course!' Jane said. 'I do like it when I have a fine idea.'

'Oh, my dear, no,' Hayden groaned. 'Surely you don't still think of that?'

'Think what?' Emma cried in confusion. Her husband, who was accustomed to his in-laws' fancies, calmly laid down a card and smiled.

'Harry St George and Helen Fallon were once nearly betrothed, were they not?' Jane said. 'And now here they are, each of them single once again. And each has something the other needs. Why should they not fall for each other again?'

'Sometimes fate parts people for a good reason, Sister,' Emma said. 'Perhaps they were not meant for each other.'

'And sometimes two people must learn to find each other at the *right* time,' Jane said with a tender smile at her husband, whom she had once almost lost. 'It was just so with us.'

Hayden shook his head. 'But Captain St George and Lady Fallon are not us, my love.'

Jane glanced at the dance floor. 'They do look well together, though.'

'He looked well dancing with Rose Parker, too,' Emma said with a sneaking smile.

'Rose Parker?' Jane said in surprise.

'Yes. And surely their personalities are rather well suited,' Emma said. 'They are both so quiet, so easy to be around.'

Jane looked at Rose, who sat at the pianoforte. She had not thought of such a thing, but Emma did have a point. And a lady without a fortune did need a home, one better than with an old aunt.

'No,' she murmured. 'Harry must surely consider Hilltop now and all its tenants. And we must find someone well settled for Rose.'

Emma looked doubtful, but she nodded. 'Just as you say, Jane.'

And while they were so occupied with romance, David won the hand easily.

Chapter Ten

⚮

Charles St George took a deep drag on his cheroot, tasting the cherry-smoke darkness at the back of his throat, before he exhaled the silvery plume into the frosty air of the small garden behind the assembly rooms. He could hear the music from the windows behind him, the stomp of dancing feet, the beat of the music, but it seemed very far away, like something in a dream.

It had been much the same on the Continent. The music and laughter in casinos and ballrooms, the subtle dance of glances and smiles, the silent language everyone seemed to understand but him. At least at first. Eventually he learned it, even mastered it. But here, back at the home he had shunned for so long—it all seemed strange again. A cacophony he couldn't quite make out clearly. All those happy couples in their contented homes—Jane and Hayden, Emma and David, and all their friends and their children. How did they do it? Charles found it such a mystery.

He thought of the people, especially the women, he had known in Europe. The beautiful, sophisticated ladies with their satins and their jewels, their brittle laughter. *That* was what he knew. Lightness, flirtations, fleeting moments. Songs and laughter around the Christmas candles he could not fathom. And yet...

Yet he longed for it, wanted it with a primitive fierceness he hadn't felt since he was a child and so wanted to belong. Yet he never had, except for his brother.

Charles inhaled from his cheroot again and stared up into the sky. It was a cold night, so crisp the breeze felt it could snap in two, but the sky was clear now, the earlier snow ceased. The stars sparkled like diamonds on a lady's black velvet gown, glittering so he wanted to reach out and feel their heat on his skin. Feel alive again.

Once, he would have longed to paint the scene, the bare trees against the candlelit windows, the elusive sparkle of the stars. Once his paintbrush could make sense of so many things around him, but now even that urge had deserted him. After what had happened to Harry on the battlefield, seeing Hilltop in such trouble, painting seemed frivolous.

Surely his father had been right. Art was useless for a man. Charles gave a bitter laugh and raised his cheroot to his lips again.

'Do you happen to have one of those to spare?' he heard a soft voice ask.

Surprised, he spun around to find Helen standing behind him. With the sparkle of jewels in her hair, the soft shimmer of her blue gown, she looked like a goddess. But silk gloves and tulle sleeves were no use in the cold wind and she shivered a bit in spite of her bright smile.

She had always been beautiful and so far above his touch. But now there was a lack of a smile in her eyes, a disillusionment like his own.

'Of course,' he replied quickly, not knowing what to say to her, how to reach her. All his skills of flirtation learned in those spa towns seemed useless with Helen. As if they would bounce right off that diamond-hard, brilliant shell that had grown around her beautiful self since he had seen her last. She no longer seemed to be the girl he had known for so long, the beautiful, fiery, adventurous Helen, the one who made him envy Harry for being her intended.

But that was a very long time ago. None of them were the same people now.

He took out his silver cheroot case and offered her one, lighting it from the remains of his own. Then he removed his velvet evening coat and tucked it around her shoulders against the cold night.

She smiled up at him and it seemed a different smile than before, softer, more tentative. More like the Helen he once knew and he felt a flash of something strangely like hope.

'It's a vile habit, I know,' she said, balancing the thin cigar between her gloved fingers. 'You must not tell anyone.'

Charles laughed. 'Your secret is always safe with me.'

Helen laughed, too, and it sounded like music on the cold breeze. 'You are clever to find such a hiding place, Charlie. Sometimes it feels as if there isn't one place left to disappear in all the world.'

'I'm surprised you would ever want to disappear. Are you not the belle of every ball?'

She smiled, her oval face wreathed in smoke. 'How can I live with such a thing all the time? It's amusing sometimes, of course. But never to get away from everyone watching...' She broke off and shook her head. 'One has to always, always smile, or the rumours will fly.'

That sounded intriguing. 'What sort of rumours?'

'Oh, you know, Charlie. I am sure that you, of all people, know.' Her smile turned bitter again.

'Helen,' he said carefully. 'What was it really like, being married to Fallon?'

Helen took a deep inhale of the smoke, not looking at him. 'Oh, you know. It is an old title that opens every door. Is that not what every girl wants? A title, a place in society, a role as a leader of fashion.'

Charles nodded. A marriage to Harry could not have given her that, it was true. 'Was it what *you* wanted?'

She shrugged. 'Of course. What else is there? To be a woman like Miss Parker, forced to be a companion or a governess?' She glanced at the party behind the windows, an unreadable expression on her face. 'But she is kind, isn't she?'

'Who?' Charles asked, unable to follow the meander of Helen's thoughts.

'Miss Parker, of course. She is sweet. Pretty, in her quiet way. She makes people around her want to smile, to feel that the world *can* be good, just as she is. She has such power, but she doesn't know it. Nice people like her never do.' She studied the stars high above their heads for a moment. 'Sometimes I wish I could be like that. Could deserve—more.'

Charles felt his heart ache at her sadness and he longed to take it away, to erase it as if it had never been, even as he knew he was not the person for such a task. He had too many ugly burdens of his own, hidden inside. 'Helen,' he said roughly. It took all the self-control he had left not to add the word *darling*, not to take her into his arms and hold her close against the cold world that seemed to hold them both prisoners. 'You deserve so very much. You deserve *everything*.'

She turned to look at him, her pale, perfect face filled with surprise. Her eyes were wide, startled. But she quickly covered it with that hard, brilliant smile. 'Charlie, you *are* a dear. But you don't know what I've done in my life.'

'Nor do you know what I have done, what I have seen. You can tell me anything you want, Helen, anything at all and I won't be shocked.'

'No, I don't think you would.' She glanced in the windows behind them, watching the shadows of the dancers pass beyond the glass. 'But what of Harry? What do you think he would think?'

Was that it, then? Helen still wanted Harry after all this time? Charles felt something he had not in a long time—sadness. 'He is your friend, too.'

She gave a bright little laugh. 'Oh, yes. My friend. Harry is so good, so like Miss Parker in some ways, isn't he? He has always put others before himself. His country, his duty. Once I thought that so boring. Didn't you, Charlie dear?'

'Maybe I did, once.'

'But we are all older now. Isn't that supposed to make us see so much clearer?' She turned away from the dancers and smiled up at him, a beacon of pure, bright light in the dark night. 'Tell me, do you still paint?'

'No. The will to see clear enough to put something down on canvas seems to have deserted me.'

Helen tilted her head as she studied him. 'I am indeed sorry to hear that. I loved your paintings. You made the world look so beautiful, like a place where one could be at peace. Do you remember a scene you did once of your mother's rose garden?'

He nodded, his thoughts going back to the summer beauty of the garden, the scent of the roses on the warm breeze—and Helen walking along the paths, a solitary figure in white he tried to capture. 'Yes.'

'It was wondrous. Like heaven should be, I think. I have never found a place to equal it. Nor, I suppose, have you.'

He shook his head. Her smile faded and she turned away to crush the end of her cheroot under her satin shoe. She slid off his coat and held it out to him.

'Thank you, Charlie,' she said simply and then she was gone, hurrying back into the crowded assembly and leaving only a trace of her exotic jasmine perfume behind.

Find an heiress for Hilltop, Charles had told Harry so blithely. So foolishly, as if heiresses were mere pieces to be moved around a chessboard. Surely their old friend Helen would do. How he regretted those words now. Helen was no mere heiress, no mere solution to a problem or childhood memory. She was so much more, had become so much more. And she deserved a fine man like Harry to make her truly smile again.

Charles look up at the cold, hard stars and found that they seemed even further away than ever before. Just like Helen herself.

Chapter Eleven

Harry stood back and studied the façade of the house with a careful, critical eye. Hilltop was not as modern or comfortable as Barton, he had to admit that. It had retained the look of an earlier time, with its rough stone walls and old towers, its wavy, thick-glass windows gazing out at the world, but letting little of it in.

But he liked the look of it and he hoped Rose would, too. She seemed to enjoy old tales, stories of fairy-tale castles. Hilltop did have just such an appearance.

Why did he care so much about whether or not Rose liked his house?

He picked up the holly wreath that lay at his feet and hung it on the old, stained, stout wooden door. It gleamed there, all glossy green leaves and bright red berries, brightening the grey stone and sending out a welcome on the cold day. It made him think of Rose herself, so warm in a cold world.

* * *

The day of the planned visit to Hilltop dawned bright and clear, cold but with a rare turquoise sky arching overhead. Rose was mesmerised by its beauty, by the prospect of the lovely day ahead, the rare treat of a ride, the chance to see Harry in his own home. She wanted to enjoy it to the fullest and not think too hard about what her feelings meant, what hurt they might bring her in the future.

Harry had ridden ahead and only Jane and Hayden elected to come along on the excursion. All the others wanted to stay near the fireplace with their cards and newspapers. Jane and her husband lagged behind Rose on the short ride, whispering and laughing together, like a pair of newly wed lovebirds free of their children and duties for a few hours.

Rose, too, felt a rare sense of freedom, of lightness. It was something she barely even remembered feeling before. She hadn't been able to ride in a long time, and at first she felt quite uncertain in the saddle, even though Jane assured her this was the gentlest mare in the Barton stable. But it had all come back to her in a wonderful rush, the power of the reins in her hands, the freedom of speed. The deliciousness of forgetting everything else for a moment.

It was so much like dancing with Harry, that feeling that her feet could leave the ground and she could fly free.

She urged her horse into a gallop along the pathway, winding their way up a hill beyond the Barton woods. She laughed as the cold wind caught at her hat and rushed over her cheeks. Yes—it was indeed like dancing, but only dancing with Harry!

She reined in her horse at the crest of the hill to wait for Jane and Hayden. From that vantage point, high above the pale rolling fields, she could see for what seemed like miles and miles. Barton Park, with all its fine, noisy company, and even her calmly dutiful life with Aunt Sylvia, were left far behind, and there was only that endless sky above her.

She remembered how she had felt once, so long ago, when she had been impossibly young and the world full of all the opportunities she had read about in books. It hadn't turned out that way at all, of course. But here, now, at Christmas, she did recall how it felt to be that girl.

Her horse pawed restlessly at the frosty ground as Rose twisted around in the saddle to look towards where she knew the chimneys of Hilltop lay. She didn't know what she expected to see beyond the grey-stone walls that bisected Barton, Hilltop and Emma's home at Rose Hill. Perhaps a different land, a fairy land of clouds and mysterious groves, like in the story Harry had said his nursemaid once read to him.

Yet it all looked much the same, fallow winter fields, hills and half-frozen streams, all laid out like a patchwork blanket sewn together with those stone walls and fringed around the outside with woods.

In the distance, though, she glimpsed old brick chimneys and towers, and a curl of smoke that seemed to beckon a welcome. The house at Hilltop, just as Harry had pointed it out to her on their sled ride.

She glanced back over her shoulder to see that Jane and Hayden still lagged behind, making slow progress up the hillside. They waved at her, laughing as if they too felt the precious, fragile power of the day, and she waved back.

She urged the horse forward, down the slope of the hill and on to a wider path, lined on either side with railed fences. Down there, in the shelter of a small valley, the light seemed greyer, more shadowed. Over the fields stood a clutch of cottages, the whitewashed and thatched houses of Hilltop tenants. When she turned through an open set of gates, once finely wrought iron in a pattern of pineapples and pomegranates but now rusted, she found Hilltop itself.

She remembered the fanciful thoughts of fairy tales and almost could have vowed she had truly found herself inside one. Unlike Barton, which had been renovated and redecorated over many years, Hilltop looked like something from a medieval world. It was built of old grey stone, overgrown with yellowing ivy, round crenelated towers still guarding its four corners, with mullioned windows staring down at her like ancient eyes. She wouldn't have been surprised to see a moat and a drawbridge, with knights galloping over it and swords drawn.

As if to prove she had entered a medieval dream, she heard the pounding of hooves behind her, like those knights. She glanced back to see that it was only Jane and Hayden, catching up with her. They were laughing, as if they had been in a merry race, and it brought her back to the present day, to the reality of where and who she was. Just plain Rose Parker, lady's companion with cloudy dreams of romance.

She turned back to the house, suddenly nervous to see Harry again.

'It is a tiny bit gloomy, is it not?' Jane said, studying the great, thick, nail-studded fortress of the front door. 'But then again, so was Barton once. It only takes a bit of style to bring it into the comfortable modern day.'

Hayden laughed. 'Only when the style has your impeccable taste, my love.'

'Nothing so easy, as you well know,' Jane said. 'What do you think, Rose?'

Rose looked up at the towers, so much like some place a fairy queen would really live in, magical and ancient. 'I think it looks enchanting. Like Sleeping Beauty's palace.'

'How right you are!' Jane exclaimed. 'One kiss and all would be well again.'

The doors opened with a great, rusty squeal and

Harry appeared at the top of the cracked stone steps. In his tweeds and doeskin breeches, he looked like the country squire he was, not the solider he used to be. Rose found she liked both personas equally.

He had that wry half-smile he wore so often, but the bright gleam in his eye gave her hope he was indeed happy to see her there at Hilltop. Just as *she* was happy to be there, to see him and his home again.

'So you found your way here at last,' he called, making his way down the steps.

'Oh, you must blame our tardiness entirely on me, Harry!' Jane said merrily as she and Hayden entered the courtyard. 'It is too lovely a day to be inside, but we are so excited to see Hilltop again. You and Charlie have become much too reclusive.'

'I fear the old place is in no shape for fine parties,' Harry said. 'But I hope old friends can start to darken this warped old door again. The housekeeper is beside herself with excitement and has laid on a splendid tea.'

'I'm happy to hear that, for I am quite famished,' Rose said. 'I don't know how you fine military men ride for weeks! I've only been in the saddle for an hour and am thoroughly exhausted.'

'We can't have that, now, can we?' Harry reached up to help her down from her horse.

They stood there for a long moment, his hands warm at her waist, their bodies mere inches from each other. Rose couldn't seem to stop herself from leaning into him and inhaled deeply of his scent, cool wind and citrus soap lingering on his coat. How wonderful it felt to be so close to him again, like a delightful, delicious forbidden treat. She had a fierce longing to throw her arms about his neck and hold on to him, to let that lovely new feeling wash over her and carry her away. She felt his shoulders stiffen under her touch, as if he could read her thoughts.

She stepped back reluctantly, feeling a sharp pang at losing his closeness. She knew she had to enjoy such feelings in the moment, to store them up for memories in the lonely future. She turned to study the house before her.

Close up, she saw it was not quite the fairy tale she had first taken it for, though the sense of being a dwelling slumbering under a spell was still quite strong. The tiles of the roof were cracked and chipped, even broken away in places, shattered on the old cobblestones of the courtyard. Some of the windows of the upper floor were boarded up and the flowerbeds that had once lined the drive in colourful profusion were overgrown.

Yet there was a wreath of holly and evergreen hung over the door, a brave note of bright colour. 'You have a holly wreath!' she said. 'When Lily and I were children, our father always said we must have holly at our door for Christmas. He said the holiday spirits would hide under the leaves to stay out of the winter cold and they would leave a blessing in return.'

Harry's smile widened. 'And did it work?'

Rose laughed. 'I don't know. Lily and I would stay up all hours of the night trying to glimpse them, but we never did. Though on Christmas morning, next to our breakfast plates, there were always extra sweets from the fairies.' She paused for a moment and in her mind she saw Lily small again, their mother's secret smiles with their father, the magical expectation of the day. 'It is strange. I haven't thought of that in so long.'

'I admit I had no thought of spirits when I had it put up there. I merely wanted you to see something pretty at Hilltop. I fear you'll be disappointed by the lack of festive decorations inside, though.' He led her up the old stone steps and swung open the doors, and Jane and Hayden trailed behind them, arm in arm. 'Most of the few servants we have left here have gone back to their families until Boxing Day and it's rather bare and cold.'

Rose had to laugh. 'You should see Aunt Sylvia's home. It is bare and cold every day, not to mention deathly quiet. This is…' She caught her breath at the sudden sight of the great hall she found herself in. 'Not dull at all. It's like something from King Arthur.'

She spun around in a circle, taking it all in. Just like the exterior of the house, the interior looked just as a fairy tale should. The great hall soared upwards, bisected by a wide stone staircase lined with an ornate iron balustrade that had fallen away in places. A huge iron chandelier hung high overhead, meant to illuminate the ancient, shredded pennants on the wall, the shields and swords hanging on the peeling walls, speaking of ancient times of St George glory.

'How very unfashionable, Harry,' Jane said with a laugh, removing her riding hat and gloves. Rose pulled her thoughts away from the Camelot fascination and followed suit. They left their accessories on the one piece of furniture, an old mosaic table, and Harry took their cloaks.

Rose fidgeted with her skirt, wishing she had a more à la mode habit, not just her old green wool one. It felt so out of place in the grandeur.

'Not much to be done about the fashion now, I'm afraid,' Harry said, a rueful smile in his tone. 'But I won't force you to take your tea in this great, chilly room.'

He led them along a long, narrow corridor, past a series of closed doors. Where one or two were open a crack, Rose glimpsed chambers shrouded with canvas covers, windows covered with dusty, faded velvet curtains, bare spots on the walls where paintings had once hung, empty cabinets whose *objets* had once been displayed.

Rose remembered the rumours that Harry needed a rich wife for his estate, for his duties, and she wondered sadly if that was all too correct.

Harry led them into a small sitting room at the end of the hallway and it was like stepping into another house altogether. The wallpaper, though much faded, was a lovely yolk-yellow with matching curtains at the windows and yellow and white striped upholstery on the chairs drawn close to a blazing fire in the white marble grate. A woman's portrait hung over the carved mantel, a lady with Charles St George's curling hair and Harry's eye colour, clad in yellow silk and pearls, smiling out at the world with her hands elegantly folded in her lap. A table was laid out with a tarnished silver teapot and china painted with small purple flowers, plates of sandwiches and iced cakes.

'Is that your mother?' Rose asked. 'How elegant she was.'

'Yes. This was her favourite room. Thankfully my father never touched it, or we wouldn't have a comfortable place to sit,' Harry answered, smiling at the painting. 'Please, everyone, do make yourselves comfortable.'

Rose perched on the edge of one of the chairs, unable to be rid of the feeling that Mrs St George was watching them, judging to see if they were worthy to be in her sitting room, in her home.

'Shall I pour?' Jane asked, reaching for the teapot. 'I fear I don't remember much about your mother, Harry, but my parents always said she used to give such lovely parties here. She was obviously a lady of fine taste.'

'Indeed she was,' Harry answered. 'Hilltop hasn't been the same since we lost her.'

Jane passed around the cups. 'They did say Hilltop was once quite the social centre of the neighbourhood! My mother said artists, politicians and leaders of fashion of all sorts came here. It must have been extraordinary.'

'Yes,' Harry said. 'Everyone loved my mother. My father could not do without her.'

'Such a sad and romantic tale,' Jane said. 'But Hilltop still has such potential. It could be that way again!'

'I fear I don't have such a social disposition, my dear Jane,' Harry said. He laughed, but Rose could sense something lurking just beneath, a tension, a discomfort. She wanted to soothe it, to tell him his home would be again as it was with his mother, but she didn't know how. Except for that wealthy heiress. She couldn't be that. Only the beautiful Helen Fallon could.

'Oh, Harry, no one expects the man to make a house a real home,' Jane said. 'That is the wife's job. I am sure your mother would agree.' She nodded towards the smiling, beautiful woman in the portrait.

'I am sure she would,' Harry said. 'But you must talk to Charlie about such matters, he is far more handsome and cosmopolitan than me. No fine lady would look twice at a battle-scarred old man like myself. Would you care for a sandwich?'

He passed around the plates of delicacies and

the talk turned to lighter matters, Jane's plans for a Christmas ball, the cold weather. The hour passed most pleasantly and, as the fire died down, Harry knelt down to build it up again.

'Oh, Harry, surely that is not your job,' Jane said with a laugh.

Harry tossed her a grin over his shoulder as he bent over the hearth stones, a wonderful, light-hearted smile Rose wanted to see again. 'I did learn one or two things in the army. I can't let my skills go rusty now.'

Rose sat back and watched as he rebuilt the fire in the grate and he soon had it roaring high enough to warm three rooms. The long, lean muscles of his back and broad shoulders shifted and flexed against his fine tweed coat and she remembered how those shoulders felt under her touch as they danced. The heat and strength of him, the way he made her feel so safe.

And she was not the only one he kept safe. He spent his life doing just that, looking after others, in the army and now at his family home. She knew he would never turn away from that duty.

She remembered his story of the young farmer he knew in the army, the one who had died and left his family behind, and Harry's longing for home, his need to do the right thing by his people. She knew those things would never change about him.

'Would you like to see more of the house?' he asked.

'Oh, yes!' Jane answered eagerly. 'I remember it in your mother's time, it was so lovely.'

'I'm afraid I don't have my mother's fine taste,' Harry said. 'But maybe you and Miss Parker could offer some female advice?'

Jane laughed, and took her husband's arm. 'Lead on, Harry!'

He took them through a series of rooms, most of them sparsely furnished or with canvas covers over chairs and tables, but it was still an intriguing house indeed, with old linenfold panelling on the walls, doors that led on to mysterious passages, vaulted ceilings with fading paintings of knights and ladies.

Jane and Hayden drifted away into another room, their voices echoing back to them, but Rose was enchanted by the paintings high above her head.

'How lovely they are,' she murmured.

'My mother commissioned an artist to make them when she first moved here,' he said. 'They are rather faded now, but I think they suit the house. The fair maidens and the castles...'

'It's so enchanting,' she said, spinning towards him. 'Just like—like you, Harry.'

He took her hand and spun her in a dancing circle. 'It suits *you*, Rose.' Something in his hoarse voice caught her, held her, and she looked up at him in a haze.

He turned his face to kiss the inside of her wrist, the pulse that beat there so frantically at the nearness of him. His breath was so warm and vital and delicious on her bare skin, a fantasy she could hardly have dared dream could come true. If only she could do the same for him, could make *him* feel safe. Help him.

But she was poor and he had to protect his home now. She couldn't do all she wanted for him.

'I—we should find Jane,' she said and broke away from him to hurry away. She felt so foolish, running away like that, but she didn't know what else to do. She needed to be near other people, to find shelter in the decorum of a group.

But she found there wouldn't be much 'decorum', for Jane and Hayden were kissing in the pale sunlight that drifted from the windows of the drawing room. They broke apart guiltily, and Rose had to laugh at the blush on her cousin's cheeks, as if they were naughty newlyweds.

Harry came up behind her and he laughed, too, putting her at ease once more. She would have to forsake his company soon enough. Surely she could enjoy that one afternoon with him?

'It looks like the sun is out now,' Harry said. 'We should take advantage of it. I was just going to ask Miss Parker if she would like to ride out with me to meet some of my tenants.'

'To visit your tenants? Really?' Rose said in surprise, feeling suddenly shy after what had happened upstairs. What might they think of her?

'I can hardly leave you to wander alone on my

estate, especially you, Jane,' he said. 'I remember what a troublemaker you were in our youth.'

'Me?' Jane cried. 'Such calumny. It was always Emma and Charlie climbing trees and scaring the grouse. Hayden, you should call him out!'

Hayden laughed. 'I can't duel with a man for telling the truth, my love.'

Jane sighed. 'I suppose not. And we *are* fortunate to have such lovely, quiet neighbours. Very well, Harry, you may live.'

Harry laughed. 'Thank you, Jane.'

'I wouldn't mind calling on some tenants of my own,' Jane said. 'Rose, why don't you go with Harry and we shall meet back at Barton?'

'Are you sure?' Rose asked in surprise. Alone, with Harry? It sounded quite thrilling.

'Of course. Someone must add a kind, tender touch for Harry's poor tenants. He must scare them to pieces with his military ways,' Jane said.

'I will take care of her,' Harry said. And she was quite sure he would.

'Jane, my darling,' Hayden said. 'What are you thinking now?'

Jane gave him an innocent smile and he quirked a dark brow. She feared she could seldom fool him after all the years of their marriage, all they had been through. 'I am merely thinking we really should call on the Porters while we are so near, since Mrs P. has the new baby. And Harry *is* quite likely to frighten someone, he does glower so since he came home.' But then again, she thought, he had not really glowered much in the last couple of days and not at all on this day.

'But that is not all you are thinking. I know you were thinking of matchmaking for poor Harry before this party began.'

'Perhaps I was,' Jane admitted. 'I just can't help it, darling. I do want all our friends to be as happy as we are.'

'And your kind heart is why I love you so much. You never give up on anyone, even on me. Harry St George is a good man and has certainly been through a great deal, war and wounds, his father dying so suddenly, the responsibilities of a place like Hilltop. More than any man should have to at once. But you and I both know a lady like Miss Parker can't help him now.'

Jane frowned. 'Rose is a lovely girl, even though she doesn't realise it.'

'She is lovely. And kind, calm and sensible. She rather reminds me of someone.'

'Really?' Jane said with a pang of jealousy. 'Who?'

Hayden laughed. 'You, of course.'

'Then why should I not try to help them along? I know I did think of him and Lady Fallon at first, but…'

'There is just one flaw in your plan, my dear, and I fear it's a large one.'

'What is that?'

'Miss Parker has no money. And Hilltop is falling down.'

'Oh. Yes.' Jane sighed, wishing she had a different, more romantic argument to make, but she couldn't find one. She glanced back at the crumbling chimneys of Hilltop and frowned. Harry St George was indeed a man who took his responsibilities seriously and his old family home was a large responsibility indeed. She knew that all too well, remembering the days when her beloved Barton was also crumbling. 'Perhaps Lady Fallon will have to be it, then.'

Still—most problems *did* have a solution, Jane told herself, if one could only think hard enough.

Rose followed Harry down the slope of a hill and along a path, narrow enough only for their horses to walk single file. Beyond the thicket of trees and out of sight of the main house, a row of cottages was laid out, near to the fields, but not as far out as the larger farms. Unlike the main house, they looked snug and tidy and recently repaired, their walls freshly whitewashed. She could hear laughter through the new windows and the timbered doors were decorated with greenery wreaths.

Harry led her past more cottages, including one that seemed to be a small shop with holiday sweets decorating the front bow window. Just beyond, in a thicket of tall trees, was a brick building. Unlike the cottages, it had no windows and the splintered door hung loose on its hinges.

'The school,' Harry said simply, solemnly, as he gestured at the building. 'My mother had it built for the tenants' children, but after she died my father closed it and it fell into disrepair.'

'Did it have many pupils?'

'A fair number. My mother thought the estate children should know reading, writing and sums, things to help them run prosperous farms and homes later.'

'She was quite right,' Rose answered, thinking of her own youthful lessons of sewing and dancing, and how little use they were. 'What of trades, such as sewing and cooking for the girls? Perhaps even training as ladies' maids or milliners?'

'That is a fine idea indeed,' Harry said, smiling as he examined the old building. 'I should very much like to repair this place and re-open the school. But such things can be—well…'

'Expensive. Yes,' Rose said ruefully. She glanced back at the half-hidden cottages, with their snug roofs and walls. 'Yet you have done so much just in the short time since you returned. The tenants' homes look so well tended. And the fields look as if they can be good producers in the summer. Jane says the soil is fine in this area. The price of corn has gone up since the end of the war and the weather this winter has been mild enough until this week.'

He gave her a surprised-looking smile. 'You're very well informed.'

Rose laughed. 'I know. Most unladylike. But part of my job is to read to Aunt Sylvia. She mostly prefers sermons and a few novels, but she does take many of the newspapers and I like to glance at them when I have the chance. Hilltop could do very well, I think, with just a bit of care.'

'Which is what I hope to give.' He gestured with his riding crop down a wider lane. 'The Perkins's farm is just this way, follow me.'

He led her down a path lined with thick hedges to a two-storey farmhouse, also whitewashed and with a thatched roof, but the paint was fresh and the thatch new, with a neat little vegetable garden enclosed by a low fence. Chickens peeked around the doorstep and the door was painted a dark green and hung with a holly wreath. Rose could feel someone watching them from the windows, studying them, *her*—the woman with Hilltop's master. Surely they were curious. Rose just wished she could be more than a visitor.

'I—perhaps I should wait for you here,' she said.

'It's much too cold for that, Rose! Besides, I assure you the Perkins family are the kindest of people. Their family has been at Hilltop for years and I know how much they love company.'

'I…' But she could make no more protests, as the door swung open. A man stood there, tall with a farmer's broad shoulders, a little girl with long, blond braids holding his hand. The man smiled and waved, and the girl practically jumped up and down in excitement. The warmth of their greeting seemed to spill right out of the cottage and wrapped around Rose like the lantern light and the scent of fresh-baked bread.

'Captain St George!' the man said. 'We didn't expect to see you here on such a cold day.'

'I got your message about the roof,' Harry said as he swung down from his saddle. He reached up to help Rose and she again seized the moment of his touch and stored it up in her memory. 'And I heard your mother was ailing. I hope she has recovered.'

'Aye, thanks to the doctor you sent to see her last week. She's doing better than she has in an age.'

'You send a doctor to your tenants?' Rose whispered to Harry, though she was not surprised at all. Being the most dutiful landlord seemed entirely like him.

'Of course. Since I've returned, it's my job. Not that there is much any doctor can do for old Mrs Perkins, I fear. She is usually much too feisty to follow his advice.'

Rose laughed, thinking of Aunt Sylvia and all the fine London physicians she had thrown out on their ears. 'I know the sort very well.'

'Captain, Captain!' the little girl cried and came skipping down the garden pathway to tug at Harry's coat-tails. 'I'm getting a new doll for Christmas.'

Harry laughed and swung the child up into his

arms, twirling her around until she shrieked with giggles. 'Are you indeed, Peggy? A fine gift for a fine girl!'

'But Papa doesn't know I know, so it's a secret.' She peeked curiously over his shoulder at Rose. 'Who is this?'

Harry gave her another twirl, and Rose laughed along with her, enchanted by this glimpse of a light-hearted Harry. He so rarely made an appearance. 'This is Miss Rose Parker, a guest at Barton Park,' he said. 'Miss Parker, this is Miss Peggy Perkins.'

Rose gave a little curtsy. 'How do you do, Miss Perkins? I am very pleased to meet you.'

Peggy studied her closely. 'You're very pretty.'

'Indeed she is,' Harry said, smiling at Rose over Peggy's head.

Rose felt her cheeks turning warm again and looked away with a nervous laugh.

'Peggy, stop chattering to the Captain and let him come inside where it's warm,' her father called.

Harry set Peggy on her feet and she led them through the doorway. 'Oscar Perkins, this is Miss Parker, one of the guests at Barton for the holiday.'

Mr Perkins didn't seem at all surprised his landlord would bring a strange lady into his house at Christmas, or if he was his wide smile didn't show it. He gave her a bow. 'You're most welcome, Miss Parker, as would be any friend of the Captain. I only wish we had a grander reception to offer you!'

Rose glanced around at the neatly swept stone

floor, the dried bundles of herbs hung from the smoke-darkened rafters that perfumed the air with lavender and rosemary, the whitewashed walls. It all reminded her of her mother's cosy cottage, the cottage that meant Rose had to work for Aunt Sylvia to make sure it was affordable.

She felt suddenly a bit sad and wistful, and silly for forgetting the real world outside even for a moment.

'Your home is lovely, Mr Perkins,' she said. 'And so kind of you to receive me so close to Christmas. You must be busy.'

'Offer the lady some tea, Oscar!' a querulous old voice called from beyond an open door. 'Show the manners I taught you.'

Mr Perkins flushed. 'My mother. She does like to, er, express herself.'

Rose laughed, again thinking old Mrs Perkins must be a lot like Aunt Sylvia. 'Some tea would be most welcome.'

'There are cakes, too,' little Peggy said. 'I helped to make them.'

'Then they must be delicious,' Rose answered. She studied the bright-eyed girl and remembered the abandoned school. How much good such a place could do for girls like Peggy! If teachers and books could be paid for and the building repaired.

'Peggy, why don't you take Miss Parker to see your grandmother while I show the Captain the roof?' Mr Perkins said.

Peggy took Rose's hand to lead her towards the open door. Rose glanced back to see Harry talking to his tenant in a low, serious voice, the two of them nodding. The light-hearted man who had swung Peggy into the air was gone again.

The sitting room was a most cosy space, small but comfortable with well-worn, shabby furnishings brightened with pretty yellow cushions and the walls painted a summery blue. A tiny, grey-haired lady sat by the fire wrapped in shawls, a white cap perched on her head. Mrs Perkins did indeed look much like a less fancy version of Aunt Sylvia, right down to her bright blue, all-seeing eyes. Rose hovered uncertainly in the doorway.

'Granny, Captain St George brought a lady to visit us,' Peggy announced. 'Her name is Miss Parker.'

'A lady?' the elder Mrs Perkins said, those perceptive eyes sweeping over Rose, taking in her plain hat and outdated riding habit. 'It's about time he did that. Past time he got himself engaged. Hilltop has been too long without a proper mistress.'

Rose laughed nervously. 'I fear I am only a guest at Barton Park, Mrs Perkins. I teach music to the Fitzwalters' children.'

'Oh. Well. That is a disappointment. But I suppose you had better sit down, anyway. Peggy, dear, go fetch the tea, will you?'

As Peggy hurried away on her errand, Rose sat

down on the stool next to Mrs Perkins's armchair. The fire was warm after the chilly day and the cottage pleasantly cosy.

'Perhaps you could persuade Lady Ramsay to find the Captain a suitable bride, then,' Mrs Perkins suggested. 'One who could make all the improvements this place needs.'

'Perhaps she could,' Rose said. 'And I would be most interested to hear what improvements you would suggest, Mrs Perkins, if the right Mrs St George could be found.'

Mrs Perkins smiled. 'I could make a long list, Miss Parker, indeed I could. The school needs to be re-opened, the fallow fields put into production again. Once, long ago, when I was a girl, the Captain's grandfather ran the estate and a fine landlord he was. Always concerned, always taking care of any problem right away. But his son…'

'The Captain's father?'

'Bah.' The old lady scowled. 'He didn't have a thought for anything but himself. Locked himself up in that house when his wife died, leaving us on our own. Running off his own sons. Master Charles—now there is a bonny young man, but I fear he takes too much after his father.'

'And does the Captain take after him?'

'Never! The Captain is a good man, a dutiful one. Look what he sacrificed in battle. Wounded like that and then coming home to a shambles. 'Tis a great shame. But we know he will always do his duty to Hilltop and to us.'

Rose nodded. She had seen that for herself. No one cared more about this place, about his duty, than Harry. 'In finding a wife?'

'Of course. Every estate needs a mistress. She would have to be the right sort, though.'

'The right sort?'

'Sensible and steady. A good, practical head on her shoulders, not like the Captain's pretty mother, rest her soul.' Mrs Perkins gave a cackling laugh. 'And rich, of course. Hilltop can't be fixed without that.'

'No,' Rose whispered. Money was the one thing she did not have to offer. 'It can't.'

Mrs Perkins peered at her closer. 'You aren't rich, are you, Miss Parker?'

'I fear not.'

'Pity.' Mrs Perkins settled back among her shawls. 'You do seem a sensible girl. Not bad looking, either.'

Rose had to laugh. 'Thank you.'

Peggy brought in the tea then, carefully balancing the heavy tray in her small hands. She was the perfect young lady as she poured out the tea and served it, and soon she and her grandmother were laughing at Rose over some of her tales of life at Aunt Sylvia's grand house.

'You all seem very merry,' Mr Perkins said as

the men re-joined them. He swung his daughter up in his arms, making her giggle.

'Miss Parker was telling us such stories,' Peggy said.

'Stories?' Harry asked.

'Oh, just about my Aunt Sylvia,' Rose answered. 'No one would believe she was quite real if they had not met her!'

'Miss Parker is quite a lovely gel,' Mrs Perkins said, chuckling. 'Won't you have some tea before you go, Captain? I have a few things I'd like to ask you about the property...'

Harry had thought he knew Rose Parker well enough by then, knew her quiet thoughtfulness, her devotion to her family, all the things that made her, well, *Rose*. A lady of such subtle understanding that one was drawn to her almost without realising it, without knowing how very addictive her warmth, her smiles, could be.

But now he saw she was fun, too, as he stood in the sitting-room doorway of that small cottage and watched her singing with little Peggy, her cheeks pink and her eyes glowing. Peggy was giggling and even her grandmother was smiling and clapping along to the song.

It was a scene of glowing, intimate happiness and Rose had created it in only a short hour. Created it because that was who she was. She could not help herself. Despite her life, her work as a companion to help her family, which could not be an easy or pleasant task for a refined lady, she still made everything about her just a bit brighter, a bit lighter.

Including himself. After the war, he had been sure he would not laugh again. But she made him want to sweep her into his arms and dance around the room with her, to protect her. And it was the hardest thing he had ever done to admit he wasn't able to.

'Now that's a fine lady,' he heard Oscar say and he turned to look at the man, somehow surprised to find he and Rose were not really the only two people in the world.

Oscar, too, watched her with a smile.

'Yes,' Harry said. 'She is.'

'I haven't seen Peggy laugh like that since we lost her mother,' Oscar said. 'The children at Barton must adore her.'

'So they do,' Harry said, thinking of Jane and Hayden's children, the way they looked at Rose as they sang, so eager for her smiling approval. The way they held her hands and laughed, as Peggy was doing now. Yes—she was a woman who brought warmth into every moment. She would surely be a fine mother.

'Captain St George!' Mrs Perkins called. 'Won't you come sit by the fire? Oscar's been keeping you out in the cold too long looking at that roof.'

Harry nodded, recalled to his duties by her

words. That was what he had to do, no matter what—take care of his home, his people.

'Peggy has made the most delicious ginger cakes,' Rose said.

'And now I've learned a new song!' Peggy cried. 'Miss Parker says I'm a—a...'

'A natural singer,' Rose said.

'Cakes *and* music?' Harry said with a laugh. 'Who could say no?'

They spent a pleasant half-hour by the cottage fire, taking tea and singing, hearing a bit of the estate gossip from Mrs Perkins, who despite her age and infirmity seemed to know everything.

By the time they left, the winter-blue sky had turned quite grey and snow had started to drift down in fat, wet, white flakes. They caught on Rose's lashes and cheeks, sparkling like diamonds as she laughed.

'See? Now it really feels like Christmas,' she cried, setting her horse to galloping down the line towards Barton. 'Race you back to Barton!'

Harry laughed and spurred his horse to catch up with her. He had almost forgotten what it felt like to ride like that, set loose from anything but the speed and the lightness, the freedom. They raced through the gates of Barton, their horses neck and neck, until Harry pulled just slightly ahead of her at the front doors of the house. The snow had begun to fall in earnest, the lights of the windows like beacons of hope in a coming storm.

But Rose's smile turned even brighter. 'I vow you must be the winner, Captain St George! What is your forfeit?'

A kiss, he thought. 'I shall have to think of just the right prize, Miss Parker—Rose.'

Her smile widened, and she laughed. 'Well, I feel like the winner myself. It has been much too long since I could ride like that. The fresh air, the snow—it's all so wondrous.'

Harry dismounted and came around to help her down from the saddle. As she looked up at him, her hand on his arm, her expression turned wistful. 'Thank you for showing me your house, Harry,' she said. 'I enjoyed it so much. It made me see—well, made me see so much about you, I suppose.'

'And were you disappointed by what you saw?'

She glanced away, her cheeks turning pink until she looked like her name in truth. A pink and white, blooming Rose. 'Quite the contrary. I just…'

A groom came to take their horses, and Rose hurried up the steps into the house. Harry followed, but he found he couldn't let her go just yet, couldn't be without her until there was no choice.

'Stay with me,' he said hoarsely. 'Just for a moment?'

Rose looked startled, but she nodded and took his hand as he led her into a small, quiet, dark sitting room off the hall.

* * *

As the sitting room door clicked shut behind them, Harry took her into his arms and held her close, so close they couldn't possibly be parted. Not yet. Rose found herself wanting to seize the moment, to make it her own and never forget it. She looped her arms around his neck and closed her eyes, inhaling his scent of woodsmoke and fresh air, the faint touch of lemon, combined with the bayberry-greenness of Christmas itself. She knew those scents would always remind her of him now.

'Oh, Harry,' she whispered. She reached up and gently touched his scarred cheek, feeling its roughness under her fingers. 'I wish—I wish…'

But she couldn't say anything else. He moaned, a low, hoarse sound in the shadows, and his lips claimed hers. She went up on tiptoe to meet him, putting all she had into that kiss. It wasn't a gentle kiss, as their first had been. It was filled with desperation, passion, need, all the feelings she could not speak.

'Rose,' he whispered, his kiss trailing over her cheek, his lips warm and firm against the life-pulse beating in her temple. 'Rose, I must…'

She was suddenly frightened of what he might say, that he could take away this moment before she could grasp it. 'You don't need to talk, Harry. I know.'

'I do need to tell you,' he said. He took a step back, but still held her hands in his, the two of them tethered in the darkness. 'I've hidden from life for too long. But you, you most extraordinary, kind-hearted woman, you make me brave again.'

'You? Not brave? Never say that,' she protested. 'You fought in battle, you were horribly injured…'

'I did fight, for so many years. It was what I had to do. But when I came home to find how I had neglected Hilltop—I have hidden from life. I couldn't face that my life had changed so much.'

How life changed, so suddenly, so unexpectedly. Yes, she knew how that felt. 'Indeed it does change, I know that.'

'I know that you do. That's why I feel I can tell you, only you, about what happened to me. How I came to be here, as I am.'

He took her hand and led her to a sofa by the high, small window that gave the room its only light. Snow still drifted down outside, thicker now, enclosing them in a silent blanket of white. She went with him, as she knew she could trust him, could follow him anywhere. But she wasn't sure she could bear to hear his words, to know of the terrible pain he must have endured.

They sat down at opposite ends of the sofa, only their hands touching in the middle. 'You know I was a soldier, of course,' he said.

Rose nodded.

'I lost so many friends,' he said. 'I could not lose my home, too. Could not let people down as I did some of those friends.'

'Oh, Harry, you could never do that,' she protested. 'I am sure you saved so many. You would never let anyone down, not at all.'

He gave her sad smile. 'Sweet Rose. You do always see the good in everyone, in everything.'

'I wish I did,' she said. 'I wish I could see—oh, Harry. We shouldn't be here like this.'

'Definitely not,' he answered roughly. But still his head bent towards hers and she instinctively leaned forward to meet him, to meet the kiss she so longed for.

The touch of his lips was soft at first, warm and gentle. When she wrapped her arms around him to draw him closer, he answered her hunger with his own and deepened the kiss. Their lips parted, tasted—and that taste sent Rose tumbling down into a new, primitive need she had never imagined before. Scandal, the past—it all meant nothing in that one perfect moment.

A moment that was all too quickly shattered when she remembered where she was, who they were. What he had tried to tell her, that his duty to his home came first, in some kind of recompense for the friends he lost in battle. In her own good honour, she could never turn him from that. She broke away from him and jumped to her feet.

'I—I should go,' she said. '*We* should go. Shouldn't we?'

'Rose…'

She shook her head. The house was still quiet as

Rose stepped into the hall, Harry close behind her. She was intently aware of his nearness, the warmth of him that always seemed to hold her secure when he was close to her.

The housekeeper Hannah came out to take their cloaks and hats.

'Have Lord and Lady Ramsay returned, Hannah?' Rose asked, self-consciously smoothing her hair as she took off her hat.

'Yes, quite a time ago,' Hannah answered with a sniff. 'And the others are dressing for dinner. Shall I have water sent up for a bath, Miss Parker?'

Rose was suddenly aware of just how long she had been alone with Harry. Being with him just seemed to make her forget all else, but she knew she couldn't do that. She had to be careful. 'Yes, thank you, Hannah.'

As the housekeeper vanished and Rose turned towards the stairs, Harry reached for her hand. 'You won't forget, Rose?'

She shook her head. 'I won't forget.' She felt him watching her all the way up the stairs.

Chapter Twelve

'What is this, then?' Mrs Pemberton cried as her long-suffering maid, Miss Powell, put her breakfast tray carefully across her velvet and lace-covered knees.

'Tea, madam. And toast with marmalade. As usual.' Powell had been with Mrs Pemberton for years and knew how every morning proceeded. She calmly crossed the floor to open the window curtains and let in the pale grey winter light.

'But what is *this*?' Mrs Pemberton picked up a small pile of letters and waved them around. The lace cap perched on her white curls trembled.

'The morning post, madam.' Powell stirred at the fire the housemaid had laid in the pre-dawn gloom.

'Why does anyone persist in writing to me?' Sylvia grumbled. 'It's probably just the usual begging letters from my useless relatives. Vultures and bores, the lot of them.' She took a sip of her tea

and thought of her relatives. She had married well
when she was quite young and he quite old, and as
they had no children and his estate was not entailed
and very extensive, she had lived a most comfortable life, one she looked back on now with much
satisfaction.

But now that she was old, cousins and step-
cousins and grand-cousins she never even knew
she possessed seemed to come out of the woodwork.

Sylvia sighed and leaned back on her piles of
lace-trimmed pillows. Growing old was no game
for the weak, she saw that every day now in hearing
that was fading, energy flagging. She had to take
her enjoyment where she could. It was amusing in
its own way to dangle those relatives along a bit.

But sometimes it was merely wearying. The
grand house was so quiet now, so unlike the days
when she was young and the corridors were filled
with parties, with friends and lovers and fun. She
had seized it all with both hands and made the most
of being pretty and rich. She regretted not a moment of it.

But what to do now? How to leave her mark on
the world?

She took another sip of tea and frowned to find
it had gone cold. Rose would never have allowed
such a thing. Rose had a quick, quiet efficiency
about her that made Sylvia's life so comfortable,
so easy. So much less lonely.

Sylvia had to admit it, even if it was only to herself—she missed Rose. The girl rather reminded her of herself when she was very young, straightforward and practical and unapologetic in a way young ladies did not seem to be in the modern world. Sylvia had been willing to do whatever she could to help her family, her mother and sisters, and so was Rose. Sylvia had married well; Rose looked after Sylvia. And Sylvia knew herself quite well enough to see Rose had a harder bargain to keep than she herself ever had.

Rose worked so her pretty, silly sister could marry her handsome, poor curate. If only there was a curate out there for Rose. Or better, a rich husband like the one Sylvia herself once snagged.

Sylvia laughed. No, she couldn't quite wish that on such a sweet girl as Rose. Sylvia had known how to ruthlessly get her way with an old husband; Rose would be too kind.

'I think there is a letter from Miss Parker,' Powell said, as if she read her employer's thoughts. 'I do hope she is enjoying herself at Barton.'

Sylvia sorted through the post, trying to conceal her eagerness. There was indeed a missive at the bottom of the pile marked with Rose's neat hand.

She opened it and quickly scanned the lines. 'It sounds as if Jane is indeed making a merry holiday this year. And Rose says the children are quite talented with their music.'

'She must be glad to be there, then,' Powell said

with a sigh, laying out Sylvia's morning gown. 'We do miss her here, though.'

'Yes. I suppose we do. None of you has her droll way of reading aloud.' Sylvia watched as Powell smoothed the creases from a grey-velvet gown and ruffled shawl. 'Whatever is *that*?'

'Your morning gown, madam,' Powell said. 'Unless you don't feel like going downstairs until later?'

'Of course I will go downstairs! I'm old, not ill. But no one will see or care how I'm dressed, anyway.' She thought for a moment about the Christmases she used to see in that house, the music and games. She glanced back down at Rose's letter.

Something among the descriptions of dinners and games caught her attention. Rose mentioned a certain name not once, not twice, but three times, and in a way that was clear she hadn't even realised it.

Captain Harry St George. Going for rides, showing them his house, sledding parties. Sylvia remembered the young man well, a war hero and certainly no fool as so many young people were. Now gossip said he was quite scarred, a recluse at his crumbling estate at Hilltop. But Rose did not make him sound that way at all.

Sylvia tapped the letter thoughtfully on the edge of her tray, a thought slowly taking form in her mind.

'Powell,' she said. 'Have the footmen bring down my trunks and for heaven's sake find something I own that isn't grey or black. It is Christmas, after all.'

Powell looked up, her eyes wide. Sylvia smiled to see that she had at last truly surprised her maid. 'Madam?'

'We are going to a party,' she said, pushing the breakfast tray aside. 'We're going to Barton Park. There's something I must do.'

Chapter Thirteen

'Snapdragon! Snapdragon!'

Everyone chanted and clapped their hands as all the light except for the fireplace was extinguished in the Barton drawing room. The footmen carried in a wide, shallow bowl of brandy with raisins and other dried fruit. After it was carefully placed on the table, Hayden stepped forward to set a match to the confection.

Rose gasped as eerie blue flames flickered across the lake of brandy. She remembered watching the grown-ups play at the game when she was a child and it always seemed so daring, everyone diving through the incandescent light to snatch at the treat. She found it looked no less wondrous now, with the circle of avid, laughing faces cast in the blue glow.

The children had been sent to bed with their nurse after their pre-dinner song, led by Rose, and dinner had been an adult event with plentiful fine

French wines. Even Rose, who had tried to sip very little since wine went right to her head and made her giddy, found herself giggling at the silly stories and jokes.

It had been Charles St George, in his King of the Bean guise, who declared cards and charades too dull for the after-dinner entertainment and instead sent for the brandy. He led the cheers as the flames danced higher.

Rose glimpsed Harry across the flames, his face half-hidden in the shadows. He smiled wryly as he watched his brother. She remembered all too well their kiss, the wondrous way it had made her feel, and now her cheeks grew warm at the memory. She told herself it was merely the fire, and not her old nemesis, her blush.

'Since you are the ruler of the evening, Charlie,' said Helen Fallon, the diamond stars in her hair glittering in the firelight, 'you must be the first to try.'

'And so I shall,' Charles answered. 'If the prize is a kiss from the fairest lady in the room.'

Helen and Charles exchanged a long, tense glance and Rose saw that Harry watched them with a small frown. Lady Fallon was an heiress and had once been almost engaged to Harry. Surely now…

No, Rose told herself as she made herself concentrate on the game. It was not her business. Yet she was much too aware of what Harry and his brother and Lady Fallon did.

'I doubt Jane would oblige you,' Helen said, turning away as if she cared not a jot what happened.

Jane laughed. 'It is not *that* kind of party, my darlings, whether the children are in their nursery or not. But, yes, Charlie, you must be the first. I see a lovely little apricot just there in the middle...'

Amid cries of encouragement, Charles dived forward to try and snatch the apricot. He was unsuccessful and fell back shaking his hand. Helen laughed. Hayden went next and managed to grab a raisin and pop it between his wife's lips.

Harry was next and he took the prize of the apricot with such ease it looked as if he barely moved. As he flung the fruit into his mouth, the tips of his fingers seemed to drip with the blue flame. In the strange, glowing light, he looked like something magical and fascinating.

Emma stepped forward to try it. She gave a little shriek, but managed to grab a raisin. 'It's hot, but it doesn't burn,' she declared. 'How is that possible?'

After the flames died down and the brandy cooled, the lanterns were lit again and the world shifted back to its everyday appearance. Rose laughed with the others, trying not to look at Harry.

'What shall we do now?' Jane said. 'Charles, you are the guide to our merriment and obviously a very good one. What game do you declare?'

Charles tapped his chin in thought. 'I say—hide and go seek.'

Helen clapped her hands. 'Wonderful! Who shall hide and who shall seek?'

'The ladies shall hide and the gentlemen seek, of course,' Charles said. 'Is that not the way of life? Jane, perhaps you will be timekeeper?'

Jane glanced at her husband. She looked a bit dubious about the new game, but she nodded and smiled. 'Just no hiding in the nursery wing. My children are too excited over Christmas to sleep as it is.'

'Very well, ladies,' Charles said. 'Get ready, get set—hide!'

Rose was caught in the midst of the crowd rushing out of the drawing room, carried with them into the hall as Jane counted off behind them. 'One—two—three…' she called, her voice floating above the giggles. Everyone scattered up the stairs and vanished into the shadows, leaving only the trace of that laughter and faint, flowery perfumes behind.

Rose wasn't sure where to go. She hadn't played the game since she was a child and even then she had usually just found a quiet corner to read in.

'Nineteen, twenty,' Jane called and Rose knew she didn't have much time. She ran up the stairs and turned down the first corridor she saw. It was only lit by flickering lights at each end, in between was shadows. She heard giggles nearby, the snap of closing doors. Suddenly rather nervous, she ducked behind some heavy satin curtains into a small window nook and pressed herself tight against the wall.

But she was not alone there for long. After a few breathless moments, someone slid between the curtains and joined her.

It was shadowy in her small sanctuary, but in the moonlight she could see it was Harry who stood there, his tall figure glowing in the phosphorescent light, his scars hidden. He stepped closer to her, letting the velvet curtain fall behind him, and they were alone in their own world.

Rose found she suddenly wasn't frightened at all. She was no longer all by herself. She could take a breath, a *real* breath, at last.

'Rose?' he asked, his voice quiet and deep, as rich and comforting as a velvet blanket. 'Are you unwell? You ran away so quickly...'

'I—no. Not at all,' she answered. 'It's just the game—suddenly I couldn't breathe.'

'I don't like such things myself,' he said. 'The darkness, the sudden noise.'

Rose swallowed hard, remembering the little he had told her about the horrors of battle. How dreadful that silly Christmas games could bring that back to him. She longed to touch him, to comfort him. 'Of course not.'

'It seems safe enough here.'

'Yes.' Rose swayed towards him, drawn by that warm, quiet strength she always found so wondrous, by the delicious winter fire scent of him.

His arms came out to catch her, drawing her close, and suddenly she did not feel safe at all. She felt her heart racing within her, making her feel reckless and full of something she hadn't known in so long—joy.

She rested her forehead against his chest, the soft wool of his evening coat warm on her skin. She closed her eyes and concentrated on the sound of his heartbeat, steady and strong, echoing her own.

In her life, she always seemed to be rushing ahead to the next moment, to worrying about the next day. Would her mother and Lily be well? Would she be able to live comfortably, safely? With Harry, in that one instant, she could just *be*, and it was a delicious feeling indeed.

She knew she should not be there alone with him, that it was dangerous indeed, but she couldn't give it up just yet. She slid her arms around his waist, feeling the strength of him as he held her up.

She felt his kiss on the top of her head and she tilted her face up to his. His gaze glowed in the darkness. His lips touched her brow, the pulse that beat at her temple, her cheek, leaving tiny touches of warmth that made her tingle all the way to her toes. She shivered with the force of emotion that flowed through her, like a flame that pushed away all the icy loneliness she had lived with for so long.

She went up on tiptoe, holding him even closer, and at last his lips touched hers. A small, questing, sweet kiss, but it made that flame burn even brighter. She moaned softly and it seemed the small sound ignited something in him, too. He groaned and dragged her so close there was nothing between them at all. They seemed to fit together perfectly, as if they had always been just like that.

Her lips instinctively parted under his kiss and his tongue lightly touched the tip of hers, as if seeking, questioning, before he deepened their touch.

She wound her arms around his neck, her fingers curling into his hair, as if she could hold him to her for ever. But he wasn't leaving her. Their kiss slid deeper, into a desperate need she hadn't even known was in her. She felt so hot, as if she would catch fire from it, and all there was in the world was the touch of his kiss. She swayed, sure she would fall.

He pressed her back against the wall and his lips trailed from hers, over the arch of her throat to touch the tiny hollow where her life-pulse pounded with need.

'Rose, I…' he gasped hoarsely. She opened her eyes to find that he rested his forehead against the wall beside her. His breath was ragged in her ear, his tall body shuddering as if he struggled with the force of longing just as she did.

Suddenly, the world seemed to crash in around their little sanctuary. She heard footsteps and muffled laughter from beyond the curtains.

She feared that if she stayed so close to him, she wouldn't be able to think at all. She slid to one side, dizzy, but his arms tightened around her.

'Not yet,' he growled. 'Please.'

Rose nodded and leaned against his shoulder, letting him hold her up. His entire body had gone rigid, perfectly still, as if he fought to regain his military control.

''Tis an enchantment,' she whispered. 'Like the spirits in the holly wreath, or *A Midsummer Night's Dream.*'

He gave a ragged laugh. 'We need Puck's remedy to set it right.'

It *did* feel like something had been set loose in Rose, something wild she had never known before. She also knew it had to be put back in the bottle before their lives were cast adrift. She could not afford gossip, not if she was to keep her position, and he needed an heiress.

'Tomorrow is Christmas Day,' she said. 'They say that is a good time for reflection and correction.'

He turned his head to look at her and she saw a small smile crook the corner of his lips. 'Oh, my sweet Rose. I think I would need more than one Christmas Day at this point.'

Rose shook her head. 'I know you. Your mistakes can surely not be many.'

He laughed roughly. 'They are many indeed. If you knew what my youth was like before the army...'

Rose heard more voices outside, laughter becoming louder, closer. She shivered with the sudden rush of cold reality and edged away from Harry, even as her whole being urged her to stay, stay, stay. She self-consciously smoothed her skirt, her hair.

It was as if mad holiday spirits had indeed taken over her world, a place she had always fought to keep so ordered and calm. She didn't *want* to go back, but she knew she had to. For both their sakes.

She slipped out of their little alcove and blinked at the sudden glow of the light. She saw that many of the hiders had been found and a crowd was drifting down the stairs. She followed them into the drawing room where Jane played at the pianoforte while several couples danced.

'Miss Parker!' little Eleanor cried, rushing out of the crowd in her dressing gown. Rose was glad of the feeling of the girl's hand on hers, an anchor to the real world. 'There you are.'

'And there you are,' Rose answered with a shaky laugh. She saw William and the other children were gathered around their father, being swung into the air in time to the music, making them shout with laughter. 'Shouldn't you all be in bed?'

'We wanted to see what you were doing, if you would sing for us since it's so hard to sleep on Christmas Eve,' Eleanor said with a winsome smile.

Rose remembered that feeling so well, when she and Lily would stay up long into the darkness, whispering about what treats might wait for them in the morning. 'Very well. Just one song, though. Tomorrow will be a long day.'

She clasped Eleanor's hand and led her upstairs,

trying to forget what had happened under the enchantment of the game. She feared it would be a sleepless night indeed.

Helen tiptoed across the upstairs landing, listening carefully to the muffled whispering and laughter of the game. She could see no one in the shadows, nor did she really want to. She tripped over one of the rugs and caught herself before she could fall, laughing at the rush of uncertainty that ran through her. She hadn't felt that way in so very long, so unsure, so filled with anticipation of the next few moments, whatever they would bring.

But she was not quite alone. Behind her, she heard the brush of a footstep, the sound of an indrawn breath, almost nothing in the silence.

'Who is there?' she called out, her heart pounding.

A tall figure stepped out of the shadows and as her eyes adjusted to the moonlight she saw it was Charles. He held a goblet of brandy loose in his hand and she remembered how he had urged them all on in their silly holiday games. He did not look so merry now. In fact, he looked quite—solemn.

'Oh, it's you,' she said and she turned to run away again. But somehow she could not leave him. She didn't want to leave him. She glanced back at him uncertainly.

A wry smile touched his lips and he raised his

glass again. 'Yes, only me. Are you so very disappointed, Helen?'

'Not at all. I merely heard laughter from this direction and wondered if Jane's children had escaped their nursery.'

'Or maybe it's the ghosts of Barton, come to haunt our feast?'

'Are there ghosts here? It seems too new a house to be haunted.' But then again, her fine London house was quite new and she felt as if ghosts followed her around there all the time. The ghost of her husband, the ghost of the wild girl she had once been.

'There are ghosts everywhere, as I'm sure you know. Especially at Christmas. That's when we remember those lost ones the most.'

Helen sat down on the nearest chair, suddenly weary. 'I thought the men were meant to be seeking, not hiding in here.'

'I prefer the quiet for the moment, don't you? You don't seem to be hiding very effectively.'

'Maybe I don't want to be found.'

'Not by anyone?'

Helen thought about that, about the gentlemen guests, some of whom she knew would welcome an invitation from her. About the hopes she had dared have for Harry before she arrived at Barton, how she wanted to bring the past to life, even when it was obviously cold and distant. 'Tell me about the Christmas ghosts.'

Charles sat down next to her and politely offered her the brandy. She had always liked that about Charles. He was so much fun at a party, but he knew how to be quiet, too, how not to press a person to talk about confusing or hurtful things. He could just—be. She had almost forgotten what that was like. With her husband, and now in her widowhood, it was always play-acting. The tales Charlie told her now, though—they felt different. She could listen to him all evening, but his words ended far too soon.

Helen took a sip of the brandy as his words faded around them, leaving only the chilly silence of the night outside the windows of their sanctuary.

'I like that,' she said. 'Ghosts of Christmas.'

'It's not the usual sort of Christmas tale,' he answered.

'That's why I like it. Sometimes it's much too easy to feel sad at this time of year, isn't it? And all the tinsel and bows make it worse, somehow.'

Charles looked at her sharply and she could tell she had surprised him. 'The lovely Lady Fallon, sad?' he said softly. 'What is it that makes you so?'

She shrugged. 'I don't even know. What *could* make me sad? I'm a rich widow now and still young. Yet I feel so alone sometimes. That's why I like the thought of your ghosts, I suppose. If they are watching—well, they're company.'

He reached up to toy with the lace trim on her sleeve. Usually when a man did that, she would laugh and turn away flirtatiously. It would mean nothing, less than nothing. But this was Charles, Charles who had known her for so long, who felt as if she herself was seeing for the first time. She could see her own feelings, her loneliness and uncertainty, in his eyes.

His touch on her arm was so light, but to Helen it burned with the glow of life itself. She found herself craving that touch so much.

'Tell me no, Helen,' he said in a low, taut voice. 'Send me away, for both of us.'

'I...' she whispered. 'I can't do that, Charlie.'

'Heaven help me, but neither can I.' His hand trailed over her arm to her waist, his touch warm and gentle through the velvet of her gown. It made her want so much more, to feel bare skin against hers again, to have that connection, to know she was not alone.

Her throat felt so tight she couldn't answer him in words. She just covered his hand with hers and pressed him closer. His other hand reached up to caress her cheek and she kissed his palm. He smelled of smoke and brandy, and it was enough to make her head whirl. There was only her and Charlie, in their own world now.

'Helen,' he said roughly. 'Every time I think I know you, you change. You're so merry, then so sad. How you baffle me.'

'But surely you know me better than anyone else ever has. I think—I think you see me.' She leaned closer to him and felt the heat of their lips hovering mere inches apart. 'And I see you.'

'I do hope not.'

She nodded and, before she could let her thoughts overwhelm her again, she closed the space between them and touched his lips with hers. The merest brush, but she felt the heat of their breath meeting and mingling, binding them closer than those ghosts could ever do.

Charles groaned and deepened their kiss, giving her what she craved. His arms came around her, pulling her close. His tongue touched the curve of her lower lip, light and almost teasing, until she parted her lips in eager welcome. And then, like the ghosts, she flew free.

'Helen,' he growled. Through the blurry heat of her desire, she felt his touch tighten, until there was nothing between them at all.

Their kiss slid over a precipice into something wild and frantic with need that had been bottled up inside of her for too long. It was something she so longed for—and something she was afraid to have. Feeling like the veriest coward, she broke away from him and ran as fast as she could. She didn't even know where she was going, only that she had to escape herself.

Chapter Fourteen

"'I saw three ships come sailing in, come sailing in, come sailing in! I saw three ships come sailing in on Christmas Day in the morning!'"

Rose followed behind the children as they walked to church for Christmas morning services, processing behind their parents with the rest of the guests and the household around them. She tried to pay attention, to make quite sure they sang in the way they had practised so carefully, but she found her attention was always wandering.

She had barely slept a wink after that kiss with Harry, a kiss that felt like a dream now, something that surely couldn't have happened to her in real life. Not quiet, sensible Rose. And yet it *had* happened and she knew she could never forget how it made her feel. She peeked over her shoulder to where Harry walked with his brother, the two of them talking together quietly. His wide-brimmed hat shielded his expression from her view, but she couldn't help but wonder if he also remembered.

How could she leave this magical Barton Christmas world and go back to Aunt Sylvia? She knew she had to, and soon, but not quite yet.

'You children do sing so beautifully,' Emma said. 'I'm sure the congregation will love it, too. Just remember—it's Christmas, so best behaviour. We don't want a repeat of last Easter, do we?'

Rose's full attention was finally captured, wondering what on earth had happened last Easter! The Barton Park brood seemed such an angelic one, in the grand scheme of children's behaviour, anyway.

'You were the one who told us to try it, Aunt Emma,' William said. 'You said they used a special lemon polish at the holidays.'

'You said that you and Mama used to lick the pews to test it, too,' Eleanor said.

'Well, do as I say and not as I do,' Emma said airily with a wave of her gloved hand. 'No more licking of pews this year, or there shall be no plum pudding at dinner for you.'

'I would never do such a thing,' Beatrice said. 'Yuck!'

'Of course you would not, Bea,' said Emma. 'You are quite an angel.'

'Not entirely an angel!' William protested. 'Was she not the one who got lost looking for the treasure?'

'Arabella's treasure?' Rose asked. 'When were you lost, Miss Marton?'

Beatrice's delicate cheeks turned bright pink. 'A long time ago. I was just a silly child. And I never found it, anyway. I am sure it doesn't exist.'

'It does!' William declared. 'We just have to narrow its location more carefully. It's somewhere over there, near the old ruins on Uncle David's estate.' He waved towards the shadow of a crumbling old chimney in the distance.

'If it *did* exist, it could certainly be helpful,' Emma said. She gestured with her fur-trimmed muff towards the semi-rusted gates of Hilltop, barely glimpsed in the distance, opposite the old ruins. 'You visited Hilltop, did you not, Rose? What did you think?'

'It was a fine old house,' Rose said carefully. 'Very medieval, like something in a story.'

'Yes. It just needs a bit of care, as Barton once did.' Emma glanced back, and Rose followed her stare to see that Harry walked with Lady Fallon now, that lady's hand on his arm as she whispered something to him. Their faces looked most solemn. 'There are tidier ways to see to necessities than digging in the dirt for lost treasure. A fine marriage, maybe? Harry certainly deserves it.'

Rose resolutely faced forward, willing herself not blush. 'He is a good gentleman indeed.'

Their little procession turned down the lane leading towards the village and the church. The solid, square stone Norman tower stretched up towards the grey sky as the bells tolled to summon everyone to Christmas. A large crowd had gathered in the churchyard amid the tilting old headstones, waiting to make their way into the warmth of the sanctuary.

To Rose's delighted surprise, she glimpsed a familiar face standing in the doorway. Her sister, Lily, clad in a pale green pelisse, bouncing up on her toes to study the newcomers. She held her husband's arm, as he stood beside her in his clerical robes, greeting the parishioners.

'Lily!' Rose cried. 'And Mr Hewlitt. How wonderful to see you! Whatever are you doing here?'

She rushed forward and Lily threw herself into her arms. Her sister was as she always had been, as delicate and sweet as a bird, smelling of lilacs. It made Rose think of home and family, and that bittersweet missing of it all again.

'He's been invited to say the Christmas service here, by the bishop himself,' Lily said proudly, standing back to take her shyly smiling husband's arm. 'We must go home very soon, as Mama is taking care of the children for us and I fear they will run her quite ragged. But Jane has insisted we stay at Barton for a few nights, as a grand treat.'

'I thought it would be a delightful holiday surprise for you, Rose,' Jane said with a laugh.

'And so it is,' Rose answered happily, drinking in the sweet sight of her sister. 'How fares Mama and the children, then?'

'They are all quite well and miss you very much. I fear I am not such a good help to them as you are and cannot take your place,' Lily said. She leaned closer and whispered, 'Hewlitt has been shown such favour of late by the bishop, I am sure he will be given a fine parish of his own soon, with a substantial vicarage and larger income. Then we can all live together again!'

Live with her family again and not worry about their safety at every moment? It sounded like an impossibly beautiful dream. 'Oh, Lily, I do hope so.'

More parishioners came along the path, claiming Mr Hewlitt's and Lily's attentions, and Rose led her charges to their place in the front pews, making sure no one licked the carved, lemon-polished wood. As they filed into their seats, she glimpsed the Perkins family, Harry's kind tenants, and waved at them. They waved back, smiling, and for a moment Rose let herself feel like she belonged there, among their community. It was quite a lovely feeling.

She sat down between Eleanor and William, helping them find their place in the hymnal as the Christmas service music soared into the old church rafters and the light shone from the ancient windows on to them in a sort of blessing. She would enjoy the day while she could and always remember it.

As the congregation sang the first song and Mr Hewlitt took his place in the pulpit, the church doors opened and a blast of cold wind swept down the aisle. Rose turned with everyone else, surprised anyone would arrive so late, and gasped at the figure who stood there, swathed in a dark fur cloak and brandishing a walking stick.

'Is it a witch, Miss Parker?' Eleanor whispered, wide-eyed.

'No,' Rose whispered back. 'It is my Aunt Sylvia!'

'So lovely!' Lily said, peering into Rose's looking glass as they got ready for the Barton Christmas ball. 'I can't remember a luncheon like that in ages. All those wonderful puddings! The children will never believe me when I tell them! I shall be twenty pounds fatter when we go home.'

Rose had to laugh, for her sister, now mother of two lovely plump cherubs, was still as tiny as she had been when they last came to Barton together. Lily was a little, golden fairy in her white muslin dress trimmed with crimson and gold ribbons. 'I'm sure Jane will send them even more puddings when you leave. Her cook is wondrous at coming up with picnic hampers.'

'I'm sure she will. And hopefully next year we shall all be together to sing your music and eat our own puddings!'

Rose smiled wistfully. 'That would be wonderful.'

Lily turned to look at her, her elfin face suddenly puckered in a frown. 'Rose, dearest, you are still in your petticoat. And you look rather tired. Was it Aunt Sylvia's unexpected appearance?'

'No, not at all.' In fact, Aunt Sylvia had been rather quiet herself after church, claiming she only needed a nap and Powell would attend to her. The reason Rose was still in her petticoat was so shallow she didn't even want to tell her sister.

Rose glanced down at the gown laid out on her bed. It was her best, a forest-green satin that had been remade from an old costume of her mother's, yet she couldn't help but wish she had something a bit—prettier. Something like the lace-trimmed confections Lady Fallon wore, stylish and elegant.

'Of course,' she said, stepping into her black evening slippers. 'We mustn't be late.'

'Rose, whatever is amiss?'

Rose tried to smile, but it felt so artificial she knew Lily would know it in a moment. 'How could anything be amiss? It is Christmas!'

'I'm your sister, Rose. I can tell something is bothering you.' Lily came to her side, taking her hand as they sat together on the bed. 'Is it Aunt Sylvia showing up like that, ruining your lovely holiday away from her? That was so silly of her.'

'No, of course not. I mean—yes, Aunt Sylvia *is* a bit silly, rushing off from her warm house like that in the middle of Christmas, but she does so often make me laugh.' Rose bit her lip. 'Lily—what is it really like to be married?'

Lily's smile turned secret and satisfied, like a cat

with purloined cream. 'I can't speak for any married people but myself, of course. Sometimes it is wonderful beyond belief and sometimes I just want to hit Hewlitt over the head with an inkwell. But mostly it is just—nice.' She clutched Rose's hand in hers. 'Why? Have you met someone Mama and I should know about? If so, you *must* tell me, so I can discover if he is worthy of you.'

Lily looked so fierce that Rose had to laugh. 'No, not really. Not yet.' She thought of Harry and their kiss in the shadowed alcove. She turned away so Lily couldn't see her expression. 'I just wondered.'

'If you really want to be married, Rose dearest, I am sure Hewlitt could find someone. He knows so very many churchmen from school, you know, and some of them have their own parishes now.'

Rose remembered her brother-in-law's friends from Lily's wedding, an earnest, well-scrubbed group, scrupulously polite. Nothing like Harry, who had seen so many terrible things and been so scarred by them, yet had emerged even stronger for it. 'I am quite all right, Lily, really. I could never be the perfect vicarage hostess, as you are.'

Before Lily could answer, there was a knock at the door and it opened to reveal Aunt Sylvia's maid, Powell, with a white box in her arms.

Powell always looked rather dour, as anyone who had worked for Aunt Sylvia for so long would, but she seemed to smile just a bit as she handed the box to Rose. 'A present, from Mrs Pemberton.'

Rose was shocked. 'A—a present? From my aunt? Are you quite sure?'

Powell nodded. 'She said she didn't want anyone to think she did not pay your wages on time.'

As the maid left, Lily bounced up and down on her toes. 'Oh, do open it, Rose! I am quite aching to see what it is.'

'I am, too,' Rose said, still bemused. Aunt Sylvia was not miserly in her wages, but she never gave gifts, either. Rose lifted the lid to find just what she had been wishing for—a new gown. It frothed with rose-coloured silk and creamy lace, quite the prettiest dress she had ever seen.

'Oh…' Lily sighed, gently touching the soft sleeve. 'You will surely be the most beautiful lady at the ball, Rose.'

'I doubt it,' Rose whispered. But secretly, deep in her heart, she hoped that just one person in particular might think just that.

'I suppose Aunt Sylvia isn't one hundred per cent an ogre after all,' Lily marvelled.

'Come along, Harry, won't you dance with me?' he heard Helen say, her voice sweet and fluting over the sound of the orchestra and the dancing feet. 'You've been standing here alone in the corner too long.'

Harry laughed as he turned to her, though he felt rather abashed. He thought he was well hidden there in the corner, behind a bank of Jane's potted palms and hothouse roses, but it seemed he was not so invisible after all.

In truth, he was waiting for Rose. She hadn't appeared at the party yet and in her absence the glow of the candles seemed dimmer, the music fainter. He was more eager than he cared to admit, keeping watch on the stairs for her.

'You know I'm not much of a dancer, Helen,' he said. 'Did you not have an example of that at the assembly?'

She laughed and offered him a glass of punch. The pearls in her hair and at her wrists gleamed, along with her cream and gold gown, but even she seemed muted there in the ballroom. He feared he was besotted indeed, and a fool for a lady who seemed to like him—but could not be his.

'I know no such thing, Harry,' Helen said. 'You were quite the gentlemanly partner at the assembly. And I do remember when we were children and took dance lessons together in my mother's drawing room. Charles was more adept, of course, but you never trod on my toes.'

'Such a compliment indeed!'

She gave an exaggerated pout. 'Oh, come now, Harry, it's Christmas, and I haven't had a dance at all tonight. You could do such a favour for an old friend.'

He glanced again at the stairs. There were more arrivals crowded in the hall, but no Rose yet. And it was clear he could no longer hide there. 'Of course.

Only because I know you will always forgive my clumsiness.'

They gave their empty glasses to a footman and Harry took her hand to step into the dance. Helen was as graceful and lively as she had once been at their long-ago lessons, laughing and twirling among the other guests. But every time they turned, he still couldn't help glancing at the door, waiting for a glimpse of Rose.

Helen suddenly tugged him under a bough of mistletoe hung in a doorway, its creamy berries set off by looping red ribbons. She stared up at him, her eyes wide and beautiful. Yet he felt—only a faint regret, a sadness at remembering the past. A longing to see a different, hazel pair of eyes before him, a different pair of lips parting.

'Oh, Harry,' she said, her own voice suddenly tinged with that nostalgic sadness. 'There is nothing left for us, is there?'

He shook his head. 'Helen—you know how fond I am of you...'

'Like a sister?'

'Yes,' he said gently. 'You are indeed like a sister to me, a very dear one.'

'But there is someone for whom you feel—more,' she said. 'I can tell. I am a lady of the world now, you know! Yet—I will never forget you, Harry, ever.'

She went up on tiptoe to softly press her lips to his cheek, the unscarred side which was smooth under her sudden kiss. He glanced over her head, to see that Rose had at last appeared on the stairs into the ballroom. She glowed like an angel with the soft candlelight behind her, a rose-pink gown floating softly around her, her light brown hair gathered up in loose curls with an ivory comb.

Her gaze turned to him and he smiled in a rush of joy at the sight. He instinctively took a step towards her, only to notice that her face bore no answering smile. She looked at Helen with wide eyes and he suddenly realised that he still held Helen in his arms. That she had just kissed him.

'Rose,' he called, but she had turned and fled back up the stairs, wiping away a tear with her gloved hand. A sharp pang pierced his heart. He struggled to catch up with her, but the crowd kept shifting before him, moving in a constant stream that made the stairs come in and out of sight. He saw her sister and brother-in-law, arm in arm on the lower step, but no Rose.

By the time he broke free of the crowd, she had quite vanished.

Chapter Fifteen

⁓⊙⊱⊰⊙⁓

'Ouch!' Rose gasped as her elbow connected with the wall, shooting a sharp pain up her arm. She kept running down the narrow back stairs, though, praying no one had heard her. She desperately needed a breath of fresh air after the crowded ballroom. After seeing Harry with Lady Fallon.

At last she tumbled out into the cold night air and its crispness cleared some of the clouds from her head. The garden was quiet, though still lit by the rows of Chinese lanterns that had led guests up the drive. The house itself was golden with light, the merry music echoing around her.

'What am I doing?' Rose murmured. It wasn't like her, sensible Rose, to run out of a party into the cold night, feeling so dizzy and strange.

She shouldn't even be thinking about Harry St George at all, not romantically. She had nothing to offer him and he had to do his duty to his home.

Yet she couldn't seem to help herself. Every time she was quiet for even a moment, he was there in her mind, her memories, and she feared he would be for a long time to come, even after she returned to her real life at Aunt Sylvia's.

She drifted towards a small summerhouse set in the garden, away from the main house, but still with lanterns outlining its steps. The rest of the winter garden was in darkness, and Rose thought of the children's tales of lost royal treasure. Could it really be out there somewhere, hidden, like fairy gold in a story? If so, how lovely it would be to find it, to help Harry solve all of Hilltop's troubles.

Still thinking of the treasure, Rose glimpsed a strange pile of stones near the far side of the summerhouse. They seemed out of place in the manicured garden.

She crept closer to examine them. They seemed to fall in a tumble, as if collapsed to hide something, like the entrance to a cellar of some sort. She nudged one with the toe of her slipper, but it didn't move. She kicked it harder and tripped, falling towards the sharp stones before she could catch her balance.

She cried out and felt someone grab her arm, like a ghost coming out of the night. She shrieked, her heart seeming to fly into her throat. She whirled around—and found it was no ghost that had caught her, but Harry. He was shadowed by the luminous lamplight behind him, but she knew it was him. Her heart beat even faster, but not from fright this time.

'Blast it, Harry, you frightened me' was all she could gasp.

He gave her a rueful smile. 'I'm sorry, Rose. I thought you heard me calling you. You shouldn't be out here by yourself in the dark.'

Rose laughed. 'I—I know. I just needed a breath of fresh air.'

'I agree. It is much too crowded in there, too much noise.'

She remembered what he had told her of his time in battle, the loud noises, the chaos, the feeling of being trapped. She reached out and gently touched his arm, hoping he knew those nightmares were no longer real, that he was not alone in a cruel, cold world. 'And I think Charles must have put something in the claret cup. I feel rather dizzy.'

Harry laughed and she was glad to see it seemed to banish some of the darkness from his eyes. 'You are right. It's just like Charles to do such a mischief. I plan to blame him entirely.' He took Rose's hand in his and she felt the warm steadiness of him envelop her until the night held no more fears. He was honourable, she knew that very well after seeing him with his tenants, hearing of his time in battle. He was a man who could be trusted, always, and she knew how rare that was.

His laughter faded and as he watched her his expression was most serious, intent. He drew her closer to him, his hands tight on her waist, and that feeling of warm safety sparked into something more. Something as shimmering and irresistible as those flickering lantern flames. It was as bright and wondrous as life itself. Not like her everyday life, grey and practical, but like a daydream come to vivid life.

She didn't want to let it go. She didn't want to lose this beauty now that she had found it.

She swayed closer to him, and wound her arms tightly around his neck so he couldn't fly away and leave her alone in this dream. She only wanted to stay here in his embrace all night—for every night, really. To forget about duty and families and treasure, and everything but him.

She gazed up at him in the moonlight, thinking how handsome he was, made even more so by his honourable scars. She had never known anyone like him at all. 'How beautiful you are, Harry,' she whispered.

He laughed in surprise. 'Of course I'm not. I was never handsome and now I'm quite a wreck.'

Rose shook her head. How could she ever convince him of what she saw, of what was true? She seemed to have no words left, her head fuzzy with the drink, the moonlight and the magic. Instead of talking, she went up on tiptoe and pressed her lips to his in a swift, sweet kiss, then another and another, as if she could never have her fill.

He groaned and pulled her closer, so close there

was not even a breath of the cold night between them. He deepened the kiss, his tongue seeking the taste of hers, and she was lost completely in him. Lost in that wild need to be just that close to him, always. To draw all he was into her until they were inseparable.

For once in her life, Rose didn't question herself, didn't draw back. She trusted Harry. She knew in that one moment he would always do right by her.

He pressed tiny, fleeting kisses to her cheek, her temple, the tiny, sensitive spot behind her ear. She shivered to feel the warm rush of his breath on her skin.

'Oh, Rose,' he whispered hoarsely. 'You know we can't go on like this.'

She nodded, pressing her face into his shoulder. She tried to breathe, but that only seemed to bring the essence of him even closer, all around her. She saw now that he was the one true thing she had always hoped for, so kind and strong.

'I know we can't,' she answered. 'But I can't—I can't go back to what was before. I can't...'

She shivered and he stood back to take her hand. 'At the very least, we can't stay out here in the cold,' he said.

Rose nodded and let him lead her across the darkened garden and up the steps of the summer-house. It was all marble, still chilly without the summer sun its stone walls usually saw, but it was out of the wind, away from anyone who might stumble out of the dance. She could see the shadow of pillars from the flickering lights outside, the outline of some wrought-iron garden furniture. It was so quiet there that she could hear her heart pounding in her ears.

She swallowed hard past her fear, past doubts. Never before had she been given the chance for a moment of such perfect happiness. She feared it would never come again. She intended to grab it now, to give herself something beautiful to remember. To be free.

Still shaking, she reached up and pulled the pins from her hair, shaking the heavy mass free over her shoulders.

As he watched her, his gaze narrowed, and she saw the quick beat of his pulse in his temple, the way his jaw tensed. 'Rose...'

'No, Harry, please.' She pressed her finger to his lips before he could say anything else. She wanted no words to shatter this spell. She was done with words, with worry and thought and being practical, even if it was only for that moment.

She sat down on the nearby iron *chaise*, drawing him with her. He wrapped his arms around her, holding her close, and she felt a burst of hope. Perhaps she was not alone. Perhaps, even though duty said they could not always be together, they *could* truly be together, just the two of them.

'I—I want you, Harry,' she managed to whisper. 'Do you want me, too?'

'Beautiful Rose. How could you ever doubt it? My feelings for you are—well, they are beyond an old soldier's words. I'm no poet. But you are the loveliest woman I have ever met.' He kissed her again, their lips meeting in a hot blur of need, and she let herself tumble into him and be lost.

She clumsily, eagerly, untied his cravat and let it fall to the floor at their feet. Something hidden deep inside of her, something urgent and instinctive, guided her as she pushed back his coat and the soft muslin of his shirt, as she eagerly touched his bare, warm skin and marvelled at the sheer life of him.

Clinging to each other, they fell back on the *chaise*, the domed marble of the ceiling whirling over her head. She rolled on top of him, not able to breathe as she studied him in the moonlight. His bare skin seemed gilded. How glorious he was, vibrant with desire and strength. It was beyond her dreams.

Her trembling fingertips traced the light, coarse sprinkling of dark hair on his chest, the thin line that led tantalisingly to the band of his velvet evening breeches. His stomach muscles tightened, his breath turning ragged as her touch brushed against it.

'Rose, my darling,' he gasped. 'Be careful. If you're not sure about me...'

'I would not be here if I wasn't sure,' she answered and she suddenly realised how very sure she was. This, him—it was the most right thing she had ever done.

She fell back into his arms, their lips meeting, heartbeats melding. There was nothing careful about that kiss, it was as hot as the sun and full of urgent, desperate need, like fireworks bursting into the night sky. She felt the slide of his hands on her back as he unlaced her gown. The winter air was cold on her skin, but she barely noticed it. Clothes were only a barrier now between her and the touch of his bare hand on her skin. She shrugged her gown away, pushing with it any last remnants of shyness.

'Rose,' he groaned, his hands tightening on her hips, warm through the thin muslin of her petticoat. 'You are so beautiful.'

How she hoped she was, for him. She kissed him again and he rolled her body beneath his, on to his discarded evening coat. She laughed as her hair spilled all around them. She *did* feel beautiful as he looked at her, felt free at last, as she knew she would when with him! There was only now, this one moment, where she was with the man she loved. Yes, *loved*, for she knew her heart was Harry's and no one else's. He kissed her and all other thoughts vanished.

She closed her eyes, and let herself revel in the feelings his touch created, the press of his kiss on her bare skin. Her palms slid over his back, so strong and warm, sheltering her under his strength. Her legs parted as she felt his weight lower between them and a new sensation she had never even imagined.

She knew what happened; she had been out in the world too long to be an ignorant miss. But the knowledge of *how* had never told her how it would *feel*, the heady, dizzy sensation of falling, falling, caught by another person and held above the world.

'I don't—don't want to hurt you,' he gasped. 'But I can't wait any longer.'

Rose smiled as she felt the press of him against her, the way her whole body ached and tingled for that final union that meant she was his, even if he could never truly be hers. 'You never could.'

She spread her legs a bit wider and he slid into her, making them as one. It did hurt a bit, a quick, burning pain, but it was nothing to the way it felt when he was joined with her. She arched her back, wrapping her arms and legs around him so tightly he could never escape her.

'You see?' she whispered against his hair as he leaned into her shoulder. 'I am completely perfect.'

'My beautiful Rose,' he gasped. Slowly, so slowly, he moved again within her, drawing back, edging forward, a little more intimate each time. Rose closed her eyes tightly, feeling all the ache ebb away until there was only pleasure. A tingling delight grew and expanded inside of her heart, warming like the sun. She had never known or even imagined anything like it.

She cried out at the wonder of it all, at the bursts

of light she saw behind her closed eyes, all blue and white and gold. The heat of it was too much. How could she survive without being consumed completely?

Above her, all around her, she felt his body grow tense, his back arch. 'Rose!' he shouted out.

She flew apart, she clung to him and let herself fall down into the fire and be consumed.

After long moments, she slowly opened her eyes, wondering if she really had fallen deep into some volcano. But it was only the summerhouse, still that pale marble in the winter moonlight.

But she was not the same. That wondrous sparkle still followed her and she held on to it with all her strength.

Beside her, collapsed on to the *chaise* with his arms tight around her, was Harry. He seemed to be asleep, his breath harsh, his limbs sprawled out in exhaustion.

Rose smiled at the sight and felt herself slowly, so slowly, floating back down to earth. She felt the iron of the *chaise* beneath his coat, the soreness of her body. But none of that mattered. Nothing mattered but this moment out of time. She had become someone different in his arms, someone beautiful and bold. Or maybe, just maybe—she had become her truest self.

Rose hardly dared to breathe as she watched Harry in the moonlight. Asleep, he looked so very young, so free of any bad memories or worries. He had a faint smile on his lips, as if his dreams were good ones. A lock of his dark hair curled on his brow.

She gently smoothed it back, marvelling at his beauty, like a warrior king in slumber. She couldn't believe what they had just done together, been to each other. It already seemed like a beautiful dream, lost in the mists, beyond her grasp. She lightly traced her fingertip across his cheek, feeling the warmth of his skin under her touch.

She didn't want to leave him. There was a physical ache inside of her, as if snapping that new, tender bond was a wound. But she knew she had to do it. She would be missed at the party if she was gone much longer, and the longer she stayed with him the harder it would be to leave.

She leaned over and pressed a soft kiss to his lips. He sighed and rolled over, but did not awaken.

'Sleep now, my love,' she whispered. Hopefully when he woke again, he would also remember their time together as a sweet dream. She tucked his coat closer around him and stood to straighten her gown and make sure her hair was once more pinned into place. She did not feel like the old Rose at all, but she had to look like her once more. She had to hide that new glow deep in her heart, keep it only her own secret.

She tiptoed to the door and could not resist a look back over once more. He still slept there, so peacefully, his face so beautifully sculpted in the shadows. She blew him a kiss and slipped out into the night.

The cold wind swept around her, as if it tried to extinguish that summer-warm glow once and for all, but Rose was determined not to let it. She hurried across the garden and up the shallow steps to the terrace of the Barton drawing room. Through the tall glass windows she glimpsed the dancers, a jewel-like mosaic of bright satins and velvets under the golden light of hundreds of candles. She could hear the faint strains of music and the patter of dancing feet, and now *they* seemed like the dream. The noise and light seemed unreal, harsh.

Rose hesitated for a moment outside, watching the crowd sweep by. Aunt Sylvia sat near the fireplace, where Lily and her husband chattered with her. Aunt Sylvia frowned as she, too, studied the crowd, tapping her walking stick impatiently, but she didn't seem to need Rose yet. Rose glanced back over her shoulder, hoping to glimpse the summerhouse, but it was hidden among the trees. She only had one way to go—forward, alone.

One of the glass doors opened and Lady Fallon slipped outside, all golden and crimson, glowing with rubies. She didn't seem to see Rose at first at first and as Rose watched her bright smile fade away she looked so much older, harder, than the usual stylish lady of society she usually appeared.

She glided over to the marble balustrade and opened her beaded reticule.

To Rose's shock, Lady Fallon brought out a thin, dark cheroot and lit it, a tiny beacon of light in the night. Rose had never seen a lady do such a thing. But her shock faded quickly. Of course Lady Fallon went her own way. She had the beauty and the money to be independent, to make many of her own choices. Rose quite envied her for that.

Yet she didn't envy the sad look that shadowed Lady Fallon's eyes as she studied the garden. Or the fact that, with all that money and independence, she could so easily give Harry what he needed, what Rose herself could not.

Rose tried to slip behind her and unobtrusively go back into the ballroom, but Lady Fallon noticed her. Her eyes widened for an instant, as if in surprise, then went back into her brilliant, blinding social smile.

'Miss Parker,' she said. 'I thought I was alone out here.'

'I just needed a breath of fresh air,' Rose answered, hoping she did not sound too breathless, did not look dishevelled.

'Indeed. Jane holds such lovely parties, but sometimes they do get so—noisy.' Lady Fallon offered her the silver case.

Rose shook her head, though she was quite tempted to give it a try. 'This all must seem quite small next to grand London balls.'

'Not at all. I think Jane knows everyone within a hundred miles, and they all want to be at her soirées. Sometimes I do think—' She broke off.

'Think what, Lady Fallon?' Rose asked, curious.

'That I would like to know what a small, cosy family Christmas would be like. I don't think I've ever known such a thing.'

Rose was surprised. Lady Fallon did not seem like the 'small, cosy family' sort of anything. 'I did always love Christmas when my sister and I were small.'

'Did you?' Lady Fallon gave her a curious glance. 'What did you and your family do?'

'Oh, nothing too exciting. Games, walks to church, gifts like dolls and sweets. My father would give us piggyback rides and sometimes Lily and I would see our parents try to sneak a kiss under the mistletoe,' Rose said wistfully, remembering those long-ago days when all seemed so safe and sweet.

Lady Fallon sighed. 'Lovely.'

Rose nodded. Maybe Lady Fallon would be good for Harry after all and not just her money. Maybe she could help him build a family for Hilltop. 'I should go find my aunt before she misses me.'

'Of course.' Lady Fallon studied the dark garden again and Rose slipped back into the drawing room. She made her way through the crowd, which was growing ever more lively as the claret cup punch flowed and the music wound louder.

She found her way to Aunt Sylvia and Lily gave

her a relieved smile. 'There you are at last, Rose,' Sylvia grumbled. 'You have quite been neglecting me. I am in need of a glass of wine.'

'Of course, Aunt,' Rose said with a rueful laugh. Her dream was quite over. 'I shall not be so neglectful again.'

Chapter Sixteen

'You are looking disgustingly cheerful this morning,' Charles grumbled as Harry joined him at the Barton breakfast table.

'Do I?' Harry said with a laugh. He *did* feel rather good-humoured, better than he had in a very long time. Perhaps better than ever before. And it was all thanks to Rose. Sweet, wondrous Rose.

When he had awakened in the chilly night to find her gone, he had felt most bereft. He wanted to tear out of the summerhouse and find her, to take her in his arms and declare that he would never let her leave his side again. That he could not be without her, now that he had finally found her, and the world shone brighter than he ever knew it could. War, the past—it was gone, melted away in the warmth of her kiss.

But he still knew she was right to go, so as not to cause a scandal. He never wanted her to think he had been forced to propose to her when he desperately wanted her by his side for all the years to come. Not because of what had happened between them in the summerhouse, but only for herself. He could no longer envision a life without her.

So he had dressed and made his way back out into the night, but he didn't return to the party. He couldn't face the crowd and the noise, and he was sure he wouldn't be able to see Rose there and *not* kiss her, not reveal to everyone there that she was his. Instead he took a long walk in the cold, deserted gardens, trying to make a plan to move forward in his life. To fulfil his duty with Rose beside him.

He hadn't slept at all, yet he felt bursting with energy. He felt—was it? Could it be happiness? It was a strange sensation and a very pleasant one.

As he ate his breakfast eggs, he studied his brother across the table. Everyone else was still in bed or enjoying the clear, sunny morning with the last of the snow, and they were alone, as they had so often been as children. Unlike himself, his brother did *not* look as if he was filled with lightness and hope. Charles's face was pale, his hair rumpled and he nursed a strong cup of tea with only uneaten toast on his plate. Harry frowned with a new worry. He needed Charles's help if the future was to work as he hoped. He wanted his brother to find such happiness, too.

'I suppose I do feel in fine fettle this morning,' Harry said. 'But you look exhausted.'

Charles shrugged. 'It's nothing at all. Just a surfeit of Christmas.'

Harry nodded. It *had* been a delightful holiday at Barton, filled with music and laughter and games, with friends all around. Surely it was the perfect setting to find unexpected love. But also to indulge in too much wine. He hoped that was all it was for Charles.

'What would you think if I went into the army again this year?' he asked as he buttered his toast.

Charles's eyes widened and he sat up straight in surprise. 'The army, Harry? Whatever for?'

'It is only an idea,' Harry said. And perhaps the only idea that would work for now. He could make some money in the army, to send home, and Charles could look after Hilltop. With Rose as Harry's wife, she would also have a home there, a place as its mistress. Harry had seen how kind she was with his tenants, how she shared his vision of a prosperous estate for them all. It would not be as quick a solution as Charles's idea of marrying an heiress, but it was something of a plan. A beginning for them all.

He wondered what Rose would think of it and could only hope she would agree. That she would take him despite everything.

'I know I can't fight any longer,' he said. 'A one-eyed, scarred officer is no good on a battlefield. But I have much experience with strategy, too, and with the logistics of moving armies. I am sure such experience could be valuable.'

'But why would you want to do that?'

'To earn an income, of course.'

Charles shook his head, as if he could not believe what he was hearing. 'What of marrying well?'

'I do plan to marry well,' he answered carefully. 'But she has no great fortune.'

'You mean—you are betrothed? But to whom?' Charles asked. 'To Miss Parker?'

Harry glanced at the door to make sure they were still alone. 'Yes, though I have not formally asked her yet. You must keep it to yourself for the moment.'

'Of course. I do like Miss Parker and she would suit you very well. Yet—' He broke off and shook his head.

'Yet what, Charlie?'

'What about Helen?'

'Oh, Charlie. Any chance Helen and I might have had was gone long ago and that is for the best. We would never have done well together.'

Charles nodded, but it looked as if his thoughts were very far away. 'So to marry Miss Parker you would go into the army again?'

'If I have to. I would have to leave someone to look after Hilltop, though.'

'You don't mean me?' Charles said, obviously aghast.

'Who else? You know the estate as well as I do and you care about it as much.'

'But—I can't run an estate! I don't know about farming and such.'

'You know as much as I do. We can learn together.' He suddenly realised how very concerned Charles had looked as he mentioned Helen. More than the concern of an old friend, mayhap? 'Or you could marry an heiress.'

Charles gave a humourless laugh. 'I doubt she would have me. You know I will help you however I can, though. No one deserves to find happiness as much as you, Harry.'

'I hoped you would say that.'

'Now you must persuade Miss Parker to marry you.' Charles smiled, a true smile this time. 'That poor lady.'

Harry laughed. 'I'm going to ride over to Hilltop this morning and fetch Mother's ring. Then we shall see.' He finished his breakfast and called for his horse, more filled with hope than he had ever been before.

'Miss Parker, are you unwell?' Lady Eleanor asked in a worried little voice. She went to Rose's side, where Rose was looking out the window of the nursery to the drive below, and slipped her small hand into Rose's. 'You look sad.'

Rose gave the little girl a smile that she hoped looked merry and reassuring, hiding the melancholy thoughts that invaded her mind. 'Not at all. I think I just danced too late last night and am now tired.'

Eleanor sighed. She looked so much like Jane in that moment it made Rose laugh. 'That's why Mama and Aunt Emma said they can't be disturbed until this afternoon.'

Rose laughed again. 'Too much Christmas will do that, I'm afraid.' She thought of her own Christmas, the night that meant she would never be the same again. She was a fallen woman and yet she did not feel 'fallen' in the least—she wanted to do it all over again. The one thing she knew could never be.

She glanced out the window, where she had seen Harry ride away from Barton only moments ago. Was he leaving for good? She had not been able to see his face, to read his expression.

Part of her feared never to see him again more than anything. And part of her was terrified of seeing him again. What would she say? What would she do? She was sure to make a fool out of herself no matter what happened. She had been unable to sleep at all last night when the dance was over, staring into the darkness of her bedroom, going over every single moment of her time with Harry, savouring every kiss, every touch, so she would always remember it.

It had made her feel so giddy with happiness. Being a fallen woman felt so wonderful that she wasn't surprised everyone preached against it so strenuously! If every lady knew how good it was, they would be clamouring to fall. She did not regret it.

But in the clear, cold light of day there was also a terrible sadness. Her time with Harry, even time just to see him or talk with him, was growing ever shorter. How could she steel herself to give that up? To go back to what she'd had before? Even knowing that she loved him and that she would always carry that love even if it was a secret in the deepest chamber of her heart.

Yet she knew that her love was exactly *why* she had to give him up. He needed so much more in his life than she could give him. He needed a fortune for his home, a society lady for his name. She would never have those.

'Shall we practise some of your music?' she said to Eleanor. She smiled down at the girl, trying not to think too much about how she would miss the children. How much joy they had brought her in her time with them. How lovely it would be to have her own little ones to teach music to, listen to their childish laughter and shrieks as they played their nursery games.

'It's Boxing Day!' William cried. 'Surely we deserve one day to play with our new toys.' He pushed his little carriage across the carpet, running it much faster than she hoped he would do eventually in real life. The others gathered close by, with their new dolls and tops and hoops.

'I'd like to play the pianoforte, Miss Parker,' Eleanor said. Rose smiled and led her over to the instrument where all their new sheet music was scattered.

'What would you like to play, then?' Rose asked. 'Whatever is your choice.'

'Something quite happy,' Eleanor said. 'I want to play something jolly while Mama gives out the gifts.'

Rose sorted through the songs until she found one she thought might suit, a lively reel that was well within Eleanor's skills. 'Perhaps this one? It's a bit harder than what we have tried so far, but you have made so much progress I'm sure you can play it very well indeed.'

'Oh, yes, I'm sure I can!' Eleanor exclaimed, her eyes shining with new confidence. 'Who will teach me once you leave, Miss Parker?'

Rose hugged her close, trying not to cry. 'I'm sure your mother will find you an excellent teacher, one much better than me.'

'But it won't be the same,' Eleanor whispered.

'Must you go, then, Miss Parker?' William said, forgetting about his carriage for the moment. 'We like *you* teaching us music.'

Rose bit her lip against those threatening tears. It would never do to cry in front of them, not on Boxing Day. 'And I love teaching you, very much. But I already have a job I must do.'

Eleanor wrinkled her little nose. 'With Aunt Sylvia?'

Rose nodded, trying not to contrast the reality

of life with her aunt and the dream she had known last night. That way could only lie sorrow and regret, and she wanted none of those. 'Yes, with Aunt Sylvia. She needs my help just as you do.'

'But what if you had another job?' Eleanor said. 'Something where you could stay with us?'

Rose hugged the little girl close. 'I would like that so much. Yet sometimes I think life does not arrange things as we would like.'

Eleanor frowned. 'Then maybe life needs persuasion.'

Rose laughed. 'Maybe. Yet for now we have music to practise. Your mama will be handing around the Boxing Day gifts very soon.'

The rest of the morning was spent most pleasantly, playing at the pianoforte and building castles out of a new set of blocks. Rose forgot her worries about the future, all her doubts, as she laughed with the children. All too soon, though, the nursemaid came to fetch them and get them ready to go downstairs.

Rose went to her own chamber to change her dress and tidy her hair. As she put on one of her sensible frocks, a pale grey trimmed with blue, she glimpsed her lovely ballgown draped over the chair where she had left it last night. She picked it up and held it carefully, as if it might shatter as easily as the dreams she had let herself grasp all too briefly. The silk felt cool and light in her hands.

She carefully folded it and tucked it into her travelling trunk. She might never wear it again, but she would always keep it.

She found her shawl and wrapped it over her shoulders, glancing in the looking glance to make sure her hair was neatly pinned. Luckily she showed little sign of her late night except some faint shadows under her eyes and paler than usual cheeks. She looked as she always did—practical, sensible Rose.

She left her chamber to make her way downstairs for tea with the other guests. She could hear Jane presenting the Barton servants with their gifts in the library and the sound of happy laughter. Rose knew that then the staff would depart for their day off and everyone at Barton would have tea and a cold supper, and then perhaps cards or charades. One more burst of merriment before the winter set in.

And tomorrow—tomorrow she would probably leave with Aunt Sylvia and the Barton Christmas would be only a memory.

Rose smiled despite the sad pang of such thoughts. It would only be a memory, yes, but what a grand one! She had never expected to have such a time in her life at all. It had been the best holiday gift.

She started down the stairs, which were deserted. Everyone seemed to be gathered in the drawing room or the library, not hurrying about as they usually were. But at the foot of the stairs she found she was not alone after all. Harry was in the hall, pacing back and forth, his brow furrowed as if he was in deep thought. She almost missed her step as she saw him, looking so handsome and strong in the daylight, and clutched at the banister.

Rose had thought she would encounter him again in a crowd, where they would have no chance of a private word and where she could prepare herself beforehand. Where, if she was lucky and her acting skills were up to the challenge, she could just keep smiling and remain composed.

Now she had no chance to prepare herself at all. He glanced up and saw her there, staring at him open-mouthed like a starry-eyed, besotted schoolgirl.

She snapped her mouth shut and tried to smile carelessly, as if she did this sort of thing all the time. She remembered Lady Fallon, her perfect, half-bored mask, and tried to copy it.

She feared it was a terrible failure. So many emotions were flooding through her, all the things she had pressed down so hard for so many years, racing free. Hope, joy, laughter, despair. And she feared it all showed on her face.

'Rose,' he said, his voice eager as he made his way to the foot of the stairs. 'I've been waiting for you.'

'Have you?' Rose forced herself to keep walking down the stairs, holding tight to the gilded banister as if it could keep her from turning and fleeing back to her chamber. 'I've been at lessons with the children.'

'We have to talk,' he said.

Rose swallowed hard past a throat gone suddenly dry. Her stomach gave a nervous flutter. 'Yes, I know.'

'Shall we…?' He gestured towards the door to the small sitting room where they had first kissed.

She didn't want to be alone with him there, as she remembered all too well what had happened the last time. Close to him there, in the half-light, she was afraid she couldn't resist him again. Yet she knew there was nowhere else they could be alone. She nodded and hurried into the room ahead of him before she could indeed turn and run away.

Once she was alone with him there, she knew it was a mistake. He was too close, too warm, the smell of him all around her. She longed to throw her arms around him and never let go.

She sat down on the sofa and tightly folded her hands in her lap.

'Rose, I—' he began, then broke off with a wry laugh, shaking his head. 'I fear I am no good at such things.'

Such things as breaking her heart? No, he had never done that. She had done it to herself, reaching for what she knew could never be hers. 'Oh, Harry,' she said. 'You need not say anything at all, I prom- ise. I know how things must be. I would never presume anything, or cause your life any trouble. We part as good friends, always.'

'Part?' he said, frowning. He sat down beside her and reached for her hand. She dared to let him, dared to feel his touch one more time. 'Rose, no. That isn't what I want at all.'

She was confused, half-hoping for—what? She didn't even know. 'Then—what do you want?'

He smiled and squeezed her hand. 'I told you I am terrible at this sort of thing. I really should have read some of those romantic novels Jane has scattered around, but there was no time.' He reached inside his coat and took out a tiny box.

As Rose watched, unable to breathe at all, he opened it to reveal a beautiful ring, a round ruby surrounded by tiny pearls. It gleamed and twinkled at her, enticing her with all it promised.

'Rose, will you do me the great honour of agreeing to be my wife?' he said, a small smile hovering around his lips. But his voice sounded uncertain. 'I know I have little to offer you, but you would have a home at Hilltop and there would be the income when I return to the army...'

'The army?' Rose gasped. To go back to battle, when he had already nearly died there? 'No, Harry, you can't do that. Hilltop needs you and I've seen how much you love your home. You belong *there* now.'

'I do love it. That is why I will return to my commission. To earn what I can.'

'And that is why I can't let you do this.' Rose reached out and gently closed the box, unable to look at it any longer without being tempted. Tempted to throw her better judgement to the winds and run into his arms. 'Your duty is to restore your home and I have no fortune to help you do that. I have nothing to offer you at all.'

He shook his head. 'Rose, you know that is not true. You have yourself. You're the kindest, bravest lady I have ever known. I need you by my side. And after what happened last night...'

'I won't use that to tie you down to something you will come to regret,' she protested. 'You cannot go back into the army. You must find a wife who can be all that you deserve and it's not me. You would despise me one day.'

'I never could do that!' he protested vehemently. His hand tightened on hers. 'Rose, please. I need *you.*'

Unable to bear being close to him a moment longer without giving in, she snatched away her hand and jumped to her feet. 'Please, Harry, I can't be the anchor that ties you down. I—I care about you too much.' She bit her tongue to keep from blurting out what she really wanted to say—that she loved him. She loved him with a force and fire she had never believed was possible. And that was why she had to let him go.

Before she could change her mind, she threw open the sitting room door and ran out. The laughter from the drawing room was even louder now, but she knew she couldn't go in there yet. Not until she could compose herself. Half-blinded by tears, she dashed up the stairs to her chamber.

At the top of the staircase, she dared to glance back. Harry stood in the sitting room doorway, watching her with a desolate look on his face. She had not expected that, that he would want her to stay with him, and it broke her heart all over again.

She forced herself to turn away and walk to her bedchamber. Only once she was alone did she let herself fall to the floor, and cry out all her sadness and regret.

'What are you doing, Eleanor? Nanny will be so angry if she sees you there, when we're supposed to go downstairs soon,' William said.

'Hush!' Eleanor hissed at her brother. One could always trust William to ruin a covert session of eavesdropping. And without eavesdropping, how would she ever learn anything? Grown-ups never told children anything interesting. She pressed her ear closer to the door of Miss Parker's chamber and waved her brother closer.

He sat down on the floor beside her. 'What's happening?' he whispered.

'Poor Miss Parker is crying,' Eleanor whispered back. Her stomach ached in a most strange fashion, she felt so sorry for kind Miss Parker. The lady's sobs, even muffled by the door, sounded like the saddest thing Eleanor had ever heard. When she had peeked out the nursery door earlier, she had seen Captain St George standing in the hall while Miss Parker ran from him. She didn't know what it meant, but she knew they were both sorrowful.

William looked just as appalled. 'But what's wrong? Is she ill?'

'I don't know,' Eleanor answered. 'But I heard one of the housemaids say she thought she heard that Miss Parker had turned down a proposal of marriage. Could it have been from Captain St George? Can you imagine that?' To Eleanor, with her love of fairy-tale castles where handsome princes saved beautiful princesses with a kiss, turning away from romance seemed unthinkable. Especially if it made Miss Parker so unhappy.

'A proposal?' William scoffed. 'You girls are so silly about such things.'

Eleanor scowled at him. 'You just wait until *you're* grown-up and have to find your own countess! It won't seem so silly then. And anyway, surely Miss Parker loves the Captain or she wouldn't be sad.'

'That's true.' William gently pressed his hand to the door, as if Miss Parker could feel their concern even through the stout wood. Eleanor placed hers next to his. 'Why do you think she turned him away, then?'

'I'm not sure. I think it has to do with money.'

'Money?'

'Miss Parker has to teach us music, doesn't she? And she has to live with that old lady. And Mama says Hilltop has a roof that is falling in.'

'But that's silly. If just a roof is keeping them from getting married...'

'Yes,' Eleanor said thoughtfully. She did so adore Miss Parker, who loved music and was always patient and smiling, and never dismissed their ideas just because they were children. She liked the Captain, too, who was just like the brave, wounded princes in her stories. Surely they were meant to be together?

Surely they just needed a fairy godmother, one who could fix their roof and help them live happily ever after?

'William,' she said with excitement. 'I have an idea. Will you help me?'

'Is it for Miss Parker?'

'Yes. If we could find the lost treasure at Uncle David's estate...'

William's eyes widened as he grinned. 'We could get Uncle David and Aunt Emma to give it to Miss Parker and she and the Captain could fix their roof and marry!'

'Exactly. And then she would live next door to Barton and never leave us.'

'But where will we start?'

Eleanor frowned. 'In Papa's library, I suppose. There are lots of old maps there, maybe one could help us narrow it down.'

'We could go out after dinner tonight, when they're all in the drawing room. The gardeners always leave their shovels in the sheds at night.'

'We'll need lanterns…'

'What on earth are you children doing?' a sudden bark interrupted them.

Frightened, they leaped to their feet and spun around. They found themselves face to face with Aunt Sylvia, who blocked their escape at the end of the corridor, all towering plumed turban, layers of fur-trimmed shawls and a most ominous dragon-headed walking stick.

William and Eleanor clutched hands. 'N-nothing at all, Aunt Sylvia,' William said. 'We were just…'

'On our way to lessons,' Eleanor said when he faltered.

'This is not your schoolroom,' Aunt Sylvia said. 'Isn't that the door to Miss Parker's chamber?'

Eleanor gulped and nodded.

'Then why are you lurking out here?' Aunt Sylvia demanded.

'We thought she might need some help,' Eleanor answered.

'Help?' Aunt Sylvia glanced at the door with a scowl. 'I see. Well, run along now. You should be doing your lessons, not pestering Miss Parker.'

Eleanor and William dashed away, hand in hand. 'Remember,' she whispered quickly when they saw the nursemaid looking for them. 'Tonight we look for the treasure.'

* * *

Sylvia impatiently pounded at Rose's door. She hadn't seen the girl for hours and she couldn't find the book she wanted. Rose always knew where to find things.

But, worse than that, Sylvia had seen Captain St George striding off down Barton's drive, his face like a thundercloud. She knew the look of heartbreak and profound disappointment on a man's face. Hadn't she caused such a thing herself more than once, when she was young and beautiful and careless in France? Those *affaires de coeur* had passed as quickly as a rainstorm.

But Sylvia had a deep suspicion that whatever was happening with Rose and Captain St George was nothing like that.

'Rose, I insist you open this door,' she called out sternly.

After a long, silent moment, the door swung open. Rose stood there, composed but pale, her eyes red-rimmed. 'How can I help you, Aunt Sylvia?' she asked.

'Oh, my dear girl. I think that for once it is how *I* can help *you*.'

Rose's mouth parted on a startled 'oh' and Sylvia realised with a pang what an old crank she had truly become. She stepped into the room and shut the door behind her. She then did something she had never dreamed she could—she took Rose into her arms and held her close.

'Now, my dear girl,' she said. 'Tell me what is amiss.'

Chapter Seventeen

Helen tried to pretend that it mattered not a whit to her that Charles had not appeared for Boxing Day tea. Neither had Miss Parker or Harry, or a few others who were obviously still recovering from last night's ball. But it was Charles's face Helen searched for every time the drawing-room door opened and her heart sank every time she saw it was not him.

She feared her disappointment would show on her face. That her reputation as the scandalous, funloving, careless Lady Fallon would be ruined if she was seen actually to care for someone.

Care for someone. What a very strange idea, a new feeling. Rather like an ague coming on, making her feel feverish and restless and giddy. She hadn't felt that way in so long. Perhaps—never. And over a mere kiss.

A kiss from Charles St George, of all people. But, yes, there it was. She wanted to see Charles again, had to see him again. Had to know if what had happened meant anything at all to him, as it had changed everything for her.

She jumped up from the sofa and went to pour herself more tea, unable to sit still any longer. Jane and Emma sat by the fireplace, Jane embroidering and Emma with a book in her lap, talking quietly while everyone else played at cards or backgammon. It was a lazy afternoon with the servants gone, everything quiet after last night's ball. A few snowflakes drifted past the window, closing them into their own cosy world as the winter weather turned colder. Yet Helen felt filled with a sparking nervous energy.

She took a sip of tea as she gazed out the window at the bare trees of the park, the lacy haze of snowflakes. She remembered Charles's kiss, how it felt on her lips, the way his touch made her feel so very—alive.

She had come to Barton half-hoping she could find something with Harry again, could recapture a bit of that girl she had once been, before Fallon and her whole shallow London life. She had only found that Harry, as brave and kind as he was, had never been for her. If they had indeed married when they were young, they would have been unhappy because they could never have understood each other.

But Charles—he saw who she *really* was, because he was the same. Seeking, restless, longing for something more.

As she lifted her teacup again, she suddenly glimpsed a figure in the grey gloom outside. Startled that anyone would have stayed out in the cold weather, she peered closer and saw to her shock that it was Charles, heading towards the house.

He wore his many-caped greatcoat, a scarf wound around up to his chin, and a hat pulled over his brow, but she knew it was him. Under his arm was tucked a leather-covered sketchbook.

Helen hurried from the drawing room, ignoring the curious looks that followed her, and found Charles handing over his winter wraps to a footman in the hall. To her surprise, he was smiling, his cheeks red from the cold, as light and merry as the Charles she had once known.

'What on earth were you doing out there?' she demanded. 'It's starting to snow. You could have made yourself ill.'

He just laughed. A *real* laugh, the kind she had not heard from him in so long.

'Would you have nursed me most tirelessly, Helen?' he said lightly. 'Brought me beef tea and bathed my feverish brow?'

Helen planted her hands on her hips. 'Certainly not. You brought it on yourself. What were you doing out there?'

'Sketching, of course.'

'Sketching? But—I thought you had given up art?'

'Yes. I saw this astonishing view when we were

out sledding a few days ago, and well—I just had to capture it.'

He opened his sketchbook, and showed Helen a scene of the winter woods, looking out over the fields to the chimneys of Hilltop beyond. It was rough, hastily drawn in quick lines, but it was exquisite. The melancholy beauty of the view was all there, the chill winter emptiness with the hope of spring to come, the promise of new life.

'Charlie, I…' she began, but words failed her. She shook her head. 'It is breathtaking.'

He shrugged. 'Just a rough sketch. When I can procure some paints, I'll really be able to do something with it. If I could just capture the layers of white in the snow. That blue undertone, not quite grey, but not azure, either. I might have lost my touch.'

'Never. It was always there, just waiting for you.' Helen flipped through the rest of the pages. Most of them were still empty, but a few held the beginnings of sketches. A tenant's little girl with her doll outside a cottage. The summerhouse in the Barton garden.

She turned a page and found that she faced—herself. A profile, a small smile on her lips, her hair waving from her brow. A smaller view of her whole figure, sad and solitary against the terrace balustrade.

Charles snatched the book back and snapped it closed. Suddenly all that sunny openness, the wonderful enthusiasm he showed over his new art, was gone.

'Charlie, I...' she stammered. 'Do you see me that way?'

He shook his head. 'You know you are beautiful, Helen. Men must tell you that every day.'

'But you are different! That sketch makes me look so—lonely.'

'And so you are. You always have been, but you have also always been strong. If you would just believe me, Helen. If you would only see yourself as I always have.' He took up her hand and pressed a quick kiss to her fingertips.

'Oh, Charlie, you are strong, too! Your talent, the way you see the world around you—it is something no one else has. If you would let me help you...'

'No one can help me, Helen,' he said starkly, turning away.

'At least let me try! Let *us* try.' She had never begged anyone for anything before, but now she wanted to. She wanted to grab his hand, to hold him with her, to beg him to show her the world as he saw it.

He smiled at her, but it was sad, quickly gone. 'Helen, you deserve so very much more than what I could give you. I've never known a lady like you, a lady with all the potential of the world inside of her. Let me do the only right thing I've ever done in my life. Forget about me and live all your dreams.'

He walked away from her, disappearing up the

stairs as she watched. She had never felt so bereft before, so hollow. So—alone.

'How dare you, Charles St George?' she whispered. She had offered him everything, wanted everything with him, and he had left her there alone.

Blast him, she thought. She wiped at her eyes and tilted her head high before she marched back into the drawing room. He was right. She did have everything. She was Lady Fallon, after all.

And Charles St George would be very sorry he ever dared to break her heart.

Chapter Eighteen

'Oh, Miss Parker! Something terrible has happened and I don't know what to do.'

Rose glanced up from the book she was pretending to read in the Barton library and saw the children's nursemaid standing in the doorway, tears streaming down her cheeks and her hands twisting in her white apron. It was raining outside, a steady, icy mist, and Rose had pleaded a headache when Jane took the other guests into the village for a musicale at the assembly rooms. Rose had hoped for a quiet evening to hide from her worries—and from seeing Harry, as he and Charles had left for Hilltop. She felt quite drained after confiding in Aunt Sylvia.

But it seemed her hopes for quiet were in vain. The tears in the maid's eyes made her own worry spring to life. She put down her book and hurried over to the girl. 'Whatever is amiss?'

'I went to look in on the children, as it's nearly their bedtime, and Lady Eleanor and Lord William are gone!'

'Gone?' Rose suddenly shivered with a cold fear. 'Are you quite sure? Perhaps they're just playing with their new toys in the day nursery. Eleanor was so determined to practise that new song…'

'Oh, no, Miss Parker. I looked there first thing. The younger ones were all asleep in their beds, but Lady Eleanor and Lord William are nowhere to be found. Their beds are still made, but I did find this.' She held out a rumpled sheet of paper.

Rose recognised it as a drawing by William, who was quite good at sketching and had been talking with Charles a few days ago about his sketchbook. It was a lady, a princess to judge by her tiara, standing by a large open chest of gold coins. The Princess held up her hands, as if beseeching someone to find her. At the bottom was scrawled, *Please don't worry, Miss Parker. We will help you. Don't leave us.*

Rose bit back a sob. 'Oh, my darlings, no,' she whispered.

'Do you know where they are, Miss Parker?' the maid asked.

'Perhaps, but I'm not really sure.' She made herself take a deep breath, to think quickly about what might be in their dear, fanciful minds. 'Send a footman with a message to Lord and Lady Ramsay, but do not alarm them too much. Say Lady Eleanor has a slight disposition. Tell her all when she arrives home. I think I might have an idea where they are and I'll go out to look for them.'

'Alone, Miss Parker?' the maid cried. 'In this weather?'

'There's no one else to go right now. Don't worry, I'll be quite well and I can move quickly on my own.' She wasn't at all sure about that, but she put as much confidence in her voice as she could. Panic would not help them now. 'Can you find me a lantern?'

She hurried up to her chamber and put on her stoutest boots and her hooded cloak. She only prayed she was right and that for some reason they had gone off to look for the treasure.

She left the house and was immediately tempted to turn around as cold, icy rain stung her cheeks. She knew she had to go forward, though. The children needed her. Harry would be brave in just such a situation; she had to take inspiration from him now. Hoping against hope that her lamp would not go out, she set off into the night.

The rain let up enough that she could just see the path in front of her, but the wind was icy-cold, biting through her cloak. She found the stone wall that divided Barton from David and Emma's Rose Hill and then led off at an angle towards Hilltop. That was where the children had pointed out to her the remains of the cold castle.

Rose carefully clambered over the wall and

rushed towards where the ruined towers rose up in the misty night. The blank windows seemed to watch her dispassionately, completely unexcited after all the turmoil and trouble they had seen over the centuries. But were they a refuge as well, a place that would shelter two children?

The ground around the ruins was a quagmire of frost and mud, and Rose picked her way carefully closer. She glanced up at the column of what had once been a chimney, the bricks now tumbling down. Rose wondered for an instant what the house must once have looked like, all pale stone and shining windows, a refuge from civil war for two fleeing lovers. How had the long-gone lady felt when she hid her treasure, hoping to reunite with her love and find a new life together?

She had a fleeting image of Harry in her mind, his smile, his hand held out to her, helping her find strength, just as those lost lovers once had. 'Are you there?' she called out.

'Help!' someone cried, a tiny, faraway sound.

Rose spun around, her heart pounding. 'Eleanor? Is that you? Where are you?'

Oh, let it be the children, she silently pleaded. Let it not be Arabella's ghost, if there was such a thing.

'Help!' the voice cried again. A very real voice, a little girl, full of fear and desperation, but blessedly real.

'Eleanor? Where are you?' she called back, scanning the ruins with desperate eyes. She could only see the fallen chimneys, hear the whine of the icy wind. 'Can you hear me? It's Miss Parker!'

'Oh, Miss Parker! We're down here.'

Rose's heart pounded even harder as a rush of panic seized her. She hadn't heard William at all. 'Down where, my dears? Keep talking so I can find you.'

'Down here, under the stones. We fell through some boards.' Eleanor started singing 'I Saw Three Ships' in a wavering, heartbreakingly brave little voice.

Rose followed the sound until she found an old caved-in area that must have once been some kind of cellar. She could hear Eleanor's voice floating up from the depths.

She knelt down at the edge of the splintered wood, holding her lantern high. It flickered alarmingly. 'Eleanor, are you there? I can't see you.'

'It's—it's dark. We only have one candle,' Eleanor said, her voice thick with tears. 'And William hurt himself when we fell.'

Hurt himself? Rose sucked in a breath. She forced herself to stay calm as she said, 'Just move towards my voice, darling. All will be well now. I'm here.'

She heard the sound of tiny footsteps, the scrape of stones moving. 'Why on earth did you come out here on such a terrible night? You gave us such a fright.'

'We—we just wanted to help you.'

'Help *me*?'

'Yes. To find some money so you can marry Captain St George and fix his roof at Hilltop.'

'Oh, my darlings,' Rose said, trying not break into tears. 'You are truly the best of friends to worry about me like that. But you should never have put yourselves in danger.'

'But you love him! You have to be together. Like in the stories.'

'We can't worry about that right now.' She held the lantern higher and at last glimpsed a pale little face below. Eleanor blinked at the sudden rush of light. She had a scrape on her dirty cheek and the sleeve of her pelisse was torn, but other than that she seemed well.

'Oh, Miss Parker,' she sobbed. 'I'm so sorry.'

'It's all right, my dear. I'm here to help you now. See that large stone over there? Can you climb up on it and reach for my hand?'

Eleanor nodded and clambered up on the fallen stone to reach up her small hand. Rose was able to grasp it and used all her strength to pull the little girl upwards. Her shoulder burned, but Eleanor was soon on solid ground next to her. Eleanor hugged Rose around the waist, her face buried in Rose's cloak, sobs shaking her tiny body. Rose held her tightly in return.

'What happened to William?' she asked urgently. 'Is he awake?'

'I think he hurt his arm,' Eleanor said. 'But he's awake.'

'Very good. Now, my dear, I need you to be very brave. A heroine princess, in fact,' Rose said, holding the girl's face between her hands. She hated to send her off, but she could think of no other way to quickly summon the needed help. 'You must run straight home and get help for your brother. Take the lantern and stay only on the path. I will climb down and stay with him until you return.'

Eleanor gulped hard and nodded. 'What if he…?'

Rose firmly shook her head. 'He will be fine. This is what you must do for him now. I know you can, I know how smart and brave you are. You are the smartest girl I know.' She handed Eleanor the lantern and gave her one more hug. 'Now run, as fast as you can.'

Eleanor dashed away. Once the bobbing lantern light disappeared into the mist, Rose took a deep breath and steeled herself to do what she must. She thought of Harry and his braveness in battle, and it gave her courage, too. She grasped the edge of the pit, its jagged wooden edges biting into her palms through her gloves, and eased herself down carefully until her feet touched the dirt floor of the old cellar. For an instant, everything looked blurry, then she realised her spectacles had been knocked askew. She pushed them up her nose.

The tiny, flickering light of the children's one candle showed her where William sat, propped up against a wall of rotting old shelves that still held dusty bottles of wine. He sat on a faded blanket and beside him was a small pile of yellowed parchment maps and a pair of shovels. They had not come unprepared.

Thankfully, he was also awake, his eyes wide open. But he held his right arm tightly with his left hand and his cheeks were damp with tears.

And the candle was burning quite low. They didn't have much time left.

'What happened, William dear?' she asked as she hurried to kneel beside him.

'I—I fell. My arm…' He gasped.

'I see that.' Rose carefully examined the arm and saw it was luckily not broken. She feared, however, that perhaps his collarbone was fractured. She wished she had some laudanum or brandy, but there was nothing. She could only hope Eleanor was very quick.

She tore a wide strip of linen from the hem of her chemise and used it to bind William's arm close to his side. She wrapped her cloak around them both and held him near, keeping a close watch on the sputtering candle.

'We just didn't want you to leave, Miss Parker,' he whispered.

'What do you mean leave, my dear? We'll always be friends, I promise.'

'We thought if you married Captain St George

and stayed at Hilltop, you could still teach us music, and tell us stories,' he said.

'Oh, William. I will always help you, no matter where I live,' Rose answered, her heart aching.

'But if you love Captain St George…'

'Sometimes love isn't quite enough,' she murmured.

'Of course it is! What of the stories you told us? About warrior knights and their fine ladies? The Captain is a warrior knight.'

'So he is.' The bravest warrior knight she had ever known. But before she could say any more, William let out a shout. Rose heard the crack of a falling stone. There was a sudden, sharp, piercing stab at the back of her head. Dizziness and pain, as well as a terrible cold, overwhelmed her as she fell to the floor. She heard William yelling, but it seemed to come from very far away.

'Harry,' she whispered. Then everything faded to blackness.

Chapter Nineteen

'Captain St George!' Harry heard a little girl's cries just as he swung down from the saddle and handed the reins to a waiting groom at Barton. He had gone to Hilltop to put his mother's ring back in storage, but he had not been able to do it.

It was still in his pocket as he went for a long ride, long after the light faded and he should have returned to Barton. But he needed the movement and speed, the cold wind on his face, trying to leave behind thoughts of Rose. Memories of how she looked after he kissed her, the way it felt to hold her close. The pain when she turned him away. But she could not be outrun.

He only forgot his heartache now, though, as he heard a panicked cry. His battle instincts went up and he whirled around, reaching for a sword that was no longer there. He saw little Lady Eleanor running towards him, her face smudged with dirt and her jacket torn.

He reached out to catch her as she hurtled towards him. 'What is it, child? Are you hurt?' He studied her swiftly, scanning for wounds as he once did in the chaos of a battlefield, but there didn't seem to be any blood or broken bones. She did, however, look terrified.

Lady Eleanor shook her head and gulped in a breath. 'No, but—our parents have gone to the village, and—and you must come with me! At once!'

'No, we need to get you inside and send for the doctor. You can tell me about it once you're in from the cold.'

'We do need the doctor, but not for me,' Eleanor wailed. 'It's my brother and Miss Parker. We fell down into the ruins of the old castle and William hurt his arm, and she came after us, but I don't know what's happened now.'

Harry froze with fear. Rose had run after the children into the freezing night, gone into the old ruins? But then his instincts took over and his mind because as clear as ice. 'You, there!' he called back to the groom. 'Who is still in the house tonight?'

The young man looked quite confused, as panicked children were probably not usually part of his job, but he answered quickly, 'Just the butler and housekeeper, sir, and perhaps the nursemaid and another footman. Everyone else has gone for Boxing Day and the family is in the village.'

'Then send for the nursemaid at once and bring as many men as you can find to follow me. We must go to…' Harry turned to Eleanor. 'Where is Rose, exactly?'

'The ruins of the old castle on Uncle David's land,' Eleanor said. 'In some old cellar. We fell in and couldn't get out.'

'Send the men after me to Rose Hill, with blankets and medical supplies,' Harry told the footman. 'And fetch a doctor at once.'

'Will they be all right?' Eleanor asked.

Harry hugged her quickly. 'I am sure they will be. Miss Parker is a most sensible lady.'

He took back his horse and galloped off towards Rose Hill. He had to make himself focus, to stay in the cold mindset that had taken him through so many battles. It was more important now than ever. Rose needed him.

He couldn't, wouldn't, ever let her down.

Rose felt as if she was sinking down into the dark waves of some warm sea, drifting deeper and deeper. She knew she had to fight against it, to push herself up into the cold world again, even though she only wanted to sleep.

But there *was* something there, something she had to battle against no matter what. If only she could remember….

Then, with a jolt, she *did* remember. She was in the old ruins, she had gone there looking for the children and something had fallen on her. She could smell the damp, earthy scent of rotting wood and darkness pressed around her. How long had she been there? She could hear a sob, seemingly from very far away, and she remembered William was with her.

She drew in a deep breath and pushed herself into a sitting position. Pain shot through her head like a bolt of lightning and she feared she would be sick. She ground her teeth against the nausea and waited for the dizziness to pass before she took stock of her surroundings.

The children's candle had burned down to a tiny stub, but it still gave a little light. She saw the old, collapsing shelves that had long ago held wine bottles, the children's shovels and the rock where she had pulled Eleanor up. Very high up, she could see a bit of the night sky and even a star or two as the mist seemed to be lifting. Surely Eleanor would be back soon. She tried not to think of the little girl alone out there.

'Oh, Miss Parker, you're awake,' William sobbed.

'Yes, my dear. I'm awake.' She shivered and drew her cloak closer around them both. She closed her eyes and thought of Harry, imagining him there with her. Holding her close, keeping her warm and safe…

'Rose! Are you there?' he shouted, and for a moment she was sure it was just part of her dream. But then it came again, so loud and strong she knew it was real. 'Rose! Please answer me.'

'We're here,' she called back hoarsely. 'Can you hear me?'

His face appeared above her, blotting out the stars, the most beautiful sight she had ever seen.

'Are you hurt, my love?' he said.

'I hit my head. I'm afraid I fainted for a moment. Poor William's shoulder is hurt. Is Eleanor...?'

'She is safe back at Barton. The doctor and some of the servants should soon be on their way. Don't worry, I'll have you both out in only a moment.' He vanished again and after a moment she did indeed hear the murmur of other voices. A rope was lowered and Harry climbed down it with a swift power and grace that quite astonished her. He did look like a warrior prince, just as the children had said, coming to their rescue.

He knelt down beside them and helped William into a makeshift sling with a blanket and the rope. The boy was quickly drawn up out of their prison.

Rose feared she would burst into tears as Harry gently took her into his arms. She clung to him, knowing at last that she was not alone. That she was truly safe. She rested her head on his shoulder and closed her eyes, all the pain and fear vanishing. It was just like in those sweet moments after they made love, all the worry and care of life gone perfectly quiet.

How could she ever give that, give *him*, up again?

She clung close to him, feeling their moments together slip away.

'Let me help you up, Rose,' he said. 'You're safe now, I promise.'

'I know I am. With you.'

'Then why did you leave me?'

'Because you deserve more than a poor companion as your wife. You deserve—everything.'

'Oh, my dear.' He pressed an ardent, tender kiss to her forehead. 'You are all I have ever dreamed of wanting. You are so kind and sweet, so strong. And I am sorry, but I won't let you leave me again, not unless it's because you truly do not love me.'

'I do love you,' Rose said, her throat tight with tears. 'So very much!'

His arms tightened around her. 'Then it's settled. We are staying together. Nothing else will ever hurt you again, my dear, sweet Rose. Not when I am here. Because I love you, too.'

She was half-afraid to hope, even as his words thrilled her to her very soul. She had hoped for things before and seen them shattered, just as her family had cracked upon her father's death and their separation. Did she dare reach out now for her heart's desire and hold on to it, no matter what?

'What—what are you saying, Harry?' she whispered.

'I'm saying I've never been happier in all my life than when I am with you. I never even thought feelings like this were real. You show me that being alive can be a joy, a wonder! I never realised before you that I was only in some grey half-world, driven by some sense of dry duty. Now I see what there can truly be.' He looked deep into her eyes, not letting her turn away. Not letting her run again. 'Please, do not send me back to that. Say you will be my wife.'

How very, very tempted she was, how filled with raw, burning longing. 'But—what will we do?'

'I could go back into the army, or learn how to be a farmer—a real farmer, who could make Hilltop profitable again. You need have no fear that I will take care of you and that we will make a true home of Hilltop. It may not be exciting or glamorous...'

'But we will take care of each other,' Rose said. She at last let her tears flow free, her emotions fly out into the world. 'I knew that day with you at Hilltop that I wanted to belong there, with you. If you want me, then I am yours, and I'll do anything I can for our life together.'

Harry laughed, a glorious sound full of a sheer joy she had never heard from him before, but which she hoped to hear again. But now perhaps she *would* hear it, again and again, every day of the life they would build together. She hardly dared believe it was true.

'Please, Rose,' he said. 'Say you will marry me. I can do anything if you are beside me.'

And she knew she could do anything with him. He was the best man she had ever met, brave and kind and strong. 'Yes, Harry St George. I will marry you.'

He smiled, like a burst of sunlight in the dank old cellar, and he reached into his coat to retrieve the box he had once offered her. 'It's fortunate I didn't lock this away again.' He opened it to reveal the ruby and pearl ring, shining and beautiful, full of promise. 'I know my mother would want you to have it.'

'Oh, Harry,' she whispered. She could say nothing else. Her hand trembled as he slipped it on to her finger. It shimmered there, like hope itself.

He lowered his lips to hers for a lingering kiss—just as they heard a clamour from the world outside. A shout, the sound of their names being called.

'It seems we must now be rescued,' Harry said.

Rose laughed. 'I must say, I am very glad they waited for us after all.'

Chapter Twenty

'Are you sure you feel quite well, Rose?' Emma Marton asked as she arranged a tea tray on Rose's bedside table. 'The children are begging every five minutes to see you, but the doctor said you must rest…'

'I am very well indeed, Emma,' Rose answered. 'The doctor just left for his second visit and he says I may even come down to dinner. My head is quite well. I have missed the children.' She had also very much missed seeing—and kissing—Harry, who had only been allowed in for a quick word that morning. She knew the days of Christmas were still going on downstairs, and she didn't want to miss a minute.

'And they miss you. They are so terribly sorry for what they did.'

'They were only trying to help. They have such good hearts.'

Emma sighed. 'I know. It does get them into

trouble sometimes. Bea and I once found ourselves in the same predicament before David and I married. David boarded up the old ruins, but now he says he will fill them in altogether.' She paused to rearrange a vase of greenery on the table. 'I understand we are to have a happier event here at Barton quite soon, though!'

'I hope so. Lily's husband has gone himself to beg a special licence from the archbishop.'

'A Christmastime wedding! How lovely.'

'Yes. I think it will be. Jane says she is bringing in even more greenery to deck the drawing room.'

'Everyone does love a romance here!' Emma said with a laugh. 'When I came back to Barton after I was widowed, I was so tired, so heartsick. I never imagined I would find someone like David here. And Barton helped Jane and Hayden find their way back to each other, too.' A soft smile lit her face. 'There is magic here. Something that brings hearts together, when they are meant to be.'

Rose laughed. 'So it does. This has truly been the most wondrous Christmas.'

'And now we shall all be neighbours!' Emma said, clapping her hands in delight. 'What do you and Harry plan to do at Hilltop now?'

'I am not sure.' She frowned as a worry pierced through her happiness, the fear that Harry would indeed go back into the army. 'There is so much to start on. I think Lily will stay and help me for a while.' As a curate's wife, Lily was well practised in making a lovely house on economies, but still Rose worried. She wanted to make everything so perfect for Harry, for their new life together.

'Well, I am glad you will be nearby. What fun we will all have together!'

As she clapped her hands again, the chamber door opened and Jane appeared with her arms overflowing with silks, satins and laces. 'I thought we might like to look through these, Rose,' she said, draping the gowns over chairs and the end of the bed, a shimmering rainbow. 'There's no time to have something from the dressmaker, of course, but Emma and I are quite handy with our needles. We could make over a few of these. Perhaps the lace from this gown on that blue silk?'

'I was going to wear my dress from the Christmas ball,' Rose said. She reached out to gently touch the blue silk, as soft and light as a cloud, and as pale as ice. Surely Harry would think she looked pretty in that! 'But this one is so lovely...'

'It will be perfect!' Jane said. 'And Lily says she had heard from your mother this morning and she should arrive later today and will bring her old wedding veil with her.'

'Mama is coming?' Rose cried. She had feared there would be no time for her mother to arrive and now the day would be perfect.

'Yes. It's meant to be a surprise, I'm afraid,' Jane said. 'Hayden has sent his fastest horses and carriage for her.'

There was the faint sound of wheels crunching on the frosty gravel of the drive below Rose's window. 'Maybe that's Mrs Parker now,' Emma said, glancing outside. A puzzled frown creased her brow. 'No, it's a carriage I don't know. And Aunt Sylvia is waiting down there.'

'What?' Rose and Jane cried. They hurried over to peer past Emma's shoulder. Aunt Sylvia did indeed wait on the front steps, swathed in her shawls, leaning on her walking stick. She looked a most formidable figure, but Rose now knew the kind heart that truly lurked beneath. She had listened to Rose when she dared not confide in anyone else.

The carriage, a plain but respectable and well-kept barouche, rolled to a stop and a man in a dark coat and hat stepped out, a leather case under his arm. Aunt Sylvia took his arm and they vanished into the house.

'How odd,' Rose murmured. She and Aunt Sylvia had had a long conversation after the doctor left, about Rose's forthcoming marriage and her former life with Aunt Sylvia. Sylvia had seemed rather out of sorts, as usual, and declared that no one could read aloud as Rose did, yet she had also talked of hiring the local vicar's youngest girl as a companion, as if she had already made the plans.

'Do you know the man, Rose?' Emma asked.

'I think I have seen him before, but I'm not sure,' Rose said. 'Aunt Sylvia does often have her men of business call, but I rarely meet them.'

Jane laughed. 'Men of business do rather tend to look alike. Hayden said Mrs Pemberton had quite commandeered his library this morning. Ah, well. We have important things to discuss ourselves. Such as—will Eleanor be allowed to be your attendant? She has made herself quite sick for begging the honour...'

That evening, Rose made her careful way downstairs before dinner. She still ached in places she had not even realised she possessed muscles after her adventure in the ruins, but the doctor said she could be out of bed for a few hours. Eleanor and William insisted on helping her, holding on to her hands. They had begged her forgiveness for running off and been thoroughly hugged and forgiven.

And waiting for her in the hall was Harry. She remembered seeing him there after she first turned away his proposal, but tonight he looked quite different—younger, his features lit with a smile. He held out his hand to her as she reached the last step and drew her close.

Rose went into his arms with joy and he lowered his head to kiss her. Eleanor sighed, while William made a dismissive snort.

'Girls and romance...*ew!*' he gasped.

'I told you, William—just you wait until you are grown,' Eleanor said. 'Then you will understand.'

Rose and Harry laughed, holding tightly to each other. But there was no time for another kiss, as

Aunt Sylvia appeared at the library door and banged her stick on the floor.

'You are not married yet, Rose,' she said. 'You have not yet stolen her from me, Captain St George. I would appreciate a word with you both for a moment.'

William and Eleanor fled from her frown, and Rose exchanged a long glance with Harry. He shrugged and offered her his arm and they followed Aunt Sylvia into the library.

The gentleman who had arrived so mysteriously earlier that day sat at the desk, papers and ledgers stacked before him. He glanced at them over his spectacles and nodded.

'Rose, you remember my lawyer, Mr Rodd,' Aunt Sylvia said, sitting down behind the desk. 'Mr Rodd, this is Miss Parker's intended, Captain St George.'

'How do you do,' Mr Rodd said. 'I must say what a fortunate pair you two are.'

Rose glanced up at Harry, who looked as puzzled as she felt herself. 'Fortunate, Mr Rodd?' Harry said.

'Indeed. Mrs Pemberton and I have just been going over the terms of her will, as well as a few current property deeds. This coal mine in Wales looks especially promising...'

Rose was now most confused. 'Coal mines?'

'And some farmland, as well as these London warehouses,' Mr Rodd said. 'Mrs Pemberton has made them over to you, effective after your marriage. If you could just sign here, Captain St George…'

'Wait a moment, Mr Rodd,' Harry said. 'Mrs Pemberton, what does this mean?'

'I am most fond of Rose, Captain St George,' Aunt Sylvia said gruffly. 'Very fond indeed. She has made my life quite a great deal brighter these last few years and I know very well I am not easy to live with. She is good girl and deserves whatever I can do to help her now. I have no children and these properties can't go with me to the hereafter, as old Pemberton found out when he left me a widow so long ago. You and your children might as well enjoy them. The leases will help Rose now and my whole estate will be hers when I am gone.'

'Oh, Aunt Sylvia,' Rose whispered. There had been so many lovely surprises in the last few days, she wasn't sure she could bear yet another. 'I had no idea you cared for me so.'

'Of course I do,' Aunt Sylvia said, waving her walking stick. 'You are a kind girl, Rose. I hope you deserve her, Captain St George, for I am loathe to let her go.'

'I don't think anyone is good enough to deserve Rose, Mrs Pemberton, least of all a man like myself,' Harry said. 'But this is too generous. We cannot accept.'

'Oh, pish!' Aunt Sylvia cried. She waved her stick again, forcing Mr Rodd to duck. 'You have no choice at all. It's already done. If you choose not to spend the income, it will accrue to your children. But I have to say, young man—if you do not allow me to make Rose's life a little bit easier now, I will be angry indeed. And you would not care to see me angry.'

Harry laughed. 'No, Mrs Pemberton, I would not. Nor would I ever do anything to hurt Rose. This will be her property to use as she wishes.'

As she wished! Rose thought of so many things— a roof for Hilltop, a new school, plenty of servants to see to the house's grand restoration, Harry able to carry out his improvements. Harry not being forced back into the army. She could hardly believe it. She rushed over to hug her aunt. 'Oh, Aunt Sylvia. How very kind you are.'

Aunt Sylvia awkwardly patted her shoulder. 'You of all people, Rose, know that is not true. I am not in the least kind. And I expect the best seat at your wedding, even if your silly mother *is* on her way to Barton.'

'Of course, Aunt Sylvia. I will even toss you my bouquet.'

Aunt Sylvia shuddered. 'No, my dear. Believe me, one marriage was quite enough.'

'So, Jane darling, do you plan to give up matchmaking now?' Hayden whispered to his wife as they sat in the Barton drawing room after dinner, watching Rose play at the pianoforte as Harry turned the pages of her music.

Jane tilted her head to study the lovely picture the two of them made, so glowing with happiness. 'I admit I misjudged what Harry needed in a wife,' she admitted. 'I quite forgot the important lesson I once learned from our own marriage. Love and friendship are the two most important things. With those, anything can be accomplished. I am happy they discovered that for themselves.'

'Then—no more matchmaking?' he said, clasping her gloved hand in his.

Jane glanced at Helen Fallon, who sat alone in the window seat. She glittered with emeralds, as beautiful as a young goddess—but her eyes shimmered with what looked terribly like tears.

'Well,' Jane murmured. 'It *would* be a shame to waste such valuable lessons in love, don't you think?'

Epilogue

'There! I think we have done quite a fine job here, don't you?' Lily said as she straightened the lace veil on Rose's curled hair. Once their mother had worn it, then Lily. Rose had never expected to don it herself.

'You have indeed,' she answered, studying herself in the looking glass. Her pale blue gown with its frothing lace train, the lace veil, the bouquet of winter greenery and white hothouse roses—it was all quite splendid. She could barely believe it *was* her. 'A silk purse.'

Lily laughed. 'You weren't exactly a sow's ear to start, my dearest sister,' she said. 'But shouldn't you take off your spectacles?'

Rose nudged them up her nose. 'I think I need to see the bridegroom.'

Lily laughed. 'Quite right.'

There was a knock at the door and Jane appeared. 'I think all is in readiness downstairs, Rose.'

Rose nodded, taking in a deep breath against the sudden nervous fluttering deep inside. 'I'm ready.'

She followed Jane and Lily to the top of the stairs, where Eleanor waited to scatter her flowers. The banister was twined with greenery and white ribbons, and she could hear music from the drawing room. It looked like a fine wedding indeed and Rose could hardly believe it was *her* wedding. That her own brave prince awaited her.

Jane and Lily disappeared into the drawing room and Rose followed the pathway of petals Eleanor laid for her. The drawing room, decorated with more blue and white ribbons and tall vases of flowers, was filled with people, including Mr Hewlitt in his cassock waiting to perform the ceremony, her mother sniffling into her handkerchief and Aunt Sylvia in her promised seat of honour. But Rose only saw the man who waited for her at the holly and ivy-wreathed altar. Her own Christmas bridegroom.

He smiled at her brilliantly, so tall and handsome in his blue coat. She smiled and hurried forward to take his hand, all nervousness forgotten, every doubt vanished. She was truly at home at last.

* * * * *

JOIN US ON SOCIAL MEDIA!

Stay up to date with our latest releases, author news and gossip, special offers and discounts, and all the behind-the-scenes action from Mills & Boon...

 @millsandboon

 @millsandboonuk

 facebook.com/millsandboon

 @millsandboonuk

It might just be true love...

GET YOUR ROMANCE FIX!

Get the latest romance news,
exclusive author interviews, story
extracts and much more!

MILLS & BOON

HISTORICAL

Awaken the romance of the past

Escape with historical heroes from time gone by.
Whether your passion is for wicked
Regency Rakes, muscled Viking warriors or
rugged Highlanders, indulge your fantasies and
awaken the romance of the past.

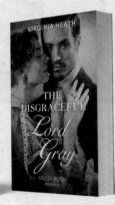

MILLS & BOON
True Love
Romance from the Heart

Celebrate true love with tender stories of heartfelt romance, from the rush of falling in love to the joy a new baby can bring, and a focus on the emotional heart of a relationship.